THE AUTHOR

GABRIELLE ROY was born in St. Boniface, Manitoba, in 1909. Her parents were part of the large Quebec emigration to western Canada in the late nineteenth century. The youngest of eight children, she studied in a convent school for twelve years, then taught school herself, first in isolated Manitoba villages and later in St. Boniface.

In 1937 Roy travelled to Europe to study drama, and during two years spent in London and Paris she began her writing career. The approaching war forced her to return to Canada, and she settled in Montreal.

Roy's first novel, *The Tin Flute*, ushered in a new era of realism in Quebec fiction with its compassionate depiction of a working-class family in Montreal's Saint-Henri district. Her later fiction often turned for its inspiration to the Manitoba of her childhood and her teaching career.

In 1947 Roy married Dr. Marcel Carbotte, and after a few years in France, they settled in Quebec City, which was to remain their home. Roy complemented her fiction with essays, reflective recollections, and three children's books. Her many honours include three Governor General's Awards, France's Prix Fémina, and Quebec's Prix David.

Gabrielle Roy died in Quebec City, Quebec, in 1983.

THE TIN FLUTE

GABRIELLE ROY

TRANSLATED BY ALAN BROWN

AFTERWORD BY
PHILIP STRATFORD

Bonheur d'occasion
Original edition
Copyright © 1945 Gabrielle Roy

The Tin Flute
Translation by Alan Brown
Copyright © 1980 by McClelland & Stewart Ltd.
Afterword copyright © 1989 by Philip Stratford
New Canadian Library edition 1989
This New Canadian Library edition 2009

Library and Archives Canada Cataloguing in Publication

Roy, Gabrielle, 1909-1983
[Bonheur d'occasion. English]
    The tin flute / Gabrielle Roy ; afterword by Philip Stratford.

Translation of: Bonheur d'occasion.
ISBN 978-0-7710-9388-3

    I. Title.

PS8535.O95 B613 2009   C843'.54   C2009-901232-4

We acknowledge the financial support of the Government of Canada
through the Book Publishing Industry Development Program and that
of the Government of Ontario through the Ontario Media Development
Corporation's Ontario Book Initiatiye. We further acknowledge the
support of the Canada Council for the Arts and the Ontario Arts Council
for our publishing program.

 ANCIENT FOREST
FRIENDLY

Typeset in Garamond by M&S, Toronto
Printed and bound in Canada

McClelland & Stewart Ltd.
75 Sherbourne Street
Toronto, Ontario
M5A 2P9
www.mcclelland.com/NCL

2   3   4   5   13   12   11

To Mélina Roy

THE TIN FLUTE

ONE

Toward noon, Florentine had taken to watching out for the young man who, yesterday, while seeming to joke around, had let her know he found her pretty.

The fever of the bazaar rose in her blood, a kind of jangled nervousness mingled with the vague feeling that one day in this teeming store things would come to a halt and her life would find its goal. It never occurred to her to think she could meet her destiny anywhere but here, in the overpowering smell of caramel, before the great mirrors hung on the wall with their narrow strips of gummed paper announcing the day's menu, to the summary clacking of the cash register, the very voice of her impatience. Everything in the place summed up for her the hasty, hectic poverty of her whole life here in St. Henri.

Over the shoulders of her half-dozen customers, her glance fled toward the counters of the store. The restaurant was at the back of the Five and Ten. In the glitter of the glassware, the chromed panels, the pots and pans, her empty, morose and expressionless ghost of a smile caught aimlessly on one glowing object after another.

Her task of waiting on the counter left her few moments in which she could return to the exciting, disturbing recollections of yesterday, except for tiny shards of time, just enough to glimpse the unknown young man's face in her mind's eye. The customers' orders and the rattling of dishes didn't always break into her reverie, which, for a second, would cause a brief tremor in her features.

Suddenly she was disconcerted, vaguely humiliated.

While she had been keeping an eye on the crowd entering the store through the glass swing-doors, the young stranger had taken a place at the imitation-marble counter and was calling her over with an impatient gesture. She went toward him, her lips slightly open, in a pout rather than a smile. How maddening that he should catch her just at the moment when she was trying to remember how he looked and sounded!

"What's your name?" he asked abruptly.

She was irritated, less by the question than by his way of asking: familiar, bantering, almost insolent.

"What a question!" she said contemptuously, though not really as if she wanted to end the conversation. On the contrary, her voice was inviting.

"Come on," said the young man, smiling. "Mine's Jean. Jean Lévesque. And I know for a start yours is Florentine. Florentine this, Florentine that, Florentine's in bad humour today, got a smile for me, Florentine? Oh, I know your first name all right. I even like it."

He changed tone imperceptibly, his eyes hardened.

"But if I call you miss, miss who? Won't you tell little old me?" he insisted with mock seriousness.

He leaned toward her and looked up with eyes whose impudence was apparent in a flash. It was his tough, strong-willed chin and the unbearable mockery of his dark eyes that she noticed most today, and, this made her furious. How could she have spent so much time in the last few days thinking about this boy? She straightened up with a jerk that made her little amber necklace rattle.

"And I guess after that you'll want to know where I live and what I'm doing tonight," she said. "I know you guys."

"You guys? What do you mean, you guys?" he mocked, looking over his shoulder as if there were someone behind him.

"Just . . . you guys!" she said, half exasperated.

His familiar, slightly vulgar tone, which put him on her level, displeased her less than his usual behaviour and speech. Her smile returned, irritated but provocative.

"Okay, now!" she said. "What do you want today?"

Once again his look had that brutal familiarity.

"I hadn't got around to asking what you're doing tonight," he said. "I wasn't in that big a hurry. Normally I'd take another three days at least. But now you mention it. . . ."

He leaned back a little on the stool and weaved gently from side to side. As he stared at her, his eyes narrowed.

"Now then! Florentine, what're you doing tonight?"

He saw that she was upset. Her lower lip was trembling, and she held it with her teeth. Then she busied herself pulling a paper napkin from a chrome box, unfolded it and spread it on the counter.

Her face was thin, delicate, almost childish. The effort she was making to control herself caused the small, blue veins on her temples to swell and knot, and her almost diaphanous nostrils, closing, pulled tight the skin of her cheeks, as smooth and delicate as silk. Her lips were still uncertain, still threatening to tremble, but Jean, looking in her eyes, was suddenly struck by their expression. Under the arched line of her plucked eyebrows, extended by a little streak of makeup, her lowered lids could not hide the thin bronze ray of a glance, cautious, attentive and extraordinarily eager. Then she blinked, and the whole pupil showed with a sudden gleam. Over her shoulders fell a mass of light-brown hair.

With no particular purpose the young man was watching her intently. She astonished more than she attracted him. And even this phrase he had just uttered, "What are you doing tonight?" . . . had been unexpected. It had taken shape in his mind without his knowing; he had tossed it out as one drops a pebble to test an unknown depth. But her reaction encouraged him to try again. Would I be ashamed to go out with her? he wondered. And then the idea that such a thought could intervene after he had gone this far pushed him on to greater daring. Elbows on the counter, eyes staring into Florentine's, he was waiting, as if in a cruel game, for a move from her to which he could react.

She stiffened under his brutal scrutiny, and he was able to see her better. He saw her upper body reflected in the wall mirror, and he was struck by her thinness. She had pulled the belt of her green uniform as tight as it would go around her waist, but you could see that her clothing barely clung to her slender body. And the young man had a sudden glimpse of what her life must be like, in the rush and bustle of St. Henri, that life of spruce young girls with rouged cheeks reading fifteen-cent serial novels and burning their fingers at the wretched little fires of what they took for love.

His voice grew incisive, almost cutting.

"You're from here? From St. Henri?" he asked.

She shrugged her shoulders, and her only reply was a vexed, ironical smile, again more like a pout.

"Me too," he went on, with mocking condescension. "So we can be friends, eh?"

He saw how her hands shook, frail as a child's; he saw her collar-bones stand out in the open neck of her dress. A moment later she forgot herself so far as to rest one thrust-out hip, hiding her nervousness in a sulk. But he was no longer seeing her as she was before him. He saw her dressed up, ready to go out in the evening, with plenty of rouge to hide the pallor of her cheeks, costume jewels rattling all over her thin body, a ridiculous little hat, perhaps even a small veil behind which her eyes would shine, emphasized by eye shadow: a girl in a funny get-up, flighty, but all in a fuss in her desire to please him. Something arose in him like a gust of a destroying wind.

"Will you come to a show with me tonight?"

He felt her hesitate. No doubt his invitation, if he took the trouble to make it sound more friendly, would meet consent. But he preferred it this way, hard and direct, as if he wanted her to refuse.

"All right, then, it's a deal," he said. "Now bring me your famous special."

Then he took a book from the pocket of his overcoat, opened it, and was absorbed at once.

Florentine's cheeks had flushed red. That was what she hated about this guy: the ability he had, after dragging her out of her depth, to banish her from his mind, leaving her like an object of no interest. Yet it was he who had, for the last few days, been making the advances. She hadn't made the first move. It was he who had wakened her from that heavy sleep in which she had lain huddled, on the margin of life, with her complaints and resentments, alone with those undefined dreams which she saw with so little clarity. He was the one who had given a focus to her hopes, which now were as sharp and torturing as desire itself.

She gazed at him a moment in silence and her heart felt a pang. She liked the boy a lot, already. He seemed elegant to her. So different from the young men she served in the store, boring little clerks, or workers with greasy sleeves and collars; and even much superior to the youths she met in neighbourhood cafés in the evening, when she'd go with Pauline and Marguerite to dance a turn to nickelodeon music and munch chocolate bars or simply sit for hours in the refuge of a booth peeking at the boys who came in, and laughing at them. Yes, he was very different from all those she had glimpsed by chance in her empty, busy life. She liked the way his thick, dark hair stood up straight and bristling. Sometimes she felt she would like to grab fistfuls of that strong, unruly hair.

The first time he'd come to the Five and Ten she had noticed him at once and managed to be the one who served him. Now she felt like running away, but also like standing up to him, to prove she didn't care. "He'll ask me out some day. He will," she had said to herself with a strange sensation of power in the hollow of her chest. Then, immediately uneasy, "Then what'll I say?"

Her companions at work – Louise, Pauline, Marguerite, all except Eveline, the "manager" – now and then accepted an invitation made during the joking and teasing over lunch. Pauline said these connections weren't dangerous as long as the fellow came to get you at home and you only went to a movie. That gave you a good chance to have a look at him and decide whether you wanted to see him again. Louise was even engaged to a young soldier she had first met in the restaurant. Since there was a war, and the newly enlisted young men felt the urge for an attachment before they left for training camp, friendships were quickly made, and under very new conditions. Some ended in marriage. Florentine didn't dare follow her thought to the end.

Even as the young man read, his lips kept something of that scoffing expression that so disconcerted her.

I'm goin' to show him, she thought, tight-lipped, I'll show him I don't care a darn about him anyway. But her curiosity to find out what he was reading was stronger than her spite. She leaned daringly over the open book. It was a trigonometry text. The rhombic forms, the triangles, the black print of the equations, made her smile to herself in total incomprehension.

"No wonder you talk like a big book, reading stuff like that."

And she went off toward the order microphone, putting on a mocking, piping voice: "One thirty-cent special!"

Her sharp voice carried the length of the restaurant and Jean Lévesque felt his forehead turn a stupid red. His eye followed her with a dark flame of resentment. He pulled his book in front of him and leaned over it, both elbows on the table, his head resting on his tanned, strong hands.

New customers were crowding toward the counter. It was the usual rush between twelve and one: a few neighbourhood working men in heavy drill; store clerks from Notre Dame Street with white collars and small felt hats which they tossed on the counter; two social service nuns in grey cloaks; and a taxi-driver and several housewives who, between shopping trips, came to perk themselves up with a cup of scalding coffee or a plate of French fries. The five young waitresses bustled back and forth, bumping into each other on the way. From time to time there was the tinkle of a spoon falling on the tile floor. A waitress would pick it up swiftly and toss it in the sink, then rush off, bending slightly forward so as to gain more speed. They were all in a hurry. Their quick footsteps, their sudden comings and goings, the rustling of their blouses, stiff with starch, the click of the toaster when the bread jumped up, the purring of the coffee pots on their electric plates, the crackling of the kitchen loud-speaker, combined in a continuous sound like the hum of a warm summer day, with the added charm of strong odours of vanilla and sweets. You could always hear the muffled rumbling of milk-shake mixers in tall chromed containers, like the interminable buzzing of flies caught in sticky paper; and then the ring of a coin on the counter, and, at intervals, the bell of the cash register like the period of a sentence, a small, high-speed knell, tireless and shrill. Though the frost had painted its arabesques on the glass doors at the front, here in the back of the store the air was torrid.

Marguerite, busy in front of the ice-cream wells, was a tall, sturdy girl whose cheeks were naturally pink, as if even in this oven they could keep the perpetual bite of some far-off country frost. She would lift off a cover, plunge the scoop into the thick of the ice cream and toss the contents into a high tapered glass with a base. She added a little whipped cream, squeezing it from a cardboard cone as from a toothpaste tube. From an aluminum drawer she took a spoonful of marshmallow and let it drip on the cream, then doused the whole creation with caramel, and crowned the summit with half a sugared cherry, red and appetizing. In no time the Sundae Special, fifteen cents, was on the counter, like a fountain of coolness on a burning summer day. She would pick up a coin, rush to the cash register and return to the ice-cream wells to start another Sundae Special. The process never varied, but Marguerite put as much care and simple joy into constructing the cunning edifice of her tenth sundae as she did for her first. A country girl who had recently come to town to stay with relatives, she was not yet disillusioned with the cheap glitter of the neighbourhood. Nor was she sated with the surprises and sweet smells of the restaurant. The animation, the flirtations continually launched around her, the atmosphere of pursuit, of withdrawal, of half consent, of seductive openings, all this amused and pleased her greatly. "Florentine's fella," as she called Jean Lévesque, had particularly impressed her. And when Florentine, carrying an order, passed near her, she couldn't resist making her usual remark, with a full, good-natured laugh:

"Your fella's givin' you the eye, eh?"

And, licking her moist lip to get a last trace of marsh-mallow, she added:

"You know, I think he's real smart, and nice, too. It won't take long, Florentine, he's going to loosen up."

Florentine smiled disdainfully. No doubt that was how life seemed to Marguerite, the big simpleton: a continuous round of sundaes after which each of the girls, without lifting her little finger, would magically be engaged, then married, in a wedding dress, with a little bouquet in her hand. As she went over to Jean Lévesque, however, she thought with some satisfaction that the young man must be showing a good deal of interest if even that great booby of a Marguerite had noticed it. Funny way to be interested, she thought, and her face twitched with resentment.

She put his plate before him and waited for him to speak, but he, absorbed in his reading, murmured a "Thanks" without looking up. Then, absent-mindedly, still reading, he picked up his fork and began to eat; while she, irresolute, stayed on, more afflicted by this silence than by the young man's earlier ambiguous words. At least when he spoke to her she had the satisfaction of telling him off. Suddenly, overtaken by an undefined but melancholy thought that moved crushingly into her life from time to time, she leaned back against the shining edge of the sink.

God, was she tired of this life! Serving rude men who insulted her with their advances, or others like Jean Lévesque, whose admiration was perhaps no more than sarcasm. Serving, always serving! And don't forget to smile, even when your feet burned as if they stood on hot coals. Smile, with rage in your throat, and aching limbs ready to collapse.

Her eyes grew dazed. On her childish features, heavily made up, could be seen, briefly superimposed, the image of the old woman she would become. At the corners of her mouth was a hint of the wrinkle into which the graceful relief of her cheeks would later fall. But it was not only this anticipation of time that flashed across Florentine's face; the hereditary weakness, the deep misery of which she was an extension and which would play its part in the work of time, seemed to well up in her dull eyes and spread like a veil over her naked, unmasked countenance.

That all passed in less than a minute. Abruptly, Florentine was on her feet again, straight and nervous, and the smile automatically came back to her rouged lips. Of the half-formed thoughts that had crossed her mind she retained only one clear impression, as bitter as her fixed smile: right now she had to stake everything that she still was, all her physical charm, in a frightening gamble on happiness. Leaning over to pick up some dirty dishes from the counter, she glimpsed Jean Lévesque's profile, and her heart knew, with a sudden dizziness as from a wound, that this boy could never again be a matter of indifference to her. She had never felt so close to hating him. She knew nothing about him except his name, which he had just told her, and a little from Louise, who said he worked in a foundry as an electrician-machinist. From the same source she had learned that he never went out with girls. This had intrigued her and was still a point in his favour.

She glanced down the length of the counter. She saw in profile all the faces leaning over their plates, mouths open, jaws working, lips greasy – a sight that always upset her – and then, down at the end, the young man's shoulders, square and powerful in his well-fitting brown suit. The skin of his cheeks was tight, his teeth strong. Young as he seemed, slight wrinkles were already to be seen on his high, stubborn forehead. His gaze, whether it touched a person or an object, or remained fixed on his open book, had a hard glint to it.

Slim, noiseless, she went nearer to him and, her eyes half squinting, examined him more closely. His suit, in English cloth, couldn't have come from a store in St. Henri. It seemed to her that even this suit was a clue to a character and a kind of life that were somehow special. Not that he was all that impeccably dressed; on the contrary, he affected a certain carelessness. His tie was loosely knotted, his hands were stained with grease, and his hair was bushy and unmanageable. But it was this lack of care in small things that gave class to the expensive things he wore: the wrist-watch, whose glass flashed with his every move, the rich silk scarf slung casually around his neck, the fine leather gloves sticking out of his suit pocket. It seemed to Florentine that if she leaned closer to him she would breathe the odour of the great, exciting city. She could see St. Catherine Street, the department-store windows, the elegant Saturday-night crowd, the florists' displays, the restaurants with their revolving doors and tables set almost on the sidewalk behind gleaming bay windows, the brightly lit movie theatres, their aisles disappearing into the dark behind the cashier's glass cage amid tall, glittering mirrors, polished banisters and potted

plants, rising toward the screen that brought the most beautiful visions in the world. Everything she desired, admired and
envied floated there before her eyes.

Oh, you could bet your life this young man wasn't bored
on Saturday nights! For her, they were nothing special.
Sometimes, not often, she had gone out with boys, but they'd
only taken her to the neighbourhood movie house or some
dingy suburban theatre, and then expected to be paid off in
kisses for such a miserly evening. She'd be so busy fending them
off that she didn't even get to watch the movie. Occasionally
she had gone to the west end of town with other girls, and in
the midst of this entirely female, chattering herd she had felt
more vexation and shame than amusement. Every couple that
passed caught her eye and increased her resentment. The city
was for couples, not for four or five girls with their arms stu-
pidly around each other's waists, weaving along St. Catherine
Street, stopping at every shop window to admire the things
they never would possess.

But how the city "downtown" appealed to her now in
association with Jean Lévesque! How this unknown young
man made the lights shine brighter, the crowd seem gay, and
springtime on the point of burgeoning in the wretched trees
of St. Henri! It seemed to her that if she had not been held
back by the great restraint the young man inspired in her, she
would have said, Let's go together. We're made to go together.
At the same time she felt that absurd impulse to reach out and
touch his dark, tangled hair. She had never encountered
anyone who was so obviously bound to rise. Maybe he was
only a mechanic now, but she was as convinced of his future
success as she was of the instinct to make an ally of him.

She woke from her dreaming and asked him in the
slightly formal tone she put on for customers:

"Would you care for a dessert?"

Jean half leaned on his elbows, squared his strong shoulders and gave her a look of mischievous impatience.

"No, but you know you haven't told me if I'm going to be the lucky guy tonight. You've been thinking about it for the last ten minutes. What did you decide? Yes or no: are you coming to the show?"

He saw the anger flash in Florentine's green eyes. But she quickly looked down. In a voice that was at once irritated, pitiful and trying to be conciliatory, she replied:

"Why should I go to a show with you, will you tell me? I don't know you! How do I know who you are!"

He chuckled, realizing that she was trying to get him to make some revelation about himself.

"Well," he said, "you can find that out little by little, if your heart's really in it."

Less intimidated by the double sense of the phrase than by his detachment, she thought, humiliated: He wants to get me talking. Maybe it's only to make fun of me. Her own laugh now sounded shrill and forced.

But he was no longer paying attention to her. He seemed to be listening to sounds from the street. A second later Florentine heard the dull beating of drums. In front of the heavy glass doors a crowd began to gather. Salesgirls who had a moment free ran to the front of their counters. Canada had declared war on Germany more than six months ago, but military parades were still a novelty in the St. Henri neighbourhood and drew crowds whenever they passed.

As the squad reached the Five and Ten, Florentine leaned out to watch with a childlike fascination, eager and surprised. There they marched, stalwart fellows, solid in their massive khaki greatcoats, their arms stiff, sugar snow drifting down upon them. Beaming, she turned to face the young man, as if to ask him to share in her childish excitement, but his expression was so hostile and contemptuous that she shrugged and turned away, attentive again to every detail of the spectacle.

Now entering her field of vision were the new recruits, still in civilian clothes, some wearing only a light suit, others in old fall coats, ragged and patched, penetrated by the bitter wind. She knew by sight some of the young men marching behind the soldiers. Like her father, they had been on relief for a long time. Suddenly, though still captivated by this spectacular evocation of war, she had the vague intuition of a wretched poverty which looked upon it as a last resort. She remembered like a troubled dream the depression years during which she had been the only one of the family bringing home a little money. And before, when she was a child, the way her mother had worked. Rose-Anna's image passed clearly before her eyes, and she was back in that daily misery and distress. For an instant she saw through her mother's eyes the passage of these men, tramps already marching like soldiers in their flapping rags. But her mind never lingered over thoughts of this kind, which led to tiring and confusing ideas. The parade seemed to her a simple distraction, a break in the monotony of the long store hours. Her eyes wide, her cheeks slightly flushed under her makeup, she turned once again to Jean Lévesque. Lively, offhand, she made her brief, pitiless comment on the scene:

"Crazy, eh?"

But Jean looked at her with such animosity that she thought almost happily, taking secret revenge: Why, he's crazy too! Passing judgement on him gave her a moment of genuine satisfaction.

His hand moved over his face again and again, as if to wipe away the cobweb of his thoughts, or perhaps simply from fatigue or habit. Finally, staring at the girl, he asked for the second time:

"Your name. Tell me your name."

"Florentine Lacasse," she answered curtly, already robbed of her small victory, and angry that she could find no escape from his ascendancy.

"Florentine Lacasse," he murmured, amused. He was searching in his pocket for a coin. "Very well, Florentine Lacasse, while you're waiting for the right soldier to come along you can always meet me tonight in front of the Cartier. Eight o'clock, does that suit you?" he added, almost playfully.

Seized by disappointment but tempted nonetheless, she did not move. This wasn't the kind of invitation she had been waiting for. But it happened they were showing *Bitter Sweet* at the Cartier. Yesterday Marguerite had been telling her about the plot, which was beautiful and very moving. She thought also of her new little hat and the perfume she'd just bought, and, more consoled every minute, of the fine couple they would make, she and Jean, almost the same height. People would certainly be intrigued at seeing them together. She even began to imagine the stories that would go around. That amused her. What did she care if stupid people wanted to talk! Really! And she saw herself with him in a smart restaurant in the neighbourhood, just the two of them in a discreetly lit booth where they could hear the flood of sound from the nickelodeon. There, she would be sure of her charm and power. That would be the place for making this insolent young man eat out of her hand. And she'd bring him around to inviting her again and again. Impudent, dreaming, the beginnings of a smile were showing when Jean stood up and tossed a fifty-cent piece on the counter. "Keep the change," he said coldly. "Buy yourself a decent meal. You're far too thin."

A harsh reply was on the tip of her tongue. She was cruelly hurt, more by her secret submission to him than by anything else, and she wanted to throw the money back, but he was already getting into his overcoat.

"You hate me, do you?" he muttered to himself. "You hate it here, you hate everything." It was as if he concentrated until he saw only the desolate landscape of her heart where nothing had yet grown but thoughts of bitterness and rejection.

Then he was out, walking quickly, decisively, strength and vigour in his shoulders. He didn't have to use his elbows to get through the crowd. It opened before him.

Florentine had a feeling that if she didn't go to his rendezvous she would never see him again. As she watched him leave she had the intuition that this stranger knew her better than she knew herself. For an instant he had cast a brilliant light in her mind, and she had glimpsed a thousand things in her life that before had lain in darkness.

Now that he was gone it seemed to her that she had fallen back into unawareness of her own thoughts. She was angry and confused. I won't go. I won't. We'll just see if I'll go, she thought, digging her nails in the palms of her hands. But at the same time she saw Eveline watching her and holding back a mischievous laugh. And Marguerite, pushing to get past with a sundae, whispered in her ear:

"I wouldn't be mad if he gave me the eye, that guy. He suits me right to a T."

The rage in Florentine's heart was appeased a little, mingling with the agreeable certainty of being envied. She had never been able to enjoy the possession of the most insignificant thing, or of a passing friendship, or even her scanty memories, except through the eyes of others.

TWO

T he whole afternoon at the foundry, Jean, who should have been giving his full attention to a motor he was repairing, was surprised to find himself thinking, I'm stupid, God, am I stupid! What do I want, getting mixed up with that Florentine. When those kids get their hooks into you they never let go. I don't even want to see her again. What got into me, asking her for a date?

He had thought he could pull back from this flirtation, which was barely started in any case. That's what he had done in the past, stopping halfway in his rare attempts at a conquest, either because it promised to be too easy or seemed like a waste of time. Striving for success, devoured by ambition, he had until now devoted his spare time stubbornly, to his studies, with no regret or sense of sacrifice.

But at the end of his working day, walking back to his little furnished room on St. Ambroise Street near the Lachine Canal, he was surprised then irritated to find how persistently Florentine occupied his mind.

She's just like all the others, he thought. She wants to have fun, make a guy spend money and time on her. That's all

she's after. It could be me or anybody . . . But then he imagined her skinny body, her childlike mouth, her tormented eyes.
No, he admitted to himself, there's something different about
her . . . and maybe that's what interests me . . . just a bit.

Then, walking alone in the darkening street, he burst
out laughing. He had just thought how he must appear to
Florentine: a joker, a bad boy, maybe even dangerous, probably attractive, like any real danger. At the same time he realized how many contradictions there were between himself and
the character he had created for other people: the smart guy
who liked to astonish by boasting about his supposed wild
life, a guy who was admired. The true Jean Lévesque was quite
different: quiet, stubborn and, most of all, hard working. This
was the one he preferred, the practical Jean who liked work for
the ambition it fed and the success it could lead to, this young
man with never a daydream who gave himself up to work as
if it were a kind of revenge.

"That's it!" he said, and thought of himself hidden in his
little room, working all evening at his correspondence course.
He took a kind of delight in this picture of himself. This was
the way to get more education. Who needed teachers? He was
his own teacher, hard and determined. The rest – the tangible
forms of success, money and respect – could wait a while. He
already knew the intoxication of success when, feeling as lonely
in his room as in a desert, he would tackle a hard problem in
algebra or geometry, swearing, teeth clenched: "I'll show them
some day . . ." A few more years and he would have his engineer's degree. Then, if they had been too stupid to see what he
was worth, they would get an eyeful. They'd see that Jean
Lévesque was somebody.

At home he went to sit at his desk, but the thought of
his rendezvous with Florentine came back to vex him.

"Damn it, I just won't go, that's all," he said to himself, and he opened his books and notes. But the thought wouldn't leave him; and at the same time the notion that he would accomplish less than usual tonight put him in such bad humour that he suddenly pushed away the papers spread before him.

One outing a week was his usual relaxation. It satisfied him, and the diversion enhanced the preciousness of his studious evenings. Once a week, preferably on Saturday, he would walk up St. Catherine Street, go to the Palace or the Princess theatre, then have a classy meal in a west-end restaurant. Afterwards he would go back to the obscurity of his suburb, light-footed, whistling, happy, as if he had received confirmation of his secret ambitions. Those were the times when he was most happy to be alone and free, without family or demanding friendships to distract him from his plan. This weekly excursion kept alive his hope for a splendid future. Just as he needed to wear soft, expensive materials, he also needed to mingle with the crowd to taste to the full his self-confidence, his refusal to sacrifice what he felt to be rare in himself, setting him off from others.

What worried him occasionally was his intense curiosity about people, a curiosity that at times came close to pity. Pity or contempt, he couldn't exactly say. But he felt vaguely that his constant need to be superior fed on a kind of compassion for those humans who were actually farthest from himself.

Pity or contempt? he wondered, and thought about Florentine again. Who was she? How was her life? There were a host of things he would have liked to know about her, without giving up any of his precious time or letting her encroach upon his life. Since the first day he saw her in the Five and Ten her face had followed him to the most unlikely places – sometimes in the forging hall when the blast furnace was open and the flames danced before his eyes; and even here at times, in his own room, when the wind rattled his windowpanes and infected his mind with its reckless turbulence.

Finally the obsession grew so intense that he could see no way to free himself of it except by showing himself purposely cynical and hard to the girl, forcing her to hate and fear him, so that she would avoid him and save him the trouble of avoiding her. But after one or two tries he still went back to the restaurant. And today he had so forgotten himself that he'd invited her out. Was it pity? Self-interest? Or just to raise a final barrier between them? – for she'd be bound to refuse such an abrupt and clumsy invitation. (Had he really thought she'd refuse?)

He remembered her pale face and that flicker of uneasiness in her eyes, and he wondered: Did she take me seriously? Is she not too timid to show up?

He knew, of course, that his curiosity had carried the day, that it now possessed him like a burning passion. It was the only emotion he would likely make no effort to master, because it seemed a necessary enrichment to his life. His curiosity was as ruthless as the wind tonight all through the suburb, along the canal, in the deserted streets, around the small frame houses, everywhere, and far up toward the mountain.

He tried to force his attention back on the work before him, but under his equations he scribbled the word "Florentine." Then, hesitantly, he added "Lacasse," and a second later irritably scratched it out. Florentine, he thought, was a young, happy name, a springtime name, but her surname broke the charm with its connotation of working-class drudgery. And that is likely how she was, this little waitress from the Five and Ten: half slum child, half graceful springtime, a springtime brief and quick to wither.

These idle thoughts, so foreign to his habits, set his nerves on edge. He rose and went to the window, and opened it wide to the wind and snow. He thrust his head outside and breathed deeply of the night air.

The wind was howling down the deserted pavement, and the snow, in its wake, powdery and dazzling white, whirled up in the air, ran to creep along the house walls and rose again in random leaps like a dancer pursued by a cracking whip. The wind was master with his whip, the snow was the wild, supple ballerina running before him, spinning on command and, at a word, prostrating herself on the earth before him. Then there was nothing to be seen but the long ripple of a scarf of white unrolled along the thresholds of the houses, silent and barely trembling. But the lash whistled down again and the dancer, in a rush of energy, rose once more to unfurl her powdery veil at the height of the street lamps. She rose and rose until she was flying over the rooftops and the plaintive sound of her weariness beat on the tightly closed shutters.

"Florentine . . . Florentine Lacasse . . . half song, half squalor, half springtime, half misery," the young man murmured. Staring at the snow dancing below him, he thought it had taken on human form, that of Florentine herself, who, though exhausted, was unable to stop whirling and spending her strength, and danced on there in the night, a prisoner to her own exertions. Those girls are like that, I suppose, he thought. They run this way and that like blind things, to their own ruin.

He turned away to change his train of thought, and as if he were trying with a single glance to gather up all the strength, all the certainty of his life and preserve his pride in his chosen path, he stared around his room. From the low, mildewed ceiling hung an electric cord pulled sideways to his table with a string. The light from the bulb fell stark and unshaded on his open books, on the bits of paper with scribbled notes and a pile of heavy volumes rising in a tier. In one corner of the room was a hot plate on which drops of dark foam from his coffee pot fell and sputtered. His bed was unmade. A few books lay on the pillow and others were strewn pell-mell along with his clothes on an ancient plush armchair. No shelves, no cupboards, no closet. No place to put anything. The room seemed in the throes of a perpetual preparation to move. But that was precisely what he liked about it. He took pains to remind himself that his presence here was transitory, that he was neither made for poverty nor resigned to it. He needed ugliness around him as well as beauty to stiffen his resolve. This room had the same effect on him as his lonely walks among the bright lights of Montreal. It excited and uplifted him, gave him an immediate obstacle to be overcome. Usually when he came into this room he felt all his projects, ambitions and delight in studying come alive. He felt all other desires fade away. Then he knew what he wanted. But tonight the spell held back. He was there like a caged animal. And always with the question, "Is she going to be there or not?"

He realized that he wouldn't stop thinking of Florentine. With a shrug he told himself there were other experiences as valuable as study, and that satisfying his curiosity had always quieted and enriched his mind.

Quickly he got ready and went out. The street was silent. Nothing is as quiet as St. Ambroise Street on winter nights. A passerby will slip past from time to time, drawn to the feebly lit window of a grocery-restaurant. A door opens, light splashes on the snowy sidewalk, the sound of a voice comes from far away. The passerby disappears, the door slams shut and in the deserted street, between the pale fire of family lamps in the houses on one side and the sombre walls bordering the canal on the other, nothing is left but the heavy power of night.

In other days this was where the suburb stopped. St. Henri's last houses had stood there facing waste fields, and an almost limpid, rustic air hung about their simple gables and tiny gardens. From those better days St. Ambroise now has no more than two or three great trees, their roots still digging in beneath the concrete of the sidewalk. Textile mills, grain elevators and warehouses have risen to face the frame houses, slowly, solidly, walling them in. The houses are still there with their little wrought-iron balconies, their tranquil façades and the faint, sweet music that sometimes filters out from behind closed shutters, trickling into the silence like the voice of another age: little lost islands to which the wind bears odours of all the continents. There is no night so cold that it does not carry from the warehouse halls the smells of milled wheat, ground grains, rancid oil, molasses, peanuts, furs, white flour and resinous pine.

Jean had chosen to live there because in that distant street, almost unknown, rents had remained very low; but also because the neighbourhood, with its rumbling, rattling and whistling at the day's end and the deep silence of its nights, switched his mind to the world of his work.

It's true that in spring the nights were not so quiet. As soon as navigation was open the deep cry of the foghorn, repeated a hundred times, came from down at the end of St. Ambroise from sunset until dawn, rising over the suburb, carried by the wind, until it even reached Mount Royal.

The house where Jean had found his little furnished room was just in front of the swing-bridge of St. Augustin street. It could watch the passage of flatboats, tankers that stank of oil or gasoline, wood barges, colliers, all of them giving a triple blast with their foghorns just before its door: their demand to be let out from the narrows of the towns into the wide, rough waters of the Great Lakes.

But the house was not only on the path of the freighters. It was also near the railway, at the crossroads of the eastern and western lines and the maritime routes of the great city. It was on the pathways of the oceans, the Great Lakes and the prairies.

To its left were shining rails. Directly in front of it shone red and green signals. In the night, coal dust and soot flew around it, amid a cavalcade of wheels, the frenzied gallop of puffing steam, the long wailing of whistles, the short, chopped blast from the chimneys of the flatboats; among these sounds tripped the shrill, broken ringing of the alarm and, prolonged beyond this clamour, the slow purring of a ship's screw. Often, when he woke at night with all these sounds about him, Jean imagined he was on a voyage, sometimes on a freighter, sometimes in a Pullman car. He would close his eyes and go to sleep with the agreeable impression that he was escaping, constantly escaping.

The house with its narrow front looked askance at the street, twisted as if to brace itself against all the shocks to which it was exposed. Its side walls sloped outward in a V, like a clumsy ship whose immovable prow strove to cleave the surrounding noise and darkness.

Jean hesitated on the threshold of the street door. He loved this house as he had likely never loved anything else in the suburb. He and the house were two long-allied forces, equally unyielding.

A gust of wind caught him from the side and sent him staggering. Pushed and battered toward the west, he went down the street hugging the house fronts. At the corner of St. Ferdinand Street the throb of a guitar escaped through a rattly store window. He went close to the steamed-up glass and saw, between the display cards, in a tiny free space at the back, the pink, beaming face of Ma Philibert, the owner. She was perched on a high stool behind the counter, one hand caressing a black cat whose tail tapped the worn and polished wood. Damp overcoats, caps and gloves, tossed over the sheet-iron that served as a fire screen, gave off a thick, hot vapour that blurred the surrounding faces. Jean couldn't see the guitarist but he had a glimpse of the instrument and the hand plucking the strings. To one side he could make out another musician playing the spoons: two tablespoons back to back giving out the staccato of metallic castanets. The gang, he thought, was having fun as usual, and on the cheap.

At the back of the shop there were two or three newcomers whose faces he could barely see. Sometimes they brought a guest to these evening get-togethers, newly hired textile workers or perhaps a few young people out of work whom Ma Philibert greeted with the same enthusiasm she showed her paying customers. Her little restaurant-store had always been the refuge of a noisy, squabbling group, usually penniless.

Jean remembered the time when he worked as a spinner and went to the little restaurant every evening except payday; for even then it seemed a tradition that on Saturday night everyone went down to the movie theatre on Notre Dame; on other evenings they returned to the soiled packs of cards, music and other cheap amusements they found at Emma Philibert's.

"Fat Emma," they called her. The most maternal and gentle influence in his life had certainly been this exuberant woman, Jean reflected. He could still hear her rough tone when she gave in to someone asking for credit: "Y' darn fool, you'll never have a penny to your name." Then, edging grumpily off her stool, she would add in a low, conspiratorial voice, "I guess it's some tobacco you want, to poison your health an' rot your teeth? Here y'are. I suppose you're goin' to pay, one of these days in a month of Sundays?" Then aloud: "D'you think Emma Philibert's stupid enough to fall for that? I don't give nothin' away, not a scrap!"

Jean was on the point of going inside. Maybe an evening here would give his mind a change, and confirm how well he had spent the last years and how far he had risen above his former companions. Ma Philibert would cluck, like a mother hen, take him in her arms, feel the material in his suit, marvel at his healthy looks. When she saw one of her former poor boys come back prosperous, she was happy as a mother superior who sees her predictions about a prize student finally come true. She'd seen all kinds in her "goodies shop" since she'd bought it to keep her husband alive during the bad years. Some of them depressed, some raging to succeed; strong men, weak men, disillusioned, mistreated, rebellious, boastful or silent men, she'd seen the whole between-the-wars generation pass by. If anybody could write about that strange time, Jean thought, it would be Ma Philibert. What experiences she must have collected! What spicy stories she could tell! But there it is, he thought, these big red-faced, happy mommas probably see nothing and understand nothing, and think everything's just lovely.

His vanity egged him on to go in and be seen by her and the little gang in all his new importance. He felt the old urge to show off to these simple young men, with his superior judgement and sometimes vehement style. But the futility of all those arguments came back to him, and the space of solitude they had cleared around him.

He came to with a start and went on toward Notre Dame Street. Nothing, it seemed, nothing tonight could take his mind off that skinny girl, with her burning eyes which he could see like an enigma behind the steaming counter of the Five and Ten.

The clock of St. Henri's Church stood at a quarter to eight when he reached the heart of the neighbourhood.

He stopped in the middle of St. Henri Square, a vast area furrowed by the railway and two streetcar tracks, a crossroads planted with black and white posts and level-crossing gates, a clearing of asphalt and dirty snow, open between bell towers and domes to the assault of howling locomotives, the peal of the great bells, the raucous streetcar gong and the unending traffic of Notre Dame and St. James streets. Almost every night now, adding to the anguish and darkness of St. Henri, came the distant tramp of heavy boots and the roll of drums, sometimes coming from Notre Dame, sometimes from as far away as the armouries up on the heights of Westmount, when the wind blew down from the mountain.

Then all these noises were drowned.

A drawn-out trembling shook the suburb.

At Atwater Street, at Rose-de-Lima, at the rue du Couvent and now at St. Henri Square, the level-crossing gates were being lowered. Here, where two main streets entered the square, their eight wooden arms, black and white with gleaming red signal lamps, met and brought the traffic to a stop.

At these four neighbouring crossings, morning and evening, the crowd of pedestrians paused to let the train go by, and impatient lines of cars idled in their stifling exhaust, many sounding their horns in fury, as if St. Henri were suddenly giving vent to its exasperation at these howling trains which sliced it violently in two with such intolerable frequency.

The train rolled by. The acrid smell of coal filled the street. A swirl of soot rose just above the rooftops, then, as it began to swoop down, the belfry of St. Henri's Church appeared, floating, without a base, like a phantom arrow amid the clouds. Then the clock appeared. Its lighted face pierced an opening in the trail of smoke, and little by little the whole church was to be seen, high architecture in the Jesuit style. In the middle of the front yard a Sacred Heart statue received the last particles of soot with open arms. The parish appeared again out of the smog, falling into place with its own tranquil durability. School, church, convent: a close-knit, centuries-old alliance, as strong in the heart of the urban jungle as in the Laurentian valleys. Beyond them, streets with low houses descended in two directions toward the areas of greater poverty, on this side to Workman Street and St. Antoine, and, on the other, down to the Lachine Canal where St. Henri stuffs its mattresses, spins its thread of silk or cotton, runs its looms, reels off its spools, while the earth trembles at the rushing trains, and the foghorns blast, and the ships, engines, screws, rails and whistles spell out the adventure of the world.

Jean felt, with a certain joy, that he was like the ship or the train, or anything else that picked up impetus as it passed through the suburb to reach its full speed elsewhere. For him it was not a punishment to spend a while in St. Henri; it was only a time of waiting and preparation.

He arrived at the Notre Dame viaduct, almost on top of the little red-brick train station. With its small tower and wooden platform squeezed between minuscule backyards, it made you think of a middle-class pensioner on a quiet vacation or, even more, of farm folk in their Sunday best, if you stopped at its rustic appearance. But beyond it, in a large notch in the suburb, the town of Westmount climbs in tiers toward the mountain's ridge in its stiff English luxury. Thus the little station is an invitation to the infinite travels of the mind. Here poverty and superfluity will stare tirelessly at each other, as long as Westmount lasts, as long as St. Henri lies at its feet. Between the two the bell towers soar.

The young man's gaze wandered from the campanile of St. Thomas Aquinas to the colonnaded tower of the convent and the spire of St. Henri, and from there directly to the flank of the mountain. He loved stopping at this spot in daytime to stare at the cold, high portals and the fine homes in grey or pink stone that stood out clearly on the hillside, and at night to see their lights shining in the distance like signals on his path. His ambitions and resentments would rise around him then and enclose him in their familiar net of anguish. In the face of this domineering mountain he felt hatred and at the same time inklings of his own power.

From St. Antoine Street there rose again the echo of those marching feet that were becoming a kind of secret texture in the suburb's life. The war! Jean had already mulled over the notion of it with a secret irresistible joy. Was this not the field where all his strong points would be deployed? How much talent lying fallow would now be called upon! He saw the war as a personal stroke of luck for him, his own chance to rise rapidly in the world. He saw himself turned loose in a life of changing values, with life itself changing every day and ready to lift him high on its crest in this raging sea of men. His strong, dark-skinned hands came down angrily on the stone parapet. What was he doing here? What could there be in common between him and a girl called Florentine Lacasse?

In his mind he wanted to diminish her, and tried to remember her vulgar expressions, her clumsy gestures. At once an appealing idea occurred to him: he would spy on her arrival without showing himself. At least he'd have the fun of seeing her caught in his net.

He crossed the street, slipped into the doorway of a store and waited, hands in pockets. He began to smile. She wouldn't come, and the whole thing would end right there. Yes, that would be the end of it, for he would stop bothering her unless she was so imprudent as to come to him now. He gave her five minutes more, and often wondered later what had possessed him to stay on under his stone shelter, watchful, nervous, but still anxious to have it over. Gradually his curiosity grew so acute that his pride began to hurt. Why didn't she come? Didn't she care about him at all? Almost all the girls he had wanted from time to time had been responsive. Could Florentine be making a fool of him? He hated to think that he might be less attractive, less sure of pleasing, than he had thought.

Peeking out of his shelter, he stared into the dark. Suddenly he gave a start.

A thin form was taking shape near the rue du Couvent, running with tiny steps.

He recognized her at once. She came toward him, doubled over against the wind, trotting, trotting, hurrying along, holding her hat on with one hand.

In that moment, from the depths of his being, from a region almost unfamiliar to him, surged a strange, new feeling, composed of more than cool curiosity and vanity, something that softened and warmed him inexplicably, filling him with the naive emotion of an adolescent.

Yes, really, he was feeling sorry for her, all of a sudden. A particle of pity had pierced beyond his rough curiosity. He was even a little moved to see her this way, hurrying toward him in the cold wind, against the storm. He would have liked to run to her, hold her, and help her to struggle against the wind and up the slope. Yet he drew back into the darkest corner of the doorway to watch her approach. Why had she come? Why was she so silly, so reckless and imprudent? Could she possibly imagine she was running to meet happiness, all alone in this furious night?

Already a dull rage, at the thought she could so easily be won, was smothering compassion in him.

Maybe she won't stop, he thought. And he waited for her to go on her way through the wind with her tiny steps, to disappear like an illusion. With the ounce of pity he still felt he hoped she would take flight.

But the girl slowed down in front of the movie house. She paced, waiting, loitering in front of the posters, stopping to examine them, then moving out again in the cold light of the sign. He saw her look left and right, then stare out beyond the lighted circle.

Well, he thought, and snapped his fingers, we'll not waste any more time on Florentine. Why should she be different from the others? I guess I can go home now. It's finished.

Florentine had begun to stamp her feet to keep them warm, and her dark coat flew back from her knees. She beat her hands together, then stood stock-still in front of the poster windows.

What do I mean, finished? What was there to be finished? And what was I feeling about her a minute ago? What's finished?

A group of girls passed the doorway in which the form of the young man was barely distinguishable. A few steps from the theatre one of them called to Florentine.

"Waitin' for somebody?"

Jean didn't hear the reply, but he saw Florentine hesitate, glancing around her. Apparently her friends were trying to coax her to go in with them. After a last searching look she went with the others into the big, brightly lit lobby. Jean was relieved. His arms fell to his sides, and his fists slowly unclenched. What's finished? If she hadn't come, would I ever have tried to see her again? Certainly not! In any case, he thought, that's the end of her. A little smile touched his lips and he went on his way, whistling.

But a doubt went with him, and after a moment he realized he was not satisfied. Did she come to meet me or her little friends? he wondered. I'm no further ahead. He could see other studious evenings lost because of this unknown girl, because he would go on asking himself dozens of questions about her. Perhaps in order to get her out of his mind he needed to be sure she didn't disdain him. "Oh, who cares about that?" he said aloud, at the end of his patience.

He had neither the desire nor the energy to go back to his studies. He felt tired, and wanted to mix with men, hear them talk, pounce on their contradictions, force them into submission and regain his certainty of superiority. To his right was the whitewashed brick façade of a little restaurant whose sign read The Two Records. He pressed the latch. Music from a nickelodeon filtered out. He stamped the snow from his feet and went inside.

THREE

The Two Records, like most of the joints of its kind in the neighbourhood, was not so much a restaurant as a combination cigar store and snack bar with soft drinks, and purveyor of ice cream and chewing gum. It took its name from a side activity unrelated to the restaurant: the sale of records – French and American songs whose popularity had waned in Montreal but was still high in St. Henri. As soon as you came in, you noticed records racked by the wall, and others hung on a long wire that spanned the room. Above the counter, suspended in the same way, hung all kinds of newspapers: dailies, weeklies, "illustrateds" and magazines. An occasional meal was served in the back, at small tables separated by partitions. They were rarely occupied, because The Two Records' customers preferred to eat their hot dogs or sandwiches at the counter and chat with the owner, Sam Latour.

Of course Sam would take the trouble to go and serve an occasional stranger in the back booth, and he did it politely; but he displayed a prodigious surprise that anyone could expect him, the boss, to interrupt his conversation and walk the length of the restaurant a couple of times. If you insisted on sitting alone, the custom was to stop at the counter, wait there for your food, and take it with you into exile.

It wasn't that Sam was grumpy or high-hat about it; but like most French-Canadians, he found serving in a restaurant distasteful, calling for a deference that went against the grain.

Sam Latour always felt a shade humiliated when his business obliged him, for example, to leave a perfectly good argument hanging while he went back to the kitchen to warm a cup of coffee or a bowl of soup. You'd have thought he ran the place so he could chew the fat to his heart's content, as they said in the neighbourhood. He had bought the shop, it was true, with the intention of turning it into a big restaurant. But slowly he had veered toward this kind of small commerce, contented, relieved to be his own boss in a place where business jogged along peacefully and profits were never too high. A stout, jovial man with full cheeks and an easy laugh, he loved talking war and politics. He was just holding forth to four or five men half sprawled across the counter when a gust of cold air came from the doorway and Jean Lévesque appeared on the threshold.

There was a sudden silence, then the conversation resumed, more muted this time. The Two Records, not far from the railway station and the taxi stand, and just a stone's throw from the Cartier cinema, was at the busiest part of St. Henri. A new face aroused much less curiosity there than in the little hangout on St. Ambroise. But on nights when the weather was bad, it was almost always the same people you saw gathered around the fat cast-iron stove: a taxi-driver taking a few minutes off between trains, a railway worker from the station, a night watchman from the switchman's cabin, a worker from the late shift. From time to time an usher from the movie house would come in on the run, splendid in his blue livery with red braid, and occasionally there would be a railway porter or messenger. A number of neighbourhood unemployed spent the whole evening there.

These men talked a great deal about the war and particularly about conscription, which they felt was imminent. The prevalent notions of the Fifth Column and the national police pervaded these men's thoughts and left them not knowing who to trust. They stopped talking and glanced at the newcomer. Reassured by his appearance they took up their discussion again. The voices quickly grew louder and were soon at their usual pitch.

Sam Latour stared quizzically at Jean, served him quickly, and went back behind the counter to pick up his argument:

"That there Imaginot line, now, that Imaginot line, you just tell me what good it is, eh? If you take an' block my road on one side, an' you leave me wide open on the other, will you tell me what good your Imaginot's goin' to do? If that's all she's got to defend herself, it's my idea France is goin' to take a lickin'."

But the man he had spoken to replied with unshakeable conviction:

"Don't you worry, Latour. France's ready. France has the Maginot line. And if she didn't have Maginot she'd still have enough friends in the world to come and save her. There ain't a country in the world has more friends than France. And those totalitarian countries with their worst kind of monsters telling you, 'I'm better than you and I'll take power, I'm the leader . . .' – no, you'll see, they're all alone, those countries like that. . . ."

He was a well-built man in taxi-driver's uniform. He seemed close to forty. But his fresh, clear complexion, his strong teeth which showed when he spoke, his eyes that sparkled with enthusiasm under the peak of his cap, and his strong, supple hands, showed that this man was in the prime of life with his strength intact, perhaps even all the ardour of his youth. He spoke loudly in a rich, sonorous voice, and he often used fine-sounding words which he mispronounced and only half understood; but he seemed to listen with lively pleasure to their resonance within his mind.

"France," he went on, and the word came out with an almost tender intonation, "no sir, France cannot be beaten. And anyway, as long as the Maginot line holds . . ."

"Now listen, Lacasse," Sam Latour interrupted, seeing an opening on the subject that interested him most, "just imagine I'm here and you're at war with me, big boy. Well, here I am behind my counter, okay? You can't get at me from the front, but what's to stop you goin' around and catchin' me on the flank? Now *that*," he went on, acting out the attack and the surprise, pointing to the breach in his defences, "*that's* war! Strategy. No, if you listen to me, it'll take more than the Imaginot to keep the Germans out. And maybe France made a big mistake getting into that war."

"France had no choice," said Azarius Lacasse in a more conciliating tone.

"No, she didn't have much choice, indeed, with England pushing her from behind," interjected a young worker in overalls, who, absorbed in his newspaper, had kept out of the argument until now.

The word *England* at once set a match to the dispute.

"Hold on," said Azarius. "We mustn't take it out on Ingle-land neither. I got no love for them, but I got like a kind of respect for Ingle-land. You can't deny it, we've been just as well off under their rule as we would have been on our own. You can't blame everythin' on Ingle-land. To tell you the truth,

Ingle-land had no more choice than France in that Munich business. You saw Chamberlain with his umberella . . ."

There were guffaws from the onlookers, but a peevish voice came from the back of the restaurant:

"According to you, then, we're not in this war to help the English?"

"I don't say that's not part of it," said Azarius. "But the main thing is to stop Germany, she's just as fierce as ever, going at Po-land that couldn't defend itself, and look at the way they chopped away at Austria and Czechoslovakia. There's more reasons than Ingle-land for going in the war. There's humanity . . ."

A short-legged man with a weasel face approached the counter.

"Don't tell me!" he said. "I suppose it's to save democracy again!"

A fresh guffaw greeted this sally.

"Yeah, democracy." Sam picked up the word. "They're still singin' the same old tune they did in the last war. What does it mean anyway, that highfalutin word?"

"Well, I'll tell you," replied the weasel-faced man, "it's soup for the old folks, and charity, and no jobs. A third of the population on direct relief and poor devils working on the streets at thirteen cents an hour for three or four days in the springtime. That's what your democracy is."

"It's the right to say what you think, too," said Azarius quietly.

"Oh, yeah," shouted Sam Latour, his ruddy face lit up by derision and his potbelly shaking with laughter under his white apron. "Yeah, a big help that is nowadays . . ." and he was on the point of adding, . . . when people are going hungry, but he held back, remembering just in time that among people he knew, Azarius Lacasse had been one of the hardest hit by the years of unemployment.

His good nature getting the better of his love of mockery, he tried to change the subject. But Azarius, untroubled, went on quietly:

"I tell you this war is for justice and punishment."

An absent-minded smile, echo of the tumbling thoughts behind these words, appeared on his lips and revealed the man entirely. Not only had he stayed young in body, he had preserved a naive and incurable belief in goodness. In that moment Jean, isolated at his table and leaning over to get a look at the taxi-driver, saw the resemblance. "Florentine's father," he said to himself. And he felt a growing contempt for these working-class men, among them this hearty innocent, who thought they had a right to their own opinions about this upheaval of human forces whose very principle was beyond them.

A murmur of disapproval around the counter had greeted the remarks of Azarius. The taxi-driver saw nothing but stern or mocking faces around him, and looked farther for support. Seeing Jean Lévesque in the back of the restaurant he called out to him:

"Hey, what do you think, young fellow? Don't you believe it's up to the young men to go and fight? I tell you, if I was twenty again . . ."

Jean had a secretive, disdainful smile that hardened his features.

"What do I think?"

He thrust his head toward the little group and then, in a calm, biting voice, went on:

"We're saying Germany wants to destroy us. And right now in Germany a whole lot of good quiet people like us, no worse than we are, they're getting whipped into a frenzy by the same story. They're being told the others are penning them into a country that's too small, and don't want to let them live. On one side or the other somebody's being sold a bill of goods. Maybe the Germans are wrong. We don't know. All I know is, I don't want to go killing some guy that never did me any harm, and who hasn't the choice but to do what he's told. I've got nothing against that poor guy. Why should I go and stick a bayonet into him? He wants to live, just like I do. He doesn't want to die."

The young man's insolent tone, his detachment, stunned the others. The ideas just expressed were beyond them and made no impression. In this densely populated neighbourhood they had grown used to many kinds of emotions aroused by the war, from indignation to self-interest, from violent opposition to revolt or fear. But from lack of any close acquaintance with war they could not conceive the impulse of pity behind the young man's judgement. His cold manner did the rest in turning the loafers in the shop against him. Their laughter, then, was in support of Azarius, when he said roughly:

"Pacifist, eh?"

"No," Lévesque said calmly, amused that these men who had a mortal fear of conscription should attach so much contempt to the word "pacifist." (He knew that some of them would gladly take to the woods to escape the call-up, but would rather be labelled draft dodgers than pacifists.) "No," he said, "pacifists are heroes. They're people who sacrifice their own interests to an idea they've got into their heads. How many do you know? I only know profiteers. Just look, the war's been on six months, and how many people are doing well off it? Starting with the ones who got a job in the army. A buck thirty a day isn't a fortune, but it's enough to get them marching by the thousands. And the guys in munitions factories, don't you think the war suits them just fine? From one end of the scale to the other it's profit makes things run. We're all profiteers, and if you don't like that word, just so we don't hurt the war effort let's say we're all good patriots."

He liked to sow confusion among his hearers, just as Azarius Lacasse liked to create goodwill around him.

"But patriotism for us," he went on, "means bigger profits for the ones who stay home than for the guys that go and get their heads bashed in fighting the war. Just wait another year, there'll be a fine state of affairs in this country, and speeches to match, you'll see what those speeches will lead to."

Azarius was pulling on his driver's gloves. Dignified, he eyed the young man from head to foot.

"One of these days," he said, "if I come across you and I have the time, we'll talk about things a little more. In the meantime don't forget there's internment camps for people that sabotage the war effort."

"And what about your freedom of speech?" quipped Sam Latour, laughing.

Azarius bowed his head to hide a smile. He had his sense of humour.

"Well, time's gettin' on," he said, ignoring Lévesque, "next train'll be in shortly."

Around him the conversation sprang up again, tame and cautious.

"Things going better at your place?" asked the owner.

"Not so bad, could be worse," said Lacasse. "My daughter's still working. Just across the road from here, by the way. At the Five and Ten."

"Oh, yes! That'd be Florentine, your oldest. She must be a big help, eh?"

Jean caught the sound of her name, and leaned forward in his booth to get a better look at her father. He felt a mixture of curiosity and animosity toward the man. An idealist, he'll get nowhere, he thought. He imagined the family of such a dreamer: anxious, unstable.

"Yep," said Azarius, "since Florentine's getting regular pay, it sure makes a difference."

He looked up suddenly, reddening.

"It's not right, you know," he said, "for a young girl to give her whole pay to help out the family. I don't like it, Latour. I don't like it one bit, and that's got to change soon. I just hope the building business picks up one of these days."

"Yeah, I don't see you drivin' taxis all your life."

"No siree," said the driver vehemently, "I'd drop it in a minute, and that's no lie. It's a dog's life."

He leaned heavily against the counter, suddenly limp, as if he heard the voice of defeat from within himself, the murmur that comes at certain times in our lives like an echo to our circumstances.

In his hesitant voice, his faltering gaze, Jean now caught a full glimpse of Florentine. Azarius, like his daughter, felt himself ill-suited to his work and unfitted for daily life; and the least forlorn of the two was perhaps not the father, Jean reflected, but rather the daughter whom he still saw running through the storm in a kind of desperation.

He reached the door just before Azarius, and went out, his head bent against the storm.

The tense, pale face of the young waitress still haunted him. Florentine, hating her work behind the counter, detesting every minute of her subjection to life, and yet giving almost all her pay to her family. A girl devoured at the same time by disgust at her daily lot and by devotion to those nearest her. This was a new Florentine!

He plunged into the dark of one of the alleys leading to Notre Dame Street. On the walls of the houses, to the right, to the left, wherever they were brightened by the pale rays of the arc lamps, he could make out "To Let" signs.

The crisis of the yearly move was already upon this unstable folk of the suburb.

Signs of spring, the young man thought.

It struck him that the signs belonged on more than the houses. *To Let* was posted on their very beings. Their arms, to let! Their idleness, to let! To let, their strength. And above all, their minds, which could be led astray at will, turned like weathercocks this way or that, ready for any risk, their forgotten energies unused, their hopes grown numb. Ready, like the houses, for the unknown. Emerging from the thaw, from the mildew! Ready for this call that was coming from abroad, spreading faster than the tolling of the tocsin. Ready for war.

And what am I ready for? he wondered. It still happened at times that he was not completely sure of his path. Two tendencies of almost equal strength struggled for possession of him, leading in opposite directions. At least he could still weigh his choices and imagine himself on the path of unselfishness which had occasionally tempted him. But he had little doubt about which way his will would eventually turn, or the final outcome that lay before him.

FOUR

While Jean Lévesque, wandering through the dark streets, was wishing he were with a friend to whom he could show off and talk about himself, another young man, the only human for whom he felt a real attachment, was making his way toward Ma Philibert's restaurant.

He reached the half-lit entrance, stumbled on a step buried in the snow and with a prolonged "Brrrrrrrr" entered the little shop like a gust of wind.

"Well, if it isn't Manuel!" cried Emma Philibert.

"Hi, Ma Philibert!" cried the young man in return, imitating the voice and gesture of the fat woman and running to join her behind the counter where, in her haste to get off the stool, she had lost one dilapidated shoe and was down retrieving it.

"Ma Philibert," he declared, "you're just as fat and round and heavy as ever . . . and just as beautiful," he added, chucking her under the chin.

"You crazy nut!" she cried, still smiling from her surprise, then laughing happily, puffing and giving a push to her hair to adjust her bun.

Then she noticed the young soldier's uniform and her face grew serious.

"Emmanuel! So it's true you joined up!"

Sitting at one of the restaurant's three tables, three young men were watching, one with impatience, like a dog, begging to play, one with ill-humour and the third with insolent boredom.

"Pitou! Boisvert! And Alphonse, you're here, too!" Emmanuel turned to greet each one in turn.

Tall, very thin, a little awkward with his hands, his face rubbed by the frost and lit by a friendly, open expression, he stood there uncertain because of the silence that had followed his greetings.

"Well, you guys, how are things?" he asked.

"Okay," said Boisvert, "first class, but you're standing in my light." Then he growled, "Why don't you shut the door right? Don't you know it's cold outside? It's twenty below! Where've you been? Is it that warm where you come from?"

"I guess," said Emmanuel, disconcerted.

Pitou had perched himself on the counter, his legs dangling, his guitar on his knees. Still shy, he watched Emmanuel and smiled aimlessly. To one side, where it was darker, sat Alphonse, a lazy smirk on his face. It's not easy, thought Emmanuel Létourneau, to pick up old acquaintances, even if you've not been away so long. And he wondered whether to sit down or simply buy some cigarettes and a chocolate bar and be on his way.

From his earliest childhood he had played with these boys despite his mother's prohibition. She would have liked to see him in better company. Then he had been lucky enough to go to St. Henri college while they, at thirteen or fourteen, were already looking for work. Before finishing school, to get away from his father's influence, he had impulsively taken a job as spinner in the cotton works on St. Ambroise. Shortly after, he became shop foreman, and this luck in those hard years had given him real prestige in the eyes of his old gang, still unemployed. Nothing in their lives held them together except the memory of the neighbourhood public school, where everybody went, whatever his class origin. There were sons of middle-class families along with ragged urchins from the canal side, and the pale, sickly children of families on relief. They sat side by side on their benches in the Christian brothers' school, and the glimpse he had of poverty at that early age never left his mind. And he never quite lost sight of the poorer kids he had liked at school: young Boisvert, intelligent and sly, but so starved that he spent more time stealing nuts and apples from other children's pockets than he did on his books; little Alphonse, already silent and bitter; and Pitou, Pitou who tore his pants and didn't dare go home for fear of a beating! Pitou, who missed three weeks of school because his mother had no thread for mending. Pitou, who turned up at last in his older brother's pants after the brother died of tuberculosis.

They had seemed to him to be the true expression of his generation – confused, wise-cracking, indolent. And on the day he left his job to join the army, the troublesome, confused recollections of his youth went with him, playing no small part, as he realized, in his decision.

It was only a few months ago that he used to stop by here at Emma's place, on his way from work, to buy a coke or a package of tobacco for the fellows sitting around in the low-ceilinged room. But as he came in just now he had felt a sullen, ill-concealed embarrassment among them. Then he understood: it was his uniform that provoked this veiled hostility. He had not been back in the suburb long before he sensed this unease, this mute disapproval. Yet as he walked around alone he had purposely sought out points of contact with his former life.

Ma Philibert, still nonplussed by his sudden appearance, made no secret of her delight. Beaming, she made him turn around while she inspected him from head to foot.

"Now, then! You sit down, Manuel," she said, fussing over him. "It's not been the same around here since you left. Sit down, sit down. You look well, you know, but you've lost weight. Do they feed you right in that army of yours?"

"Oh, yes," said Emmanuel, smiling, "we get lots to eat."

The smile gave his face its natural expression of gentleness. He had dark eyes, rather high cheekbones and a forehead narrowed at the temples. As he spoke he tilted his head slightly to one side, as if his neck had trouble holding it straight. His slim hands nervously dug into his greatcoat pockets. He drew out a lighter and a pack of cigarettes which he passed around before taking one. He lit up and settled comfortably in his chair. In the middle of the narrow room the cast-iron stove was red-hot, and Ma Philibert's face was framed as usual between the jars of peppermints and pink candies lined up on the counter. The small bell above the door rattled with every puff of wind. Boisvert, faithful to his obsession, took out his jackknife and started paring his nails. Emmanuel thought, I'm the one who's changed. He stretched his legs toward the stove's heat, sighing contentedly.

"You always were a soft touch," said Pitou.

He was smoking sparingly, watching with comic despair as his cigarette grew shorter.

"Yeah," he went on, "you've always got a cigarette to lend a guy. Not like Boisvert, he goes and smokes all by himself so he won't have to give us a puff. At least you're one of the guys."

He had moved to his regular place on top of the soft drink ice-box. Sitting on the red metal square, he held his guitar between his legs, reached for Emmanuel's forage cap and slapped it rakishly on his own head.

"You're wet behind the ears," said Boisvert. "All you know is how to bum cigarettes. When did I ever see you pass them around?"

Pitou shrugged, made a face, then, dropping to his feet, leaned over the shining lid to admire his reflection as he tried on Emmanuel's wedge-cap in different styles. Straightening up, he asked suddenly:

"How long you been in the army now, Manuel? Four months? How do you like it? Does a guy have a good life in the army, Manuel?"

"Not bad."

There was a pause. Alphonse had shifted his position, and as always when a trace of life animated this gangling body, everyone turned to look. He sat stretched out, his feet against the apron of the stove, his hands clasped behind his neck.

"Tell me, Manuel, why did you join up?" he asked in his drawling voice. "You had a good job. You were doing decent work. You didn't need the army to keep you alive."

"No," said Emmanuel, laughing, "not a bit of it."

"Is that right, you left your job to join up!" cried Ma Philibert. "I didn't believe it. Now why ever did you do that, Manuel?"

"There's a war on, you know, Mama," Emmanuel said.

"I know that, but the war's a long way off. Is it really our business?"

"Come on," said Pitou, "we're not goin' to let everybody get knocked around like the Poles."

"The Poles, the Poles, they're not our folks, are they?"

47

"There's not two kinds of folks on earth," Emmanuel said absent-mindedly, as if he had been following his own train of thought.

"You're not goin' to tell me," said fat Emma, "that the Polocks and them Ukrainians are just like us. Why, they beat their wives and they eat garlic."

She was tapping the counter with the tips of her plump fingers. The black cat, taking this for an invitation to be caressed, offered his pink nose. Emma scratched him behind the ears for a moment, her large bust heaving.

"Do you want me to tell you what I think?" she went on angrily. "It's those smooth talkers there, running around the streets getting young fellows to join, they're the ones you listened to. Don't try to tell me they didn't get you drunk to make you sign."

Emmanuel smiled, but the smile had no fixed place on his thin face. It wandered past his lips, touched his eyes, then disappeared in their depths to give way to an expression partly meditative, partly bitter, partly tender. Right here before him he felt he had the sad indifference of the human heart to the universality of unhappiness. An indifference that was not selfish or egotistical, that was perhaps nothing more than the instinct for self-preservation: ears stopped, eyes shut for survival in the poverty of her daily life.

"But Mama," he said, "if the neighbour's house was burning down you'd be the first one to go and help."

"Well, sure I'd go . . ."

"Come on, there's enough houses burning down and filth and misery right here around us every day," Boisvert broke in, "you don't have to go far to find that."

"I know," said Emmanuel. "And it wasn't to save Poland that I joined up, believe me."

"What for, then?" Boisvert demanded, disconcerted.

He was short, with long, dull-blonde hair that flopped down straight on both sides, and bright, shifty eyes. He went on paring his nails as he spoke, then stopped and pointed his knife blade at the others. But he frowned and went back to a gnawing attack on the flesh at the base of his thumbnail, chewing furiously, his eyes wide open and suffering behind his ravaged hand, then spat invisible bits of skin on the floor. Through the blue haze from their cigarettes Emmanuel stared at him. A shade of contempt showed in his eyes, then understanding. His face hung slightly forward, pale, almost too handsome, his thin cheeks hollowed. His dark eyes, deep-set, shone gently after his irritation passed.

"Did you ever think," he said, "that a guy can help himself sometimes by helping other people?"

"Like fun!" Boisvert replied. "A guy has his work cut out these days looking after himself."

He nibbled off a refractory bit of skin, snapped shut his jack-knife and stepped into the middle of the room, a disdainful curl on his lips.

"I'll tell you something," he said, "for twenty, thirty years society doesn't do a thing for us. It tells us, look after yourself, it's up to you. Then one fine day it remembers we're there. All of a sudden it needs us. Come and defend me, it's shouting. Come and defend me!"

He stopped in front of Emmanuel, solid on his short legs, a lock of blond hair hanging over his forehead.

"Now you, you were lucky. If you want to play hero, that's your business. Everybody's got his own business. But what about us, what did we get from society? Look at me, look at Alphonse. What did it ever do for us? Nothing. And if that's not enough, look at Pitou. How old is he? Eighteen. Well, he never got paid for a day's work in his life. An' it's almost five years since he left school with a good kick in the you know where and he's still lookin' for work. Is that fair, eh? Five years running right and left and all he's learned is playin' the guitar! Our Pitou smokes like a man, he chews like a man and he spits like a man, but he hasn't earned one red cent in all his dang life. Do you think that's pretty, now? I think that's damn awful, that's what I think."

Pitou, a flighty, impressionable creature, waggled his round head with its fuzzy hair and plucked the odd plaintive string on his guitar. Boisvert's honeyed sympathy, theatrical as it was, touched the very core of his torment. Another time he would have stuck out his tongue at him, but now, held up as victim, he felt obliged to support Boisvert.

"It's true, you know," he said. "I haven't been able to get a day's work since I quit school. I'm too old to deliver papers, and they won't take me on in the factories. Nobody wants any part of me, nowhere."

"What did I tell you?" said Boisvert. "It comes back to what I always said. Society gave us nothing. Nothing."

"Aren't you ashamed," cried Ma Philibert, "saying that in front of me, after all the time you've sat here evenings warming your feet at my fire, with my wood?"

"That's not what I'm talkin' about," said Boisvert. "Society . . ." he was about to go on.

"In my time," she scolded, "we didn't talk about being given nothin'. We talked about giving."

"That was your time." Boisvert was getting angry. "Nowadays it's not the same. As I was saying, society's given us nothing . . ."

"Wait a minute, wait a minute," Alphonse murmured lazily. "That's not quite true. Society gave us something. It gave us something, for sure. You know what it gave us?"

He was sitting almost in the dark, and spoke with his eyes half closed, barely moving his lips, so that his voice seemed to come from someone hidden behind him.

"All right, I'll tell you. It gave us temptations."

"You're crazy, you're all crazy," cried Ma Philibert.

"No, not so crazy," Emmanuel said gently. "What were you going to say, Alphonse?"

There was a pause. They could hear Alphonse laughing derisively. Then he went on, his thick voice rising through the dark, like a part of it:

"Did you ever go walking along St. Catherine Street, an' you didn't have a penny in your pocket, an' you look at all the stuff in the windows? Yes, eh? Well, so have I. An' I saw some great things, my friends, just like a lot of other people have. I had time to look, lots of time. The great things I've seen, just bummin' along St. Catherine, you couldn't make a list of it. Packards, Buicks, cars for speed, cars for fun, and all those big wax dolls with fancy dresses on, and some with not a stitch. There's nothin' you can't see on that street. Furniture, bed-rooms, more dolls in frills an' silk, and sports stores, golf clubs, tennis racquets, skis, fishin' poles. If anybody has time to have fun with all those things, it must be us, eh?

"But all the fun we get is looking. And the way people stuff themselves! Did you ever have an empty gut and walk by a restaurant up there where there's chicken roasting in the window? But that's not all, my friends. They put all that under our noses, all the very best. But don't ever believe that's all they do!

"They tell us to buy, as well. You'd think they're afraid we won't be tempted enough. So they dun it into our ears that we gotta buy all their junk. Turn on your radio a minute and what do you hear? Sometimes a gent from the loan company, he wants to lend you five hundred bucks. Boy! That's enough to buy an old Buick! Or you see a billboard that says how well they're goin' to dry-clean these rags you've got on. And then they tell you you're crazy, you're stupid not to get in fashion and have a frigidaire at home. Just open up the paper nowadays. Buy cigarettes, buy good Dutch gin, buy little pills for your headache, buy a fur coat. Nobody should go without, they drum it into you night and day. This is progress, everybody's got the right to have fun. Then you go out in the street. And they're tempting you with big lights every time you look up. Good cigarettes, good chocolate, lots of them, all in those little lights dancing over your head, here, there, everywhere."

He stood up and came out under the hanging light bulb, a tall, thin boy, his eyelids red with sties, his big ears standing out from his head.

"Yeah, temptations, that's what they've given us," he went on. "Nothing else but. This whole cheap show of a life is fixed to tempt us. And that's how society gets a hold on us, the cheater, and gets us good. Don't fool yourselves, you guys, we'll all be sucked in. It doesn't take much of a temptation either to make us decide to give our little beggarly lives. I know a guy went to join up, do you know why?"

He searched in his pockets and came up with a toothpick which he stuck between his lips.

"So he'd have a winter coat. That kid, he'd had enough of buying his clothes from the Jews on Craig Street in a rag shop that stinks of sweat and onions. That kid, it just hit him all of a sudden, he had to have an overcoat with brass buttons. And you can bet he's rubbing and shining them, right now, those brass buttons of his. But look what they cost him, eh?"

He stared for a second at Emmanuel.

"Do you want to hear another one?" he said. "Another of my stories?"

An impatient smile flickered on Emmanuel's face. He knew that it was as hard to interrupt Alphonse when he had a bee in his bonnet as it was to draw him out of his morose silence at other times.

"Go to it," he said. "It's not dull, anyway. You're off the track a bit sometimes, but you're always funny."

"Sure I'm funny," Alphonse agreed with a bitter smile. "I'm funny to look at and funny to listen to. And I'll make a real funny corpse one of these days."

He opened wide his sickly eyes, a thing he seldom did, and his whole face was transformed. Strangely enough, all the interest of this wretched face had fled into its eyes which were deep, almost tender at times, dark violet in colour.

"All the ones that are still good for anything, don't worry, they'll volunteer on their own," he went on bitterly. "It won't be long. Look, I know another guy. He joined up to get married. Listen to this now, isn't this terrific? Ten days' leave and then a little allowance for the lady and the guy goes off to get his head bashed in to pay for the wedding. For five years that guy went to see that same girl and wandered around the parks and back streets, no place to sit."

"You forgot one thing," the young soldier said after a pause. "You forgot the biggest temptation."

"Now you don't say!" murmured Alphonse. "Is that right?"

"The temptation," Emmanuel went on, "of animals in a cage or dwarfs in a circus. The temptation to break the bars and get out into life. A temptation you've forgotten: the temptation to fight."

"To fight!" said Boisvert, furious. "What the hell for?"

"Because," replied Emmanuel, looking him in the eye, "it's your only chance to he a man again. Come on! Don't you see?" His voice grew violent. "That's why you have to fight."

He was growing heated, and in his effort to convince and say just what he meant, his fists clenched, he hesitated, frowned – then his eyes lit up with enthusiasm and his voice rose, trembling:

"Don't you see that the guys that go and fight this time are goin' to want something better than little copper medals?"

Alphonse looked up slowly, indolently, at Emmanuel, and sneered: "Yeah, and what are they gonna get? Lots of luck, just like before. Millionaires up on the hill and guys out of work down below, fighting with each other."

A fleeting smile played over Emmanuel's face. Boisvert was no longer in the conversation. He had flopped on one of the tables, and emitted the occasional dull groan.

"No. They'll get life," said Emmanuel.

"Life in a shell hole, with grenades bursting!" Alphonse exclaimed. "You've thought of everything!"

"Aw, shut up," Boisvert barked suddenly. "You're talkin' to hear yourself. We've just got one chance. That's if enough guys like you join up, there'll be more room here. That's what we need, room! Too many people on earth."

Three strokes of his hand and his hair stayed up. He smoothed it, and looked arrogantly around at the others.

"No, go on, Manuel," Pitou shouted, "you're right. I'm listening anyway. Go on."

"Well," said Emmanuel, now talking only to the red-head, "you know, Pitou, what keeps us all in the circus behind bars, it's money. The guys who have the money decide if you're going to work or not, depending how it suits them. But the war, this war, it's going to destroy that damned power of

54

money. You hear them say every day, the countries can't go on spending I don't know how many millions for ships that go and get sunk, or planes that get shot down or tanks that last three days. Money invested in destruction destroys itself. Great! That's just fine! 'Cause money isn't wealth. Wealth is our arms and our brains, the masses. And that's the wealth that'll last after the war. That's what's going to feed the world, and all men, in justice."

His voice growing softer, he went on: "We've always given all we had to give, in wars. We'll do it just once more. But not for nothing this time. Some day we'll have to settle our accounts." And then, as if his thoughts had stumbled on something and he was unable to give form to his conviction, he hesitated, smiled and finally dropped his sentence.

"Yes," said Alphonse, who had noticed this hesitation, "there's a lot would like to believe the same thing, but . . ."

His eyes wavered. He was silent; then, seeing that Emmanuel was about to leave, he hoisted himself to his feet. "Wait for me," he said haughtily. "I'm goin' your way."

He mumbled as he went for his coat: "All that's a lot of malarkey anyway. What good does it do a guy who needs a buck or a mickey. A buck and a bottle of Scotch, that quiets your mind."

Emmanuel leaned over the counter to say good night to Ma Philibert. She had just dozed off, her elbow bent, one finger supporting her sagging double chin.

He made for the door, followed by Alphonse. Behind them, Pitou's voice rose, soaring, oblivious, in a song that told of the soft prairies, the freedom of the deer, gentle fawns with wide, innocent eyes, the quiet elk coming to drink at sundown among the reeds, the splendid horizon of loneliness. He sang the words to the sketchiest accompaniment on his guitar.

The plaintive music followed the young men for a minute or two, then was lost in the wild cry of the wind.

Winter had returned to whip the passersby with its fine, icy thongs. Alphonse took Emmanuel's arm to get a little borrowed warmth.

"If you're not in a hurry, come with me," he said. And he went on, with no transition: "Pitou's a lucky little guy. He's always got his music. Boisvert, now, when he's finished picking away at himself, he goes back and minds his business. But all he really wants is to make his comfy little spot in life. He's okay, that guy."

He walked faster, keeping up with Emmanuel.

"But you and me, we think too much. And where does that get you?"

His brief laughter had a snarl in it.

"There's three good ways," he said, "to give up thinkin'. The first way is to go out in a rowboat, all by yourself. The second is to empty a bottle of Scotch. But that's nothing for the down-and-out. Maybe there's a third way. . . ."

"What then?" asked Emmanuel, intrigued.

"I'm gonna tell you in a minute," said Alphonse. "Don't want to get your hopes up till I know I can deliver."

They turned onto St. Ambroise Street toward the grain elevators, which rose up suddenly out of the storm and faded again behind heavy gusts of snow.

After a moment Alphonse forced himself to speak.

"You got any money on you?"

"Come on, out with it, how much do you want?"

"One buck," said Alphonse, resentful. "I never borrow more than a buck at a time, what do you think I am? I'd get into debt!"

Emmanuel opened his greatcoat to take out his wallet. "No hurry," grumped Alphonse.

He was puffing by fits and starts, pushing Emmanuel from behind to speed him up.

They turned into an ill-lit street. Alphonse slowed down. He was looking at the house numbers. A feeble light shone in the second floor of a shoddy building. Downstairs was a laundry. When he saw the reddish glow behind the shutters, Alphonse gripped Emmanuel's arm. He seemed not to feel the cold now. He had even opened his wretched coat and mopped his forehead several times. The wind blew his clothes tight to his thin body and spilled around him in a torrent.

"Well! It's a go!" he said. "Old Charlotte hasn't moved yet."

Then Emmanuel understood. He hesitated a second, gave Alphonse the dollar bill he had been holding in his hand, and went silently on his way.

He came to Notre Dame Street, and went on walking straight ahead without a goal. A need for tenderness had come over him. He tried to recall the features of the girls he had taken to the movies or met at parties. He could easily remember their names, but their faces remained a blur. "Claire, Aline, Yolande," he murmured to help his memory. No emotion stirred. They all seemed like phantoms from another life, the carefree life he had as a young man, a lightweight life, perhaps, which he had left for good when he put on the uniform. It was true. He'd never really been in love. Sometimes he'd thought he was drawn to a pretty face, but each time a dream took shape in his mind, asking him to wait.

The farther he walked the more conscious he was of a need for friendship, something new and unforeseen, measuring up to his strange expectations. Was it really friendship he was searching for? Or a part of himself which he only half understood, and which would become clear in the light of friendship? However it was, he felt so isolated and exasperated that he would gladly have spoken to strangers in the street. And he knew from fellow soldiers who had told him of it that this need grew stronger on each furlough, more acute and urgent.

Suddenly he thought he recognized Jean Lévesque walking ahead of him. He hurried to catch up with him. At school they had been inseparable. Since then, despite their differences of opinion, their odd comradeship persisted because of this very attraction of opposites.

The dark shape ahead of him hesitated, then went into a tavern. Emmanuel followed. There, at a table in the back, he found Jean.

"Hey!" said Lévesque when he saw him. "I was just thinking about you – the volunteer! Doing some recruiting in St. Henri?" he joked, his cynicism softened by friendship.

"Yeah, I've come for you," Emmanuel jibed.

There was a pause, then Jean, his forehead between his hands, said softly:

"There's one big difference between you and me. You think it's the soldiers who change the world. And, well, I think it's the guys that stay home and make money out of the war."

Emmanuel, provoked, waved away the other's remark. Nothing would make him regret his decision. He felt emptied of everything except a trembling of anxiety. His previous lengthy explanation of his reason for joining had only released his natural tendency to cheerfulness, tenderness and joy, but he could see before him not the slightest prospect of happiness or affection.

He ordered two Molsons and turning to Lévesque suddenly remarked, his voice a little sad:

"I've been home for three or four hours and I'm bored already."

"What about Fernande, and Huguette and Claire and Yolande?" Jean rhymed off the names, poking fun at him.

Emmanuel looked down to hide a twitching muscle in his face.

"Did you ever . . . did you ever meet a real girl, a real one?"

"There's no such thing," said Lévesque.

He gulped at his beer as soon as the waiter had put down the glasses, then stopped in a daze. He had had a mental glimpse of Florentine running toward him in the wind.

"Aha!" said Emmanuel, who had caught his expression. "Who were you thinking about?"

Lévesque lit a cigarette. He was on the point of saying Florentine's name. But he broke his match into splinters and threw the pieces in the ashtray. He was frowning, but smiling at the same time, showing his strong teeth which gave the impression that he was taking his bite at life.

"About a girl in the Five and Ten," he said. "A waitress. Too thin, but cute just the same. Her waist's like that," he added, with a descriptive gesture. "And she's as full of hellery as a drowning cat."

Emmanuel looked away. He was remembering, he didn't know why, nor why he felt a catch at his heart, a waitress he'd seen in a railway station restaurant, pale, harried, thin . . . And to keep her tips coming, or maybe just to keep her job, she had for everyone the same sad, tired, humiliated smile. A hard life, he thought. Leaning toward Jean, envious of his detached, nonchalant air that the girls liked so much, he asked:

"How far have you got?"

Jean sat back in his chair and burst out laughing.

"Come on, are you kidding? You know the kind I like. No, no," he protested, so vehemently that he was surprised at himself. "I know her name, that's all. I just mentioned her for fun, just for laughs."

"Oh! Just for laughs!" said Emmanuel. His voice sounded strange. "What's her name?"

Jean hesitated a second.

"How long are you staying in St. Henri?"

"A week."

"Okay, come and have lunch at the Five and Ten some day next week. You can have a look at her . . ."

Then he leaned his head against the back of his chair and gave the half-full ashtray a petulant shove.

"Let's talk about something interesting," he said. "What about this war, eh? If I could find something in the army that paid better than the munitions, I might go in myself. Maybe. But with my specialty in mechanics, I'm not worried about them coming after me."

And as he talked he drew designs in the spilled beer on the table.

FIVE

Not far from Rose-Anna Lacasse the children were sleeping on the two sofas and the pull-out bed in the dining room. She herself, on her bed at the back of the double room, dozed off from time to time but always to wake with a start and check the small clock on her bedside table. She was not concerned about the little ones sleeping under her care, but about the others who had not come home. Florentine! Why had she left so suddenly tonight, without saying where she was going? And where did Eugène spend his evenings? And Azarius, poor fellow, he'd never learn, what new idea did he have up his sleeve? True, he was working and bringing home his pay – not much, but enough to make ends meet. Yet day after day he was dreaming up new projects, wanting to quit his job as taxi-driver, try something else – as if you could be choosy when you had children to feed, and fresh worries at home every minute of the day. As if you were free to say, in such a case, That job suits me, I have no use for this one . . . But that was Azarius all over, always ready to give up a sure thing for something new, his whole life long!

All the little everyday cares were reinforced tonight by Rose-Anna's mistrust and terror of the unknown, which for her was worse than sure misfortune. Depressing memories, still heavy to bear, came to seek her out in the shadows where she lay defenceless, her eyes closed, her hands abandoned on her breast. Life had never seemed so threatening to her, and she couldn't have said what she feared. Some undefined misfortune it was, stalking the little house on Beaudoin Street.

Finally she heard a man's footsteps thumping in the entry of the narrow building. At once her haste to know the worst or be reassured impelled her to get up. She put her hands to her heavy waist and stood stretching in the dark.

"Azarius, is that you?" she asked, keeping her voice low. All she heard was a man's breathing in the hall behind the door-curtain, and, in the low room, dimly lit by a night light, the regular breathing of the children.

Weary, unsteady, a little giddy, as she often was after a few minutes lying down, she moved forward to pull back the faded curtain. She saw Eugène, her eldest son.

"Oh!" she said, with a sigh of relief. "You frightened me, you know. Somehow I thought it was your father and he didn't want to let me see him because of bad news."

The wind was moaning loudly. You could hear it rattling a pail hung from the barrel outside the kitchen door. Rose-Anna wiped her damp forehead.

"I must have been dreaming," she said apologetically. "I thought for a minute your father was coming with bad news. The things you imagine when you're all alone and the storm's outside!" she said, confiding in this tall young man as she had not done for a long time.

As she looked at him she was astounded to see that he had almost become a man. It was a fact that they felt like strangers, this young man who only came home to eat, and herself, who these days saw nothing of him but the clothes she mended. Now her instinct to recapture him spoke louder than all her fears. She thought rapidly, in a kind of panic. He's been growing up for years, and we've drifted apart like that and I never even noticed it. And he surely has worries too, and I haven't a notion of them!

"I must have been dreaming," she said again, "and I don't know if it was about you or your father. Well, it was your father," she admitted. "And that tells me he's going to lose his job."

At last the young man broke the strange, suspicious silence that followed him like a secret transgression.

"That figures," he said harshly. "He's going to lose it, too, if he goes on shooting his mouth off in the restaurant across the road instead of looking after his customers. The boss has just about had enough of our father. And on top of that he tries to set everybody straight . . ."

They were standing face to face, speaking softly so as not to wake the children. In any case, there was nowhere in this tiny, cluttered house where they could have been alone. All their lives they had talked like this, hastily, cramped, whispering in secret. Confidences waited for silence, dark, the night-time. But it had been a long time since Eugène had come like this, seeking out his mother in the dark. The last time, she remembered, was when he had stolen a bicycle. It's always when he needs me for something, she thought. And this time she wanted to anticipate the confession he was contemplating.

"Listen," she said, thinking it was his enforced idleness that bothered him, "your father told me this morning he wants to go into the taxi business for himself. He thinks he can make more money like that. And give you a job."

The young man was working up to his confession. But he didn't yet dare to make it, precisely because of his mother's confidence in him. Confidence! How could she cling to such a slim hope?

"Another crazy move, Mother," he said. "Where's he going to find the money? Why can't he stay still? Hasn't he put us into enough misery? He had his relief, why couldn't he stay on it?"

"Relief?" sighed Rose-Anna. "No, anything else but that, Eugène."

"Yeah," he repeated, "anything but relief."

He wandered restlessly about the room, spotted a chair strewn with children's clothes and sat down on it, crushing a little dress hung over its back. Stockings were drying on a cord strung parallel to the stovepipe. He looked around him with the feeling of animosity that overwhelmed him as soon as he came home. Then his mouth relaxed in a soft, embarrassed smile. He ran his fingers through his brown hair, thinking, staring at the corner of the linoleum. But then he stood up, delivered, liberated. His voice was low, almost timid:

"Listen, Mother, I've got something to tell you. It wasn't about Father I wanted to talk. He can do whatever he wants. But I . . ."

Caught up in her idea, Rose-Anna began automatically picking up and tidying things, which helped her to think.

"If your father could give you a job, Eugène . . ."

"Hell of a time to think about that," he said mysteriously. "Ma, you might as well know right now . . ."

His hesitant gaze, like that of Azarius, stood up for a moment to his mother's silent questioning, then wandered off to nowhere.

In the glow of the night light Rose-Anna finally saw how pale he was. Then she knew it was serious, whatever he had come to tell her. Seized with anguish, stammering, she went over to him. She smelled alcohol on his breath.

"What is it, Eugène?"

There was silence, suspense. Eugène looked away, then grew angry and admitted, "All right, I just joined up."

"You joined up!"

Rose-Anna's knees grew weak. For a second she was giddy. The pictures of parents and saints whirled in the feeble light, and the knick-knacks on the buffet, and the indistinct faces of the children, and the raw light of a street lamp seen through the cotton curtains, and the driving snow. In the midst of this vortex she clearly saw Eugène, but as a small boy leaving to go to school.

"Is it true?" she murmured.

Her voice was trembling, incredulous. She couldn't shape the words that tumbled in her head. But her dizziness left her. She suddenly felt firm and ready for the fight. It was not the first time she had had to defend Eugène. His little offences as a boy – his petty thievery, his lies – she remembered them and the things she had done to cover up for him. But all that seemed like nothing compared to what she was ready to accomplish now to save him.

"Eugène," she said, "you've been drinking, you don't know what you're talking about. Aren't you ashamed of yourself, scaring me like that?"

"It's no scare, Ma. I tell you I just joined up."

She leaned toward him, her eyes shining with determination.

"In that case, you're going to get out of it. It's not too late. You're too young, you're not eighteen yet. You can tell them you didn't know what you were doing, that your family needs you. I'll go myself, if you like. I'll go, I'll explain . . ."

He stopped the hot flood of her protests.

"I signed." And he added, louder, "And I'm glad."

"Glad!"

"Yes, glad! I'm glad!"

Rose-Anna could only repeat the word, turning it in her mind, trying to understand.

"You're glad! What kind of crazy nonsense is that? And you're telling that to me!"

She went on folding the pieces of clothing, smoothing them out with quick, absent-minded gestures, keeping her hands busy as she always did when emotions grew too strong. She looked up at him.

"Is it because I didn't give you enough money for cigarettes, or just pocket money?" she asked, almost humbly. "You know, I'd have given you more if it didn't come from Florentine. She brings almost every pay home, it wouldn't be fair . . ."

"Let her keep her money," he interrupted roughly. "I'll be making as much as she does now."

"Anyway, I gave you as much as I could, it seems to me."

Eugène exploded.

"It's not that! Listen, Ma, a guy gets fed up, you know, bumming ten cents here and a quarter there. You get fed up always hanging around looking for work. The army's the right place for a guy like me. No trade, not much school, it's the best place."

"Oh, Lord!" Rose-Anna sighed.

And yet she had always known the day would come when Eugène would be so disgusted with doing nothing that he would give in to some dreadful impulse. But join the army! No, she'd never thought of that.

"I didn't really think you took it so much to heart," she

said. "You're still so young. You'd have found something too, if you waited. Look at your father, he sat around for years . . ."

"Yeah, and I didn't want to do the same."

"Not so loud!" Rose-Anna begged. "Don't wake the children."

Little Daniel moaned gently in his sleep. She went over to the narrow bed and tucked him in.

Eugène found the gesture unbearably moving. He followed his mother, and took her apron strings and tied them, as he had done when he was small. And he thought, It's the first time in my life I'll be able to give her something.

His voice was caressing:

"Listen, Ma," he said in her ear, "it's going to be a help, you know. All the time I'm in the army you're going to get twenty bucks a month."

His emotion came through in his words, a sort of innocent, proud, astonished joy. Like his father, he had a marvellous capacity for enthusiasm, and for believing that he was being guided by worthy sentiments. Like his father, he was not clear as to where his own interests ended and generosity began. At this moment he was almost certain that he had acted out of pure altruism. He was so pleased with himself that tears came to his eyes.

"Twenty bucks a month, Ma, that's not so bad, eh?"

Rose-Anna turned slowly toward him, as if she didn't want to recognize too quickly what she knew. The street light outside shone in where they were standing. Her face was ashen, with deep shadows for eyes. Strands of hair fell down unkempt on her cheeks, and her lips moved soundlessly. She seemed old and ready to collapse.

"Yes, I see," she said, her voice coming from far away. "I see why you joined up, poor child!"

She raised her hands toward him without touching him and went on in a voice that was plaintive, almost resigned, a soft voice, without resentment, lifeless, barely audible:

"You shouldn't have done it, Eugène. We'd have got along."

She stated this with a surge of courage, even a gentle welcoming of well-known ills, tried and familiar as day and night, and less to be feared than others hidden in the mists of the future.

She was holding back a sob, tugging at her apron. Suddenly all her resentment about money, her misery for lack of it, her fright, and her great need for money poured out in a pitiful protest.

"Twenty beautiful dollars a month!" she was murmuring through her sobs. "Just think, isn't that lovely! Twenty dollars a month!"

Tears as pale as her face ran down her thin cheeks. Her hands, white and tightly clasped, seemed to reject the offered money.

Eugène shook his head, as he always had when he didn't get his way, and went to the kitchen. She heard him take out the little camp bed that was folded behind a door during the day and set up each night between the table and the sink.

Wiping her eyes, she made her way to the back of the double room and lay down fully dressed on her bed. She had still to wait for Florentine and Azarius, and then bar the doors and be sure that everyone was asleep before she herself undressed and tried to get some rest. In the shadows, at the foot of the bed, the bleeding face of a Christ with his crown of thorns darkened a patch of the wall. Beside it, completing it, a *mater dolorosa* offered her transpierced heart to the ghostly light that flickered through the window.

Rose-Anna searched for the words of prayer that she recited every night, alone, but her mind was absent. Instead of the statuette of her childhood, which often came mysteriously before her eyes when she meditated, she saw paper money, rolls of bills peeling off one after the other, flying, twisting, disappearing in the night, carried away by the wind.

SIX

The salesgirls were starting their escape from the Five and Ten into the darkening street. Some went out in groups through the front entrance, doing up their coats, adjusting their hats. At the curb they stopped for a second, stunned, their faces whipped by the wind, then, with little nervous screams, holding each others' arms, they dashed off toward St. Henri Square. Others, heads bowed against the wind, crossed the street and took quick refuge at the streetcar stop and waited there, stamping the hardened snow. As one group disappeared into the cross streets or froze at the car stops, a new lot would pour out the revolving doors and rush toward the square. The streetcars, already crammed, came down St. James and Notre Dame and somehow managed to take aboard the crowd that was flooding the street.

Jean Lévesque huddled in a doorway stamping his heels on the cold stone. The flood of shadows passed by in front of him. It was a tired but hurried flood, rolling silently toward its evening rest. It came from far away, from every corner of the neighbourhood, ending up on St. Henri Square, where it divided up again. Masons, white with mortar, carpenters with their tool boxes, housewives hurrying to get home before their husbands, workers in their caps, lunch boxes under their arms, girls from the textile or cigarette factories, mill hands, puddlers, guards, foremen, clerks, shop-keepers. The six-o'clock flood caught in its stream not only the workers from the neighbourhood but those coming home from Ville Saint Pierre, Lachine, Saint Joseph, Saint Cunégonde and even Hochelaga, as well as those who lived at the other end of town and started here their interminable tram ride.

At regular intervals a raucous bell jangled from up Notre Dame Street and a streetcar passed by. Through their steamed-up windows Jean could see the raised arms of straphangers, opened newspapers, bowed and weary backs, a mass of exhausted humanity; and sometimes among the mass he would see a face look out, melancholy and dejected. Perhaps this was the face of that whole crowd! Its expression stayed with Jean long after.

But he was becoming impatient, and began to stare at the exit of the Five and Ten. Did I miss her? he wondered, and was angry at himself. Just as he was growing worried, the heavy door was pushed outward by a small, bare hand and Florentine appeared. Alone, as he had hoped.

He adjusted his scarf, a gesture he would have laughed at in anyone else, and quickly caught up with her.

"Well! Florentine!"

He wanted this encounter to seem quite accidental, but he didn't fool her for a second.

"Oh! It's you!" she said with a little contemptuous laugh. "You're hangin' around these parts quite a bit these days."

Jean smiled, not admitting a thing.

"I wanted to tell you . . . about last night, Florentine . . ."

"Don't put yourself out making excuses," she interrupted.

And she hugged her purse tight to her body. Her nose trembled, and her fine nostrils, blue with cold, moved with her rapid breathing.

"What do you take me for? Did you think I took you serious and went to meet you? Not me, that's for sure."

"Is that right?"

He took her arm gently, smiling warmly.

"So you'd have made me wait in the cold!" he teased her. "I didn't think it of you. Two friends like us, just made to get along . . ."

He pressed his arm slightly against hers. She must have sensed a force too strong for her, because she suddenly tried to pull free.

"Anyway, I don't want to see you again," she said.

"You wouldn't leave a guy all by himself to get bored, would you?" he protested. "Come and have dinner with me in town tonight. Will you?"

Behind the tiny veil her eyes crackled with indignation, but in their depths a small, defiant flame lit up in response to the young man's bold look.

"Well, that beats all!" she said.

Her small, white, pointed teeth bit at her lower lip. Such cheek! And yet his invitation bothered her in quite another way, at first in the back of her mind, but it was on the move and already her vanity was awakened. What was more, it was very cold, and she was trembling so hard she barely had the strength to think.

"I'm not dressed for town," she said, in a tone of childish anger.

And as soon as she had uttered these revealing words she looked up, pouting, half persuaded.

He was steering her toward a streetcar stop.

"That's all right, Florentine, you're fine the way you are. What difference do a little paint and powder make?"

The streetcar was stopping. She turned to him suddenly with a look full of anxiety.

"I'd rather not go there today," she said, very directly.

People were climbing on board. She was caught in a press of bodies and in a moment was sitting in the tram.

She thought, Maybe I didn't wait long enough yesterday. Maybe he came to meet me. Standing in front of her, strap-hanging, Jean was examining her. She met his look and saw herself in it as in a glass, and her hands went up to straighten her little hat. Her thoughts were racing. She had imagined herself going out with him like this some day, but dressed fit to kill. With distress, real distress, she thought of her pretty new dress, tight at the waist, which made her small breasts very round and emphasized her hips just enough. She felt a pang in her heart as she thought of her little jewel box, from which she could have chosen a pin for her hair, and bracelets, four or five, to jangle on her wrist, and maybe a brooch for her blouse. Wasn't it the very end, she thought, going in to town wearing her poor work dress and not a piece of jewellery on her?

A new concern was suddenly added. Did she at least have her lipstick? Frantically, hands trembling, she opened her imitation-leather purse and rummaged in it. Her fingers slid over the comb, the compact, a few pennies. She grew frantic, pulling things from the bottom and pushing them to one side. Her mouth tightened and her eyes shifted uncertainly as she stared across the car. Finally her fingers found the little metal tube. She gripped it with joy and was relieved, so relieved. She was close to taking it out and redoing her lips then and there, but Jean was watching.

Yet she felt comforted. She had her lipstick. Any minute now, when Jean looked away, she would take out the tube, which she was holding ready in one hand deep in the bottom of her purse. She could wait, there was no hurry. She started to smile, but crossed her legs instead. Then, where the hem of her skirt was pulled up over her knee, she saw a run in her stocking, and again she pouted. That was just swell, going to town in your worst dress and a run in your stocking into the bargain. At home in a drawer of her dresser she had a lovely chiffon pair. The finest you could get. She'd been crazy to buy them, they'd cost two dollars, but they were the nicest silk and the colour matched her pale skin.

Jean weaved slightly back and forth above her with the movement of the tram, a mocking smile on his face.

"If you pulled your skirt down a little or uncrossed your legs the run wouldn't show at all," he said softly, leaning down to her ear.

Choking with indignation, she sought in vain for a comeback. Her thoughts grew confused. The damp heat of the tram, the heavy breath from all these mouths, the noise, everything made her groggy. With Jean nothing ever happened the way you planned it. What a pain!

But then she stopped worrying and stayed quiet, her head loose, wobbling with the jerky motion of the tram, occasionally allowing the lids to droop over eyes burning with fatigue. The whole trip was a torture of warmth and torpor.

When they got out of the streetcar and ran to catch a bus, the cold seized her. But soon they were rolling along with a quiet rumble. Everything was waves of cold, heat, subdued voices, waves of wind, of doubt, of hope, up to the moment when they entered a discreetly lit restaurant, where white tablecloths and glittering crystal danced before her eyes. Then everything turned to a dream, and bravely she entered the dream to play her part in it. Yet in order to live at the height of her dream, every move cost her a painful effort.

"Oh," she cried, emerging from her torpor the moment she crossed the threshold, "I never been here before. It's classy, eh?"

She felt immensely flattered, and had already forgotten her poor woollen dress and the ladder in her stocking, which was running. She looked up at Jean, ecstatic.

A waiter in tuxedo with a stiff shirt-front bowed and led them to a small table. There were flowers. She thought they must be paper, until she was astonished by their feel and smell. The waiter pulled out a chair and Florentine sat down, awkwardly taking off her coat, raising her elbows too high. Then she was handed a menu and Jean, across from her, was saying in a polished, courteous voice she'd never heard:

"What would you like, Florentine? An apéritif?"

She'd never heard the word. She wondered if Jean was showing off. She nodded, avoiding his eye.

"And after that?"

With fingers bleached by years of dishwater she turned the pages of the menu. All those funny words, which she deciphered syllable by syllable, pronouncing them laboriously to herself, left her worried and hesitant. Her heart beat quickly. But she took her time, searching up and down the page, and when she found a word that looked familiar, she pounced:

"Hey! There's roast lamb, I like that."

"No, no Florentine, you're going to start with soup. Just leave it to me."

Trying to keep on top of things, she murmured:

"It's all right, I'm going to take that, up there on the left, the consommé."

Now she was fiddling with the menu, pretending to think it over. Jean could see only the top of her face, and, peeking around the edge of the menu, her fingernails, from which the polish was cracking and coming off in flakes. On one finger there was hardly any polish left, and this bare white nail, beside its scarlet neighbour, fascinated him. He couldn't look away from it. Long, long afterwards, when he would think of Florentine, he would see that pale fingernail, stripped of its polish, naked, marked with tiny ribs and white spots – a symbol of anemia.

For her, the enchantment was beginning. For him, pity had already killed desire. I could never hurt her, he thought. No, I could never make up my mind to that.

"You wouldn't like some hors d'oeuvres?" he asked her.

At that moment, and to his profound embarrassment, he saw that Florentine was digging in her purse and bringing out, piece by piece, her whole artillery of beautification. Beside the cutlery and crystal gleamed her lipstick, her compact and even a comb . . .

"Not here," he said, humiliated, looking sideways to see if people at the next table were watching. "There."

He pointed to a heavy curtain with gently illuminated letters above it.

"Oh! I see!"

With a defiant smile, as if she found his embarrassment out of place, she dumped her things in the purse again and went to the rear of the restaurant. He was furious when he saw her coming back, her lips smeared red, and preceded by a perfume so harsh that people on both sides of her path looked up and smiled.

Why did I bring her here? he thought, gripping the table's edge. Of course, I told myself often enough: to see her as she is and have no more illusions about her. He watched her approaching in her tight dress. Or was it to see her eat her fill for once? Or was it to dazzle her . . . and then take her, and leave her worse off than she was before?

He stood up as she reached the table. In her cocktail glass swam a cherry which she examined and at last put to one side on her plate. She tilted back her head and swallowed the whole drink at a gulp, and then began to choke.

Her cheeks grew red. She began to talk. She talked volubly, her elbows on the table, her eyes lively and happy at times, at others distant and vague. The courses came and went, the *potage Julienne*, the hors d'oeuvres, the filet of sole, the steak, the salad, the French pastries. And she didn't stop talking, except once in a while to peck about in her plate like a bird. She tasted everything and said, "It's good." But she was too excited to be aware of the taste of food. What really intoxicated her was in a great mirror behind Jean: her own reflection, which she frequently leaned forward to observe. There she was, her eyes shining, her complexion smooth and clear, her features slightly blurred; and because she liked herself like this, each time she leaned forward she seemed to want to communicate to him her moment of triumph. How could she fail to love someone in whose company she felt so beautiful?

Toward the end of the meal she began to call him by his first name. She didn't notice that he barely listened, that he cast covert glances of boredom in her direction. She was really talking to herself, bending her body toward those eyes of flame encouraging her, egging her on, intoxicating her from the depths of the mirror.

Later in the evening, when they left the bus and continued on foot, she grew calm, almost silent. It had suddenly turned warmer, as often happens near the end of February.

The air was soft. Snow was falling, powdering their clothing and hair and hanging, fine and silky, on their trembling lashes. Immense flakes floated slowly down and as they passed beneath the street lights Florentine saw that their shapes were infinitely varied. Some were great stars, others reminded her of the monstrance on the altar. She no longer dared to speak, and felt occasional pangs of doubt: had she really made a good impression? Jean seemed so far away.

They turned onto the Notre Dame viaduct in front of the St. Henri station, and Jean stopped. She saw him looking up toward the mountain, whose lights you could mistake for clusters of early stars.

"Did you ever see that mountain?" he said slowly.

She smiled in embarrassment, but ironically, for she sometimes had no notion what he was getting at, this strange young man; then her thoughts flew to the restaurant where she had known a moment of happiness. And like him she leaned on the parapet to dream. She too stared at the mountain, her eyes shining in the snow, blinking in the snowflakes; but what she saw there was the great mirror in the restaurant and her own face with soft lips, and hair as fluffy and light as if it had been reflected in still, dark water.

Jean turned to contemplate her. She now left him almost indifferent, almost calm. He scarcely even thought of kissing her. And that was as it should be. Now that he no longer felt a brutal, irresistible attraction to Florentine, he could talk to her about his ambitions. He could clearly show her the great distance that lay between them.

He took her thin wrist in his hand and began to laugh.

"You know, beautiful," he said, "it won't be long before I have my foot on the first rung of the ladder . . . and then, good-bye to St. Henri!"

A strange anxiety came over her, and she stood pensive, her hands still folded on the parapet. A shunting locomotive wrapped them in a cloud of steam. For a moment Florentine felt lost in an infinite mist. Then she was calm again. What did she have to worry about? Things were going as they should. When they came out of the restaurant and Jean took her arm, she had been worried, it was true. She had wondered, Where's he going to take me now? She had bristled at the thought of defending herself against him. But when she realized he was bringing her straight home, she regained her assurance. A thought had blossomed in her mind: He doesn't hate me. He wants to be my boyfriend.

At that moment, standing straight beside him, enigmatic, smiling to herself, she savoured the words "my boyfriend." And with the boldness she had gathered from the thought of being loved, respected, by this unusual young man, she held her own incipient feelings in check. It's not that I've got the big love for him, she reflected, no, I can't say I love him truly. He's a show-off with his long words and all his crazy ideas, but he's not like the other guys in St. Henri either.

Slowly they resumed their walk, each lost in his own thoughts.

Jean: I won't see her again. Maybe once or twice more, so there are no hard feelings, but this has to end soon.

And she: I must arrange to invite him to our house. It seemed important to her to maintain the kind of respect he was showing her tonight. That was the right way to go, especially as their adventure had had a very imprudent beginning. Invite him home . . . But how? It's so small and ugly and full of children . . .

And Jean again: Oh! The poor kid in her little dress! Why don't I drop her right now?

On Beaudoin Street she stopped before the naked, poverty-stricken façade of a frame house. At the right a low, damp opening led to a small interior yard where windows, faintly lit, cast their glow on accumulations of junk. There were twenty or so such houses on the street, pierced here and there by covered passages leading to hidden courtyards. At the street's end an embankment rose to the level of the railway.

"Do you live at the end?"

"No, here."

Florentine pointed to the house which rose directly from the back of the sidewalk. It stood in range of the street lamp which shone accusingly on the faded, depressing grey of its paint. She too was standing in the lamp's raw light. Her cheeks looked hollow; her lips too red, too bold.

"Get away from there," he said.

He pushed her into the shadows. And the shadows were kind to her. They wiped out all trace of makeup, and made of her a frail, almost childish thing; they dressed her in mystery and gave her distance and value. He held his breath, staring at her for a moment, then swiftly put his arms around her, around her shadow, this smiling mystery. He drew to him Florentine's pale smile, her weakness, her credulity, her deep eyes in the darkness. His lips touched her cheeks. They sought for the form and warmth of her mouth. And the wind sported around them, and the snow slid down between their touching faces, melted there and ran between their lips in tiny streams.

Florentine melted into his arms. He had the impression of holding nothing more than a bundle of clothing, something soft, inert and damp. He held her closer and could feel how bony her shoulders were under the thin coat. His hand ran down her slender arm, and he gently pushed away this little creature veiled in shadow, polka-dotted with snow and smelling of frost and winter's cold.

She was standing in front of him, her eyes still closed. He leaned forward and pressed his lips against each of the closed eyelids. Then he pulled back and walked rapidly away. He almost felt like whistling.

And Florentine, her head in a whirl, was dreaming: He kissed me on the eyes! She remembered other kisses but she had never felt the caress of lips on her closed eyes.

Feeling her way like a blind thing, she found the doorway. In the little room, lit by a trembling ray from the street lamp, she began to undress, taking care to make no noise that might wake the household, noting the thumping of her heart, dreading any interruption of the memory: He kissed me on the eyes!

From the depths of the double room, however, where she could just see the outline of the bed, came a voice that was weary.

"Florentine? Is that you? It's late."

"It's not so late," she murmured.

Sitting on the edge of the sofa-bed, she took off her stockings, only half aware of what she was doing. She was floating on a great wave, rising with it in a joy that almost choked her heart.

"Your father isn't back yet. I don't know what he's up to," the plaintive voice went on. "I'm really scared he's quit his job. I know he didn't get his pay yesterday. And Eugène's joined up, Florentine. Oh, God, what's going to happen to us?"

But Florentine was still riding the crest of her great wave. . . . When it lifted her high she had to hold her breath. How could she ever again be bothered by these petty everyday cares? Would she ever again feel the old anxiety on hearing these dreadful midnight confidences, in the silence heavy with breathing? The wave that bore her was like a long, slow swell. There were hollows into which she sank with all her thoughts, all her willpower, where she was no more than a wing, a feather, a fringe, borne off ever faster, ever faster. . . . He kissed me on the cheeks. On the eyes!

"What's going to happen to us, Florentine?"

On the cheeks, on the eyes, and his lips were so soft. . . .

"If your father's gone and lost his job again, we'll have to live on what you can give us, poor Florentine. We can always go back on relief. . . ."

There was a silence, long and distressing, broken by the gusts of wind and snow rattling at the windows. Rose-Anna raised her voice again. This time she was talking to herself in the heavy solitude of the great bed. She had given up hope of reaching Florentine. Perhaps she was too tired, too weary, to talk. Or half asleep already. She bore her no grudge, but she had to talk. She couldn't lie there in the dark like that, alone with what was weighing on her heart.

"The landlord's given notice, we have to move in May," she said.

And her heart was so full of anxiety, so weighted down with troubles, that she would have spoken aloud to herself in this way even if she had been alone. "What are we going to do if your father doesn't get another job and there we are having to move again? The rents are going up and up, and now . . ."

She hesitated on the verge of one last confidence. And in the dark, the deep dark that seemed so empty and filled with gloom, eyeless, earless, pitiless, she came out with it: "When there were only ten of us it was hard enough to get along, but now there's going to be eleven. . . ."

Florentine was jolted back to reality. The wave of ecstasy vanished and left her a castaway.

Her throat dry, she said roughly:

"Not another one!"

For some time now she'd been keeping an eye on her mother. She imagined her growing heavier day by day; but Rose-Anna, her figure misshapen from so many childbirths, always seemed to bear a burden beneath her loose and swelling clothes. Florentine had been suspicious at first, but she had thought, it can't be. Our mother's over forty.

"It'll be in May, the end of May," said Rose-Anna.

She seemed embarrassed to admit it. But she recovered quickly and said, "You won't mind, will you, Florentine, if you have another little sister?"

"Good God, Mother, don't you think there's enough of us now?"

The fatal phrase had slipped out. Florentine was already sorry for it, wished she could take it back, but in the warm silence of the room, with the wind beating the windows, the memory of it hung. The dark seemed to repeat it, to echo it again and again.

Rose-Anna turned on her sweaty pillow. "Easy, child, easy!" she begged. Then after a long silence she whispered into the shadow: "There's no help for it, Florentine. We don't do what we like in this life, we do what we can."

It's not true, thought Florentine. I'm going to do what I like. And I won't have troubles like our mother.

The rolling wave was there again, lifting her high and singing in her ears with the sound of a thousand clear streams, music of her dreams that promised a happy life. Naked under her nightgown, she crept into bed beside her younger sister, Yvonne. The child kept her eyes tightly closed, but her lips were trembling. At thirteen she was trying to go her own way in her search for the key to the mysteries of human life.

Florentine tried to warm her frozen feet on those of her sister, and, half asleep already, called softly to her mother:

"Never mind, Ma, don't worry, we'll make out all right. We've been through worse."

Beside her Yvonne, stiff and wide awake, was breathing jerkily. Her eyes stared at the ceiling, and with her hands clasped before her, she tried to push a suffocating weight from her thin chest.

SEVEN

S he watched him smoking his cigarette with short puffs
as he sat quietly by the kitchen stove, yesterday's newspaper spread out on his knees, and she was bitter.

From the heavy knitted jacket half closed over his strong
chest his neck rose white and smooth as that of a young man.
His complexion was fresh and almost free of wrinkles. She
begrudged his staying young and handsome, with his unfailing good health, while she bore such obvious marks of fatigue
and wear. He was just two years younger than she, a difference
that had not counted when they married. Now he looked at
least ten years younger. Rose-Anna, at the end of her tether,
said nothing more as she went about poking the fire. Her lips
trembled as she bent over the light of the open stove-lid.

The flame sprang up with a shower of sparks. Azarius
looked up. He sniffed the odour of dry wood shavings – a
small supply lay on the oven door – and that of toasting
bread, which he loved above all. He sighed with well-being,
thinking of the cold mornings when he kept an eye on the
passersby from his taxi station. It was more than Rose-Anna
could bear.

"Why did you have to go an' quit your job! Was this a time to get hard to please? You don't see Florentine quitting her job, eh?"

This was the start of their day. A touch of sunlight rose behind the kitchen window. Thus had begun many of their days in the past. Rose-Anna, listening to her own voice, wondered if her words had not been their own echo from the past. But Eugène's camp bed, standing against the partition, reminded her that her eldest son was gone, that she was growing old and that Azarius never changed.

"What's more, you're right in my way," she said. "How do you expect me to get the meals? Pull back your chair, can't you?"

He gave a little smile, half embarrassed, half surprised. He could no more get used to reproaches than he could to the awareness of being in the wrong.

"Just give me a little time," he said. "I've got prospects. Let a man think a bit about his business, will you?"

"Yes, you think about your business, sittin' by the fire. Go right ahead."

"Come on, Mother, might as well sit here as anywhere, as long as I'm sittin' jugglin' things around."

"Juggling!"

She had caught up his word derisively, and the shuffling of her slippers on the floor stopped abruptly.

"Juggling, is it? Can't you do anything else? You've spent your life juggling. And after all your juggling things in your head, where did it get you? D'you think juggling's going to help the poor souls that need it?"

She felt a sudden dull pain. It cut off her speech, and she laid a hand on her swollen body.

"Go and lie down again, Mother. I'll do your chores today," he said gently.

His boastfulness was gone. Not his painful certainty of being misunderstood, not his latent self-confidence, not even his fund of easy optimism. But there was an end to showing off. What was left was an overwhelming desire to be forgiven. It would have been hard to recognize the speechmaker of The Two Records restaurant in this contrite man hunched beside the fire. This was how he was at home, without resilience, as if he were in a nest of thorns trying to pluck them away one by one as they multiplied around him. Even his voice was not the one he used outside to state his opinion or give his generous and daring views. Now it had a conciliatory tone, almost humble, in which from time to time you could hear a note of defeat.

"If you really want to know the truth," he said, sighing, "I'll tell you, wife. I was fired. But it's just as well. I wanted to quit. How can I look after my business when I'm tied up in that outfit morning and night!"

She looked away. She'd had time to cool off, but didn't want to show it too soon. Straightening out the kitchen table-cloth, she remembered something old Madame Lacasse had said: "With Azarius, my girl, you'll never hear one word louder than another. And that's worth forgiving a few faults for, child."

It was true, thought Rose-Anna. Azarius had never said an angry word to her.

"All right! That's it, make yourself useful," she said mildly.

She sat down to eat in her turn at the corner near the oven. This was how she managed to give bigger servings to the children and keep only a crust of bread for herself without anyone noticing. She began to rock gently, which she often did even in a straight chair as an aid to reflection.

She quickly came up with a plan. Always full of ideas, once she had thought of a project she pursued it tirelessly. She took a last gulp of tea and set her cup down decisively.

"Listen," she said, "how would it be, now you're here to see to the kids, if I got out and started looking for a place to live?"

She wasn't asking for advice. The moment her idea was expressed it seemed to her reasonable and excellent.

"You know," she went on, "however bad things are, we've still got to live somewhere."

Drops of saliva ran from the corners of her lips. She sucked them back in and got to her feet: a little woman, rounded out everywhere, her forehead still handsome and her brown eyes courageous, with delicate, mobile furrows between her eyebrows.

Over her housedress she pulled on her old winter coat, its original black turning green. From the buffet in the dining room she took her hat and a shabby purse that Florentine had passed on to her. Florentine was just waking up, and her mother brought her shoes and stockings and told her to hurry, it was after half-past eight.

Florentine, emerging from her sleep, looked around, frowning, then, remembering her joy, was sitting on the edge of her bed with a single sprightly jump.

"That's right, don't you be late now," said Rose-Anna.

She bustled across the kitchen as if she had to catch a train, and went out, pushing back the little ones who clung to her skirt shouting, "Bring us a chocolate rabbit, Ma. Bring me a flute, Ma!"

They were all of school age, except little Gisèle, but Rose-Anna had kept them home for a few weeks, Lucille because she had no rubbers, and Albert because he had a bad cold. As for Daniel, for two months now he had been in a slow decline without showing any serious symptoms. Philippe, who was turning fifteen, stubbornly refused to go back to school at all.

Rose-Anna had caught him smoking his father's cigarette butts and reading detective stories. He looked unhealthy, with rotting teeth, and eczema on his face.

From the sidewalk Rose-Anna turned back to see them all piled into the doorway, even little Daniel who was half dressed because his pants and shirt had not dried overnight. Only Yvonne was missing. Up at dawn, she would wash at the cold-water tap in the kitchen, dress quickly, snatch a crust and stow it in her schoolbag beside her books, then silent as a shadow she would be off to an early Mass before going to the convent school. She took communion every morning. In any kind of weather she was the first to leave the house. When they had tried to keep her in because of extreme cold, she had flown into rages that were extraordinary in such a nervous, self-effacing and gentle child.

Then, one day when they had tried to keep her in by force, she had begun to weep, explaining through her sobs that she would leave Our Lord in suffering if she missed a Mass. Rose-Anna had understood the artless story: in Yvonne's classroom there was a sacred heart, and each girl who went to Mass was entitled, as she came into her class, to remove one of the thorns from this suffering heart. Yvonne had said, with the tears running down her pallid cheeks, "Oh, Mother, there are so many bad people putting thorns in Jesus' heart every day. Please let me go to Mass!"

Her mother had not tried to dissuade her after that. But the same evening Rose-Anna had taken some old material and made her a good, warm coat, with layers of quilting. Then when the child left in the cold dawn she would say to herself, "At least she has something warm on her bones."

The children in the doorway were astonished to see her go out, for she never left the house. Daniel had shouted in his

GABRIELLE ROY

thin voice, "A flute, Ma, don't forget!" And Gisèle had begun
to cry, until Azarius took her in his arms and told her to wave
good-bye.

All Rose-Anna's resentment had melted, her ill-humour
had disappeared like magic. She went on her way, determined
to buy perhaps not the flute that Daniel had asked for, but at
least four little chocolate rabbits to keep for Easter. Walking
was hard in the soft snow. Occasionally she stopped to get her
breath, leaning against a wall or a fence.

Since the early days of March the sun had shone stronger
over the neighbourhood and the old snow had begun to melt.

She made her way slowly, tired and heavy. Already old
memories were attacking and eating away her courage. She
saw the futility of her hopes. The clear sky and soft air meant
nothing to her. Springtime! What had it ever meant to her?
In her married life it had meant two things: being pregnant,
and going out pregnant to look for a place to live. Every spring,
a move.

In the first years it had meant looking for something
better. She and Azarius would get tired of their cramped space
and by winter's end would start wishing for something newer,
fresher, brighter and bigger, for the family was growing. Azarius
especially would be full of wild ideas. He would talk about
a house with a garden for his cabbages and carrots. And she, a
country girl, would be delighted at the notion of seeing vegetables growing beneath her windows. But it was always smokestacks or shantytowns that she saw when she looked out.

Later, when Florentine and Eugène had started school,
they no longer moved because they wanted to but because they
were behind in their rent and had to find something cheaper.
Year after year this search went on, as rents went up and decent
housing grew harder and harder to find.

Before, when she went off to find a home, she had a clear idea of how it should look. She wanted a verandah, a yard for the children and a living room. Azarius would encourage her: "Get nothing but the best, Rose-Anna, nothing but the best."

For a long time now her efforts had been limited to finding a place to live, anything at all. Walls, a ceiling and a floor. All she asked was shelter.

A bitter thought crossed her mind: the bigger the family, the smaller and darker grew their lodgings.

The depression had affected Azarius early on, as he was a carpenter. Too proud to take just any work, he had tried to find it only within his own trade. Then he had become discouraged, and, like so many others, had finally accepted government relief.

The worst days of their life! thought Rose-Anna. The rent allowance was practically nothing. Landlords laughed when you offered them ten dollars a month for four rooms.

Then Azarius would agree to pay the difference, just a few dollars. Always the optimist, incurable, he'd say, "Oh, I'll make a buck here and there, we'll find a way." But he wouldn't find work, or the money would go to fill another vacuum. He would never manage to keep the agreement, and next spring another furious landlord would put them into the street.

The sun was already a bright, running brook. From the gables of the houses hung sharp-pointed icicles, like gleaming crystal. From time to time one would break off with a snap, and crash at Rose-Anna's feet in shining shards. She progressed very slowly, afraid of falling, always seeking a hand-hold some-where. Then she would be in soft snow again, which meant harder work but less fear of a slip and fall.

How she had loved spring in the first days! She'd had two beautiful springtimes in her life. One, when she met Azarius, such a happy fellow in those times, about whom her mother, Madame Laplante, had prophesied, "He'll never amount to much, that boy, he's too sure everythin's goin' to turn out rosy." Then there was the spring Florentine was born, her first. She remembered how sweet those two springs had been. Sometimes she even thought she could smell the fresh leaves of those first years. She saw herself going out, in the little free time she'd had, pushing Florentine in her small carriage in the sunlight. Neighbours bent over the ribbons and lace and said, "My, you do take a lot of trouble. When you're at the tenth you won't bother."

Rose-Anna made an effort to hurry. People were sweeping or shovelling snow in front of their houses. Some who knew her shouted gaily, "Good-day, Madame Lacasse! You out house-hunting?"

Others looked up at the fair sky and jerked their heads: "That's it this time. Spring's here!"

"Yes," said Rose-Anna, "but you never know."

"We'll have a cold snap yet, but it's great while it lasts."

"Oh, yes," she'd agree, forcing a smile, "and you can save a little on the heat."

She went on, picking up her old train of thought. It wasn't that houses were scarce. Everywhere she looked Rose-Anna saw "To Let" signs. It seemed that once a year the neighbourhood gave in to a folly of escape stimulated by the passage of trains and the blowing of locomotive whistles, but, unable to afford a real voyage, settled for a move next door. Two houses out of five had their much-used signs up: "To Let, To Let, To Let!"

Rose-Anna met several workers' wives who were, like her, walking slowly as they scrutinized the houses. In a few weeks there would be hundreds of them on the march. She must hurry, she thought, to avoid the great April rush. But she couldn't make up her mind to knock. She would go up to the steps, glance inside and trot back to the sidewalk. Either she was discouraged by her glimpse of the inside, or the house was so clean and well-kept that she thought, no use asking how much, it's too dear for us.

On St. Ferdinand Street, however, she forced herself to go inside a certain brick house. She came out in a daze, barely walking straight. The smell of diapers drying over the stove and the sight of the windowless toilet opening onto the kitchen had been so disgusting she was afraid she'd be sick. And for that they want seventeen dollars a month! The only light inside came from the front windows, for the others looked out on a yard as narrow as a well. Seventeen dollars a month, she thought. It can't be done. We can't manage.

Yet she began again with her patient calculations. Rose-Anna knew by heart the exact amount of their small income, the largest part being Florentine's salary. And she also knew what their expenses came to, those that were strictly necessary. She could tell to a penny "how much I need this month . . ." and she would surely have added: ". . . to make the grade."

Even in her most obscure thoughts she used this expression from the world of success and ambition, an instinctive working-class way of defying arithmetic. . . .

She passed by several houses without seeing their signs, preoccupied by her battle of the sums. She was walking firmly now, striking out some expense or other – only her eyes showed the regret she felt – but running full speed into a total which always exceeded their resources. And at that point Rose-Anna, who still had her imagination, began to soar beyond this prison of worries, torments and intractable calculations. She created a rich uncle she had never known, who died and left her his great fortune; or she saw herself finding a well-packed wallet which she would, of course, return to its owner, but for which she would get a generous reward. This fancy became so insistent that she began feverishly to search the ground. Then she grew ashamed of these childish notions.

Whatever the dream, Rose-Anna was brought back to earth by her arithmetic.

She arrived at St. Henri Square and crossed it for once without fear of the streetcars, the warning bell of the rail crossing, or the sharp smoke that bit at her eyes. A passing truck just missed her, and she looked up more surprised than terrified, like an absent-minded accountant disturbed at his books.

Safe on the sidewalk again, she started her accounts over from the beginning. And now, for the first time since Eugène had joined up, she thought of the twenty dollars a month he had mentioned. But, with a tightening of the lips, she refused to take them into account. Only to realize a moment later that she had already engulfed them mentally, committed them to the last penny. Ashamed of herself, but relieved just the same, she took a deep breath.

As if it was meant for her, she noticed a poster stuck on a store wall showing in broad strokes the figure of a young soldier, bayonet fixed, his eyes shining, his boyish mouth open in a rallying cry: "Let's go, boys! The country needs us!" were the words in striking black on the blue background above his head.

Rose-Anna was stunned. The boy looked just like Eugène. *His* mouth, *his* eyes! Spelling out the words, she thought they read, Let's go, boys! Our mothers need us! She clasped her hands over her coat. Eugène was crying out in anguish from his high wall, shouting their poverty down to the four winds.

Her gait was not as sure, not as courageous, as she turned to the most wretched areas, behind St. Henri station.

She soon arrived at Workman Street, which earns its name. "Work, workman," it says, "wear yourself out, bend your back, live in filth and drudgery."

Rose-Anna ventured along in front of the slum of grey brick which forms a long wall with identical, equidistant doors and windows.

A crowd of ragged children were playing on the sidewalk among the litter. Women, thin and sad, stood in evil-smelling doorways, astonished by the sunlight. Others, indoors, set their babies on the windowsill and stared out aimlessly. Everywhere you saw windows plugged with rags or oiled paper. Everywhere you heard shrill voices, children crying, cries of misery coming from the depths of this house or that, doors and shutters closed, dead, walled up against the light as if it were a tomb.

All the houses – but how can they be called houses when only the number over the door tells one from the next, a pitiful appeal to individuality – all the houses in the row, not just two or three out of five, were for rent, every last one.

Every spring that hideous street was emptied, and every spring it filled again.

A persistent wind carried the sweet penetrating odour of tobacco up from the nearby cigarette factories, along with a bitter whiff of hot paint and linseed oil which she could taste as well as smell. It left her tongue thick and her throat dry.

No, Rose-Anna thought, Florentine would never want to come here. She turned back the way she had come and tried Convent Street. This was a peaceful avenue of middle-class houses. There were lace curtains over stained-glass windows. The cream-coloured blinds were half drawn. On the house fronts you saw brass sign plates; and here and there on the inside sill of a window, robust plants that had more air and space, Rose-Anna reflected, than the children she'd just glimpsed on St. Ferdinand Street. She knew that this oasis of silence was not for the Lacasse family. For that matter, there was nothing for rent here. But she could breathe easier. Workman Street had restored her courage after all. It was some comfort to know that they were not yet reduced to extreme poverty. To her right rose the Church of St. Thomas Aquinas. Because she was tired and needed to rest and think, she went inside and sank exhausted into the last pew of the nave.

Her thoughts wandered and scattered at first, but then her strength returned.

She thought, I must pray, this is a church. She slid gently to the edge of the bench and knelt, telling her rosary.

But as she murmured her Ave's she was unable to concentrate. Her lips moved but in fact she was launched on a silent plea which at first was addressed to no statue, no relic, not even to a presence.

"It's not fair to my children," she said. "Not to Eugène, he never had a chance, and not to Florentine. When I was her age, did I have to think about keeping my parents alive?" And she added, "Lord, listen to me!"

It wasn't often that she prayed directly to God. She preferred to ask the intercession of saints that were familiar through statues and pictures. But of God, God himself, she had no conception. She had had no notion of him for years because of the effort it called for, and anyway no matter how hard she tried she still couldn't see him, or anything more than a pile of clouds like cotton batting and a dove flying over them. But now she had brought to life the immense old man-with-a-beard of her childhood – the one above the holy family who is supposed to be God the father. Her need was too urgent to allow for intermediaries.

She said all kinds of things without trying to put them in order, but with a natural tendency to justify herself and disarm the divine power. "I've done my duty, Lord. I've had eleven children. I have eight alive and three that died young, maybe because I was too tired. And this little one that's on the way, Lord, is he going to be as sickly as the last three?"

Then she remembered that God knew all about her life, and she was wasting time telling him that. But she said to herself as well: "Maybe he forgets things. There's so much misery goes up to him." This was the first crack in her faith – the candid supposition that God, as absent-minded, tired and harassed as herself, couldn't manage to give more than cursory attention to human needs.

She came around to material things, but not too hastily, because it seemed to her that a certain adroitness was as necessary in prayer as in any other petition. All of that was instinctive and came about in the depths of her being. She would have been embarrassed to ask any favour for herself, but for her family she was not afraid to say what she wanted; that was how she marked off the dividing line between spiritual and temporal goods.

She thought fleetingly of Yvonne, and felt a sudden pang. Was not she herself one of those creatures her daughter talked about, who thrust their thorns into the Saviour's flesh?

But on second thought she rejected the idea. At heart she had an intuition of God that was gentle and not unlike herself. Her whole life separated her from the sickly piety of Yvonne. She felt relieved. Her prayer was less an attempt to escape from her burdens than a humble way of putting the responsibility on the one who had given them to her.

With a firm step she reached the holy water basin, crossed herself, then went outside, breathing a first breath of spring air with a kind of naive surprise.

On the platform before the church she already felt encouraged. If it had to be, now that Azarius wasn't working, she could take the whole day, and other whole days, to find a proper dwelling. Her energy came back, along with her old habit of making the best of the smallest advantage.

The street was sunlit. She put sunlight into the house she hoped for. Timidly at first, she couldn't have told you how, she began by imagining a little room with windows facing south, where she could set up her sewing machine. Then the sun reached the dining room; it lit up the kitchen doorway and moved inside. It landed on the geraniums in their clay pots. It glistened on the pots and pans. It shone on a white tablecloth. It brightened the face of a little girl sitting in her high chair.

Rose-Anna shook her head. The corners of her mouth moved in a melancholy smile. What she had just glimpsed was her house as a newlywed, it was Florentine, it was the sunlight she had known when she was twenty.

EIGHT

Florentine was serving Emmanuel and Jean Lévesque, flashing her best smile at them both.

From end to end of the counter all the stools were full, and behind the row of hasty diners others, standing, watched out for a gap in this stockade of rounded backs. Housewives, determined to grab the first empty seat, clutched their parcels and kept an eye out, right and left, or staked out their claim behind a customer who was almost finished. Workers, their caps still on, stood a little farther back from the wafted gravy smells, all of them serious, sad, somewhat resigned, with the grave and worried faces they wore at the factory entrance punching in, or hesitating just inside a beer parlour when the tables were full.

The moment a sated customer rose to go, another took his place and the counter in front of him was wiped and set as if by magic. The waitress would shout an order in the microphone, the dumb-waiter would squeak into motion and a well-filled plate would appear steaming in the mouth of an opening just below the mirrors, coming directly, it seemed, from a deep and inexhaustible cavern of supplies.

The cash register was ringing almost continuously. Diners hustled the waitresses along or caught their attention by snapping their fingers or, even more rudely, with a loud "Pssst!"

But Florentine refused to be hurried. The midday rush no longer made her nervous. Now it was more like a respite from the noise and bustle, the moment when she started looking out for Jean or, when he had arrived, letting her thoughts spin about his presence. Her hip leaning against the inside of the counter, she was now chatting with the two young men. Sometimes in the rattle of the dishes she would miss what they were saying and lean toward them, lip-reading out of the corner of her eye. Then, pretending not to care, she straightened slowly as if she were, in any case, privy to everything that mattered. Her ear, beneath the pink paper flower stuck in her hair, caught every sound meant to catch her attention: a spoon rapping on the imitation marble, a boot scratching impatiently on the tile floor, the call of an angry fat woman. Florentine shrugged and her nose grew pinched; then she went back to smiling at Jean and Emmanuel.

This morning her face showed an animation not quite vulgar but a little forced, nervous and obvious, almost defiant. Her expression was radiant, so that the makeup for once seemed natural, answering the sparkle in her eyes. On her small, thin face, with its shining, elongated eyes, cloudy in the steam of the broilers, Jean could see clearly as the shadow of a memory passed: the falling snow, their kiss in the snowstorm. Then he saw how she grew suddenly vivacious and all her movements became lively.

Occasionally her eyes would rest on him, and a precise, passionate, living reminder would flash across to him. Then she would turn to Emmanuel to distract Jean and put him off the scent with her flirtatiousness, addressing the other in a very friendly way, with just a touch of daring, as if her being Jean's friend gave her certain rights over his chums. She was too greedy for admiration not to encourage Emmanuel's spontaneous reaction, and so excited by Jean's presence, so anxious to try out her power over him, that she thought she could attract him all the more by winning Emmanuel.

Her glance flew from one to the other, and the half smile in suspense on her lips seemed to hesitate between them. Emmanuel, caught up by the game, teased her:

"Haven't we seen each other somewhere, Mademoiselle Florentine?"

"Could be," she said, and laughed, tossing her hair back. "The sidewalks aren't that wide in St. Henri, and they're not that crowded neither."

"But haven't we talked to each other already?"

"Maybe. But not that I remember."

Then she began to question him in her quick way. He answered her, but absent-mindedly, paying more attention to her vivacity and curiosity about him than to her words, high-pitched and with sharp notes that hung above the rattling of the dishes.

"You been in the army long?" she asked. And she polished the tips of her fingernails, held them up to the light, rubbed them again against her uniform and put on a friendly, detached air.

"Six months," he replied.

Each time he spoke he leaned forward over his plate to be sure she heard him, then retreated, and this constant movement was beginning to make him self-conscious.

"How d'ya like it?" she asked.

"Oh, not bad . . ."

"Must be awful after a while, though, eh? Drilling an' all that stuff?"

Emmanuel only smiled.

"Think you'll be goin' overseas before long? I hear there's some took the boat already, eh?"

She asked without any secret longing for adventure, with no tremor of curiosity or admiration. But he misunderstood the sparkle in her green eyes and imagined that she, like he, felt the attraction of the unknown.

"Oh, I hope so," he said. "Yep, I sure hope I get over there."

"You're goin' to get to see some awful things there, ain't you?"

Then, with a smile, "What was your name again?"

"Hey! Don't tell me you forgot already!"

She was not embarrassed, simply pretended that she was trying to remember, and murmured:

"Létourneau, eh? Isn't that it?"

She glanced slyly at Jean, her eyes telling him:

See! He likes me too! You're not the only one, but all the same you're the one I like best. I just want you to know you're not the only one in the world . . . even if you are . . .

Her eyes grew soft, their lids fluttered, and for the space of a glance she tried to draw him into the memories that were burning in her mind, full of the wind, the cold, the snow, and the two of them alone together. Then she steadied herself and continued the conversation with Emmanuel, self-possessed and sociable.

"It must be nice to be on leave. How much did you say you have?"

"Just a few days."

"Oh! Just a few days! That goes by very fast. . . ."

"Yes," he murmured.

Intrigued by the mockery that occasionally shone in her green eyes, and by the jerky motions of her hands, which she folded, unfolded and crossed again, he wondered if she wasn't letting him know he could meet her. . . . He blushed, and hated his shyness so much that he let the conversation drop, dissatisfied with himself, irritated by his own silence. He began to crumble a piece of bread.

"Is the chicken okay?" she asked, playful and sprightly.

"What about you," Jean broke in, "have you got lots of boyfriends?"

Florentine managed to keep her smile, but her small, strongly veined hands clutched each other and turned white. Why was he insulting her this way? Hadn't she been nice to him? And to Emmanuel because of him? Hadn't she been friendly the whole time, looking after them and making other people wait? How she hated him, as much as she had the first day she saw him, with his mocking, bottomless brown eyes full of mischief, and his mouth, so hard and determined! And how she loved that very mouth! And to think that with all its arrogance it had touched her eyelids! She was excited, upset and humiliated at the same time. Would she never be able to make *him* suffer as he was doing to her now – but without risking losing him? Yet she was not going to swallow her shame without a comeback.

"That's my business," she said, but she had been taken by surprise and her smile began to falter and her small bust rose and fell quickly under the thin cotton of her uniform, and all the animation left her face. Her gaze was rivetted to a scratch on the pink marble, where her fingernail scraped to and fro; her feet shifted aimlessly behind the counter, and she was wretched and upset, wretched from an old nightmare that was always ready to return like a cruel shadow.

"I guess you don't want to tell us, eh," Jean went on, "whether you meet some guys from the Five and Ten after hours. Right? D'you think we'd have a chance, me or Emmanuel?"

"That," she said, looking him straight in the face, "is a stupid thing to ask."

Angry, she shifted about the bottles of sauce and the salt cellar and wiped them, all the while feeling a chill in her shoulders, as if someone had laid an icy hand on the back of her neck; and she was so miserable at not finding the right words to defend herself that she turned her face away to hide it. Usually she wasn't at a loss for words. What was happening to her? What a stupid feeling, not to be able to strike back!

"Don't pay any attention to him, Mademoiselle Florentine," said Emmanuel. "He's just trying to get you goin'. He doesn't mean it."

"Well, he almost made me mad," she said, half smiling now, clinging to the hope that Jean had only wanted to tease her. "I'm next thing to mad. An' it wouldn't take much to make me real mad. And then I'd tell him where to get off at."

"Where to get off at!" Jean repeated, and he burst out laughing.

"Yes, where to get off. I say what comes into my head. I don't make up fine speeches."

"Don't mind him," Emmanuel intervened again.

He stretched his hand partway across the counter.

"No, I won't mind, sure I won't," she said, then, trying to speak with more style, she repeated: "Certainly I won't," and was petrified with embarrassment. "But the fact is . . . that you . . ."

Her smile as she looked at Emmanuel was lukewarm and barely grateful.

"The fact is, you're better mannered than he is."

"Well, well now!" Jean sneered.

She stiffened.

"If you don't mind," she said, "you might tell me what you want for dessert. I haven't got all day to talk." She looked into space and rhymed them off: "There's apricot, raisin and apple pie, and banana custard and lemon pie too." And she shook her curls impatiently, bored with the menu and still angry. "Well, all right, if you've not made up your minds yet, do it now."

She turned on her heel and left them, swinging her shoulders a little as she went, and her moving hair shone in the reflections of nickel and copper: long, brown and silky.

"Why don't you try and get a date," Jean whispered to Emmanuel.

"Are you crazy?" said Emmanuel.

They could see themselves in the mirror against a background of pale-pink lingerie. Their eyes met in the reflection. Emmanuel's expressed hesitation.

"She'll put us in our place, but good," he said.

But he wasn't ready to turn down the game completely. Emboldened by Jean's self-confidence, he was thinking of some small kindness he could show Florentine, some gentle, charming word that might win her. He saw himself in the mirror, his right shoulder slightly advanced, not so much in impudence as signalling an effort at gaiety.

"Want to bet?" asked Jean.

He was on the verge of telling how he had got to know Florentine. Words like "It's easy, you can't imagine how easy it is" were on the tip of his tongue, but he changed his mind. He felt an urge to destroy the scrap of friendship and confidence in others, the vestige of attraction he still felt toward humanity, in order to remain in a loneliness he found uplifting because in it he found the full expression of his own being.

"Ask her!" he insisted.

"Aw, I don't know," said Emmanuel, uncertain again, and saddened.

Florentine, at the far end of the long space behind the counter, was leaning over to pick up a pile of dirty plates. Her arms looked frail and were marked by swollen veins. Weariness had left its lines around her mouth and at this moment shadowed her eyes.

"I don't know," said Emmanuel.

Leave her alone, he thought. They should all leave her alone. Let her smile be a quiet one, as it must once have been. And let her eyes be calm when she comes face to face with life. And let everyone leave her alone!

"Ask her," Jean persisted. "If she turns you down I'll ask her myself . . . Hey! Florentine!" he called.

From a distance she made the beginnings of a gesture that might have meant resentment or impatience or submission – a little signal that was totally Florentine. She picked up more plates on her way toward them, and there she was before them with a pile of dirty dishes up to her chin and a wet lock of hair sticking to her cheek.

"Well, what do you want now?"

"Emmanuel wants to ask you something."

She put down the plates, brushed back her straying hair and stared at them mockingly, no allurements in her challenge.

"All right, let him ask!"

Why don't people let her alone! Let her be natural, let her get rid of that look of being greedy and on her guard at the same time, thought Emmanuel. I'd like to make her happy somehow, and I don't know why but I'd like to dance with her too. She's thin and willowy, I'll bet she can dance.

"Do you like dancing, Mademoiselle Florentine?"

"Is that all you've got to ask me?" she said.

A shadow of irritation showed in her face, but a glint of curiosity lit up her eyes. She looked at him sideways, breathing jerkily, excited as she always was by the least attention from a boy, excited and on her guard.

"So that's all you had on your mind!" she said scornfully.

We should let her alone, he thought. And get out of here.

"So it's true, eh? You like dancing?"

Despite herself, her hips began to weave as if to the echo of distant jazz. And all she thought of was dancing in Jean's arms. It must be Jean who put Emmanuel up to asking her what she liked. But what if it was a trap?

Her eyes wandered toward Jean.

"Depends who with," she said.

Emmanuel, embarrassed now, and bothered more by Jean's ironic attitude than by the girl's agitation, carried away by his own timidity, rushed into his next question and was sorry for it even before the words were out.

"Are you doing anything, Mademoiselle Florentine, say, tomorrow night?"

"Such as?"

Her delicate nostrils quivered. Suddenly it seemed she could see Jean's hardness, as if it had become visible, and her own as well, which she recognized: a hardness that would never flinch. She raised her arm and pointed a finger straight at Jean.

"It was him, eh? He put you up to asking me that!"

She pouted in disdain. Why not show Jean right now that she didn't care a snap about him? She too could pretend that their kiss in the snowstorm had been just a game, and that it was already a thing of the past. But if he went away and never came back! What good was revenge in that case?

"Oh, you guys are crazy!" she said bitterly. "There just isn't anybody crazier than you two."

Her lips were still smiling, but a desolate expression of anger and loss trembled on her face. Then she stared at Jean and her mouth grew tight.

"I say no," she said. "If you was to ask me to the Normandy Roof, why, I still wouldn't go."

"Come on," said Jean, "you don't really mean no!"

"Oh yes I do. No to the two of you, and I mean just that."

Her voice grew shrill. Some of the younger customers nearby were watching, and egged her on with nods and laughter.

"That's right," said one, "give it to 'em, Florentine!"

"I said no!" she went on, still louder. "Who do you think I am?" She bit her lip. "Seems like some people think we're dumbbells. And they're not far away neither. I could tell you their names."

Marguerite, noisily dragging a tub of marshmallow along the floor, interjected as she passed by:

"Hey! Don't get mad, it's only fun."

She had a loud, rough voice, childish and friendly.

"It's only in fun, come on!" she said, and glanced in gentle reproach at Emmanuel and Jean.

"I'll get mad if I like," said Florentine. "Fun! You call that fun, making a fool out of people? For fun! Some people go pretty far for their fun."

"I wasn't joking," said Emmanuel.

"No? Then what *were* you doing? We're not just here to be laughed at, you know!"

"That's right, you tell 'em, kid," said a younger worker, laughing.

"You can be good an' sure I'll tell them."

"There's nothing to get mad about," Emmanuel tried to explain.

"No. Nothing at all!" she said sarcastically. "That's what you think, you guys."

But she was not talking to Emmanuel. Her eyes and their devouring flame were on Jean's face. He was looking down, smiling coldly, out of her range, languidly tapping his cigarette ashes to the floor. Oh, she thought, you belong to me just the same, you do. And so great was her fear of losing him, so violent her rebellion at her own attachment, such was her rancour at the distress of her heart, that everything she did became too difficult and she was saying anything that came into her head.

"We're here to serve you, that's okay, we've got to do it," she went on. "But we don't have to listen to your stupid remarks, eh? None of that stupid stuff, okay? We just can't stand that!"

Her cheekbones were shining, and she kept swinging her shoulders and tossing her head to keep her hair back. Then she took her long locks in one hand to hold them in place and, bending her neck slightly, flashed a smile that was at once defiant and expectant.

"Now get mad. Go on, get mad," she said. "See if I care!"

"Oh, but you're the one that's mad," said Emmanuel gently.

Her two arms raised, she was tucking strands of curls behind her ears.

"Me? Not a drop. Not even that much."

"I wouldn't want you to be," said Emmanuel.

"I'm not mad."

"You sure? Really not?"

"If I say so."

"'Cause if you're not mad," said Emmanuel, "I'd really like to see you again."

He was thinking of the party his parents were going to give for him before he left. Impulsively, without even waiting for advice from his mother, he wanted to invite Florentine. Why not? he thought. She must have a nice dress that would do. And she's pretty. He was happy already thinking of things he could do to please her and wipe out the ugly impression of their first meeting. He imagined how he would introduce her to his friends. "This is Mademoiselle Florentine," he would say, and perhaps he'd even add, "my girlfriend." Why not? If she was awkward or made little mistakes in company, he wouldn't mind. The prospect of the party, which had bored him, now seemed full of the mysterious and unexpected. He could see himself being attentive to her, discovering other aspects of her character.

He leaned forward over his plate and gave the girl a smile full of impatience, friendliness and honesty.

"Do you know what would please me, Mademoiselle Florentine?"

"No, I don't know."

"What would really please me?"

"I don't know. No idea."

"My mother's giving a party tomorrow night . . ." and he touched Jean's arm. "We just wondered, my friend and I, whether you'd like to come."

"At your place!"

"Is it yes?" asked Emmanuel.

A smile of satisfaction touched her lips.

"Wait a minute, will you?" she asked. "I don't know yet. I . . . I don't know . . ."

But already she could see herself in her pretty dress, her

best stockings and her patent-leather shoes. At last Jean would see her dressed up, and not as poor as he thought. So that's what the two of them were cooking up. She purposely put off the moment of decision, tasting the power of being able to make her answer a haughty no.

"Will you come?" asked Emmanuel.

"Well, I haven't said yes, not quite. I've got to think . . ."

"Say yes," he insisted gently, "and don't think about it."

"Well, I'm going to feel like an outsider. I won't know anybody there."

She was enjoying the suspense, thinking that Jean would admire her for prolonging it, and taking pleasure in teasing Emmanuel. But she began to worry that he'd grow tired of asking her, and made up her mind with a little pout.

"Okay then. I'll go. I'll go, yeah, I'll be there." And she added in a tone that was half grateful, half sulky, "It's very kind of you to think about me. Thanks."

He began to laugh, relieved and happy.

"Should I come and pick you up?"

She thought it over, wondering about Jean's silence.

"The thing is, I gotta work late this Saturday," she said. "It is this Saturday, isn't it?"

"That's right, tomorrow."

She was waiting for a word from Jean, a look, an implicit promise, a word of encouragement. But he was getting up to leave, knotting his scarf.

"No, I'll go . . . I mean, it's okay, that's it, I'll get there by myself."

"Don't forget now!"

Emmanuel smiled at her, his head cocked to one side, his arms hanging awkwardly.

"And above all," he said, "don't change your mind."

Her eyes followed Jean. She leaned toward him, devoured by the fear of losing him that she felt each time he left. Jean. She had the impression that it was as cold in his heart as the winter night in which they had warmed each other. Jean was the hard, whipping wind, he was winter, the sworn enemy of the sudden softness you feel at the approach of spring. He and she . . . they'd recognized each other the night of the storm. But the storm and cold would come to an end. And although he had come into her life like a destroying gust of wind, perhaps when the first storms were past it would turn out that he had come to help her see more clearly all the ugliness and poverty around her. Never before today had she noticed the long-suffering resignation on her clients' faces, or at least never had it seemed so obvious, along with her own resemblance to them and her fury as she recognized the fact. Never had all these smells of hot grease and vanilla turned her stomach so. And Jean was marching off as if his mission were accomplished and he had nothing more to do here. Yet Jean was her own escape, which she had struggled against so long. He was the one she had to follow, to the ends of the earth, forever. She would never let him get away.

Long after the two young men had disappeared, snatched away by the street where a burst of sunlight was struggling against the grey sky, Florentine was still inventing a thousand pretexts for rejecting an aspect of truth which she had almost glimpsed just now. Oh no! She would never give up loving Jean. She could never be resigned to that. And anyway, wouldn't it be stupid to give up just when she had a chance to see him again, to show herself proud and radiant, to dazzle him so that he would never in his life see anything but the face of Florentine? Already she was imagining his attitude and her own role at Létourneau's party, all the men surrounding her, the lights converging on her in the middle of a big room. For this was how Jean would really find out her worth, when all the other young men took notice of her.

It must be a fine house, Létourneau's. She remembered only scraps of what Emmanuel had told her . . . "Phone me when you're free tomorrow, I'll come and get you. We live on Sir Georges-Etienne Cartier Square. . . ." Very impressed, she kept repeating the address, imagining a modern drawing room with discreet lighting, well-mannered guests, and hosts who circulated pleasantly serving a distinguished late supper. She grew sentimental at the thought.

Her hands deep in dishwater, she was singing to herself, because she was no longer Florentine the waitress who was angered and humiliated by her menial job. Let them call for her with rough words, plague her with vulgar approaches, that didn't bother her now, she was warmed against all the disgust she had felt at her dull daily life. She was a new Florentine, unknown even to herself, freed from the past the night she ran to meet Jean in the storm – oh! how she liked herself in this whole undertaking!

Her weariness had left her. She had flown so far in her own thoughts that when, just after one o'clock, she saw her mother enter the store, she was shocked and felt a kind of stunned vexation. Her mother . . . She was coming through the store, blinking at all the glitter. Her gait was slow, and she was upset as she saw herself in the mirrors, and busy hiding her old gloves with the holes in them.

NINE

Florentine stared, amazed to see her mother there. She realized that her first feeling had been one of relief that she hadn't come earlier, before Jean and Emmanuel left. But she regretted this thought so sincerely that she leaned over the counter and called out to her mother with an effort to be jolly:

"Maw! What a surprise!"

She couldn't get over her mother's appearance. As often happens to members of a family who see each other every day, she had ceased to observe Rose-Anna's face, and now saw all the changes that had escaped her: the faint wrinkles around the eyes, the listlessness in her expression, the suffering and courage inscribed on her features. At a glance she realized all that had slipped in between today and the remembered image.

For years she had seen her mother at home, working away in the half-light of evening or early morning. Rose-Anna had only to turn up now in the blaze of this bazaar for Florentine to see her clearly at last, with her poor smile and timid manner that gave away her intention to take up as little room as possible.

Florentine was stunned. She had helped her mother out of fairness and pride, but without real tenderness, and often with a sense of injury to herself. For the first time she had occasion to be glad that she had never acted meanly toward her family. She felt a sudden desire, akin to happiness, to be good to her mother, to show herself more attentive, gentle and generous.

She felt the imperious desire to mark the day with some special kindness, the memory of which would stay intact. She now perceived her mother's life as a long, grey voyage which she, Florentine, would never make; and today, in a way, they were saying good-bye to each other. Maybe their paths were beginning to separate this very minute. Some people need the threat of parting to make them attentive to their own feelings, and in that moment she knew that she loved her mother.

"Mamma," she said warmly, "come on, sit down!"

"I just dropped in, I was going by," Rose-Anna explained. "Your father's at home, as you know. And out of work, eh?"

Oh, that was their mother, starting right off with their troubles! Away from home she had this embarrassed smile, and she didn't mean to dampen youthful spirits – on the contrary, she liked to warm herself by their fire and often adopted a forced gaiety – but her words of complaint came out all by themselves. They were her real words of greeting. And perhaps they were the right words to reach her family, for apart from their worries, what kept them together?

She went on, speaking more softly, ashamed to talk of these things in the presence of strangers:

"So . . . I got away early this morning to look for a house, Florentine."

She'd told her all that this morning. Florentine frowned at her own impatience, but she caught herself in time and answered kindly:

"You did right to stop by. And I've got just the thing for you. We got chicken today, forty cents. I'm treating you."

"Nothing of the kind, Florentine! All I wanted was a cup of coffee to perk me up."

You could almost hear her murmur, Forty cents! That's a fortune! All her life, with her knowledge of the cost of food and her ability to make substantial meals from nothing, she had kept her peasant horror of paying in a restaurant for a meal she could prepare at home for half the price. At the same time she had always repressed a secret desire to treat herself some day to this extravagant pleasure.

"Oh, very well then," she said, giving in to fatigue and temptation, "but just a smidgin of pie or maybe a doughnut. I could eat that, I guess."

"No, no!" said Florentine, losing patience.

Compared with her mother's fear of spending she saw Jean tossing down a tip. What she admired most about the young man was perhaps the way he threw his money on the counter. While her family kept their eyes on their money after it was gone, like a part of themselves, torn away and lost. Sometimes Rose-Anna would drag up for no apparent reason the reckless use to which she had put a few pennies on some past occasion.

Florentine looked up, stung to the quick by these recollections.

"No, no," she said again, "you're goin' to eat a big meal, Mamma. It's not often you get a chance to eat at my place, eh?"

"That's true," said Rose-Anna, touched by the girl's gaiety. "It's the very first time, I do believe. But just the same, I'll just have a cup of coffee, really, Florentine, that's going to do me just fine."

She watched the rapid movements of the waitresses, impressed by their youth, and stole a look at Florentine, who seemed to have risen far above her family here in the glitter of mirrors and the colourful crowd. She was silent, feeling almost as much embarrassment as pride. In a confused way she realized how imprudent it was always to bother Florentine with their troubles, casting her shadow on this girl's youth; and suddenly, clumsily, she decided to put on a happier front.

"I'd better not get in the habit of going out, you might get tired of seein' me here. It's so warm and nice in your store. And does it ever smell good! And don't you look pretty now!"

This compliment was like balm to Florentine's heart.

"I'm ordering chicken. You'll see, it's good," she cried, back to her first resolve to be kind to Rose-Anna.

She wiped the counter in front of her mother, brought her a paper napkin and a glass of water, and lavished on her all the attentions she had to pay to strangers day after day without the slightest satisfaction. Today they filled her with joy, as if this was the first time she had ever wiped a counter or set a place; and a distant sound of music caught her, gave its rhythm to her body, and lightened her heavy chores.

"You know, you got a nice job. You're well off here," Rose-Anna said, misinterpreting the happiness on Florentine's face.

"That's what you think!" cried the girl, forgetting her resolve. But then she laughed:

"Had good tips today, though," she said.

She thought of Jean and Emmanuel. Not seeing that their generosity toward her emphasized the distance between them, she could still be delighted at the coins they had left beneath their plates.

"You know something?" she went on. "It's always me gets the most tips."

Then she brought a plate piled high and, as the crowd was gone, took a few minutes to keep her mother company and watch her eat.

"Is it good? Do you like it?" she kept asking.

"Just first-class," said Rose-Anna.

But she also kept saying, with the tenacity that ruined the smallest extravagance for her:

"My, that's expensive though, forty cents. Seems to me it can't be worth that much. Just think, Florentine! That's a lot!"

When she finished the chicken, Florentine cut her a piece of pie.

"Oh, I couldn't!" said Rose-Anna. "I had too much already."

"It's all included in the meal," Florentine insisted. "It doesn't cost any more."

"Well, just a taste then," said Rose-Anna. "But it's not out of hunger anymore."

"Try it anyway," said Florentine. "Is it good? Not up to yours, eh?"

"Better," said Rose-Anna.

Then Florentine, seeing her mother relaxed and almost happy, felt a tenfold desire to add to the joy she had already given her. She reached into her blouse and took out two new bills. She'd been keeping them to buy stockings, and the moment her hands touched the crisp paper she felt a terrible regret, but she sighed and held her hand out to her mother.

"Here," she said, "take that. Take it, Mother."

"But you gave me your week's pay already," Rose-Anna objected.

Florentine smiled. She said:

"This is a little extra. Come on, take it!"

She was thinking: I'm good to my mother. I'll get it back. It'll be counted in my favour. She was still sad at giving up her silk stockings, but she felt a new certainty that she would be happy immediately. She thought of tomorrow's party and in her innocence believed that because of this generous act she would shine brighter there and earn Jean's complete submission.

Rose-Anna had turned red. "Oh," she said, her fingers busy chasing bread crumbs from her coat, "I didn't come in to get something from you, Florentine. I know you don't get to keep much of your pay."

She took the bills just the same and put them in her change purse which she slipped into the inside pocket of her bag. Carefully folded and buried so deep, they seemed almost safe from all the pressing needs making their calls upon them.

"To tell the truth," she admitted, "I needed that money almost right now."

"Oh, Maw," said Florentine, less pleased with her generosity than she had expected to be, "and you wouldn't have said a word!"

She saw the dejected look on her mother, grateful and full of admiration for Florentine, saw her stand up with an effort and go away among the counters, stopping here and there to touch some material or examine an article.

Her mother! Getting old. . . . She moved slowly, and her coat, too tight, made her belly stick out more prominently. With the two dollars deep in her purse she wandered off, more uncertain than ever, for now she saw the shining pots and pans and the cloth, so soft to the touch. Her desires grew vast and many, and she left, poorer certainly than when she had come in the store.

Suddenly all the joy Florentine had felt turned to gall. Her happiness at being generous gave way to an aching stupor. What she had done had led to nothing.

At the back of the store Rose-Anna stopped at the toy counter. She was looking at a little tin flute, but she quickly put it back when a salesgirl approached. Florentine realized that between Daniel's wish and the shiny flute there would always be her mother's good intention – an intention repressed. And between her own wish to help Rose-Anna and the impossibility of doing so, nothing would be left but the hurting memory of today's small, vain attempt.

She made herself smile at her mother who, in the distance, seemed to be asking her advice: Should I buy the shining flute, the slim and pretty flute, or the stockings, the bread, the clothing? Which is more important? A flute like a ray of sunshine in the hands of a sickly boy, a flute breathing sounds of happiness, or the daily bread for the family table? Tell me, Florentine, which should I buy?

Florentine managed another smile when Rose-Anna, finally making up her mind to leave the store, turned to wave; but, she would gladly have destroyed within herself all her impotent good intentions. Wary of its own softness, her heart was hardening again.

TEN

In a high brick house, the upstairs apartment cast the cozy light of its bright windows through the falling snow out into the quiet darkness of the square. At the foot of the iron staircase that climbed toward these lighted openings in the austere façade, Florentine listened to the party sounds, muffled by the soft snow. She hated arriving alone at the house of people she didn't know.

Until the moment her store closed she'd hoped that Jean would come for her. She had counted on it, all ready with her silk dress under her uniform and her patent-leather shoes in a paper bag. Then at nine o'clock she had left by herself, so angry at being alone that she had decided several times, as her feet took her willy-nilly toward Sir Georges-Etienne Cartier Square, not to go to the Létourneaus; but just as often she decided that she would go – and in both cases with a single end in view: to make a show of her indifference to Jean.

But she knew she was determined not to miss this party, for Jean would be there sooner or later, and she mustn't lose this chance of seeing him. After all, this was her prettiest dress, and he hadn't seen it, and anyway it would be terrible just to go home now that she had it on, and felt her heart rustling with murmurs of a celebration, her heart, like her dress, all disposed to please.

The shadows passing, passing by the yellow windows up there – they must be dancing. The snowflakes also danced; outside in the shafts of light, they fluttered like moths around a lamp. Millions of flakes, soft and white, flew down and struck the windows, dying there, clinging to the light and warmth.

Florentine ran up the stairs and rang quickly so as not to lose her nerve at the last moment. Emmanuel opened the door. He was in his uniform, as he had been the day she met him in the Five and Ten. He stood on the threshold and his vague smile sought her in the shadow into which she had withdrawn. Then he recognized her and the smile grew real.

"Hey! Mademoiselle Florentine! You came after all!"

She seemed so uncertain, ready to turn and flee, like an aerial form, a vision on the landing, created out of a play of light and shadow, that he hesitated to offer his hand. But then he drew her inside the warm house, full of smoke and succulent smells from the kitchen. Now he was looking at her with his friendly smile, finding again her ardent, stubborn face as he remembered it. Snowflakes were melting on her cheeks.

"You really came!" he cried happily.

He pulled off her gloves, took her purse while she unbuttoned her coat, then shook off the snow still hanging on the thin fur collar.

"Come into Mother's room," he said.

Leaning close to her as he guided her down the hall, he asked:

"Come this way . . . I can . . . Hey, can I just call you Florentine?"

THE TIN FLUTE

"If you like," she said with a smile and the shade of a self-conscious pout. "I don't mind."

"And will you call me Emmanuel?"

"If you like. I don't mind."

She was listening with anxiety to the voices from the living room.

"Sounds like a lot of people!"

"You're used to that," he said. "At the Five and Ten you see them from morning till night. You're not scared of people, are you?"

"That's not the same," she said.

"No?"

"Course not. At the Five and Ten you're serving people. You get tired of serving people. You get fed up serving them. But at night, people . . . Oh, I don't know how to say it . . ."

She frowned and stopped abruptly. Why was she getting into this kind of explanation with Emmanuel? Was it the warmth inside that made her imagine, across time and space, that she was chatting with Jean? With a Jean who, like Emmanuel, was attentive and willing to listen, trying to understand.

"Oh! I don't know why I'm telling you stuff like that with no rhyme or reason," she said roguishly, slapping his hand lightly with her glove.

She had just thought, I can afford to be nice to Emmanuel. It doesn't matter how I act with him.

She had no need to fear that through him she would feel that tightening around the heart, the dizziness, the misgivings. . . . It would be easy to confide to him all the secrets she saved up for Jean. She could be affectionate with him, in small ways. She might even let him kiss her if he was gentle, just so as not to forget Jean's kisses.

123

Emmanuel drew back to let her go in his mother's room. It was papered in mauve, and the bed cover, drapes and doilies were in the same thick, silky corded cloth.

"If you want to powder your nose, you'll find everything on the dressing table, I think."

"Oh," she said indignantly, "I've got my own things. I have my powder."

She went straight to the table with its gathered skirting and its mauve-shaded lamp which cast a pale light below it.

She avoided touching things, but looked fascinated at the phials and pots of makeup. She took out her comb and began arranging her waves, amused at seeing herself from different angles in the three-panelled glass. Her arms, raised shoulder-high, pulled the hem of her dress above her knees, and her slip appeared, trimmed with a narrow strip of fraying lace.

Emmanuel, thinking he might be embarrassing her, murmured:

"I'm going to get Mum to introduce you around."

She felt a touch of panic.

"No, you introduce me. Stay with me."

He took her arm gently, drew her close and, without trying to kiss her, looked long into her face. He knew that he had been a little free with her in the restaurant, and was surprised that she had actually come to his party. Now he was afraid that his parents might not give her a warm welcome. But the thought that she might feel out of place in his home made her more attractive to him, more vulnerable. He liked the blind confidence she placed in him.

"Don't worry," he said, "I won't let you get bored."

"Oh, I won't be bored," she said. "I don't think so anyway. But I don't want you to leave me all alone."

As she spoke she was listening to the voices from the

other room, trying to single out that of Jean. The effort brought a flush to her cheeks. Her eyes dimmed, she clung to Emmanuel's arm and she looked coaxingly up at him. What she really wanted was for Emmanuel to appear so taken with her that Jean would be upset. Could she not succeed in that? Could she not, just this evening, be the one most spoiled and coddled?

They went into the living room, Emmanuel holding her hand. Folding chairs rented for the occasion lined the walls of two adjoining rooms whose glass doors stood open. The twenty or so guests who occupied the chairs looked more like spectators than participants in a jolly evening. The rug had been taken up and the heavier furniture pushed back in a corner. In another corner stood the radio. Some of the young people glanced expectantly toward it, others, equally anxious for the dancing to start again, tapped out a rhythm with their toes.

In front of each group Emmanuel murmured, "Mademoiselle Lacasse," then ran quickly through five or six names. And she, her nostrils pinched, would make an effort to smile and say:

"Oh, I don't think I'll be able to remember all the names. . . ." and then in a whisper to Emmanuel: "You told me there wouldn't be many people!"

At the kitchen door she was confronted by the young man's parents: Madame Létourneau, small and plump, with a sweet doll-face; and Monsieur Létourneau, with the hint of a paunch, a fine, smooth moustache, a courteous smile, more polite than affable, looking very like a portrait on the wall nearby which must have been of his father. His pose was thoughtful, one elbow on the arm of his chair, the hand beneath his chin occasionally giving a twist to his moustache. His business was the sale of devotional articles, ornaments and communion wine, and in the process of serving prelates and country priests he had caught an unction in his speech and a slow dignity of movement, with broad, benign and measured gestures, as if each time he raised his arm it lifted with it a heavy, embroidered sleeve. In order to tempt the young priests who were drawn to his store, he would put on a shining chasuble or a lace surplice and parade up and down in front of the counter, showing off the beauty of a material in the discreet light that fell among the statuettes and plaster Christs, bathing his shop in the sacral glow of the vestry.

After business hours he was involved in traditionalist movements and occupied positions of honour in several religious and nationalist societies. His veneration for the past caused him to reject anything that was flawed by modernism or foreign elements. Yet he tolerated parties in his house, receiving young people whose language, customs and frivolity he deplored, partly out of curiosity and partly out of an urbanity he liked to think he possessed.

For some time now Emmanuel's relationship with his father had been polite but devoid of friendship. As for Madame Létourneau, her timid soul, weak and loving, had tried for so long to reconcile these two that she had become like a mirror that gave an exaggerated reflection of her son's vivacity and her husband's dignity. She wavered between childish effusiveness and a sudden and unexplained rigidity which seemed to express her respectful devotion to Monsieur Létourneau.

Emmanuel introduced Florentine to his sister Marie, a gentle, serious girl; to his brother in college uniform, looking very like Emmanuel; and to a great-aunt with pious, fearful hands whose ceaseless fumbling with the folds of her dress seemed to have to do with an unseen rosary.

Florentine had never felt so out of place, so lost and desolate. She knew now that Jean was not at the party, and from her first glance, which stamped them all as boring, she doubted that he would come. Madame Létourneau, on an impulse of kindness, tried to make her feel at home. She chatted endlessly in a nervous, cooing voice.

"Do you know, Emmanuel's been talking of nothing but you since yesterday? These nice curls now, tell me," she went on, "are they natural?"

"Yes," said Florentine.

Monsieur Létourneau took his turn at questioning her with the appearance of paternal interest. She was irritated by the fact that he made her admit things she had never wanted to admit. It was as if he were proving to her, very gently and with a courteous smile, that she had no business in his house.

She was not slow in catching certain nuances in his voice or in grasping their meaning, and she was hurt and furious. If I was in love with Emmanuel, she thought, it's not this old boy that would change my mind. And the certainty that if she wanted she could lead Emmanuel to face anything for her sake pleased and consoled her.

Emmanuel was chatting with some friends in the bay of a window decorated by a tall fern. Florentine, to boost her confidence, took out her compact and dabbed at her nose with the powder puff. She caught Létourneau Senior's mocking glance, and continued at her task deliberately, her head high.

Suddenly she noticed Emmanuel. He was alone now, staring vacantly into nothingness. She thought he seemed as lonely as she was, as if this were not his own home, as if he wondered what he was doing here, as if he were waiting for someone, had been waiting for a very long time. Then his gaze fell on her, and his face brightened. Jean, she thought, never looked at me like that. Just now Emmanuel looked at me as if he'd known me forever. Every time I see Jean he looks as if he's trying to remember who I am. . . . She was amazed at her own discovery.

Conversation was desultory along the wall. Guests from the city were carrying most of the burden; those from St. Henri were mainly tongue-tied. A medical student who had been at college with Emmanuel astonished everyone by his precise and elaborate way of speaking. Near him was another student, thoughtful and intelligent-looking, whom the girls found much more intriguing. They nudged each other, clutching their evening bags, and whispered:

"Who's that one?"

"He's a painter," somebody replied.

"No, he's a writer."

None of them sounded very sure of her information. But these whispers and murmurs grew animated in the corner where the girls were concentrated, while the young men chatted among themselves, some of them making a getaway into the hall or even the stairway where they told jokes and laughed loudly as if some restraint had been removed.

Florentine kept an eye on the living-room doorway. She was still hoping for the bell, for Jean to appear . . . with his dark hair tousled and powdered with snow, as she saw him in her memory. Oh, how she hoped for that, and for the half-smile he might have for her when he saw her, his lips barely parted.

Emmanuel turned on the radio. A furious jazz melody with noisy saxophones filled the room. The girls hurriedly pushed their hair into place, and taking out their compacts reassured themselves that they were fit to dance. Then Emmanuel was standing in front of Florentine. He took her hands and drew her to him.

"This is our dance. Do you know how to swing?"

He was laughing. Normally he was slightly awkward and

reticent, but as soon as he was caught by an emotion, his mettle showed. His head no longer slanted toward his right shoulder, and his smile came to life like an offering to his joy. When Madame Létourneau saw him like this – exuberant, his head high – she was as disappointed as he that an eye defect had kept him out of the Air Force.

Florentine followed him perfectly from the very first steps. She who was so rebellious and strong-willed showed an astonishing docility when she danced, her slim, supple figure submitting to the rhythm and her partner's movements, abandoned, passionate, childlike, almost primitive.

"What kind of nigger dance is that?" Monsieur Létourneau wanted to know. "Where on earth did Emmanuel learn that?"

"They dance very well together. Doesn't look like the first time," murmured his wife. Then, leaning toward her husband, she pleaded gently, "But, my dear, we don't give enough parties. We've lost touch with the young people."

Emmanuel held her close, then let her go to arm's length. For a time they moved forward, shaking their legs from the knee like light weights that had their own life. Holding Florentine's hand above her head, he twirled her until her skirt flew high and her necklace and bracelets rattled. Then he held her waist again and they jumped in a jerking rhythm, face to face, breath to breath, mirrored in each other's eyes. Florentine's hair, floating free, flew from shoulder to shoulder and blinded her when she whirled.

"Where did Emmanuel meet that girl? Did you say she was a Lacasse? Was that it?" asked Monsieur Létourneau.

"Why, don't you remember," his wife murmured, "that poor woman who used to come here by the day sometimes, it was years ago."

"So that's her daughter, is it?"

"Of course . . . but you'd never know it. Her Florentine is quite a classy little thing."

"Does Emmanuel know?"

"He must. That wouldn't bother him anyway."

"Stupid!" muttered Monsieur Létourneau, twisting his moustache. "The boy will never keep up his station in life."

"I could dance all night with you, do you know that, Florentine?" said Emmanuel. "I could dance with you all my life!"

"Me too," she said. "I just love dancing!"

"I'll never dance this with anybody else but you. And would you believe it, I'll not let you get away."

She threw her head back and gave herself up to him with a smile. If there was one thing she liked better than dancing, it was to be the centre of attraction in a crowd. The others around them were quiet now; everyone was looking at them. She thought she heard some say, Who is that girl, anyway?

With a shiver she imagined the reply:

Oh, some little waitress from the Five and Ten.

Very well, she'd show them that she knew how to make Emmanuel like her, and not just him, if she felt like it. She'd show them who Florentine was! This feeling of defiance, along with the speed of their dancing, lifted up her heart and put colour in her cheeks. You'd have said her eyes were lit by two tiny lamps whose flickering light set a point of fire in each pupil. Her thin coral necklace like a light chain flew around her small neck; and her arms, another chain holding Emmanuel, and her rustling silk dress and her high heels tapping the bare floor – this was Florentine! And she was dancing out her own life, she was defying her life, burning her life, and other lives were bound to burn if hers did.

Emmanuel's devotion and his obvious infatuation were

the proof of this, and his tense smile, his face grown pale – yes, these were proof that she, Florentine, had a rare and genuine power over men. That wiped out so many humiliations that had left their mark on her heart. Good. It was like a promise that Jean himself could not help being in love with her.

Now it was Jean she was dreaming of, half out of breath, her lips parted showing her small, straight teeth, panting, her silk dress clinging to her delicate form; and she loved feeling Emmanuel's heart beating fast under his heavy wool tunic. Gently, caressingly, she went so far as to let her cheek touch his, and then, through her thin dress, she felt such a thumping that she wasn't sure if it was her heart or his beating at such a rate.

The music stopped. Emmanuel noticed that the brooch on her dress was undone.

"Your pin," he said, "it's going to fall off."

Clumsily he tried to replace it where her neckline widened.

Florentine stiffened, took a step back and fastened the brooch herself. She was trembling a little.

When she looked up again she saw Emmanuel's eyes on fire.

"My darling," he murmured, very softly, and caught his breath.

Now they were playing a waltz. He took her in his arms almost roughly.

The music, much slower, was less to Florentine's taste. Emmanuel was holding her too tightly. His moist hand was crushing her fingers. Clumsy couples bumped into them at every second step. The room seemed too small now that all the young people were dancing. Their many-coloured mass was swaying without advancing or retreating, as if they were searching for a way out. The seven-branched candelabrum still gave off its feeble light through coloured bulbs, but the serried group of dancers cast confused shadows on the walls and seemed to darken everything.

The movement was no longer so fast as to prevent Florentine from thinking. How boring it was, this slow music! She laughed at something Emmanuel was saying to her, but didn't hear the words. She wasn't listening to him. All that she could hear was an evil foreboding. Jean . . . he hadn't come. And it was on purpose, so as not to see her. He'd decided that he didn't want to see her anymore. And what good did it do to be loved if the one she wanted never came back?

Her arms and legs hurt. It would have been all right if she had been able to go on and on in a frenetic whirl, turning and turning, never stopping, keeping ahead of her fatigue. But now weariness was seeping into her limbs and forming a heavy weight dragging after her like a life enchained, a life afraid of not attaining happiness.

Emmanuel was holding her too tight. He was warm, and his coarse wool uniform scratched her bare arm. She looked up at him and detested him. He had called her "darling." What did that mean to her? He was not the one who had a right to say such words to her.

Later she returned to reality. It was stifling hot in this big room with its radiator. The flowers on the piano were wilting. She looked around her, dazed, and caught a phrase from Monsieur Létourneau: "The French-Canadian race . . . the family . . ."

Around Emmanuel a group was discussing the war. She heard scraps of a bitter argument. "Poland attacked . . . the democracies . . ." Tired, she allowed her eyes to close. Then she opened them and caught the cold, smiling gaze of

THE TIN FLUTE

Mr. Létourneau fixed upon her. This man seemed to see in her the waitress exposed to public coarseness, born to that state and destined to stay in it all her life. The moment he looked at her she felt herself relegated to the greasy steam of the sink, and she felt her hands plunging into tepid, soapy dishwater, with the smoke of pork sausages rising all around her.

A tart question came from a girl sitting beside her:

"Have you been going out with Emmanuel for long?"

Yet the voice had a touch of distress in it.

Florentine heard her with a start. She would have liked to be rude to this stranger with her anxieties. Hurting some-one would have been a relief. But all she did was accentuate her pout.

"He's not my steady, in any case."

"Who is your steady then?" persisted the girl whose eyes were drowned in chagrin. "You love him," she said hastily, in an attempt to narrow the distance between them.

She was small and dainty and despairing, and followed Emmanuel with a heart-broken look.

"My steady!" Florentine repeated the words, and felt a rush of anger.

My steady, she thought. I haven't even got one. Here I am nineteen and I haven't even got a boyfriend to take me to a show on Saturday or come to parties with me. I'm nineteen, and I'm all alone. . . .

"Where did you buy your dress?"

It was the voice of the girl beside her again.

The question was probably not ill-meant but Florentine thought she heard a shade of condescension in it. As she hes-itated to reply she suddenly saw her mother busy cutting the cloth one winter night, the material laid out on the table in the large room, the lovely black silk, supple and rustling, and

Rose-Anna puffing, excited at making the first slash with the scissors – and the wind outside whistling in the cracks of the small, frosted panes! Oh, how the silk had seemed beautiful to her that night, and she remembered the first try-on, before the sleeves were added, ducking down before the sideboard mirror then climbing on a chair, so as to see the whole dress even if it were half at a time.

"I don't remember where I bought it," she said, barely audibly.

But it was as if she had denied Rose-Anna's work of all those evenings. That was an end to her belief that she had a pretty dress. Now she knew it was a poor girl's dress. She would never wear it again without hearing the crisp sound of the scissors in the expensive cloth or seeing it, half sewn, with white basting thread, a dress of sacrifice, of work done by poor lamplight.

While she was dreaming, a set expression on her face, Emmanuel had crept up behind her and played the childish trick of clapping his hands on her eyes.

"Guess who!" he cried, laughing. Then: "What were you thinking?"

"Oh," she said, "that's not hard to guess," and she pushed his hands away impatiently, but somehow left him holding one of hers, and joined in his laughter.

Dancing had lost its charm. Her shoes, too small and barely broken-in, were hurting her feet. It seemed to her that only her high heels held her up, and that they were boring from beneath into her feet. But they mustn't think she was unhappy or worn out. And so she laughed a little louder than before and made her eyes sparkle – she'd discovered how to do it. They'd think she was having more fun than anyone; nobody was to know she was dying of weariness and distress. And maybe if she pretended hard enough she'd end up having fun. She murmured something.

"What did you say?" asked Emmanuel.

"I said, I'm really having a good time."

"Are you glad you came?"

"Am I? Why, sure!"

"Not too tired?"

She frowned, irritated:

"Who, me? I'm never tired!"

"Do you often go to parties?"

"Pretty often. Just depends."

"I should have met you long ago, Florentine. We've wasted a lot of time."

"I'll be around," she teased.

A shadow of melancholy passed over Emmanuel's face.

"Yes, you'll be around," he murmured, "but I've got to go back pretty soon."

She was aware of a gentle, unfamiliar feeling around her like an aura.

"Why did you join up?" she asked. "It doesn't seem to make your parents very happy."

"It doesn't make anybody very happy," he said, something pathetic creeping into his voice, and he looked for approval as he met her glance.

But she lost interest in the subject, swung her shoulders and got into the rhythm, her vivacity reviving.

As it was Lent, supper was served just after midnight. Marie Létourneau, along with Emmanuel and her mother, passed around paper napkins, soft drinks and paper plates containing thin sandwiches, just like a picnic, two or three olives, a celery stalk and a leaf of lettuce. Marie Létourneau looked exhausted. You could guess from her pale, serious face that she took little joy in these festive occasions, but that she wore herself out in the exacting preparations they demanded.

The dancing started up again, and the party went on until dawn. Couples were still on their feet when Madame Létourneau disappeared, to come back a moment later dressed for out-of-doors.

"It's Sunday," she said. "I might as well go to Mass now and sleep later."

The guests from the city, including the student and his mysterious companion, had left hours ago. Only the couples from St. Henri were left, and they all agreed with Emmanuel:

"Let's go to Mass together!"

ELEVEN

They wrapped themselves up and went out into the early morning. The air was mild. They walked two by two under the dripping trees. The tall trunks of the maples, their branches bare and grey and shining with melted snow, already showed their forms clearly in the half-light of the square. Underfoot the soft snow was deep and slushy. The houses were still dark. From cellar to attic the windows were black holes in the cold façades. Over their roofs a scarf of watery blue unfurled in the retreating night sky. The stars were melting.

The party crossed the square together, quiet now, except for one couple who laughed too loudly as they teased each other. Their two silhouettes went astray for a moment among the trees. Then you heard them laugh again, and suddenly the laugh was muffled.

On Notre Dame Street a few lamps gave off their trembling light behind windows shivering under sudden gusts of wind. The air was almost warm, but heavy. You could feel a March downpour in the offing. But to lungs clogged from cigarette smoke the morning was like a blessing.

Emmanuel was breathing deeply, ecstatically. He was astonished at how mild the morning was, and even more at the peace it brought him. Walking beside Florentine, holding her so that she wouldn't slip, he felt a relaxation and serenity that he had never known. They seemed to be starting on a real friendship, more than a friendship, a budding affection, ill-defined, delicious, but uncertain and changeable as the day-light whose colour was just breaking through the veils of night.

The massive Church of St. Zotique appeared in a white vapour like a cloud of incense rising from its steps. Shadows crept toward the doors. Behind two or three old ladies come to hear the early Mass, Florentine and Emmanuel were inside.

They were enveloped in the pleasant warmth of the place. Florentine, after a rapid genuflection, sat down wearily, barely able to struggle against sleep. Yet even in this torpor her thoughts made her suffer cruelly. Unlike Emmanuel, who from the first hint of dawn had realized the enchantments of the night just past and felt cheerful and miraculously transformed, she had become aware of an acute disappointment. The day, beginning dull and grey, reflected her feelings.

Emmanuel . . . What was he doing, kneeling here beside her, as if he were her fiancé? Fiancé . . . The word afflicted her with an inexpressible desire to see Jean again. He was the one who should be here, not this stranger, this Emmanuel, who didn't even arouse her curiosity. Every small attention he paid her now became a vexation. She had no more use for his attentiveness. A little more and she'd detest him altogether. She'd repulse his kindness as a destructive thing that could only increase her distance from Jean.

Why isn't Jean here, close by me? she kept thinking. An image came to her tired brain which made it wide awake. She was remembering the day when Jean had first invited her out.

She recalled how he had said she would have to get to know him little by little, and she saw him leave the counter, squaring his shoulders.

Then she realized that this sight was imprinted on her mind, like certain poses that impress us in childhood and follow us all our days, unchangeable and fixed forever.

She began to feel panic. The first thing was to dismiss the vision, choose something else her mind had held fast. Impossible. She continued to see him from the back, a passerby growing more distant, indifferent to what he had seen in passing.

That was when she recognized love: this torture on seeing someone, the greater torture when he was out of sight, in short, a torture without end. Breathing harder, she murmured to herself, with the secret desire of inflicting on Jean this arid thirst rather than curing herself of it: I could make him love me too if I had half a chance. By that she clearly meant: I'd make him suffer as he's making me suffer now.

At her side Emmanuel was praying. His lips were moving and his fine features expressed a cheerful peace. Florentine slid forward onto the prie-dieu beside him, and she too began to pray. But her prayer was almost an order, a challenge: I have to see him again. Let me see him again, dear Holy Virgin, I want so much to see him.

Then she grew more calm and began to use a hundred feminine wiles to get the Virgin on her side. I'll make a novena, she said, if I see him this very day. The fear of committing herself without succeeding froze her heart. She added: I'll do the first nine Fridays of the month as well. But only if I see him today. Otherwise it doesn't count.

She was begging with all her heart, yet her eyes remained hard and her mouth stayed motionless.

At the elevation she caught Emmanuel's eye as she bent her head. For the briefest of seconds she felt another longing: she thought of praying to have this consuming love extirpated from her heart. But as her bowed head touched the next pew she saw Jean again, his back, as he went away. Then she became one with her torment. She clutched it as a drowning man grasps a fragment of a wreck.

She would do other, more difficult things to obtain the Virgin's intercession. She'd go to Mass every morning, she'd even – oh, that would be hard! – give up the movies for six months, maybe more. What wouldn't she do? She'd go to the Oratory on the mountain and climb the steps on her knees like some poor devil seeking a cure, though her cure would be to stay intoxicated with a bad dream, and infect another with it, give it to him like an illness. She stared at the lighted candles with eyes that in this flame seemed hard and resolute, not for a moment thinking that her desire for Jean's kisses might be an obstacle between her and the pale statues that peered out from the shadows of the apse. This very day I'll start a novena if I see him, dear holy Virgin. And that was her prayer until the end of the Mass.

As they came out of the church Emmanuel noticed her great fatigue and her faltering steps.

"Honey, you're done right in. Do you want to take a taxi?"

A cab was just slowing down near the group of the faithful coming out of the portico.

The Lacasse house was only five minutes' walk away, but Florentine was so spiteful that she didn't mind making Emmanuel spend the extra money. She could imagine her mother's astonishment at seeing her come home in a taxi. She nodded in agreement, exaggerating her shivering and helping her teeth to chatter.

The sun was rising, round and sulphurous. Soft snow had begun to fall, threatening to turn to rain. Emmanuel turned up Florentine's fur collar and, protecting her as best he could, steered her to the taxi.

She smiled to herself as she snuggled like a cat into the warm seat.

"You really were cold!" said Emmanuel, covering her legs with a flap of his coat.

Now she was shivering with pleasure at seeing herself cared for and spoiled with nothing demanded in return. Warmth blew her way from the heater. The radio, through the crackle of static, was playing an insignificant love song. The church atmosphere was already swept away from Florentine's memory. Why panic? If she was patient she'd get what she wanted. And while she waited, why not let Emmanuel be kind to her? Slowly, giving no hint of her train of thought, she asked him:

"Your friend, Lévesque, the guy at the store with you the other day, you'd invited him, hadn't you? Why didn't he come last night?"

As if she were unconcerned, she looked out as the houses paraded by and allowed Emmanuel to take her hand.

"Don't you worry about Lévesque," he said, frowning and at the same time moving a little closer.

She dropped her purse, bent down to retrieve it and went on with affected playfulness:

"Oh, I was just wondering why he didn't come. It seemed funny to me. I thought you were great friends. Where's he from, anyway?"

"We were friends," said Emmanuel simply. "We still see each other sometimes. He's a guy . . . he hasn't had it easy in life. You'd think he was taking it out on anybody that reminded him of the bad days. But let's talk about us, Florentine. We haven't got a lot of time."

Again she pushed him off on the pretext that she was too warm, laughing as if she'd made a joke.

"He's a funny one," she went on, still in her mocking tone. "Where does he live, anyway?"

"He's got a little room at the corner of St. Ambroise and St. Augustin. He likes living alone. He spends most of his time studying and hasn't much use for girls. The funny thing is, they seem to like him."

He emphasized the last words and tried to catch Florentine's expression.

She looked at him, wide-eyed, sounding his mood, then laid a hand over her heart and said with a forced laugh:

"Not me, that's for sure." Her voice was shrill and sharp. "I think he's . . ." She searched for a word that would wound Jean, a word that Emmanuel might even repeat to him. "I'll tell you. He's just not my type. Not my type at all."

Her vehemence made him smile.

"That's good. Good for me, I mean. I owe Jean a lot, and he's a friend in spite of everything, but if you were my sister I wouldn't like to see you go out with him."

"Why?"

His answer was simple and direct.

"Because you'd be running after your own unhappiness."

"Oh!" she said, amused and half incredulous.

"There's another reason," he said, taking her hand again.

"What?"

"Luckily you're not my sister. And I think a lot of you."

"As much as that?"

"A lot," he repeated.

The taxi halted outside the girl's house. He got out and

paid the driver, then joined her. She had started shivering again, genuinely this time, staring with a lost look down the ugly, deserted street which echoed the suffering this day held for her. The two of them were the only living things, patches of murmuring light, in this gloomy corridor.

"D'you want to give me a kiss, Florentine?"

She started, seeming to emerge from a troubled daydream, and looked at him with distaste, not knowing what to say. He was the only one who hadn't tried to get her into dark corners at the party. And she'd been expecting him to want to kiss her. But right here . . . with the memory of Jean . . . She made a little face and turned her head just in time for his lips to brush her cheek. He was dizzied by the faint caress, and immediately wanted more.

"Not like that, Florentine, better than that."

He caught her by the waist so abruptly that she lost her balance. Red-faced and trembling he struggled with her and found her lips.

A door slammed in the distance. Quickly he let her go, but held her by the wrists.

"I won't see you before I go, Florentine. I'm leaving tonight. But from now on you're my girlfriend, eh?"

She said neither yes nor no, thinking, I've time to decide about it. I don't have to make up my mind now.

But as soon as he was gone she wiped her mouth. She watched him, noticing that he walked with his head tilted to one side. She wanted to laugh and she wanted to cry.

TWELVE

The end of the winter was signalled by clouds and gusty winds. Early that afternoon masses of low clouds hung over the south slope of the mountain and the wind charged at the lower town.

Around eight that night the powdery snow was loosed on the city. Shutters slammed and from time to time one heard the sound of ripping zinc from the roofs of houses. Dark trees twisted and dry cracking sounds were heard from their knotty trunks. On the windowpanes came rattling fistfuls of shot, and the snow whirled and sifted beneath ill-fitting doors, slid in the cracks of windowsills and searched in a frenzy for any refuge against the fury of the wind.

There was no more earth or sky. The houses were massive shadows with here and there what looked like the pale blinking of a lantern. You'd have said that a vigilant hand fumbling through the tempest lit an occasional street lamp which at once went out, tried a new bulb which gave off a hasty flame, and, untiring, continued this vain struggle against the dark. On Notre Dame Street the flashiest signs cast only a dim glow into the roadway, and from the sidewalk across from the movie theatre came no more than a reddish light like that of a distant fire.

Pushed and harried by the wind, Azarius emerged from a patch of dark, passed quickly through the turbulent halo of a street light, and then, with short, quick steps, leaning into the gale, made his way toward The Two Records restaurant. Its white façade blended into the storm. Three yards away you'd never see it. With the sure hand of habit Azarius found the latch.

The place was almost empty. Sam Latour, sitting by the roaring stove, was smoking a cigar and blowing smoke rings whose ascension toward the ceiling he observed with satisfaction. Behind the counter his wife, a charmer with freshly waved dark hair, was leafing through an illustrated magazine, her elbows on the unpainted wood and her chin on one hand. There was only one customer, visible from the rear, immersed in the reading of his newspaper.

"Oho! It's our do-nothing big talker!" shouted Latour good-humouredly. "Did the storm blow you in? Nita was just sayin' she bet we wouldn't even see a cat in here tonight."

"Happens there ain't much doin' tonight, you're right," said Azarius laconically.

Leaning on the counter, he unbuttoned his overcoat and ordered a coke. He didn't seem anxious to talk. Contrary to his custom, he remained silent for some time, giving excessive attention to wiping the bottle-neck on his sleeve. His forehead was smooth, his cheeks red and healthy from the cold, but he was looking restlessly around, bewildered and uncomfortable.

"That's right," said Anita Latour, picking up the nickel Azarius had left on the counter. "Sam was just saying there can't be many folks out and about tonight."

This affectionate couple had the habit of giving each other mutual support even for their least compromising statements. What one said passed at once into the conversation of the other, prefaced by a good-natured "Sam was saying . . ." or "As Nita said . . ." Each borrowed phrase was paid for with a smile.

"And that's just what I thought, too," Anita went on, "when I saw this storm. Sam's goin' to be all alone the whole night, says I to myself. So I just up and come along."

Sam was laughing slyly.

"Tell me, Lacasse," he said, "did you ever in your born days seen a good girl like my Nita? You could almost hate her, she's so darn good."

Azarius took a long swig from the bottle and wiped his mouth with the back of his hand. For a moment he remained undecided, his eyes shifting nervously. He remembered Rose-Anna, not as she was now but as she had been: happy, with tender eyes as soft as velvet, and a cordial voice. But she changed while he remembered, and he saw her hunched by the lamp, patching children's clothes. He saw her straighten up to get closer to the light and take a few stitches, holding the dark material close to her eyes.

He had tried to help her, offered to thread her needle. He had asked her humbly to tell him how he could be useful and she had answered not a word. Then for the first time in his life he had said to her "one word louder than the next."

"Dang it, it's enough to drive a man to drink, do you know that?"

To that also she made no reply. And he had dressed to go out, but so slowly as to give her every chance to hold him back. He could stand reproaches but never silence.

The atmosphere of the house had suddenly grown unbearable.

"I'm just goin' to take a little turn outside, Mother, if that's the way it is."

Nothing.

Outside, he had automatically turned toward The Two Records. Now, in the warmth, he was calming down. He was in his element here. They'd listen to him in a minute, when he started talking. Sam would contradict him, but he'd listen. And above all he'd hear the sound of his own voice reaffirming his confidence in himself.

"How's things at your place?" asked Anita.

Azarius started. He managed the shadow of a smile.

"Well, not bad, not bad ay-tall, thank you, ma'm."

"You gave up the taxi business?" asked Sam. "Your boy Eugène was sayin' so the other day he was in. So he's in the army now, your boy! What do you say to that?"

"As far as I'm concerned, it's fine. He did well, Eugène. He's young and smart. I wouldn't mind bein' in his place."

"Yeah?"

"Yeah, and quick about it."

"Well now. And look at the mess the Russians have got into with the Finns, eh? And not much new apart from that. You'd think both sides is scared to take a hold. The French are playing cards in their forts and the Germans on their side too, looks like."

He stroked his chin and sighed. "It's a phony war, for sure, eh?"

Azarius had his turn to sigh:

"Yes, she's a phony war, all right."

Then, looking up, he said, "The taxi business, it don't pay at all. Six or seven dollars a week! There's a limit. A man's not goin' to go on workin' for nothing just because he's short of cash." He was warming up, and by the end of his speech had recovered his assurance.

But suddenly he seemed to hear the hollowness of his own words and his shoulders slumped. He went on:

"Besides, you're just as well off not to work and stay on relief."

Sam had left his chair and was striding up and down in the lighted part of the shop.

"Yes, but don't forget they're going to put an end to that. There won't be no relief anymore. They'll stop it cold," he said, clasping his hands behind his back.

"We asked nothing but a chance to work," Azarius replied vehemently.

"Of course! And that's just the trouble. You and a lot of others like you wanted nothing more than a job and a bit of a salary just to keep body and soul together. Instead of that you were doin' nothing and the rest of us who were making a dollar, well, we were paying for that. We paid to keep you doing nothing. In Canada, here, it got so that two-thirds of the population kept the other third idle!"

"An' yet there was no lack of work to be done," interrupted Azarius. "People still needed new houses."

Sam Latour laughed and pulled at the collar tight around his thick neck with the impatience of an ox straining at his yoke.

"Well I should say! Houses and roads and bridges too!"

He finally loosened his tie and went on, relaxed:

"There never was a lack of work. Or men neither. I've seen fifty men, by gum, after the same job. I wonder what we did lack."

"Money," said Azarius.

"That's right, money," thundered the owner. "There was none for the old folks or for schools or orphans. And none to give people work. But just take a look right now, there's money for the war. It's there now, all right."

"Yep, there's money there for the war, sure enough," said Azarius.

He tipped back his head to finish off the bottle, then looking down he murmured:

"I figure we're bound to get our hands on some of it."

"Could be," said Sam, sitting down again.

There was a pause, broken only by the crackling of the fire in the big iron stove.

The little man at the back of the room, a stranger to Azarius and Sam, suddenly spoke up.

"Business is picking up," he said, "but mostly in armaments. Now, that's a good line to be in these days. If I could start over again, that's what I'd take up. But I'm a builder by trade. I'm a mason. And do you know how many years it's been since I practised my trade? I don't mean just odd jobs patching a hole in a wall – they don't even pay you to go there and back. I mean a real job, do you know how long it's been?"

He was speaking quietly, seated at his table in the back, his hands flat on the table-top, staring ahead of him in a way that was at once pitiful and comic because of a twitch that afflicted his right cheek and his chin.

"I'll tell you: eight years. Eight years since I worked at my trade." His voice was calm and unexcited. "But I've done a pile of other things. I've done gardening for the nuns, I was a paper-hanger and I was a bed-bug exterminator once when there was a plague of them, disinfecting lousy mattresses."

Unaware that his deep voice and timid manner had a comic effect (did he think it was his words?), he went on:

"An' that ain't all. If you want to see a fellow that's been a jack of all trades, just look at me, I'm your boy. After I worked on those mattresses I had an idea. An' it was a good one. You'll laugh, 'cause you can see I'm not the kind of a good-lookin' fellow for door-to-door work. Anyway, I turned travelling salesman just the same. You can't name something I never tried to sell: insurance policies – you always start out like that, you think you're smarter than you are – then vanilla extract, green tea, Christmas cards, floor brushes, rupture belts, horse medicine and whatever you care to mention! I used to tell them . . ."

And he stood up suddenly and drew Sam Latour aside as if he were going to put over a big sale, looking small and puny beside the big man. Then he went into his spiel:

"So you don't want any powder, mamzelle. Well, perhaps your mother, there, that fine, big lady I see behind you, maybe she'd like to see my new baking powder, it raises your cakes four times as high. And you, sir, what about trying my corn remedy? You got no corns? What about heartburn? Try one bottle and if you're not cured in three days . . . What! No heartburn neither? Well, now, you can always use a little floor brush. Maybe I'll be back next year . . ."

He waved good-bye half-heartedly, with mock discouragement, and went back to his table.

"There ain't no work I haven't done," he said to no one in particular. "No work except my own work. Mason. They say you've got to specialize to get work these days. Well, I can tell you a trade nowadays it's no good anymore. You spend half your life learnin' it and the other half forgetting how to do it. No, sir, the good days for a man with a trade, they're gone. The only way you can get along, it's doin' little jobs. . . ."

The touch of comedy during the man's demonstration was forgotten, and gloom settled on the group again.

Azarius stared at the stranger, whose life was so like his own.

"There's something in what you say," he said. "Now, me, I'm a carpenter by trade. Yes, sir, a carpenter," he repeated, as the little man looked up with interest. "When building dropped to nothing, I had the notion of earnin' a living by making small furniture. The smallest things, stools, smokers' sets, they sold pretty good at first. But one day I realized I wasn't getting paid for my time. Like my wife, she's a first-class dressmaker. When we got married she was making dresses, and that's a lot of work, she was makin' them for two bucks each. Nowadays she can't even get that much. You can buy a silk dress ready-made for a buck and a half. A buck and a half for a silk dress! Now what are they paying them there in those factories if they can sell a dress for a buck and a half!"

"Why, sure," said the mason. "It's the same whatever you go to do. The skill's disappearing. No experience. Everything's mechanized. But just the same . . ."

His grey eyes under the thick tufts of eyebrows began to blink compulsively, as if his myopic vision had been riddled by a series of blinding rays.

"Just the same, there's nothing as fine on this earth as the builder's trade! Now you take your mason, there, plastering a nice new wall with a good, well-mixed solid plaster, eh, mister, I'm goin' to tell you!" he said, half smiling at Azarius.

"Yes siree!" said Azarius, as enthusiastic as the other, suddenly filled with memories of his working days and warmed by the man's approval.

He had taken a step toward this mason who could have been a fellow worker in the good times gone by. He lifted his hands toward the light, carpenter's hands that had loved the feel of bare wood, and his wide nostrils quivered at the fine smell of the fresh-cut boards just beyond his grasp.

"Just to be up on a scaffolding," he said, "between the sky and the ground, and hear the hammers going the whole day long! And you see the wall go up straight as a die, all of a piece on a good strong foundation, and first thing you know there's a house there by the sidewalk where there was nothing but a field of weeds. That's the life all right."

"Yep, that was the way to work," said the mason.

"The way to work," echoed Azarius.

There was silence.

After a moment Anita made a sign to her husband.

"Hey, Sam, wasn't there somebody here just this morning lookin' for a man to drive his truck? Who was that now? Do you remember?"

"You're right, that was Lachance, Hormidas Lachance. Why don't you look him up, Lacasse?"

Azarius' face grew dark red.

"Lachance!" he grunted, with a disgust intensified by his train of thought so suddenly interrupted. "There's a big shot that's earned his name. I know him, all right. He's one of those guys that thought he could hire a man for next to nothin' a few years ago. He liked getting a fellow who was on relief, they'd work for peanuts. And then if they quit he'd turn in their names and they'd lose the relief."

"Well, who knows," said Anita gently, "maybe he's not so cheap nowadays."

"We'll see about that," said Azarius with a roughness that was unlike him.

He took off his cap and jammed it down tighter on his head. He seemed to hesitate. Then, suddenly, looking at the clock on the wall, he whistled between his teeth:

"By golly, the time goes fast. Well, I've got to get goin'. Good night. And thanks just the same for the tip, Madame. Good night, Latour . . ."

On the threshold he turned and looked back, staring at the mason who had returned to his paper, holding his head in his hands, appearing once more as the image of the little, quiet man you'd take for a retired clerk, totally satisfied with his life.

"A good night to you too, friend," said Azarius, a shade of distress and commiseration in his voice.

Brusquely he opened the door and disappeared into the dark.

Usually so easy-going, tonight he strode along at a great clip, muttering bits of angry phrases. He suddenly felt resentful toward the mason. Now he saw him bitterly as the personification of his own wasted life. He was angry at Sam Latour for mentioning Lachance, because now he might be put to the embarrassment of thinking about applying, though he knew he was incapable of doing so. Like all indecisive men, he put up a little fight, just for form's sake, against what he knew was an irrevocable refusal by his conscience. Perhaps, too, he was more angry at himself than at anyone else for having looked back with nostalgia on other days. He had lived for so long in this sluggish state, renouncing his regrets and keeping going on the strength of vague hopes! And now he'd have to start over again, struggle to figure things out and regain his peace of mind. He walked along energetically, his head hunched down between his shoulders. The storm was quieter, exhausted by its own violence. A few rare stars shone through the gaps between the clouds.

When he reached Beaudoin Street he forced his pace still more. His anxiety at having left Rose-Anna alone with sick children on her hands had grown acute on his way home.

He went in the house as if he had a presentiment of disaster.

"Rose-Anna! Are you there?" he shouted. "Is everything all right?"

She was in the kitchen, sorting the children's washing. The things that were not too dirty she put on one side, and tossed the others in the sink. She glanced, astonished, at her husband, and looked away again without speaking.

"The washing could wait till tomorrow," he said. "You're killing yourself, Mother."

He had these sudden revelations of her fatigue and ill-health, at times when he himself felt the pangs of discouragement.

"It's got to be done," she replied curtly. "They have nothing else to wear, you know that very well."

Sitting at a corner of the table, he began unlacing his boots. He took one off and let it fall heavily.

"I saw Sam," he said after a moment's silence. "He said something about Lachance wanting a man to run his truck."

Knowing how Rose-Anna had hated Lachance, he hoped to hear an instant protest from her, as well as credit for his near-sacrifice.

But she whirled on him, her eyes bitter.

"All right, what are you waiting for? Go and see him!"

"But Mother!" He was surprised. "Don't you remember what he did to us? Have you forgotten how he made us lose the relief?"

A small voice called "Mamma!" from the next room.

"What's the matter with him?" asked Azarius, struck by the whining, exasperated tone of the child. "That's Daniel again. Isn't he any better?"

"I don't know what's wrong with him," said Rose-Anna.

"He had a nosebleed just now. We've got to get him to the doctor."

She went out with a glass of water for the child. Azarius heard her exhorting him to go to sleep. A moment later he saw her watching him, leaning on the door frame. He couldn't repress a twinge of shame as her clear gaze took in him and his weakness.

"Listen, Azarius," she said, her voice implacable for once, "this is no time for getting all proud. Not when the kids need things to wear and maybe medicine next. Dear Jesus, no! Go and see him just the same, Azarius!"

"You can't mean it, Mother!"

The wind moaned in the cracks of the window. He added evasively:

"I'll go tomorrow, early. But I almost think it's nonsense, Rose-Anna. Something better might come up, and if I've signed on with Lachance I'll miss out. If you really want, I'll go tomorrow. First thing in the morning."

"No, Azarius, if Lachance is in a hurry he'll have somebody by tomorrow morning. And I know you! You'll have changed your mind again. You go there right now."

"Right now! There ain't all that hurry! It can wait."

He saw her untie her apron strings and quickly smooth her hair.

"Then I'm going," she said.

"Hey! Are you crazy? On a night like this?"

She went into the next room. He thought she was testing him, that she'd just gone to get her sewing and in a minute she'd be sitting beside him in the kitchen where it was warmer, and they'd talk it all over more calmly. He pulled off his other boot and sat there silently, one elbow on the table, staring vaguely. Maybe I'll go tomorrow, he thought, but I'll try my luck first with Holliday, the contractor. Anyway, I'll think it over.

And there was Rose-Anna in front of him, dressed to go out, slowly tying the inside belt of her coat. Instinctively he got up to bar the way.

"You're not going out in a storm like that. I'll go, I tell you."

"No, let me go, Azarius."

He caught her eye. She had the same grave, energetic expression she had had in the days when she went out doing housework and sewed for others and, from morning till night, struggled to alleviate their poverty. He bowed his head.

"You know right well it's better if I go," she said in her quietest voice. "Lachance is bound to feel ashamed of himself when he sees me there. I'm going to rub his nose in everything he did to us. I'm going to explain everything to him. I'm going to make him give you a job. Don't you worry."

"Tomorrow's soon enough . . ." Azarius began.

But Rose-Anna already had a firm hand on the doorknob. She said:

"Fill up the tub and put it on the stove, if you want to help. I'll finish the wash when I get back."

And she said something else which was lost in the storm. He saw her almost lose her balance outside, caught in a gust of wind as she closed the door. Then there was no sound but the slow, measured dripping of water from the tap.

He reached behind him for the chair-back and sat down. His arms hung loosely as he stared at the pile of dirty clothes that overflowed the sink. His physique had not suffered from the years of unemployment and odd jobs. His hair was still as bushy as a young man's, his wide smile came easily, his complexion was fresh and he was a fine figure of a man. He was a good talker, he knew how to carry on a discussion, he made a good impression when he went after work, and he wasn't really lazy. What had happened to him then?

He buried his face in his hands.

What on earth had happened to him?

He saw his life pass before him rapidly in images sometimes precise and clear, sometimes blurred as by a fog. He saw his early days as a carpenter, building houses in the neighbourhood. In those days Rose-Anna would make him a lunch and pack it in his tin lunch box. At noon, sitting high on a beam, he would open the box, which invariably held some special surprise – a fine, rosy apple whose seeds he could spit down into the street, or a meat pie wrapped in layers of wax paper and still holding some of the oven's heat. Or a bunch of green grapes, or some of those buckwheat cakes of which he never tired. Those high-flown snacks in the burning midday sun, its heat beating down on his neck, formed a clear, well-defined part of his memories. He couldn't understand why so many insignificant details stuck in his mind, such as the sound of the hammer, the taste of nails in his mouth, the squeaking of a new door opened and shut for the first time, and those tasty lunches. . . .

Then came a sudden break in his life. He felt that he had to get back to that very moment in his existence if he wanted to know what had become of him. . . . But then the images began to come thick and fast, implacably.

He wasn't building now, and saw himself vaguely in a series of jobs that had nothing to do with him. He saw a man that must be Azarius, but was not. He sat high on the driver's seat of a delivery van, climbing down to leave bottles of milk at door after door. Then the man quit this monotonous chore and started looking for something else. The milkman became an iceman, then a clerk in a neighbourhood store. The clerk faded away, and there were no more little jobs, just single days' work here and there for a dollar, for thirty cents, for ten cents a day. Then, nothing. A man sitting by the stove in the kitchen, stretching his legs lazily. "Might as well let them pay us to live, Mother, till something turns up. So long as I can't work at my own trade!"

Azarius was surprised at the sound of his own voice. He had spoken aloud without knowing. For a time he listened to the whine of the wind, listened carefully, wondering if he had not been half asleep.

Then this jobless man that he was tried to renew some contact with the other, the first man, the one who was still suffering at his own decline but didn't want to show it. At that time he had turned into a big talker, a speechifier, hanging around the tobacco stores and the little restaurants of that part of town, and he had developed his innate talent for rhetoric. That, too, was when he began to boast about the convents, churches and presbyteries he had built, and the others, if you could believe him, that he yet would build. In fact he had never built anything but little bungalows for newlyweds, but the more he talked about churches and convents the more he actually believed he had built hundreds of them.

In those days he had always thought he was on the verge of some great undertaking. Thus he had not hesitated to squander the two hundred dollars Rose-Anna had inherited from her father on a set of tools for building small and fancy pieces of furniture. He had remained certain he was doing big business until the day when he found himself staring at a workshop full of articles that would never sell, and a heavy debt to the lumberyard.

Far from being discouraged at this, he was pushed by

failure to even greater risks. He had thought he was handy at every trade and just about to make his fortune one way or the other. He had scraped together a hundred dollars and sunk the lot into an ironwork and repair shop, along with a man whose name he barely knew. The little shop on St. James Street bore both their names on its sign: Lacasse and Tremblay. Then the partner had cleared out, leaving Lacasse in bad shape with their creditors; and a new sign was painted in black letters on the shop front.

But Azarius had still not lost his optimism. He still refused the odd jobs offered by friends through Rose-Anna's mediation, saying that he wasn't born to do chores for peanuts. That made his reputation in the neighbourhood: a heartless husband who sent his wife out to scrub floors rather than taking an honest job. Yet this wasn't true: every time he saw Rose-Anna go out as a cleaning woman he had been revolted. But he had said nothing. He'd show them all that he could earn a living for his family, and a good living at that. Just give him a little time. And first chance he had, he'd gone into a skid, as Rose-Anna called it.

He had squeezed the last cent of credit out of his brothers-in-law to try his luck in organizing a kind of sweepstake. This time he almost had trouble with the police. He had tried it again, lost again, and tried again.

He stood up, oppressed by the leaden weight of his thoughts. He wasn't stupider than other men, surely! Why couldn't he succeed? He'd been unlucky, that was it, but some day luck would be on his side, and his great undertaking, one of his great undertakings, would be his revenge for all the contempt, all the shame he felt loaded upon him.

He looked at the wretched lodgings around him with eyes that blinked as if he were just awaking. Rose-Anna doesn't believe in me either, he thought. She never believed in me. Nobody does. He was afraid to wake up and see himself as she had seen him for the last twenty years, perhaps as he really was.

Suddenly he wished he could run away. He wished it with such acuteness that he thought of a thousand projects, all of them absurd. He saw himself packing his bundle and making off before his wife returned. He'd jump a freight train and go get a job in the mines. Or he'd just start off along St. James Street till he was out of town and there he'd take the highway until fortune smiled on him at last – a man born to high adventure. He'd walk through rain and snow, under the stars and under the sun, all his possessions tied in a kerchief on the end of a stick, and somewhere, at a fork in the road, sometime, he'd discover what he had been searching for since his childhood. He wanted to run, with such intensity his throat grew tight and dry. He wished he had no wife, no family, no roof over his head. He wished he were a tramp, a real old-timer, sleeping in a straw stack in the open air, his eyes wet with dew. He wished for the dawn that would find him a free man with no ties, no cares, no love.

Then he glanced at the sink. The rusty metal basin had filled up with the drops from the leaky tap and was running over in a thin, continuous stream. Azarius pulled his sleeves up to his elbows and slowly plunged his hands into the wash. The clock struck.

With stiff and clumsy movements he began to scrub a little black skirt, full of holes and so worn that the cloth came apart in his fingers.

THIRTEEN

The hum of the sewing machine nibbled at the silence. It stopped at times and then you could hear the kettle whistling. Rose-Anna, her lips pinched, was concentrating on her sewing. She would press on the pedal and the voice of her labour would be heard again, muffled, tireless and somehow plaintive.

Mother and daughter both sat within the circle of the lamplight. Every time Rose-Anna looked up she saw Florentine sitting nearby on the leather sofa, her legs tucked under her. The girl was holding a yellow magazine, reading a few lines at a time with seeming boredom, then staring in front of her, frowning, noisily chewing her gum. She was nervous and irritable, but Rose-Anna didn't even notice, she was so happy to have the girl beside her.

The children were asleep. Rose-Anna had put them in the big bed for the moment, until she finished making her quilt, and early, so that she would have quiet and room to work. The room looked neat and cosy, with its cretonne-covered couches lined up along the walls. Rose-Anna, as tranquil as this room which she had arranged in her own image, was hurrying at

GABRIELLE ROY

her work. Azarius would be home soon . . . Azarius, who, thanks to her efforts, was working again, and even seemed happy to do so. What more could she ask? The house was once more living with a heart as contented as Rose-Anna's own.

For the last two weeks she had been getting up first in the morning, very early, so as to make Azarius' breakfast. He often reminded her that he could make coffee in a jiffy, and told her to stay in bed, but there was a trace of hesitation and hope in his voice that she knew very well. She knew it was a comfort to him to hear her old slippers dragging on the kitchen linoleum while he shaved in the first grey light of dawn. She knew he liked coming into the room when it was warmed, where the fire was crackling and the steam fogged the windows. She was sure that even his bread tasted better when she gave it to him buttered, and the coffee when she poured it for him, holding back the broad sleeve of her kimono. Their eyes would meet then, briefly, eloquently. Rose-Anna wanted no other reward. What was more, for a man going off to work – and his hours were long – no sign of respect was exaggerated. She would go to the door with him and open it for him, then, shivering and making room for him to pass, give him a kiss that was not overtly tender or exuberant, but had a kind of dignity that called for courage. Then she would shut the door behind him and go back to sit in Azarius' chair in the kitchen, allowing herself a few minutes' rest, her hands crossed on the tablecloth.

Despite her hurry, she did the same thing from time to time this evening. Her hands would suddenly lie still in front of her and her thoughts, distracted from her work, flew elsewhere. The light, falling straight from the ceiling, showed the marks left on her face by work begun in the early mornings and ended late at night; but her mouth was relaxed, almost at rest. And now Rose-Anna, to tame the sudden hope she felt, a brand-new hope, which experience had taught her to treat as the most fragile of possessions, began to count its causes. First of all, Eugène had paid them a brief visit. On a twenty-four-hour pass, he had barely done more than drop in. But she had been struck by his healthy looks and, in general, felt reassured about him. Daniel was still very pale and weak, but she thought he was recovering some of his old desire to play. And for Rose-Anna a child that played games, however strange and serious they seemed, was a healthy child. Thus she never noticed that Daniel was very serious for his age. She saw him writing or pretending to read the whole day long, but if she paid any attention to the fact she was merely amused. Last of all (and wasn't this her greatest joy?), Florentine stayed home almost every night, and, though they were absorbed by different things and hadn't much to say, it was consoling to feel her daughter's presence, even if she was silent and sullen. She's got something on her mind, Rose-Anna thought. She'll get over it, and I'll have my happy Florentine again. But then she thought, What is bothering her so much? Could she be in love? She tried to remember the words Florentine murmured sometimes when she was daydreaming, and the occasions on which she had gone out evenings. But she had no memory for such things, and found it easy to reassure herself.

She was leaning with her elbows on the machine, gazing into the dark corners of the room. Then, ashamed at shirking so many chores that awaited her, she pressed her foot down abruptly on the pedal. The sewing machine hummed again, accompanied by the whistle of steam from the kitchen. A gentle wind whispered at the window. It was no longer the raucous gust of winter, but a spring wind that shook the last puffs of snow from the trees and made the wet branches rub together.

"Your father should be home soon. It's almost eight."

She would often make some unimportant remark like this in the midst of the silence, with a trace of intimate satisfaction. Her words would fall with no continuation, and she would go back to her thoughts again; sometimes she would sigh, and the bib of her apron would quiver.

For there was, alas, a dark spot in her ease of mind, and she couldn't think of it without foreboding: they still had not found a proper place to live, and the date of their move was coming closer. Azarius kept telling her there was no rush, they should wait until they had a little cash to pay down for the first month's rent. That way, he said, they'd get a nicer place. Maybe he was right. She'd have liked nothing better than to believe him. Yet the memory of many disappointments warned her that in anything requiring common sense she had to rely on herself.

In fact, the greatest suffering in her married life was occasioned by her feeling that in important decisions she could rely on no one else in the family except Florentine, and she herself was not born to lead, for her character was gentle, and despite her efforts she had remained too much of a dreamer.

She had to try to be the family helmsman. When she thought of her efforts, undertaken timidly enough, she felt more embarrassment than pride, and it seemed that when she had proved Azarius in the wrong she had widened the gap between them.

What was more, she noticed an increasing tendency in her children to imitate their father's penchant for living in the clouds. What dream world, closed to her, did they escape to? It wasn't that she lacked imagination. Little Yvonne had been the first, in her excitable way, to detach herself from the family.

Even when she was there under the lamp, poring over her school books with her pale, stubborn face, Rose-Anna knew that she was far away and inaccessible, and this child's escape for some reason was more irritating to her than any other's. Luckily there was Florentine, so practical, so different from the rest.

As she sewed, Rose-Anna cast a glance at the girl, taking care not to prolong it. She was not often demonstrative, either with her children or with Azarius. Her tenderness was almost always concealed behind a look that was discreet or words that were so common as to be unnoticeable. She would have disliked expressing herself in any other way. Yet this evening her heart was filled with an awakening of affection and a sudden clairvoyance. Florentine was indeed the only one of her children who lived in Rose-Anna's world and who was not a stranger to daily cares. A flood of emotion warmed her, and at the same time she felt a kind of surrender to Florentine's judgement. Once again the idea crossed her mind: Florentine, who was so capable, so sure of herself, would be their salvation. She'll do this. . . . She'll decide that. . . . It'll be up to her because she helps us out so much. . . . Rose-Anna moved her lips as if she were talking. All her interior monologues were helped along by unconscious movements of her face. Then she prepared a new start at conversation, aware of the abyss between her thoughts and her usual turn of phrase.

"Your father got his pay tonight," she said. "If only he comes straight home and don't go spending it first."

She was sorry she had said it, sounding suspicious.

"I shouldn't say that," she murmured. "Your father doesn't spend on himself, you've got to give him that. But robberies, accidents . . ."

On reflection, that seemed silly. So she changed the subject:

"Are you sure his supper's in the warming oven, Florentine? He'll be here with an appetite like a bear. . . ."

That was as if she had just said, her equanimity restored, He's coming home, he's done his day's work, he's got his self-respect back and a line of sweat on his face, and I've always liked those things, but he's going to have ten times his normal appetite because of the fresh air and being tired and swallowing his pride, and I won't fail him now any more than he's failing me. I'll accept what he brings, whether it's his simple weariness or some unexpected joy.

"Azarius!" she said aloud, carried along by her reverie.

"Who are you talkin' to?" asked Florentine, without looking up.

She was bored in this silent room. And she was tormented less by her boredom than by her hatred for this poor house, which was like a prison wall dooming all their attempts to escape. For three weeks now, ever since the day when Jean had come to the store with Emmanuel, he had not been there. He had disappeared with the last rough storm of the winter, like a squall which leaves nothing behind it but the trace of violence. Oh, the misery, the exasperation of waiting for him day after day, without being able to whisper a word about it, like a secret illness. You try, though, to discover things by roundabout means, and you learn that the one without whom life is impossible has the gall to go on breathing, sleeping, talking, walking, as if nothing were wrong with the world. Then rage grows in the midst of love, through and through love, like thorns through a flowering bush, until the flowers which could have flourished die one by one in this rough tangle.

The bitter feeling, like an abrasion, of growing spiteful

while losing everything she had desired was so strong that Florentine wanted to cry out. But who would hear her complaint? Everybody in the house was far away in his own dream.

Boredom submerged her and she seemed to sink deeper into it with every tick of the clock resounding in the silence. And just as the fire smouldering in the room responded to every gust of wind outside, her heart's fever answered the least whisper from the street, rising at a voice or a man's footstep on the hard snow before the door.

Oh, how bored she was this Saturday night! To calm her nerves she would have liked to smoke, but because of her mother she didn't dare.

She had a small pack of cigarettes under a cushion, however, and after much hesitation took it out, put a cigarette in her mouth and, on the point of striking a match, said:

"You don't mind, do you, Mother?"

Rose-Anna was shocked. Florentine, her legs crossed, lit her cigarette and sent a puff of smoke toward the ceiling. Slim and bold, she looked like a boy. But Rose-Anna thought, I mustn't be after her about everything. She merely said:

"Do you really like that stuff?" and coughed a little. "Well, it's your business, Florentine."

And she set about her sewing again. Had they ever had time in all their years together to stop working and get to know each other? The wheel of the machine was whirring. It was invulnerable to Florentine's boredom, as it was to Rose-Anna's dreaming; it turned as the years had turned, as the earth turned, unaware in its blind course of what takes place between its poles.

The house was caught in this tireless motion of the wheel. Work filled the house, killing speech and understanding. The whirring wheel turned and the hours turned with it, and with the hours the confidences missed, the voices that had failed to speak, the thoughts left unexpressed. . . .

Sometimes a surprise, a word or a complaint came to break the spell of silence. Tonight it was Azarius' homecoming.

About eight o'clock the kitchen door slammed shut more noisily than usual. He came in whistling, tossed his cap on a nail in the wall, plunked his lunch box down on the table, and you couldn't tell if he brought good or bad news until he came into the living room, beaming with joy at being home and with something else that shone in his eyes.

"A good wind brings good surprises, Rose-Anna!"

As she looked up at him she didn't know whether to smile or take alarm. She heard the tremble in his voice, tried to finish a seam, bit the thread off and asked:

"What is it, Azarius?"

He stood leaning against the door frame, his teeth flashing. His hair fell, as it used to do, in damp, flat locks where the cap had marked his forehead. He looked young and happy, as if in counting his treasures he had found one he'd never seen before – buried under all the monotonous days.

Rose-Anna looked at him in silence for a few seconds. She could hear her own heart. There were times when Azarius, with a rush, took her back to her youth.

"Well, my big silly boy, what's this news of yours? If you've got news, out with it."

She was still half leaning over her sewing machine, keeping an eye on her husband, but less severe than usual, with the shadow of a smile she always had when she used the tender, mocking expression "silly boy" that was a souvenir of their courtship.

Azarius laughed aloud.

"You're curious, eh, old girl?"

Because he didn't often have great joys to offer, he liked to gild his surprises and make them appear as big events, surrounded by the suspense he enjoyed creating. And he liked to see Rose-Anna smiling. And above all, how he loved to be able to give her something beyond all expectations! To this man peace and security of living, which were all that Rose-Anna wanted of him, didn't seem adequate to make those around him happy. Happiness had to be something bigger and better!

He planted himself in front of her.

"Get the kids' duds ready," he said.

"Get them ready? What are you talking about?"

"I tell you, get them ready. We're leaving tomorrow, old girl. We're goin' to visit your folks. We're taking a trip, we're having a holiday. The whole day. And tomorrow, off we go!"

She held up her palm toward him, pale with excitement and surprise.

"Don't play tricks on me, Azarius!"

"It's no trick, my girl. I've got the truck. We'll leave tomorrow first thing at the crack of dawn. Off to the country. Oh," he said, pleased with himself for anticipating one of her secret wishes, "I know you've wanted to go there for a long time and see the Laplantes. Well, we're going. First thing in the morning. Your mother, your brothers, you'll see them all. And you know the sugaring-off is just beginning. Maple sugar, Rose-Anna!"

How well she knew this voice which had never been able to soothe her pain or reassure her in her anxieties, but which, perhaps five or ten times in her life, had known how to lift her up to the highest peaks. Through him she had known cold and hunger, through him she had lived in miserable quarters and felt the fear of each new day gnawing at her being; but through him, as well, she had come to hear the birds at daybreak – "D'you hear that little robin on the roof, Mother?" he'd say to her as they awoke. And through him she had known that spring was coming. Through him she had kept something of her youth, a tremor, perhaps a hunger that withstood the years.

Could he imagine the way she felt now, Azarius, this extraordinary man? Had he not discovered again the spot where her repressed desires hid as if afraid of their own existence? "Maple sugar! . . ." The two words had barely reached her ears but she was off on the secret path of her dreams. And so it was joy that she had foreseen when Azarius came home. It was almost as upsetting as a misfortune, because so unaccustomed. It took her breath away. Come now, be reasonable, she told herself. Don't give way like this. But she could see herself there already, in the place where she had spent her childhood. She was walking through the maple woods toward the sugaring cabin, and – what a miracle! – she was taking long strides with the buoyancy of a slim girl. The snow was soft, and her feet crushed the twigs beneath it as she passed. She could have told you, *that* old tree gave sap for six years, *that* one's not as good, and *that* one over there just runs for a few days each spring. But the thing that moved her most she could not have spoken of: the big sunny clearings among the trees where the snow had already melted, exposing the reddish-brown earth and last autumn's rotting leaves; the tree trunks where drops of water glinted like dew; and the wide roadway slashed through the woodland, airy and spacious, open to the sky between the leafless treetops.

The delights of her childhood followed each other in rapid succession in her mind's eye. Around the roots of the biggest trees snow and shadow still prevailed, but each day the sun rose nearer and penetrated farther among the maples, where busy forms were seen going rapidly about their work. Her uncle Alfred urged on the horses, bringing cordwood for the great fire in the cabin. The children in their red, green or yellow tuques sprang about like rabbits, and their dog Pato followed them through the clearing and into the underbrush, barking until the hillsides echoed.

The scene was gay, brightly lit and joyous, and Rose-Anna's heart beat faster as she saw it come to life. There were tin buckets gleaming where they hung from the tree trunks, and a little metallic thud as those that were brimming with sap were carried off and dumped in a barrel on the sled; and all around there was a thin murmur, softer than the softest rain of springtime falling on new leaves, and this was the sound of a thousand drops of sap dripping one by one.

Rose-Anna could still see the crackling of the great fire under the tubs, filled with pale sap that boiled thickly, sending bubbles to the top. She felt the taste of the syrup on her lips and its sweet odour in her nostrils, and all the noises of the forest sounded in her memory.

Then her vision changed. She was in her parents' house with her sisters-in-law and brothers and all their children, half of whom she had never even seen. She was talking to her old mother who was in her rocking chair in a corner of the kitchen. Old Madame Laplante had never been very demonstrative or good-natured, but still had a warm welcome for the daughter she hadn't seen for many years. She said a few encouraging words and the two of them were together for a confidential moment in the warmth of the room. The house was filled with an echo of the sounds of the maple woods. A great tub of snow sat on the table, and they poured hot syrup on it, which turned into marvellous honey-coloured candy. Rose-Anna trembled. She saw the children regaling themselves on bread dunked in

GABRIELLE ROY

syrup, and maple toffee on sticks, treats that were totally new to them.

She came back from her long, magnificent voyage and, her eyes falling on the piece of sewing in her hand, she sighed.

"Seven years!" she murmured.

"Yep," he said, "it's seven years since you saw your mother."

But what she had been thinking was, It's seven years that I've been holding back this desire to see them all down there. . . . Seven years! Can a person go on forever struggling like that?

She looked down, then said hesitantly:

"Father, have you thought about how much it costs?"

"Sure, Mother, that's all taken care of. The truck is free."

"Lachance is letting you have it?"

Azarius flushed.

"I guess he's lettin' me have it! I do enough for him, it seems to me. But it ain't just that. I'm goin' to bring back thirty or forty gallons of syrup and pay for the trip. I've got orders for syrup to pay for it. I've got orders for more than that."

"You've got orders?"

She was afraid for a moment that Azarius was plotting one of his wild schemes. His enthusiasms could spring from the slightest of expectations. The greater the risk and the clumsier his approach, the happier he was. But she had been deprived of joy for too long not to give in at once. Perhaps she had given in already and only found small objections as self-punishment for such a surrender to temptation.

"And what about the children, Father?" she said weakly.

"We'll take 'em along, that's what. Let them see it all too."

She could put up with their poverty courageously as long as her family were not there to see. But show up with her children in rags? Never! Her family had no idea of their poverty, and this had always been a consolation to Rose-Anna.

"I don't suppose you've got time to patch a few things together by tomorrow, Mother?"

Silent, she thought that poverty was like a sickness you put to sleep inside you, and it didn't hurt too much as long as you didn't move. You grew used to it, you ended up not paying much attention to it as long as you stayed tucked away with it in the dark; but when you took the notion of going out with it in daylight, it became frightening to the sight, so ugly you could not expose it to the sun.

"I don't know," she said. "They hardly have a thing to put on their backs."

"Tell you what," he said. "I'll help."

He rubbed his hands together, filled with an irresponsible joy, for in their trip he saw nothing but escape, while she was left with her burden whether they went or stayed.

Azarius went over to Florentine who was following their conversation, silent, astonished and hostile. He leaned over and tugged affectionately at her long, chestnut hair.

"You too, little girl," he said, "tiffy yourself up! Just you wait, those country boys'll have a fit."

Florentine had drawn back, frowning. Her mouth turned down in an irritated pout.

"No, I won't be going," she said. "But you all go ahead. I'll look after the house."

Azarius noticed the glint of determination in her eyes, though she had turned away from him. He wondered what was behind it. This pretty, slim creature was his pride and joy; and, so he thought, wouldn't easily lose her head. As he was driving home tonight he had thought how he would like to introduce her to his in-laws, the Laplantes. Beyond the road illuminated by the headlights of his truck, he had envisioned her with her new spring hat, her straight, tapered legs, running ahead of him as he drove.

Usually it was Rose-Anna's image that kept him company on the way home, when, his hands lax on the wheel, he would half doze, humming to himself to keep from dropping off completely. Twelve hours of driving on the dirty roads! But tonight it was Florentine who had accompanied his thoughts. Florentine, so small, so willowy, it broke his heart! Florentine, dressed up as if for a party, running breathless along the great, dark road! It was then that he had decided, in order to rid himself of a vague uneasiness, that he would be more generous with Florentine. This had allowed his daydream to take a more placid and agreeable path. He never failed to notice her trinkets, her saucy little hats or the fine silk stockings she bought. And although she bought them out of her waitress' pay after giving most of it to her mother, he had always felt, when she arrived with her purchases, that they were somehow due to his own generosity. He felt he was a good father because she managed to dress flashily. She was not an advertisement of their poverty. Like him, she knew that their streak of bad luck was not permanent. How grateful he was that she shared his faith in better times to come!

In this mood, his conscience clear, he had arrived home proud of having a fine surprise for her as well as for Rose-Anna. At heart, what he wanted was to have his revenge on the cold mistrust of the Laplante family. Florentine would be their pride and joy when they showed her off at the farm. He had never thought she would lack enthusiasm for his splendid plan.

"Hey, little girl," he said teasingly, "don't you want to try the sugar and toffee and pick yourself a handsome country boy?"

"What's that to me?" she answered, lighting another cigarette.

Strange that at this moment the picture of Florentine running wildly along the road pushed its way again into his mind! He scowled. Anita Latour, well-placed behind her counter to know all that went on in the neighbourhood, had hinted that Florentine might have a boyfriend.

"What is it? Have you got a beau?" he asked.

But he was always afraid to get to the bottom of things, and let his question drop. Florentine got out of the situation abruptly.

"Let me be," she said. "I just don't want to go to your sugaring-off, that's all."

Azarius stood helpless, his hands hanging. Then he covered his disappointment by retreating.

"Well, that's it then, Florentine will keep house. The rest of us can leave with an easy mind. What're you mulling over there, Mother? Don't you want to put on your best bib and tucker? We can't miss a chance like this!"

"A chance like this . . ." she repeated.

She met his glance, young and shining, the traces of annoyance melting away already. Her own fears disappeared. She was reassured by Florentine's impassivity, and gave herself up to the promised pleasure.

"No," she said, "sometimes you're right. If we always go putting things off we end up with nothing."

She felt a need to explain herself further, and sat gently wringing her hands: "I think we just have to make up our minds all of a sudden."

She didn't want to show too openly that Azarius had persuaded her with his crazy idea. For once she'd go along with his folly – she who had always had common sense on her side and had defended it alone.

"Listen," she said, and the tremor in her voice revealed a resolution that was foreign to her, "the stores aren't shut yet, it's Saturday. If you hurry you've got time to buy me a few things. Now listen," she repeated, and her voice grew so grave that you could hear in it the call of all the trips they had postponed, of all their desires frustrated for so long, "listen, you have to buy . . ."

There was a long pause after this frightening, spellbinding word. She heard herself say it as in a dream, unable to believe that it had come from her.

"You're going to buy . . ."

They were in suspense – even Florentine – wondering which of a thousand articles the poor woman was going to choose. They could see her ticking them off in her mind. And, sure enough, she quickly ran through a long list which she had put together in that instant.

"You're to buy," she said, "two yards of blue serge, three pairs of cotton socks, a shirt for Philippe if you see one, no, four pairs of cotton socks and a pair of shoes for Daniel. Don't get the wrong size, he's a seven . . ."

But something was bothering her. She added, upsetting her list:

"You know, it's not Daniel needs the shoes the most, he likely won't be going out to school this year. Maybe we can save a little there. Shoes cost so much! And Albert's growing out of his."

A confused concern for justice made her decision difficult. Like many mothers in the neighbourhood, she thought there was no hurry about sending a child to school. She had never had scruples about keeping the youngest ones at home if they had no warm clothes to wear; but she had put all her energy into ensuring that the older ones made their classes, even at the price of seeing the little ones cry at the preference given to their elders. Daniel had suffered most. It seemed to her that because of his sickness he had been deprived of his new shoes for far too long.

"Size seven," she murmured, her hands at her throbbing temples. "What did I say, the serge, stockings, a shirt . . ."

Albert, whom everyone had thought was fast asleep, begged:

"And can I have a tie?"

"And me!" yelped little Lucille. "You've been promising me a new dress for a long time now, Mamma!"

Daniel, dragged out of his sleep by the small, begging voices, not knowing what was going on but convinced that it was the time for putting in your orders, stammered in his childish want:

"Is it Christmas?"

And everyone laughed just the same, with tears not far.

But Rose-Anna felt cornered, overwhelmed by all the desires she had unleashed. She took fright, and scolded:

"Go to sleep, the bunch of you, or we won't go tomorrow."

"Where are we going tomorrow?"

Excited, the children were leaning out of bed in clusters, and Albert was telling them:

"Shhh! I think we're going to Grandmother's to eat maple sugar!"

All of them, big and small, were so worked up; they had left far behind their own house with its dim lights and creeping shadows; they were in such a lovely landscape that it seemed natural for Azarius to ask:

"And what about you, Mother? Seems to me you need a new dress!"

She gave him a smile tinged with reproach, as if she measured her husband's improvidence from nearby, having taken flight along with him, and now being able to reply tenderly:

"D'you see me in satin and velvet?" she tried to joke. "That would be a sight!"

She laughed a little with him. It was still time to laugh and look at each other with new eyes and follow the same path to adventure. Then her eyes grew serious again.

"Remember what I told you now, and don't let them put it over on you. And don't buy the dearest thing in the store."

Azarius took out a little notebook and wet his pencil:

"All right now, if I'm goin' to do it right I'd better make a list. You said a shirt, two yards of blue serge, shoes . . ."

Rose-Anna, realizing these notions, born of dreams and excitement, meant the spending of real money, now hesitated, then beat a retreat:

"No, leave out the serge – unless you see some real cheap . . . Do you think you know enough to do it?"

Thus, at the last moment, she transferred her burden of fear to Azarius.

Neither of them, concentrating on their task in the circle of light around the sewing machine, noticed that Florentine was swiftly getting ready to go out.

Rose-Anna reread her list, putting a price after each item, then added them up. When she saw the total she froze, terrified, and yet unshakable in her determination not to shorten the list.

The kitchen door opened from inside. A gust of cold air curled around her legs. She looked up, astonished.

"Who's that going out? Florentine? Where on earth is she off to at this hour?"

Her face clouded, but then, taken by the fever of their project, she held out the list to Azarius with a trembling hand, not daring to look him in the face. And seeing the future clearly, measuring what pain each joy would cost, hearing from every fibre of her being that every joy exacerbates the pain, she said:

"Go on, get out of here before I change my mind. It could be we're trying to eat our cake too soon, Azarius, but Lord in Heaven, we don't get cake every day, let's have a taste of it when it's going around!"

And in the modest lodging the hum of the sewing machine started up again. The children, gone back to sleep, would not be roused from the big bed because that hum, the voice of work itself, would accompany Rose-Anna's task, tireless, buzzing in the silence like the promise of fulfilment, mingling with the breathing of those who lay asleep.

Her shoulders sagging, her back hunched, her eyelids tired, Rose-Anna sewed for the feast, not daring even to sing for fear of frightening off her joy.

FOURTEEN

The windows of the Montreal Metal Works on St. James Street were brightly lit. In the clear, soft air of night you could hear continuous hammering, the squeaking of winches and a hundred mingled noises, strident and dull, which spread out over the sleepy neighbourhood.

Florentine kept her distance from the foundry, though each of its windows caught her in its glow as she passed. She didn't dare go near the entrance leading to the forging shop because of the armed guard standing in the sentry box. Motionless on the other side of the street, she peered into the hall on the ground floor. Through the sooty, lurid windows she could see moving shadows and, from time to time, when strips of red hot metal were drawn from a gaping furnace, bursts of reddish light in which the shapes became clear silhouettes, rushing urgently about their work. She took a few paces this way and that, keeping close to the wall, always wary of attracting the guard's attention. After a time she saw a worker emerge, his lunch box under his arm and his cap pulled well down. She went up to him and in an almost unintelligible voice, as if the whole atmosphere of nocturnal labours had terrorized her, asked:

"Is this where Monsieur Lévesque works?"

Saying Jean's name was even more intimidating.

The man stared at her from under the peak of his cap, which almost covered his forehead.

"Lévesque? The machinist? Yes, ma'am – mademoiselle – he must be in the forging shop."

Then, after a pause:

"Do you want me to go and get him? If it's urgent . . ."

Florentine shook her head hastily.

"No, no, I'll wait."

Collecting her courage, blushing, she added:

"D'you think he'll be long?"

The man shrugged.

"Don't know. There's an awful lot of work these days."

He touched his cap and went on his way.

Soon other workers came out in groups, probably apprentice casters and polishers, as Florentine judged from their harsh comments on working conditions. As their voices faded down St. James Street, Florentine saw a single form silhouetted in the doorway of the shop. From his thin waist and powerful shoulders she knew that it was Jean. Her heartbeat grew faster and her forehead broke out in sweat. She waited until he had taken a few steps, then came out of the shadows to meet him.

She found not a word to say, but stood in front of him with a silly smile, her breast heaving.

"What are you doing here?" he asked.

He stared at her with a touch of impatience, frowning.

She began to trot along beside him.

"It's a long time since we saw each other," she said. "I was just going by this way tonight, so . . ."

He said nothing to help her along, and she cut off her explanation, realizing it meant nothing to him. Her hands clutched her bulging purse of imitation leather. Avidly she searched Jean's face for some reaction. His jaw-line was hard, though it weakened at times as if from fatigue.

After a time Jean rubbed a hand across his forehead and slowed his pace. Then he spoke listlessly:

"That's right, it's been a while. We're working double shifts these days. I even did thirty-six hours in two days this week. A guy doesn't know if he's still alive or turned into a machine."

He shrugged, and talking to the empty night in front of him added:

"They stuck me with four new apprentices again. Guys that hardly know a thing. And then they complain. They're never satisfied. 'What're you chewing the rag about?' I asked them tonight. 'Before you came here you were getting fifteen or twenty cents an hour. Now you get thirty, and forty cents when there's overtime.'"

He stopped, out of breath, so beaten by fatigue that he had trouble finding words. He repressed a yawn.

"Oh, it's a funny life! Either you earn peanuts and you've got lots of time to spend it, or you get twice as much and you haven't time to enjoy a cent's worth."

"Is it as tough as all that?" she asked, saying anything to get his attention. She knew that he was not talking to her but to himself.

He glanced at her furtively and went on with his indifferent monologue.

"And now I'm the boss of my department."

Without really admitting to himself that she was there, he asked:

"Did you know that? . . ."

But he didn't wait for an answer.

What use to him now was the admiration of this girl who'd come pestering him? Before, when he was less sure of himself, he might have found her tolerable. God, was he tired! Could hardly think straight. But his head was busy with a hundred things, so many that it was a bother. Head of his department! That was a good start . . . and if he had to give up his studious evenings, it wouldn't be to the detriment of his promotion.

"Yeah, these days," he went on, "they judge a man by his competence, not by a piece of paper. I'm not afraid of anybody. It takes a war to show people up."

Totally disconcerted, Florentine glanced at him hastily, anxiously. Under a street lamp she noticed that his eyes were drawn like those of a man who has not slept for a long time.

"You've really had it, eh, Jean?" she said.

She tried to take his arm, wanting to seem kind. Her hand caught empty air. Jean had pulled away.

"Why did you come here tonight? I thought you were great pals with Emmanuel! What about that? A little war bride! A ten-day marriage! A pretty wee soldier! And then a pretty wee pension from the government. . . ."

He laughed cruelly and then, after a moment, added without even seeing her, or so it seemed:

"You know, you'd be better off with a guy like me, a guy with a head on his shoulders, eh?"

She said nothing. Then Jean noticed the girl's shadow gliding behind his own. And the morsel of pity he felt, along with a touch of jealousy, impelled him to renew his attack:

"Emmanuel, there, you kind of threw yourself at his head that day in the Five and Ten."

"I don't hate Emmanuel," she said in a strangled voice. "But he means no more to me than that."

She tripped in her attempt to keep up with him, and her chin trembled.

"But why did you come, though?" he insisted.

A humble smile crossed her face, but he didn't see it because he was staring in front of him. The smile left no trace except in the girl's clumsy phrase:

"They told me you were working late tonight. An' I just thought I'd wait for you. I don't know, we hadn't seen each other for a good three weeks. An' you didn't come to the party at the Létourneaus' either, like I said . . ."

She prolonged her thoughts with an awkward gesture, then licked her lips and said with all the daring she could muster:

"Sometimes I thought maybe you were mad at me."

He flinched. Then she pushed humility down to a level she would have thought impossible. She begged:

"Did I do something bad to you, ever, not intending?"

He shook his head emphatically.

"Never," he said, "but I'm not your boyfriend."

He was walking quickly. She had to hurry to keep up, almost running, but her shadow still glided behind his.

She was angry with herself for not having found a better explanation. It was so hard to explain what she had done on the spur of the moment. But she wasn't sorry, though a small voice told her: He doesn't care about you. You don't count for him. But this was advice that she didn't want. She had to stick to her plan. She tried to start up the conversation again.

"Even if you're not my real boyfriend that's no reason to stay mad."

So much candour and tenacity made him smile. It was such a cruel smile that Florentine, when she saw it, lost all her self-control. The little pride she still had rose in revolt. She bit her lips and her nostrils flared.

"But you don't need to worry," she said. "I'm not going to run after you, you'll see."

She added, as the tears began:

"You were the one started it."

At this he took her arm.

"Good," he said. "Now you're here, you're going to have supper with me."

It was his turn to hurry after her, for she was tripping along, her head high, her teeth biting at the edge of her lip. She kept trying to break loose, and at times her eyes blurred so that she could barely see where she was going.

From a large window bright lights shone just ahead of them. They went into a brand-new restaurant which still smelled of paint and wood. Jean led her to a table at the back and helped her off with her coat. She was passive, saying not a word, but her lips were working. It was then that something changed in him.

Florentine ceased to be a troublesome, tenacious shadow tagging along at a time when he wanted to be alone, and became a living creature trembling in the glaring ceiling lights. Her maroon sweater clung to her body, outlining her small, pointed breasts. She was wearing none of her costume jewellery tonight, and hardly any powder. For once she was there before him with no affectation, no defences, and her whole being took on an unaccustomed life, fearful and almost submissive. Stripped of artifice and coyness, she awoke distant memories in him, memories filled with sadness. He was more embarrassed by all this than he was surprised.

For the last three weeks his work had helped him to banish the thought of the girl. And, seeing Emmanuel drawn to her from their first meeting, he had resolved never to see her again, content with a solution that put an end to his indecision, left a clear field to his best friend and gave him the illusion of unselfishness. In fact, on the evening of the party he had walked back and forth a few times under the brightly lit windows and then had left. After all, he wasn't such a bad fellow as people made out. He'd pushed Florentine Emmanuel's way – a guy who could really love her. But he hadn't foreseen that they might meet again . . . either by chance or in the Five and Ten. And still less at night in a deserted street. He began to look at her with some annoyance, and a half-formulated thought flashed through his mind: Her tough luck. It's her own doing.

She had caught the change in Jean's expression. She laid one hand on the table, a hand that offered itself to him. Already she was preparing a new plan. She would no longer disdain the slightest advantage. Her hand crept across the table. He took it in his.

"You're not scared, Florentine?"

Scared? Yes, she'd been afraid, madly afraid that Jean would turn away from her, but now that she saw him agitated and less able than herself to hide the fact, her self-assurance returned.

"What of?"

She was smiling vaguely, as in those dreams where one is guided by an unknown hand; and as she shook her head with a free and graceful movement, her hair fell loosely over her shoulders.

"Scared of a guy like me," he said.

Her eyelids fluttered and her shining eyes devoured him. Yet as she watched him so closely it happened that she saw with perfect clarity that the more he desired her the fewer illusions he had and, perhaps, the less he liked her.

In her silence she heard Emmanuel:

"With Jean you'd be running after your own unhappiness." That was important, and worth thinking about. But not now, she thought. Oh, not now! Not now, when after such a long time of boredom, waiting and regret she had begun to breathe again! Anyway, what had she to fear? If he was the dashing fellow he pretended to be, wouldn't he have tried to take advantage of her? Instead of that, he'd taken her home and his kiss had been no more than gentle. Whether he liked it or not, be was going to be her boyfriend, her real one, her steady! They'd laugh together at the movies every Saturday night, maybe twice a week! And a lovely life would open out before her if only she was stubborn enough and not too proud just now! Later, she could get things under control.

Her hand was trembling in his, and suddenly she lifted it to his mouth and pressed hard, turning in her palm to the caress of his lips.

The restaurant owner appeared at their booth. Jean made a movement to pull her hand away but, grown bold, she held it there. She was no longer afraid to be seen with him like this; for her these demonstrations of tenderness – almost in public – were a kind of homage. And in any case, she was carried away by a moment of real passion. Believing herself so close to Jean, she was entering on a total solitude. Her passion had already made her blind.

They ate little. From time to time he looked sharply at her, occasionally with a tepid smile that played over his lips for a second and then disappeared.

When dessert arrived he moved around beside her. He encircled her wrist with his hand, seeming to measure its thinness. He dug in his fingers near her small, swollen veins, then looked at this bruised wrist as if fascinated. Then his hand slid up the inside of her arm to the elbow and stiffened as it reached that smooth flesh. She felt his hand burn her. Her eyelids grew heavy and she leaned her head against his shoulder, her hair brushing his face. It was then that a darkening mist surrounded her.

"Let's get out," he said suddenly.

She took her coat and hat like an automaton, smiling, her eyes glazed. Once outside, the breeze, which had turned bitter, brought her back to a certain calm.

"You know, it wasn't just to see if you were mad at me that I came tonight," she murmured, leaning against him.

She looked up at him, a little intoxicated, and pulled at the sleeve of his overcoat. Touching his clothing, breathing the smell of hot sand, of the forge, of the cooling moulds, left her helpless with emotion.

"I came to invite you to my place. Tomorrow. Sunday," she added dreamily.

In spite of everything, she was still able to concentrate on the importance of following her plan through to the end: persuading Jean to visit her on Sunday while her parents were away, so that they would be free to kiss each other. It was a daring plan. She suspected that his desire for her would be provoked beyond measure, but thought she could be sure of his respect because of the trust she placed in him. Her plan was only half conscious but firm, and it pleased her.

"Will you come?" she insisted.

He replied with a slight pressure on her arm. In silence they emerged into Sir Georges Etienne-Cartier Square. Among the elms and maples, stiff with cold, a few shadowy forms passed, two by two, then returned. The benches were empty. This March evening, half winter, half spring, forced lovers to walk slowly with only brief and furtive stops where the dark lay thickest.

Jean was on the lookout for a dark spot. He saw a great tree that cast a pool of shadow near the corner of the square. He disappeared with Florentine into the black arabesques projected by the branches.

At once Florentine shut her eyes. She held up her lips. But in that moment he was struck by the fragility of this closed face and murmured, with fright and shock:

"My God, you're thin!"

He let her go abruptly. And withdrew from her. She opened her eyes and saw him in front of her, a few steps away, his hands deep in his pockets. So that it was she who had to run to him, leaving the shadows, emerging in the half-light, throwing her arms around his neck, dreading the idea that her plan was falling through and Jean might still escape her. Almost sobbing, with the little strength that remained, she burst into plaintive explanations that came out in fragments, as if through a nervous laugh:

"I love you so much, Jean. It's crazy, it's not my fault, but I love you so much!"

His arms hanging at his sides, he was looking over Florentine's head, over the rooftops, over the square, at the pale crescent moon in the sky. His eyes were hard and dry. The expression of his mouth was nervous, irritated. He was deeply, intolerably embarrassed by this unforeseen drama.

"What good will it do you if I go to your place tomorrow?" he asked.

But without looking up she made a sign with her head that she wanted him to come, and wanted nothing else. At every movement her chin dug into his chest. He felt her growing quiet. She was sure now that he would come to her house just to get out of this ridiculous dilemma.

He held up her chin and forced her to look at him. Then, almost gently but aware that this was the last time he would be patient with her, he said:

"I'm not your boyfriend, you know. Don't go getting ideas just because I took a little shine to you at the store. Because marriage, for me, you know . . ."

He was on the alert for some withdrawal on her part, and was hoping for it. But she held him ever tighter with her thin arms. She stood on tiptoe so that her cheek could touch his chin. Her breath mingled with his and she smiled at him feebly through the tangled hair that veiled her eyes. Jean, afraid that a passerby would see them like this, and filled with a sudden cowardly urge to put a speedy end to the scene, promised evasively:

"All right, if I don't have to work all day tomorrow, I'll come and see you."

FIFTEEN

To the children's eyes the countryside was nothing but snow-covered space, greyish-white, with occasional patches of bare earth, and tall, dark-brown trees rising in their solitude. But Rose-Anna and Azarius often exchanged a glance, smiled with complicity and seemed to share each other's daydreams.

"Remember, here?" one would say.

"Yes, it hasn't changed," the other would reply.

Small memories that led to small, pleasant reflections.

Rose-Anna delighted in the pure air that came in the open window. She had lowered it as soon as they left Victoria Bridge behind and taken a deep, long breath.

"Now, that's clean air for you," she said.

They were making good time along the highway. Despite her night at the sewing machine, Rose-Anna didn't look too tired. Her eyes were a little heavy, but the lines around her mouth were relaxed.

One by one she recognized the villages along the Richelieu Valley, and something like her youthful joy prompted remarks that only Azarius understood.

Then, suddenly, she was silent. With a powerful, mute greeting from her heart she recognized the river that tumbled past the foot of Fort Chambly, and from then on was on the watch for every curve in the road, every turn that brought them closer to the Richelieu. Hills and rivers alone had little attraction for her, except when they were associated with her own life. The St. Lawrence thus meant little to her, but she knew everything about the Richelieu because it had flowed through her whole childhood. She didn't hesitate to tell her children, "It's the most beautiful river in the country." Or, describing a landscape, "It's not as nice as the strips of land down home, down beside the river."

As soon as the Richelieu appeared on their left, she sat up straighter. Her hands on the edge of the open window, she leaned out and shouted the names of the villages they passed through, bumping along in the livestock truck: Saint Hilaire, Saint Mathias, Saint Charles. The riverbanks lay ever lower and the water flowed so quietly and with such restrained force and life that you could only guess at its great, dark depths beneath the thin crust of ice.

Now here's Azarius, half turning toward the back of the truck where the children huddle on their blankets, and shouting:

"Look there, now, you Lacasse kids! Your mother and I came here once in a rowboat!"

And Daniel, whom they'd kept between them in the cab so he wouldn't get too cold, wide-eyed, still a little feverish, stretched to have a look. "Where's the river?" He was too small to see out the windows. For him the Richelieu could just as well be the strip of blue sky that he saw flying by through the windshield, with occasional arabesques of dark twigs and branches.

"And what's a rowboat?" he asked seriously and with a great effort to imagine it.

From time to time he tried to sit higher on the seat in order to discover and understand all these things his parents were talking about. Yet somehow the Richelieu must have remained in his memory as a strip of azure high above his head, such a blue as he had never seen, with streaks of snow-white clouds which might be rowboats.

Brought down to earth for a moment, Rose-Anna took time to wrap him carefully in his covers. She had felt him shivering as he cuddled close to her.

Then, at the end of a tree-lined avenue, her village appeared.

"St. Denis!" shouted Azarius.

And Rose-Anna strained forward, her eyes dimmed by tears. Memory aiding, she anticipated the corner, and farther on, the little hill at the end of the village. Finally the landscape made its last concession and gave her the house where she was born. You could see the gabled roof behind the maples, then the railed verandah with what was left of its climbing cucumbers, shrivelled by the winter. Rose-Anna, thrown toward Azarius by the movement of the truck, murmured with a shudder of physical pain and more than a trace of emotion:

"Well now! Here we are! You know, it's hardly changed!"

Her joy had lasted this long, and was to last a little more, for the door burst open and her brothers and sister-in-law appeared, and she could hear the warm exclamations like a distant rumbling:

"Would you look at that! See who's here! Well, land's sakes! We've got visitors from Montreal!"

But just as she was getting out of the truck, shaky and dizzy from the sudden gust of fresh air, trying to smooth out her old winter coat, a heavy attempt at humour by her brother Ernest marked the first attack on her joy.

"Well, I'll be darned, Rose-Anna! If it ain't you!" said the farmer, taking her in with a hasty glance. "And would you look at her! You must be tryin' to bring up fifteen of them, just like our mother, eh?"

Rose-Anna was shaken by this strange greeting. She had laced her corsets as tightly as she could and hoped her pregnancy wouldn't be noticed, not out of false shame but because she had always been in this state when she visited her family and this time would really have liked to have a quiet day, a day of rediscovered youth – perhaps a day of illusions. But she tried to smile and pass it off as a joke.

"Why, it runs in the family, Ernest. What do you expect?"

Yet she had realized how fragile and easily threatened was her joy.

A harder blow came from her sister-in-law, Réséda. Helping her to take off the children's coats, Madame Laplante Junior cried:

"Say, your kids are pale as ghosts, Rose-Anna! I hope you give them enough to eat, at least!"

This time Rose-Anna was angry. Réséda was just being spiteful because her own children were so badly dressed; they looked like ragamuffins with their coarse, home-knitted stockings and shabby pants hanging down over their knees.

Rose-Anna called over Gisèle to comb up the big wave in her hair and hoist her hem above her knee as fashion would have it. But as she was hastily tiffying-up her children, she glanced over at Daniel and Réséda's eldest, chubby, pink-faced Gilbert. The farm boy had grabbed his city cousin and was trying to roll on the floor with him like a healthy puppy. Rose-Anna gave a scream. Her sickly child was struggling hopelessly. What he clearly wanted was to be left alone.

Rose-Anna controlled herself.

"He's older than mine, of course."

"He is not," the young woman protested. "They were born the same year, you know right well."

"No, no. There's six months' difference."

And there was a long discussion over birthdays.

"Albert, now, he's more the age of yours," Rose-Anna insisted.

"Not a bit of it," said Réséda decisively. "You know they were both summer babies."

As she talked she paced up and down the room, trying to pacify the baby at her breast who was clamouring for his meal and trying with his strong little hands to unhook her blouse and get at her round, firm breasts. Réséda went on:

"No, no, you can't change my mind. I know they were born the same month."

The women stared at each other, almost hostile. There was insolent pride in the eyes of the farm wife. Rose-Anna gave way first. Her anger abated. She glanced around at her children, fearful and confused, wondering if she had ever really seen them as they were, with their thin, small faces and skinny limbs.

Réséda's second-last was crawling toward her, his legs short and fat, bowed and dimpled. Suddenly, above the baby, she saw a row of bony little legs – those of her own children, sitting docile along the wall; and she saw nothing of them but their legs, dangling, long and almost emaciated.

Then a final wound came from her mother. After the hectic dinner in two sittings, during which she had helped her sister-in-law as best she could, Rose-Anna found a moment alone with old Madame Laplante. She had been waiting for this time, when Réséda would be busy with her breast-feeding and the men would be talking of important things around the stove, to have a quiet chat with her mother. But the old woman's first words were filled with fatalism:

"My poor Rose-Anna! I thought as much. I was sure you'd had a bad time. Of course I knew it. Why should it be better for you than for anybody else? And now you see, my girl, you can't just make things happen as you like in your life. There was a time you thought you'd have your say about it, but now . . ."

All this in a sharp, high voice devoid of bitterness or any other emotion. Old Madame Laplante, sunk in her squeaking rocking chair, seemed to have been transmuted into the negation of all hope. It was not that charity had had no place in her life. On the contrary, she liked to think that she was on her way to her Creator laden with indulgences, her hands filled with good deeds. It was almost as if she saw herself achieving paradise like a careful traveller who had taken life-long precautions to ensure herself a comfortable stay in that last resort. She had, as she said, "put up with her purgatory here on earth."

She was one of those people who listen attentively to tales of woe. Any other kind she met with a sceptical smile. Nothing surprised her like a happy face. She didn't believe in happiness, and never had.

At the other end of the kitchen the men were talking, their voices growing louder. Rose-Anna had pulled her chair close to the old woman. Awkward and ill at ease, she clasped and unclasped her hands on her knees. She felt almost ashamed to have come to her mother, not as a married woman with her responsibilities and her own burdens, and the strength they presuppose, but like a child in search of help and wisdom. What she got was bits and pieces of advice in a sermonizing tone as cold as the old woman's white, angular face: advice that reached her ears but touched her heart with nothing but a feeling of total solitude.

What had she expected, anyway? She no longer knew, for as she chatted with her mother, their voices subdued, she found herself forgetting the image she had created of her over time and distance, rediscovering her as she really was, as she had always been; and wondered how she had been able to practise this self-deception. From this old creature she could expect not the slightest sign of tenderness.

Madame Laplante had raised fifteen children. She had got up in the middle of the night to attend to them; she had taught them their prayers and heard them their catechism; she had clothed them by spinning, weaving and sewing with her strong hands, and she had fed them well. But never had she looked down at one of them with a transparent flame of joy in those hard, iron-grey eyes; never had she taken them on her knees, except when they were in swaddling clothes. She had never kissed them, except for a peck after a long absence or perhaps on New Year's Day, and then with a chill of seriousness accompanied by the empty formulas of her good wishes.

She had held fifteen round heads against her breast, fifteen little bodies had clung to her skirts; she had had a good, affectionate and attentive husband; but all her life she had talked about the crosses she had to bear, her trials and burdens, her Christian resignation and the pain she must endure.

On his deathbed her husband had murmured, his voice thickened by the approach of his last sleep:

"Well, you'll have one cross less to bear now, poor wife!"

"And how's your Azarius making out these days?"

Rose-Anna started, and came back to present anxieties. Then she leaned close to her mother again. She realized that the old woman, in her dry, distant way, was asking about Rose-Anna's family. She had always said, "Your Azarius," or "Your Florentine, your children, your life. . . ." She had felt even less warmth for Azarius, a city boy, than for her other sons-in-law who all came from the country. At Rose-Anna's wedding she had declared:

"You may think you're running away from poverty, that you're going to play the fine lady in town, but you mark my words: poverty finds us out. You'll have your miseries too. But it's your choice. Let's hope you won't be sorry for it."

The only good wishes she'd ever had from her, Rose-Anna thought.

"Oh! Azarius!" she said. "Well, he's working these days. He's feeling better about things. And Eugène joined up, I told you that. He looks pretty good in his uniform. It makes him look grown-up. Yes, we're getting along. Florentine gets paid regular."

The old woman blinked. For each remark she said:

"Well, well! That's fine. That's fine if things are as good as you say."

But her dry, yellowed fingers rubbed at the arm of her chair, worn at that spot by this gesture which seemed to express her constant scepticism.

Rose-Anna went on defending her husband with the same harsh voice she had used in former times when her mother had unkind things to say about him.

"He gets by," she said. "When one thing doesn't work out, he tries another. He doesn't stay idle long. He's just taken up truck driving to fill in. He's counting on the war to start him up in his trade again. There'll be building to do."

She was surprised to hear herself using the expressions Azarius used, and when she mentioned his trade she spoke with almost as much passion as he did. But at other times her voice sounded distant and artificial. She heard it, and wondered if it was indeed herself talking this way. Through the window that looked across the fields she saw the children taking off for the sugar bush with Uncle Octave. Daniel was scuffling through the snow, far behind the frisky group. Rose-Anna's voice grew still and her eyes were anxious until she saw Yvonne turn back to help her little brother. Then Azarius' voice came to her, as if through a dream:

"Look here, if you think you're goin' to have a big run of sap, you can let me have some syrup. I can sell it for you, and I won't make but pennies on the deal. On my route there, it's easy as pie."

He was showing off, putting on airs, slouched on a kitchen chair with his feet up before the fire. Rose-Anna had pressed his only decent suit the night before, and he was playing the city slicker in front of his brothers-in-law in braces and shirtsleeves, their ties loosened.

Rose-Anna saw that they were taking his proposition seriously, and she was concerned. As soon as they had a little bit of luck, Azarius was too encouraged and ready to launch into some undertaking about which he knew nothing at all. A part of her dreaded the least good fortune that came their way. She would have liked to caution Azarius, and her brothers too. And she was bothered by Philippe's attitude, rolling cigarettes under his grandmother's disapproving eyes, hanging around the men and using coarse language every time he opened his mouth. But instead of checking him,

Rose-Anna turned, embarrassed, to her mother, and went on in a monotonous tone with the recital of her family's life:

"Yvonne's first in her class. The sisters are very pleased with her. Philippe is just about to look for a job. It seems they'll take on boys like him in the munitions factories. So altogether we won't be too badly off."

From time to time she straightened in her chair to see better out the window. The children were just entering the maple woods, a small blotch of colours that broke up and disappeared in Indian file between the trees. She regretted so much not having gone with them that her eyes filled with tears. She hadn't dared after her mother, lecturing her like a child, had said, "You're not going running around the woods in your condition!"

Run around the woods, indeed! thought Rose-Anna. This was not how she had imagined their expedition. But perhaps she had for a time been unable to see herself as others saw her, and had dreamed of something impossible, misled by her desire. She was now so frightened of finding her dream ridiculous that she put away the thought of it, telling herself, I knew I wouldn't be able to go to the maple bush, of course I knew . . .

Yet when old Madame Laplante sent someone to the cellar for a big cut of salt pork, fresh eggs, cream and preserves, Rose-Anna was touched by her mother's generosity. Knowing how the poor old woman couldn't stand to be thanked, she was at a loss for words. And this made her really sad. She watched her mother get up with difficulty to add a loaf of home-made bread to the box of food, rummaging around in the box, rearranging its contents and grumbling to herself. She gives us so much every time we come, thought Rose-Anna. I'll bet she doesn't believe a word I tell her. Poor old thing, she wants to help us, in her own way. And it makes her mad that she can't do more. She'd never let us go hungry if she knew we were badly off. All her life, whenever we needed her, she's given us food and things to wear – and good advice. It's true. Rose-Anna frowned. Was this all a mother was supposed to give her children?

But then she turned this thought against herself. Could I do more for Florentine once she's married and needs somebody to talk to, the way I do now?

And she suddenly fancied that she understood her mother's austerity. Did it not come from the terrible awareness of not being able to defend her whole brood?

Because she was no longer sure that she could help Florentine, either now or in the future, because she was possessed by the fear that Florentine would never ask for such help, and because she had just realized that it was very hard to come to the rescue of one's children in their secret woes, Rose-Anna shook her head and lapsed into silence. Effortlessly, as if she had always had the habit, she began to stroke the arm of her chair with her aged mother's futile gesture.

SIXTEEN

In the house on Beaudoin Street there was not a sound to be heard but the rattle of the kettle lid in the kitchen and from time to time the tapping of Florentine's high heels on the linoleum.

A vague melancholy and heavy silence hung in the dining room.

For Jean's visit the girl had scrubbed and waxed and dusted, whisking out of sight all the bits of clothing and the ill-used toys that testified to the cramped life of the family in these rooms. She had arranged the chairs around the table according to her own fancy, exposing certain light-coloured areas on the wallpaper which revealed its fatigue and age. She hid away the knick-knacks that had littered the buffet; in their place she laid an embroidered, heavily starched runner, and on it, right under the holy picture, a clay vase with a few forlorn paper flowers. The picture showed the Christ-child half draped in scarlet cloth, grasping with his chubby arms a Madonna dressed in dark-blue robes. It was at this picture that Jean was staring just now in a state of morose embarrassment.

Florentine was fussing about in her housewife role. She

had thought it an excellent idea to show herself in this light. She hadn't dared for a minute to doubt that he would come, though she had gone to the window from time to time, peeking out and crumpling the curtain in her hand, then slowly letting it fall.

Now that she had him there, she harnessed all her energy to defy the young man's will rather than to please him; and she played her role with caution. Brightly coloured jewellery rattled at her neck and on her wrists, the nervous voices of her willpower. Over her black silk dress a little oilcloth apron slid and rustled with every movement.

One minute she would be there with Jean, asking if he wasn't bored. Lively and attentive, she would bring him a cushion, a magazine or some snapshots of herself in an album. Leaning on his shoulder she would give him the needed explanations. Then, a second later she'd be in the kitchen, singing as she busied herself at the stove.

Jean was exasperated by these attentions. She was treating him with the consideration and confidence due a fiancé, as if there had been a tacit agreement between them. She left him alone to make some fudge, and went on chatting from the kitchen in a friendly way, slightly detached but polite. Her attitude bespoke a wakeful, prudent reserve. She avoided touching his hand, and when he asked her to sit down she chose a chair that was not next to his. And she put on a serious, preoccupied air, playing with her bracelets, not looking when she felt his eyes upon her.

Florentine's ruses forced a smile from Jean. You're smart, he thought. If I didn't know better I'd think you hadn't a single trick up your sleeve. But her comings and goings were driving him crazy. She slipped through his fingers with great skill. As soon as he made a gesture in her direction, she drew back and invented a new errand in the kitchen.

The footsteps of a solitary passerby outside echoed in the house and slowly faded away.

Jean looked around, uneasy. Through the kitchen door he could see Florentine buttering the inside of a saucepan. Her apron whispered against her dress, the metal rattled on the counter. Then he could hear the sugar sizzling in the pan. All these sounds seemed to come from very far away. They irritated him, arousing his defensive instincts against all domestic order. Again he found himself staring at the Madonna and Child on the wall above the buffet. He understood why this picture attracted and bothered him. It called up his whole past, his unhappy childhood and turbulent adolescence. A flood of memories returned and things he had thought safely asleep came back to his consciousness.

First it was the Church-Art image of the orphanage that came to life; and with it an impression of drowsiness, in which black silhouettes passed his dormitory bed. There were the cold dawns in the chapel and, mysteriously, his shrill choirboy's voice which he seemed to hear out of the depths of memory.

This image led to a host of others. He saw the orphans' grey twill pinafores, coarse and grey as their days deprived of tenderness. He saw himself ripping his to strips. His need for individuality showing already.

Then the scarlet and blue picture on the wall changed size. It became a tiny souvenir that the nuns slipped in his missal the day when a lady had come to get him at the orphanage. She was a silent, embittered woman who had made a vow to adopt a child if her own, an only girl, recovered her health. Thus he had been a part of this barter with the saints, but the girl had died in any case shortly after.

His mother, or rather the woman who had insisted he call her that, had not been hard on him, but after the death of her child she had become so distant, so inaccessible, that Jean remembered feeling even more lonely than in the orphanage.

There had been no indulgence, even for his slightest peccadillos. He remembered hearing words exchanged in the night when they thought he was asleep, precise, cruel words like, "Well, it's no wonder. What do you expect? He's a foundling. . . ." "That's not true, he had parents, you remember that poor couple that died in the accident." "That's as may be. Nobody's really sure. . . ."

Then Jean saw himself in college, taciturn and rebellious by turns, but with an intelligence and a curiosity that astonished his professors. His adoptive parents, while they showed no affection for him, were not stingy with material things. In those days he was well dressed and always had pocket money, which he jingled with satisfaction as he thought of the long humiliation in the orphanage. Occasionally, more out of pride than generosity, he would share his wealth with poorer boys. Already he knew that money buys prestige and respect.

In a few years, thanks to a healthy and copious diet, he had grown amazingly, acquiring solid muscles, strong shoulders and a glance that was piercing and determined. Nothing about him recalled the puny orphan he had been. A mysterious heredity was expressing itself triumphantly in him. From two strangers who had died shortly after his birth he had inherited this awakening power, and he would have liked to wrest their secrets from his dead, for he had few bonds with the living.

His character had undergone a transformation as total as that of his body. There were abrupt transitions from apparent submission to rebellion. He affected an attitude of disdain and sarcasm. He enjoyed expounding to all comers his personal opinions tinged with caustic humour. He loved provoking arguments for the pleasure of contradicting others.

His curiosity was insatiable, and he began to devour all the books he could lay his hands on. On his walks he would stop and talk to working men, believing that, like him, they must be tortured with the desire to know and understand. One day he would feel a great love for them, and wanted nothing but to devote his life to social reform. The next day he would be filled with contempt for the masses, feel himself above them and predestined for higher things.

As time went on he became still more solitary. The character of his mind, hard and precise, his sudden spells of silence, his unexplained reversals of position, all combined to disconcert his friends. Out of a spirit of contradiction he began to frequent only the most unfortunate. In the college his reputation was made: he was stuck-up. To give him a lesson in humility his teachers, at the end of the year, held back all the first prizes that should have been his.

Jean flushed as he remembered this affront. Then one night he had left his adoptive parents' house after a final stormy disagreement. He saw himself packing his things and plunging out into the dark. Running away had re-established his moral balance. From that time on he was a young man like so many others, concerned only with carving out a position for himself at a time when there were ten applicants for every job. The satisfaction of owing his success only to himself filled him with pride. A small room rented anywhere, a job as puddler, another job, a new room, and the rest of his life had come quickly and easily. He was now in a relatively calm period in which, like a Robinson Crusoe, he saw everything around him as a means which he could bend to his own purpose. Ahead of him he saw years of struggle and poverty, after which he would have only to stretch out his hand to take the fruits of his labour.

Jean stood up. He looked around the room astonished

because he had forgotten the starting point of his train of thought. The silence made him nervous. The humble arrangement of domestic things, reminiscent of a certain kind of life, upset him. He would have liked to run away. In the kitchen he glimpsed Florentine, on tiptoe in front of the mirror above the sink, curling her hair around her fingers. He was irritated at being alone with her and at feeling an unexpected renewal of curiosity which threatened to flood his common sense. Impatiently he called her. She came at once, holding a plate of candy as a shield. He grabbed it from her almost roughly. She seemed to want to tame him, and this he could not bear.

"How is it your parents aren't here?" he asked. "Are they away for the day?"

Her eyes were artless, clear.

"I don't know, really. But I think they could be back any time now."

"Did you invite me because you knew you'd be alone today?"

She took fright at the expression in his eyes.

"No! Of course not! They only decided to leave this morning."

"Where did they go?"

"To the sugaring-off, I think. That's right, Dad was talking about it this morning. So that's what they must have decided."

The words stuck in her throat. She could see that he didn't believe her. But she still tried to mislead him, getting tangled in her own lie.

"When Mamma saw it was so nice this morning, you know . . ."

Again she had to drop her eyes, then suddenly began to appear angry at his disbelief.

"I suppose you think you know everything!" she cried.

He had grasped her wrists, and now wrapped his arms around her as if to break her. His desire exasperated him. He had come here certain that her family would be around, and much against his will – imagining a family scene that would bore him stiff, at the same time determined to put up with it, just out of pride at keeping his word. And that wasn't all, either. Why had he come if it weren't for the fact that the girl, weeping as she had last night, had disarmed him for a moment and wrung a drop of compassion from him? And here she was, more tenacious and cunning than ever! That's where weakness got you! She was simpering at him, trying to conquer him, instinctively making use of all the devices she had used to catch his attention in the restaurant.

Disturbed by his own violence and his regret at having given in to her yesterday, he devised an escape:

"Come on, get your hat. We're going to a movie."

But still he held her tight. He knew now that Florentine's house reminded him of the thing he most dreaded: poverty, that implacable smell of poor clothing, the poverty you could recognize with your eyes shut. He realized that Florentine personified this kind of wretched life against which his whole being was in revolt. And in the same moment he understood the feeling that drew him toward her: she was his own poverty, his solitude, his sad childhood, his lonely youth. She was all that he had hated, all that he had left behind him, but also everything that remained intimately linked to him, the most profound part of his nature and the powerful spur of his destiny.

It was his own wretchedness and sadness that he held in his arms, his life as it might have been if he had not ripped it off like a cumbersome rag. His head fell to her shoulder and he remembered the great torment of affection that had been his when he was very small. Without thinking, as if he had known her in that past time, he murmured:

"Just a tiny little waist. I could put my hands around it."

At the same time he remembered that occasionally during his life he had tried to do a good turn, that as a child he had willingly shared a treat with a small friend. He still felt such surges of generosity, and gave in to them if they didn't cramp his style. That was it. He could be kind if his kindness caused him no problems. How many friendships had that cost!

Florentine was cowering as his dark eyes stared down at her with a kind of madness. Her own imprudence had become so obvious to her that its consequences closed in around her.

She tried to escape, and his fingers ripped one of the thin straps of her apron. This torn bit of clothing, half hanging now, made him pause. With a great effort of will he whispered in her ear:

"Go get your coat, get your hat. . . ."

But he didn't release her. Out of the corner of his eye, over her shoulder, he stared at the old leather couch.

She fell back, her knees bent, one foot kicking feebly. Before she closed her eyes she caught the glance of the Madonna and that of all the other saints bent upon her. She tried to rise up toward these sad countenances which came to her from all parts of the room, begging her, supplicating, mute and terrible. Jean still seemed ready to let her go. But then she slid down into the hollow of the couch where she slept each night beside her small sister Yvonne.

Outside, above the neighbourhood imbued with its Sunday calm, the church bells rang out vespers.

SEVENTEEN

For a long time that Sunday evening Jean Lévesque wandered the streets aimlessly, filled with self-hatred. Not because of Florentine's suffering face, which floated before his eyes, but because he felt very clearly that he had irrevocably compromised his freedom. With an irritated gesture he tried to unlace two invisible arms from around his neck. Would he now have the feeling, wherever he went, that another life was linked to his? That this intrusion made his former solitude a thousand times more precious than he had thought? And, more precisely, what would Florentine's attitude be now? What would she expect of him? But what troubled him most was his inability to regain that self-possession which excluded all sense of responsibility. What on earth had he been thinking about? Until now he had been able to limit his curiosity to prudent moves, semi-advances that called for no diminishing of the self. He felt a vague disgust, and admitted awareness of the motive that had lain behind his fear of a liaison with a young and inexperienced girl. Not those old ideas! he thought, with more disdain for his own hesitations than for his conduct toward Florentine.

Walking quickly, he reached St. James Street. The light of a street lamp came like a slap, but as soon as he had crossed the pavement he was again wrapped in the dark of Beaudoin Street, which grows more shadowed and wretched as it goes down toward the Lachine Canal. Soon he was on St. Emilie, with its shops, ornate balconies and pinnacled roofs at every street corner. When he passed a blinking arc lamp Jean would see wet façades with long rust-coloured zigzags where the water had found its easiest descent. The snow was melting in a soft south wind. You could almost hear it dissolving and escaping in rivulets of blackened water in the silence of the deserted street. From every roof and every softened twig, far and wide, it ran in a sound like rain, continuous and melancholy.

The need to justify himself, with all its bitterness and confusion, directed his thoughts along a single track: had he really wanted to hurt Florentine? Even today he'd wanted to spare her. And was it not the frustration of that wish that enraged him now? It might even be that he had wanted to keep a memory of her that he would not despise, mingled with some sentiment of pity and anguish that he had felt at another time in his life. What other time? He wasn't sure. An illusion, perhaps.

But between Florentine and him there was no longer any cloudy, snowy night that would remind him: I let her go because she was throwing herself away, the ignorant scatter-brain! What they held in common now, and would forever, was the creaking of an ancient sofa, the squeaking of springs, the glow of a cracked centre light. Florentine's image might fade in his memory, as his youth itself might fade: never would he forget the horrid poverty that had been the setting of their moment of love. That was the unforgivable thing staining his cherished superiority, an embarrassment to his ambitions, a vision that could sour every future success.

Jean's pace was rapid, his hair was blowing in the wind, his cap tucked under his arm. He could not hide from himself the fact that he was shattered by the experience, for there had been only one woman in his life before Florentine, a woman older than he who had led him on, but who had no face in his memory. But Florentine! He could still see her anxious move, devoid of pride, to keep him from taking his hat and coat to leave, so fearful had she been of finding herself alone with her thoughts after his departure.

Poor little fool, he thought, less in compassion for her than in regret that he, of all people, had become the bearer of her pain and disillusion. He no longer doubted that it had been her extreme ignorance which led her to compromise herself so rashly. Knowing this, he understood at last her pose of bold-ness. And how timid and clumsy she actually was! What childish hesitation he had displayed! No . . . he didn't want to think about it. That meant giving in to pity or, what was worse, to this feeling of his own diminished freedom.

The St. Henri Church clock showed after midnight when he reached Notre Dame Street. He crossed Guay Square, half asleep with its phantom trees casting anxious shadows on the stone, shadows blurred by a thin fog and drizzle of the kind that heralds spring.

Jean's thoughts had already passed the mark where the vision of an offence brakes the mind, holding it in suspense, as if life from then on must take a new turn. He saw himself no more able to think of the consequences of his conduct than the wind of the plains can pause to consider the destruction it has left behind. He fled from the sight of Florentine's total disarray when he left her, saying in her small voice, "I'll see you tomorrow, won't I, Jean?"

That voice reached him now over an ever-widening

distance. At the time he had consciously hesitated to reply. Now her voice echoed distantly inside him, but like a call that had no meaning and could not distract him from his dominant idea: to find a way out that would protect him against any weakness so far as she was concerned – a return within himself.

"Knock it down, everything that's past, knock it down!" he shouted, the violence of his thoughts making him express them aloud. "Knock it all down!" And he knew that he was attacking not just a memory that was painful to his own conceit, but a whole section of his life which, tonight, had ended. It's time, he thought, time to break loose from all that. And his determination was all the more violent because the hindrance in his path took on the shape of a young working girl who had come to follow in his steps, timidly, tenaciously and with not a trace of pride. It flashed across his mind that perhaps she really loved him, that only passion could have led her so far astray. But this thought, far from calming him, poisoned his reflections. Indeed that would have been the last indignity, if her blind stubbornness had dared to pass for love.

He reached St. Antoine Street, which was vibrating from the passage of a distant streetcar. The bright lights, after the dark alleyways, made him blink. The show windows cast on the sidewalk a light that seemed intense. He was glad of the glare, which helped him shake off the counsels of the dark. Even more than the memory of this evening, he wanted to rid himself of any notion that he was loved by Florentine.

It began to rain harder. The last snow was under attack by these heavy, wide-spaced drops. All that remained underfoot of months of frost and freezing was a light crust that crumbled as he walked. The sidewalk was soon completely washed by this slow, tenacious rain. Its smooth, shining surface reflected the midnight lights and tangles of naked branches.

Springtime! What would it bring, he wondered. He felt a greed for the unknown, the beginnings that new seasons bring. A woman's footsteps tapping behind made him turn.

He saw only a solitary shadow behind him, but it reminded him irritatingly of Florentine's hand on his arm, and how she had come trotting toward him one stormy night. And for a brief moment he understood clearly that through the biting wind, from the depths of her misery, from the depths of all her uncertainties, she had come running to him, scatterbrained, daring, but bringing him her whole life, since he no doubt represented something solid and successful to her and her poverty. He watched his shadow stretching before him on the sidewalk. Stupefaction and resentment brought him to a halt. What was he supposed to do with such a gift? What did it matter to him? Never had the cool solitude he had built around himself felt more precious.

Spring, which sharpens the sensitivity of many people, excluded him from its magic. On the contrary, it filled him with renewed determination never again to give in to his need for friendship.

Springtime! What a season of thin illusions! Soon there would be leaves in the light of the street lamps, the poor would set out chairs on the sidewalk before their houses. In the evening the squeak of rocking chairs on concrete would be heard. Babies, for the first time in their lives, would breathe outdoor air; older children would trace chalk squares on the cement and sing a rhyme as they hopped from one to the other. And in the inside courtyards, by the light of kitchen windows, neighbour families would chat or play at cards. What did these needy folk find to chat about, with their lives so plain and monotonous? Elsewhere men would gather on a vacant lot to throw horseshoes, they too pretending to forget. The clang of metal would ring in the evening air along with shouts from the children, loud puffing from the locomotives and the choppy voice of the boat whistles. And that's what spring would be, down where the smoke came from, at the foot of the mountain!

He imagined the end of April. That would be the great exodus toward the street. From all the apartments, the damp basements, the garrets under the zinc roofs, the slums of Workman Street, from the big houses of Sir Georges-Etienne Cartier Square, from the sinister alleys down by the canal, from the peaceful squares, from near, from far, from everywhere, the crowd would come, and its multitudinous voice, contained on one side by the mountain, on the other by the ring of factories, would rise toward the distant stars. And the stars would be the only spectators to this inconceivable propensity of man for his sustaining joy.

Everywhere in the dark, narrow streets, in the obscurity between houses, in the shadows of trees, there would be silhouettes of couples. Two by two they would stroll through the odours of hot molasses, tobacco, rotten fruit, vibrating with the trains, covered with soot, stubborn and pitiable shadows. On some spring nights, when the wind blew softly and a folly of hope lay in the air, they would begin again to go through those motions which ensure the perpetuity of human suffering. And Jean dared to rejoice at this passivity of men which makes it so easy for the daring ones to rise. He looked down at the dark mass of roofs, each of which hid its share of dreams and misery, and it seemed to him that between himself and Florentine a poor man's springtime was breathing its disenchantment.

A door opened somewhere down the street. A burst of jazz escaped, soldiers emerged, staggering, accompanied by hatless women who laughed loudly and jostled one another. The young men were trying to get them to come along. They resisted half-heartedly, then gave in. The group disappeared, singing. Jean, striding quickly now, was surprised to find himself smiling. He was thinking about what he was escaping by avoiding Florentine: a hidden love, furtive encounters, long, wandering walks out-doors, and the fear on his part and hers of having to pay dearly for such a paltry sin. He felt a glow of self-satisfaction. His brutal, relentless domination of Florentine had left him, in fact, with a taste for other conquests, more exotic and challenging. But that'll come, that will come, he said to himself, enjoying the rhythm of his own stride.

He had completely lost his sense of time when he reached the corner of Courcelles and St. Ambroise. He noticed a dull rumbling under the pavement, and through the grill of the gutter realized that it came from rushing waters. A network of underground drains came together here at a main sewer, and the roar of its flood filled the street and rushed away like a torrent. This was the first and truest voice of the season's freedom in the neighbourhood, and the young man tasted a kind of relaxation and expansiveness. He felt liberated.

Instinctively he had chosen the way to his own dwelling. His footsteps awoke the echoes sleeping in the deserted street. On his right rose the massive rows of grain elevators. He looked at them as at old friends, but with new interest and insistence, as if these imperious walls, these concrete towers, owed him a final confirmation of his destiny.

Farther on, the heavy mass of the cotton factories dark-ened the sky, rising on both sides of the street and joined by an elevated gallery that bridged the roadway. Jean was making his way in their shadow when he noticed a couple strolling hand in hand like children. By the light of a watery window he recog-nized Marguerite L'Estienne whom he had seen at the Five and

Ten, and Alphonse Poirier. As he left them behind he smiled, partly at their attitude, which he found ridiculous, and partly at Alphonse who had recently tried to borrow money from him. Suddenly he began to understand what had been nagging obscurely at his mind all evening. Now it took on the form of a decision, ready-made. That was it, yes, he'd leave St. Henri. I need a change of air, he thought. The whole place had become hateful to him. Not just the memory of a jilted girl, but worse: the thought that he had spent the whole evening justifying himself. What did he have to justify? Already, beyond his departure he could glimpse what the ambitious ones in a big city see in their onward flight: new lands to conquer! Something was waiting for him in this world turned topsy-turvy by the war. Exactly what, he didn't know, except that it would reward him for his patience, marking time here in St. Henri. For a moment he was dazzled at being borne off toward the unknown with such self-confidence, such unconcern, as if he had just cast off a load of ballast. It was only later that he understood what he had thrown overboard that night. His old and sterile pity was no more an unconscious burden to him.

Carefully he went up the creaking staircase. The peace of his little room settled over him without dampening his haste to be on his way. For a second, as he groped in the dark for the hanging bulb, he saw Florentine as he had left her, white-faced, her eyes fixed on his in a kind of mute and frightful supplication. It crossed his mind that he was taking the most commonplace way out of his difficulties – and perhaps the most unworthy. But it was too late to pass judgement on things of this sort. If he felt righteous indignation, it was rather directed at Florentine than at himself.

As soon as he had turned the light on, he began searching among the papers on his shelf. There it was – an application form for one of the biggest munitions factories in the country. His pen scratched swiftly over the blank spaces, and his mind occupied itself with consequences. With his experience as a mechanic he would get a better job. If necessary, he'd ask for a recommendation from his boss. He should have an answer in a week. And he mustn't weaken in the meantime, whatever happened.

But what was he afraid of? He quickly wrote an accompanying letter, slipped both papers in an envelope, addressed and sealed it.

Then, fully dressed, he lay down on his bed. And an unworthy, almost vulgar thought glided through his mind, telling him something new about himself: After all, if I wanted to, just once more before I leave . . .

He refused to listen to this voice, but his refusal was tainted with anger and humiliation, for he did not know how long his flesh would still cry out in the dark, in his solitude, for that child of poverty with the narrow hips. Florentine Lacasse! How often would he suffer for having let her escape so easily!

EIGHTEEN

For a good hour now Rose-Anna had been walking toward the mountain. Her steps were slow and stubborn and her face was bathed in sweat, and when she finally reached Cedar Avenue she couldn't tackle it at once. Carved out of the rock, the road climbed rapidly. The April sun was warm. Here and there, out of the damp cracks in the stone, tufts of grass were pushing up with their fresh green blades.

Rose-Anna, catching her breath, was able to look around her. On her left a high iron grill rose in front of a vacant lot. Between the bars she saw clearly the whole lower town. Ribbons of smoke flew from the tips of grey factory chimneys. Great hanging signs cut the horizon into sections of blue and black; and, fighting for space in that town of work and prayer, the roofs descended in steps, tighter and tighter together until their monotony came to a halt at the river's edge. Toward the middle of its iridescent waters a light mist obscured the distant view.

Rose-Anna rested as she took in the panorama of the city. It didn't even occur to her to try to place her own house in the distance. Instead, she took the measure of the slope still to be climbed before she would arrive at the children's hospital she had been told was at the very top of Cedar Avenue.

Daniel had been taken there shortly after their excursion to St. Denis.

One night as she was undressing him Rose-Anna had found large violet patches on his arms and legs. Next day she put him in his sled and dragged him to a young doctor on the rue du Couvent for whom she had done some housework. Everything else happened so quickly. The doctor had whisked Daniel off to the hospital. Rose-Anna remembered only one precise detail: the child had not cried or protested. In his weakness he had confidence in this stranger who was taking him away. Daniel had merely waved with his bony little hand.

Rose-Anna started up the hill again.

All that she knew of Mount Royal, stretched out above St. Henri, was St. Joseph's Oratory and the great cemetery where the people from the lower town came to bury their dead, just like those who lived on the hill. And now it seemed that the children of the poor also came to live on this mountain when they were sick, protected by the crystal air from the smoke, the soot and the foul breath of the factories which hung around the low-lying houses like the breath of a monster straining at its work. That the hospital and cemetery were both in these parts appeared to her as an evil sign.

The size and luxury of the private houses, which she could see in the depths of their gardens, she found astonishing. From time to time, as she slowed her pace to rest and marvel, she murmured to herself, Good Lord, it's rich here, and so fine! What's Daniel doing up here?

It didn't occur to her to be delighted that the child had been brought to where the air was so clear and pure. On the contrary, the farther she walked the more she imagined him isolated and so small, perhaps missing, in all this silence, the rumble of the trains that shook their house in St. Henri each time they passed. She remembered his simple game, which he persisted in playing every day: putting the kitchen chairs in a row and taking his place gravely on the first one, the proud engineer of his own railroad. Sometimes he would try a weak imitation of the train whistle, or shield his eyes with one hand as if he could see through the trembling wall of the kitchen the curve of the shining rails that cut through their neighbour-hood. The kitchen was small, and Rose-Anna admitted to herself that she had often upset his pleasure, pushing the chairs back in place and sending him to play elsewhere.

Again she was panting, too tired to go on. As she rested she thought of all the misfortunes they'd had in the last few weeks. As they whirled through her mind she wondered, opening her eyes to the clear sky above, whether she had just had a bad dream. But as the beating of her heart grew quieter she found strength to recognize and admit those misfortunes.

What a mad thing it had been, going to the sugar shack! It wasn't for them to run after such pleasures. Hadn't that always brought bad luck? And how absurd and incomprehen-sible it seemed now, that frenzy of happiness that had pos-sessed them all!

It was a muddle in her mind: first the accident a few miles from St. Denis and the return in the dark to her mother's house. From Azarius' hangdog face she had soon gathered the truth. He had taken the truck without permission, and now that he must be discovered, he was afraid of losing his job, which was exactly what happened next morning. And, thought Rose-Anna, perhaps that wasn't the worst of their troubles. A neighbour had told her that in their absence Florentine had been visited by a young man, and that the man had not left until late Sunday evening. Florentine had put on a defiant air when she was questioned.

Weary and broken, she turned her mind to her most pressing worry, Daniel's illness.

The doctor had talked about red corpuscles, about white corpuscles, and some were multiplying, she couldn't remember which. And vitamin deficiencies as well. She hadn't understood much of it, but she could still see Daniel's half-naked body mottled with violet, his belly swollen and his arms hanging helplessly. And she felt ashamed.

Her other children, it seemed, were in equal danger. She remembered that they'd talked at the clinic about the right kind of diet to make sure the bones and teeth were properly formed and to ensure good health. What a joke! And they'd said that kind of food was within the reach of every budget! They had shown her clearly what her duty was. She felt a twinge of anguish. Perhaps she hadn't tried hard enough. She finally convinced herself of her own laxity, and her eyes were dry and hard.

But then she wiped this idea from her mind, because she would have to attack her problems one by one if she wanted to solve them. She shook her head and continued up the hill, trying to be quicker. She had walked all the way because the streetcar often gave her nausea, but now she was afraid of missing visiting hours.

Daniel was half sitting, half lying there, supported by two or three pillows. Toys were clustered everywhere in the folds of the covers: a tin flute, like the one he had always wanted, a teddy bear, a rattle, a box of wax crayons and a drawing book. In a single day he'd had more toys than in all his life, probably too many for him to love; or perhaps he felt too grown-up for any of them. What really held his attention was not the bear, not the flute, but a large boxful of alphabet cards. He was lining them up, tired but engrossed, and when he made a mistake his face showed a twitch of pain.

At the doorway Rose-Anna met a young nurse whose clear eyes, magnificently blue, took her in with a look of surprise mingled with pity. It made her feel old, and she instinctively held her well-worn purse like a shield in front of her protuberant coat.

Then she approached the bed on tiptoe because of this very white hospital with its wide, bright windows, so cheerful despite all the suffering; and also because her rough soles squeaked on the polished floor.

Daniel smiled timidly, then went back to searching out his letters.

She tried to help him, but his stubborn little hand blocked hers.

"Let me do it alone," he said. "That's how the Brother showed us at school, don't you remember?"

He had been in his class for only a few weeks, but his memory of it was persistent and gave him no rest. He remembered two or three days at the very beginning, in September, when he had been especially happy, going off to school with his new bag hanging on his back, holding Lucille's and Albert's hands. What they had taught him hadn't been too hard, and when he came home his great joy had been to get out his spelling book and show Azarius what he had learned that day. He would walk around, sometimes following his mother step for step in the kitchen, reciting behind her his "ba, be, bi, bo, bu," and driving her out of her mind. She had told him kindly to be quiet, yet this was enough to drive him into solitude with the great restlessness that quivered within him.

At night he would try so hard to retain every scrap of new knowledge that he would murmur his lessons, half asleep.

One morning he woke with a headache and nosebleeds. Rose-Anna said, "He's too little to be going to school." And she kept him home, despite his tears.

Later, when there were heavy rainstorms, she kept him home again because he had no rubbers. When he returned to his desk he had trouble understanding, had forgotten things, and when the teacher spoke to him directly he would break out in a sweat. It wasn't his fault; he was trying to do everything right. After a few days, he slowly began to see the lovely light that had reached him once before.

Then a cold wave hit the neighbourhood. There was always some reason for not going to school. Rose-Anna set to work sewing: first a coat for Yvonne, who was far ahead in school, then a windbreaker for Albert. Last of all Rose-Anna had made a coat for Daniel out of old cloth. And Daniel, who hated to see her leave her sewing machine to do other tasks, followed her stubbornly, pulling at her apron strings and repeating, "Ma, finish my coat?"

It was so important to finish that coat! It lay on the table, still without sleeves, shapeless, dotted with white basting thread. Daniel kept trying it on, despite his mother's words: "Daniel! You'll rip out my stitches! Hey, busybody!"

She couldn't understand why he'd want so desperately to get back to school.

After a while the sleeves were added. And Daniel loved his coat.

One morning he tried it on in secret, fetched his schoolbag and attempted to sneak out. But Rose-Anna caught him at the door. She wasn't angry, she was saddened, and told him plaintively: "I can't make it any faster. I have too many things to do."

But that day she neglected her housework. She even let the dishes pile up in the sink, and sewed for a long time. In the evening, when the dining room was tidy and the sofas pulled out flat and made up, she was still sewing. Daniel went to sleep to the humming of the sewing machine, and dreamed of his overcoat. A strange thing: in his fantasies he had seen it with a fur collar. And when he opened his shining eyes he saw his coat on a chair-back trimmed with old black wolf skin that had been one of his mother's wedding presents.

But he didn't go to school that day. Feeling his forehead, Rose-Anna was sure he had a fever. For long weeks he had lain on two chairs that formed his small bed in the midst of all the traffic, with his overcoat beside him as a consolation.

When he finally went back to school after the holidays he was lost. The Brother's words remained incomprehensible this time. All his efforts were useless. Between him and the modest tasks that he was set came a face that was severe and dissatisfied. And how you had to try to please that face! This time he could not. He sat in despair at the back of the classroom. He knew nothing, understood nothing. The chalk and the pencil slipped from his hand. He would pick it up and make some vague scribble, but he no longer knew what was expected of him.

Rose-Anna now saw a glimmer of anguish in her son's eyes. Old fears, ill-defined obsessions, came and went in his half-closed eyes.

"Why don't you forget your letters for a while," she said. "You're just tiring yourself for nothing."

But Daniel again pushed his mother's hand away and patiently, wide-eyed, went back to his work. That's my son, thought Rose-Anna. He'd never give up a search or a chore or a duty. In the dark of night, in his solitude, he'd follow his stubborn notions.

She tried to make his self-imposed task a little easier, but as she stood up to do so the box of letters slid to the floor. Daniel called frantically:

"Jenny!"

Rose-Anna turned around, surprised. The young nurse she had seen as she came in was running to answer Daniel's call. So, thought Rose-Anna, when he needs help he turns to her now, not to his mother.

The nurse picked up the letters and put them back in the box within his reach. She pulled up the covers and, as if she were speaking to another grown-up, asked:

"All right now, Danny?"

And Daniel smiled in his slow, timid way. Jenny with her blonde hair in its sober headband, Jenny with her grey-blue eyes and her smile that made a dimple at the corners of her mouth, Jenny who came to him with a rustling of starched, white linen, Jenny, always patient, was helping him in his struggle against the disapproving face of his days in school. In his suffering and distress there would always be these two faces, and sometimes one would win, sometimes the other, but he never succeeded in dissociating them or in seeing only the face that brought him peace of mind.

Rose-Anna dimly understood these things for all their mystery, though they lay far outside her usual preoccupations. She was silent for a long moment.

When the nurse had left she leaned over toward the bed. She had a fear that her child couldn't make himself understood in this place. And another sentiment made itself felt, as cold as steel.

"Does she only speak English?" she asked, with a touch of unfriendliness. "When you need something, can you ask her for it?"

"Yes," said Daniel.

"But aren't there any other children here that speak French?"

"Sure, that baby."

Rose-Anna saw a tiny child, his hands gripping the bars as he stood up in his crib.

"That one there!"

"Yes, he's my friend."

"He's too small to talk. You've got nobody to talk to?"

"Yes, Jenny."

"And what if she doesn't understand you?"

"She understands."

He was getting just a shade impatient. His eyes sought Jenny's smile at the other end of the ward. She was something wonderful and gentle that had come into his life, and they'd always understand each other, language or no language.

To get him back Rose-Anna put on her happy voice, and reminded him of their excursion to the country:

"You had a real feast, eh, that day we went to the sugar shack? Did you like your snow candy?"

"Yes."

He was thinking about the best day in his life, but it always got mixed up in his imagination with Jenny's name. There was "grandmother's country" as he called St. Denis, with all the blue he'd seen through the windshield and which was perhaps the Richelieu, a word he loved, fine-sounding and distant, and he thought, I should have brought back some sugar from there for Jenny, for his thoughts were blurred and he didn't remember that he hadn't even known Jenny when they went on their ride to the country.

"You call her by her first name!" Rose-Anna said suddenly.

"Yes, Jenny," he said, breathing with difficulty. "She's Jenny."

He was searching among his letters again. After a moment his mother asked cautiously:

"Do you like her?"

"Yes, she's Jenny."

"But you don't like her better than us, do you?"

A shadow of hesitation crossed his tired face.

"No."

She was expecting him to complain about something and ask to be taken home. But he was only interested in sorting out his letters. And it was Rose-Anna who, after a long silence, broached the subject:

"Aren't you in a hurry to get well and come home, and . . . go back to school like before?"

She caught his gloomy look and hastened to add:

"I might just find enough money to buy you a little cap, if you want one, to go with your nice new overcoat. That was what you wanted most, wasn't it?"

"No."

But she thought she had touched his weak point, for she remembered how he had wanted to be a little man, from his first days in school. She pulled her chair closer to his bed.

"Then you tell me what you'd like most!"

A tiredness shadowed his face. Precocious, he may have vaguely understood his family's poverty and his own need to be reasonable; or perhaps he was too tired to think about it. He looked around, taking time to smile at the baby who reached toward him through the bars of his crib. Daniel shrugged.

"Nothing, I guess."

When Rose-Anna spoke again her voice took on the

melancholy tone that comes instinctively when one speaks through bars or in a convent parlour.

"Those are nice toys. Who gave them to you?"

"It was Jenny!" he said triumphantly.

"No, no, it wasn't Jenny. There's rich ladies who bring toys for sick little boys, or other children that have too many toys themselves."

"That's not true! It was Jenny!"

Rose-Anna was surprised at his anger. Daniel's eyes were shining. His lips trembled. She was perplexed and saddened. Then, remembering that the doctor had said impatience and irritability were symptoms of Daniel's illness, she tried to mollify him.

"Gisèle and Lucille miss you something terrible," she said.

He nodded, but his lips were still tight. Yet a moment later he asked about Yvonne. His mother made too long a story out of her answer, and got everything mixed up. His gaze wandered. Here too he was loved, he thought, and had lots of chums who didn't try to drag him into tiring games. The more active ones played a kind of hockey, tossing the puck from bed to bed. Jenny had invented the game, and Daniel loved it, following it with a true spectator's eye. And though he never raised a finger in his bed, Jenny said he was the goalie, and gave him points on the blackboard.

Here he was in a world made for children. There were no grown-ups with their conversations to trouble his sleep. No one whispered at night, and he never woke suddenly to hear people talking about money, about rent, about expenses, words vast and cruel that came to his ears in the darkness. He could lie here at ease, and no one would fold or move his bed each morning. For the first time he had a few things of his very own. And, above all, he'd never had such windows at home, nor such sunlight on the walls. It was enough to make him forget his new coat, which Jenny had taken from him on his arrival in the hospital and locked up along with his new St. Denis shoes and other small effects. He'd never have given up that coat to anyone but Jenny.

He breathed heavily, and with an effort. He had just finished a group of letters and shouted happily:

"Look what I wrote. . . ."

Rose-Anna had already seen it on the covers: Jenny's name.

"Can you write anything else?" she asked, her throat tightening.

"Sure," he said kindly. "I'm going to write your name."

A little later she saw in the folds of the sheet five letters which made "Mamma." She wanted to help him finish the word, but he grew angry.

"Let me do it myself! The Brother doesn't want you to touch it!"

His eyes stared wide, full of fear. His mouth trembled.

The nurse was at his bedside in a moment.

"He's getting tired," she said in English. "Maybe you can stay longer tomorrow."

Rose-Anna blinked. She understood vaguely that she was being dismissed. With the docility of the humble, on discovering she was just a visitor she stood up unsteadily. It was now, after a few minutes' rest, that she felt the strain throughout her body. She took a few heavy steps, no longer on tiptoe but letting her weight fall flat-footed on the slippery floor. It's a long way from home, it's not the same here, she thought, her mind skidding into nonsense; she felt trapped and yet stubborn.

Then she caught Jenny's glance, and looked down as if her secrets had been revealed.

Another hesitant step or two, hating to leave, and she stopped, trying desperately to remember a few words of English. She wanted to know what treatment Daniel was getting. She would have liked to describe his character so that the young nurse could care for him as well as possible, seeing that she herself had to abandon him. But the more she thought, the more she realized that she was incapable of such an explanation. She settled for a brief smile in Jenny's direction, and turned around for a final look at Daniel. His head was buried in the pillow.

On the foot of the bed was a card on which she read: *Name: Daniel Lacasse. Age: six years.* Then came the name of his illness, which she couldn't decipher.

"Leukemia." Was that what the doctor had said? "A wasting disease . . ."

She had not been too frightened, because he had neglected to add that from this disease there was no return.

Yet in the doorway of the ward a presentiment seized her, penetrating to the fibres of her soul. She wheeled around with the violent desire to take the child in her arms and bring him home. An old mistrust of doctors and hospitals acquired in childhood from her mother's sayings came to her mind.

Jenny was tucking in the covers. Daniel, quiet again, was smiling. Rose-Anna made a timid gesture – a child's "Bye-bye . . ." – and the baby, gripping the bars of his crib, found it irresistibly funny. He laughed loud and clear, and a dribble ran down his chin.

Rose-Anna was in the dark corridor. Her step was hesitant because of the feeble light and her fear that she wouldn't find the exit. One thought filled her mind with reproach: Daniel had all he needed here. He had never been so happy. She didn't understand it and tried to find the reason. A sentiment with the taste of poison stuck in her throat. So they've taken him from me too, she thought, and it's easy to take him, he's so small! Her body stiffened as she walked. Daniel's new peace of mind, marvellous as it was, pursued her down the stairs like an unforgettable shame.

At the front entrance a blinding ray of sunlight struck her face, and she stretched out her hands that searched their way into the sun. Never had she felt her poverty so intensely.

She opened her purse to find a tram ticket; she was too tired to walk. She was dumbfounded to see a ten-dollar bill tucked in behind the torn lining. Then she remembered: this was all she had been able to save, to "hide away," as she put it, out of the twenty dollars sent by the government after Eugène had joined up. The money had seemed so tainted by sacrifice that she had not wished to use more than half of it; not for food or clothing or even a treat for Daniel. Stubbornly she had kept it for their move, for what she called "rent money," so precious that she had concealed it from herself.

NINETEEN

Rose-Anna got off the streetcar at Notre Dame. In front of The Two Records she saw a freshly printed news bulletin. A small group of men and women crowded around it. From where she was, over the heads and shoulders crouching as if in astonishment, Rose-Anna could see the coarse lettering on the yellow paper of the notice:

Germans invade Norway.
Oslo bombed.

She stared, dazed, pulling at the strap of her purse. At first she didn't know the source of her paralysis. Then, trained to misfortune, her mind flew to Eugène. In a way that was inexplicable but hard as rock, she was sure that her son's fate depended on this piece of news. She reread the large letters, syllable by syllable, barely forming the words with her lips. At the word "Norway" she stopped to reflect. And this distant land, located somewhere over there, seemed linked once and for all with their lives, incomprehensible as that might be. She left aside the fact that Eugène had assured her in his last letter that he would be in training camp for at least six months. She simply saw the far black letters spelling out immediate danger. And this woman, who never read anything but her *Book of Hours*, did an extraordinary thing. She crossed the street, fumbling in her purse for change, and in all haste offered three cents to the newspaper vendor, quickly opening the damp pages he had given her. Leaning against the entrance to a store, she read a few lines, pushed this way and that by housewives shopping at the fruit store, holding her purse under her arm. After a moment she folded the paper and stared in front of her with eyes heavy with anger. She hated the Germans. She, who had never hated anyone in her life, felt a sudden, implacable hatred for this people she had never known.

She started toward Beaudoin Street and home. All at once she knew them well, all those women in far-off countries, whether they were Polish, Norwegian, Czechs or Slovaks. They were women like herself, women of the people, as needy as she was. For centuries they had seen their husbands and sons march away. One age passed away, another came, and nothing changed: the women of all the ages waved good-bye or wept in their kerchiefs, and the men marched off. It seemed to her that on this bright late-afternoon she was walking not alone but in the ranks of thousands of women whose sighs breathed in her ears, the weary sighs of the poor, the ordinary women, from the depths of the centuries to her own time. She was one of them, one of the women with nothing to defend but their men and their sons, who had never sung when it was time for them to leave. One of the women who had watched the parades with dry eyes, secretly cursing war.

Yet she hated the Germans more than war itself; and this troubled her. She tried to dismiss the feeling like an evil thought. It frightened her, for she saw that it gave her a reason for accepting the sacrifice of her son. She tried to pull back, to remain outside of hate as well as pity. We're in Canada, after all, she said to herself, it's too bad about what goes on over there, but it's not our fault. Fiercely she tried to disown the forlorn procession that had joined her, but though she walked more quickly she was unable to lose this crowd emerging mysteriously out of the past, from all directions, from far but also nearby, for new faces not unlike her own kept appearing. The women from elsewhere had misfortunes to bear that were greater than hers. They were weeping for their devastated homes. They came toward Rose-Anna, and when they saw her made the motions of a prayer. In every age women have known each other by their mourning. Their supplication was silent; they raised their arms as if to ask her for help. Rose-Anna hurried on. She saw the despair of her sisters, saw it clearly and without flinching, looked at it squarely and understood all its horror; then she put her own child's life in the balance, and he won. Eugène seemed as powerless and forgotten as Daniel; she saw that they both had need of her. Her defensive instinct awoke, she regained all her energy, knew her goal and ceased to think of anything but that.

She had planned to stop at the Five and Ten to tell Florentine how Daniel was getting on, and to buy a few provisions for supper at a grocery on Notre Dame. All that was forgotten now. She went straight home, her hands clenched, her eyes resolute, as though some pressing danger awaited her, a danger to be cornered, forestalled if she could.

But when she saw their house she felt a relief that made her smile.

She went directly to the kitchen, taking off her coat. For all her anxieties she didn't forget that she had supper to prepare. Her eyes, still accustomed to the glare outside, at first saw only the familiar shapes of the furniture. She went to the dining room and hung her outdoor things in the closet. Then, tying an apron over her Sunday dress, which she had no time to change, she came back to the kitchen. She was pushing her sleeves up and approaching the stove when she saw Eugène sitting at the table with a broad smile on his face.

She stretched trembling hands out toward him. Then, moved beyond words, she stepped back to examine him from head to foot. She was not particularly surprised to see him. She knew that if she had come home in haste, thinking constantly about Eugène, it was because some telepathy had warned her that he was there and needed her.

The children were playing outside; but to guard against any interruptions she led him into the dining room. In any case, it seemed to her that the kitchen was not the place to receive this handsome young man in uniform, his cheeks rosy with health and exercise, quite unlike the picture of Eugène she had kept in her mind's eye.

"Now, let me get a look at you!" she said, going ahead of him into the brightest room in the house, turning around at every other step to inspect him. Her voice, do what she would, betrayed her pride at seeing him like this, standing straighter, his skin fresh and healthy.

As soon as they were sitting on the leather couch her fears returned. Eugène, despite his new well-being, was not lighthearted. At once she took his visit to be a desertion.

"I suppose they wanted to send you over there!" she said bitterly.

She pointed to the crumpled newspaper on the buffet.

Eugène laughed. His laugh was half-hearted, joyless, a little bored. He ran a hand through his thick, wavy hair.

"Not a chance, Ma. You're always the darndest one for getting ideas in your head."

Silence. He felt it was his turn to make conversation, and told her a few details about life in camp. He said he liked it fine. Then he stopped, not knowing where to go next.

Rose-Anna had more questions for him. How was the food there? Was he homesick? Who were his friends? Eugène replied absent-mindedly, smiling at times at the childish questions, then looked around the room, impatient. God, it was poor and ugly in this place! He saw the camp bed that his mother used to open out for him, covering it with a thin mattress when he wanted to go to bed. He remembered the hot dishes his mother had kept for him when he came home from bumming around the neighbourhood. He saw her drawn, white face the day she had gone to the police station to excuse and defend him. He had returned the stolen bicycle and she had done whatever had to be done so that no charges were laid. Oh, he could even see the wilted hat she'd had at the time, and her good dress, her Sunday dress, which she'd worn that day, so determined to make a good impression and win their sympathy. All that was a pain in the neck because he'd have preferred to recall some injustice from his mother: it would make it easier to ask for what he wanted.

He felt that every fleeting minute worked against him. The cares, frustrations and sufferings of his mother would soon take over again, entwine him, paralyze him, if he stayed too long in this house. It was true, the house frightened him, with all its reminders of childhood. And the poverty that was written over every corner of the place! He'd wanted long enough to run away. And it seemed so long, in fact, since he had left! Never to come back! Oh, to get out the door and into life, the life which even tonight might offer him the exciting wine of forgetfulness!

He stood up. His temples were throbbing. The face of a girl floated before his eyes. He paced a few steps then marked time as if treading on his memories. Suddenly he turned toward her. His eyes had hardened. It was such an effort to smile that his face looked strained, and he held his hand up before it, speaking with the faintly humble tone he put on when he talked to his mother.

"Did you get your twenty bucks, Ma, first of the month?"

She nodded, still sitting in her corner of the sofa.

"I even managed to hide ten of it," she confessed. "Your father's still out of work. He counts on starting again soon. But I'm keeping the ten dollars just in case. At least we'll have that to put down on the first month's rent. I saw a place that wasn't all that bad," she said in a moment of optimism. "I've got your ten dollars to make a deposit if we decide to take it."

She said "your ten dollars" with an inflection of deference and gratitude, she who had for so long refused to count on this money.

"You know," she went on, "the first thing is to have a place to live. After that, well, we'll see! Once you've got a roof over your head there's time to think about the rest."

She was explaining her intentions in great detail as if from now on she had to account to him for the way she spent the money he brought into the household.

"That money," she cried, almost vehemently, "you can be sure I won't lay a hand on it unless there's terrible need."

He looked away. He couldn't bear to hear her talking about rents and poverty. Would the two of them ever talk about anything else? Was that what he'd come home for? To hear more complaints? Outside people were hurrying past, almost racing toward the busy streets of town. Others were on their way to the movies. Girls were going out to meet their boyfriends. There was music, there was youth in the streets, and all of that was waiting for him.

With a nervous hand he pulled from his pocket a new cigarette case engraved with his initials, which he couldn't help giving an admiring glance.

Frowning, he took a deep drag of his cigarette. But then he threw it down and crushed it with his heel. Looking out the window, he said without turning around:

"I'm a bit short, Ma. You couldn't let me have a few bucks? There was the trip, and all the extras, you know. . . ."

His slim hips were silhouetted against the window. Rose-Anna trembled. Her heart went out to him at once as it had when he was a little boy and asked her for a nickel, his face turned away from her as it was now, looking out at passersby in the street.

"Sure," she said. "But all I've got is those ten dollars, and a few bits of change. Maybe I could scrape up fifty cents for you. . . ."

Eugène's eyes glittered. He moved quickly toward her.

"No, no, don't leave yourself short. Just gimme the ten, I'll bring you the change."

His request was like a bullet. Was he going to leave with all that money, weak as he was, and with no sense of its value? She saw her bitter, stubborn plans come crashing down. Then she reassured herself. Lord, how she jumped to conclusions! Of course Eugène was just going to run down to the corner and bring her back the change!

She opened the buffet drawer where she kept her purse and took out the crisp new bill.

"It's your money, after all," she said. "If you hadn't joined up we'd never have had it. But . . . Eugène . . . please don't spend it all."

This time she held his gaze, her eyes supplicating, her hands stretched out toward him.

He took the bill, impatient with all these nagging demands that were such a torture to him.

"Hell," he said, "I'll pay you back. It's payday soon, and you'll get this back and more."

He became confident once the money was in his pocket. Everything was going to change in this house. It was his turn to take things in hand. His father hadn't been able to do a thing to save the family. Well, it was up to him now.

"You know, Ma, we're not going to be poor much longer," he said. "I'm probably goin' to be promoted, and it'll be more than twenty bucks you'll get then, you just wait. You'll have enough to live on, Ma. You won't have to scrape all your life, the rest of us'll see to that."

The colour came back to his face and his eyes glowed as he invented such a fine future. He bent to kiss his mother's cheek and murmured affectionately:

"What would you like, anyway? What can I buy you? A dress? A new hat?"

Her smile was pitiful, she had seen enough, she was cured of false hope. Her voice was soft, and her words followed a single, humiliated train of thought:

"It's for the rent, you know."

Her hands fell to her sides in a gesture of total dejection.

He jammed down his wedge cap on his wavy hair and went over to study his reflection in the mirror over the buffet.

"What! You're not staying for supper!" she cried.

His face took on an expression of regret. His sensual mouth, with its soft, feminine lines, tightened, and again he was indecisive, sad and confused.

"Well, you know . . . er . . . I got some people to see. Tomorrow for sure, eh?"

And he started out very quickly, away from his mother's hurt look.

"Gotta see some people. But after that . . ."

He had his hand on the doorknob when the noisy gang of children burst in.

"Hey, Gene!"

In a second they were hanging from his arms and legs. Lucille and Albert were searching his pockets, and Gisèle was pulling at his sleeve. Lisping, she asked:

"Did you bwing me a pwesent, Zene?"

Philippe, in the doorway, watched his brother enviously.

"How about a few cigarettes, if you got too many?"

Eugène was laughing, obviously flattered by the welcome. Even this artless admiration was pleasing to him.

"Here, ya little bum!"

He threw an almost-full package to Philippe. Then he took out a handful of change and tossed the coins one by one into the air. He missed his mother's stern expression as he did this. Lucille and Albert caught them in the air or scrambled under table or chairs to fight over them.

Gisèle, less active, was sniffling:

"Zene, I din get any!"

And she stamped her feet, ordering him around in her shrill, thin voice:

"Give to Gisèle!"

Eugène took her in his arms, wiped her nose with his big khaki handkerchief and put a shiny new penny in her fat little hands, which trembled with pleasure.

"There now. That one's all for you."

The house had become noisy, excited, happy. The children pushed at each other as they counted their coins, ready to deal a foul blow. Rose-Anna, surprised and embarrassed, watched them rush off to the corner store. Eugène slipped out after them.

Alone with the little girl who was singing now, safe beneath a chair, Rose-Anna leaned on the table and indulged in a moment of piercing regret. It had hurt her terribly to see that money flying through the air.

TWENTY

Eugène's hangdog look disappeared the moment he left the house, and he went off whistling toward Notre Dame Street. At the corner of Beaudoin he took a deep breath and smiled to himself at the success of his ruse. He touched the ten dollars in his pocket to make sure it was safe, then unfolded a scrap of paper with a name and phone number. He thought of a pair of very red lips, eyes that were bold and full of mischief, and a small beret cocked over long, tangled hair.

His cheeks burned. He saw again the railway station crowded with soldiers, a girl off to one side who had smiled ever so slightly at him as he passed, smiled with her eyes, fringed with long, dark lashes which were raised almost imperceptibly. A moment later he was sitting beside her, daring to ask her name. As he stared, she crossed her slim legs and laughed softly.

"Does your mamma know you're out?"

He'd show her that he wasn't such a baby as she thought. He crumpled the scrap of paper torn from her address book. If only she hadn't been fooling, if only this were the real number!

He hurried to the nearest cigar store and into the phone booth. Panting a little, he dialled the number. A moment later he was surprised to hear an unfamiliar voice. Someone was asking who he wanted to speak to. "Yvette," he managed to get out, terrified that more questions would be asked. There was a pause, then the sharp voice he knew sounded in his ear. He was so relieved that he laughed nervously, then gave his name and took the plunge:

"Wanta get together tonight?"

There was a silence, then a peal of laughter. At last: "Okay!"

"Where?" he asked, barely able to speak.

She named a place and time for their meeting. Eugène's voice faded to a murmur. He hung up, stayed for a moment with his arm resting on the small shelf, then emerged, his face red, throwing his shoulders back as if he were on parade.

In the street, he reflected that he had two hours before meeting Yvette. What a nuisance! How would he kill the time? He hesitated at the curb. For a second his mother's sad, tired face appeared in his mind's eye. Sullen, he set off walking to escape her image. Approaching The Two Records, he went in and asked for cigarettes.

Sam Latour was listening to the news, leaning close to a small radio that he had placed among some cardboard displays on a shelf. He was grumbling as he came over to the counter:

"Son of a gun! Things are bad there in Norway!"

His voice was excited.

"When are they going to stop those damn Krauts?" he said, talking to himself, as if the news were a personal affront.

"Just you wait till we get there!" cried Eugène. Nonchalantly he snapped his ten-dollar bill and tossed it on the counter.

"By gosh, you're in the money today!" said Sam. "Those ten-buck bills don't seem to stick to your fingers, young fella!"

"There's more where that came from," said Eugène.

He picked up his change very casually, and stuffed the bills in various pockets. Then he lit a cigarette.

"Yep," Latour went on, "looks like you're doin' just fine, my boy."

"About time," said Eugène, leaning on the counter, his legs crossed, looking toward the door, in a posture that seemed to mimic Azarius.

Beneath his low forehead with its growth of thick, wavy hair, his eyes glinted with vanity. They were the same shade of blue as his father's but, closer to his short, thin nose, they gave his face a different expression. The father's gaze was open and enthusiastic; Eugène's was shifting, liquid, changeable and ready to take flight.

"Yep," said Sam Latour again.

A customer came in, then two workers stopped in front of the shop and, hearing the newscast, entered. From time to time Sam nodded or shifted his weight with his shoulders to punctuate the broadcast, or tightened his belt with an aggressive gesture. He had undergone a change since his futile discussions with Azarius Lacasse. His indifference had given way to outraged astonishment. He heard the description of the invasion of Oslo with bent head, savagely chewing at his cigar. His good-natured, peaceful character could turn, when he was moved, to a sudden, childish rage. Incapable of anything underhand, any tale of trickery troubled him.

There was deep silence at the end of the broadcast. Sam switched off the radio. At once a hubbub of voices filled the restaurant.

"Those sneaks!" said Sam Latour. He came out to serve his customers, head down like an angry ram.

"Sneakin' into a country dressed up like the local folks and then grabbin' everything off before they know what happened! Those treacherous bastards!"

As he handed out cigarettes, gum or cokes, with hard blows to his cash register, he emitted an uninterrupted flow of invective.

The passing customers were in no hurry to leave. A few near the door were reading the papers for more details. Others were studying a map of Europe which Sam had pinned to a wall.

"Norway!" mused one. "They're good people up there. They never went lookin' for war."

"No more than we did," said one of the workers.

"It was a very advanced, modern country, too," said another who seemed well-informed.

"And they still had their traitors," roared Sam Latour.

"Traitors!" said the first customer. "Seems like they're all over the place. Funny business, that, selling your own country."

"What do you expect?" Latour broke in. "There's people who'd sell their own mother for money or a bit of ribbon."

He chewed away at his cigar, straining at his collar like a restive horse.

"I just wonder if they can stop them," said a thin young man, looking up from his newspaper.

Eugène assumed a theatrically aggressive stance. He had noticed that these working men, full of common sense and moderation, glanced at him occasionally with unspoken admiration. He was carried away as he saw himself through their eyes, proud to represent that valiant, bellicose youth in whom the older, more mature, the weak and undecided saw their salvation. A defender of women, of the aged and oppressed, that's what he was. The avenging arm of society outraged. A fighting spirit shone in his eyes.

"You bet we're goin' to stop them," he said loudly. "Just like this. . . ."

He made a savage motion, as if to stab a bayonet through the wall. His face was tense, his lips tight, as if he had met with stiff resistance. Then, with a grunt, he removed the imaginary weapon, stood straight and looked around him, highly satisfied with himself.

"Yep," said Sam Latour.

"Yeah!" said Eugène.

The door opened. Léon Boisvert came in, decked out in new clothes, a newspaper tucked under one arm, his manner cautious and affected, putting out his feelers before venturing farther inside. He wiped his feet carefully on the mat by the door.

Eugène stared at him, mockingly.

"What! You're still in civvies, are you?"

Boisvert was disconcerted. Five weeks ago he had succeeded in landing a job as bookkeeper in an office nearby. His fear of conscription had become a constant obsession that tormented him even in his dreams. He had always had a frightful notion of war, seeing bodies pierced with bayonets and himself pursued by men trying to thrust a weapon into his hands. To all this was now added the fear of losing his precious job, the first good luck in his life, which he had sought for years. An unhealthy pallor pervaded his features.

"When you can't get a job there's always the army, that's true," he said disdainfully.

Eugène strutted, an arrogant smile on his lips.

"It won't be long till they have the call-up," he said. "I'm in a good spot to know these things. Only one thing you can do: head for the woods. . . . Or get married," he added mockingly.

He butted his cigarette on the counter.

"But I'll tell you this," he said, "it's the guys who volunteered that'll get the good jobs after the war."

Swaggering, he took his leave.

Outside, the air seemed light and heady. He felt that he was master of his life and floating sky-high. No more indecision or scruples. What the heck, he thought, life owes me something, what with the risk I'm taking. With his long, easy stride he made for the streetcar stop and elbowed his way to the front. He felt that the weary crowd was looking his way, paying attention to him. His joy rose higher, higher. And his demands on life soared. He thought, they shouldn't charge us for anything, it's a darn shame. If they've got no worries, all those people, it's because of us.

The wait by the Maisonneuve monument on the Place d'Armes seemed interminable. His nerves on edge, he smoked cigarette after cigarette. Yvette was late. He saw from the clock on the Aldred Building that he'd been waiting a good ten minutes. And all that he had coming to him, his youth, its amusements and giddy pleasures, were due this minute, no time to waste. He began to pace to and fro, and suddenly, very clearly, saw his mother's face as she had given him the ten dollars.

He took out what was left of it, counted the bills, and felt a feeble urge to go home.

"Ma," he murmured softly, with a touch of tenderness, imagining now that he wanted nothing so much as to console Rose-Anna and win back her admiration. He saw himself returning what remained of the ten dollars, and his mother, reassured and proud of him, going to lock it up where she had kept it. The greatest thing was not his mother's profound relief, but his own part in the transaction, his generosity, and Rose-Anna so sorry that she had doubted him. She really was scared I'd spend it all, he thought. And he fondled his good intentions in a maudlin way as if they were already made good, and was just as pleased with himself as if it had been true. At that moment a streetcar coming from the west opened its doors. He saw Yvette, dressed in a long, full coat that hung open to reveal her slim hips in a clinging, bright-red dress fit to knock his eye out. Rose-Anna had lost. He threw away his cigarette and, whistling, crossed the square to meet this bright, skin-tight, flashy dress. . . .

TWENTY-ONE

Florentine had grown more or less immune to the charms of spring. April was gone, May was making a timid start in the neighbourhood of St. Henri, and the old trees along the streets, imbedded in cement, had budded and grown green without winning a single glance from her as she walked twice a day between her home and the store. But tonight, as she left the Five and Ten, she couldn't help stopping in wonderment at the softness of the air, as if she had awakened to a transformation that had taken place while she was absent, missing its different stages. The sun still warmed Notre Dame Street, despite the late hour. Above the cobblers' shops, the fruit stores and other small establishments, apartment windows opened on interiors which added their intimate murmur to the sounds of traffic outside. Between the loud passage of a train, a heavy truck or a streetcar, the faint sound of a distant church bell might find its way into those open windows.

Beside St. Henri's railway station with its little tower, a few flowers had forced their corollas up through the coarse earth. High above, beyond the church steeples which escaped from the layers of drifted soot, rose the mountain with its green slopes woven like a living network of pale, floating leaves. It was indeed spring, all around her, verging already on the dust and heat of summer.

Florentine was now obliged to recognize this flight of time. Her fear began to sound an alarm within her like a runaway bell that refused to stop, ringing louder than all the church towers in the city – the fear that she had long felt approaching, perhaps even since Jean was at her house.

Could she subdue it? That would have been as impossible as trying to quiet the great bells pealing out over the rooftops. She knew it well: she couldn't use arguments or reason against the unceasing rattle of this alarm. Today she'd have to do something. But what? For a while she'd had one thought in mind: to tell Jean what she suspected. But she had rejected this. Now it came back to her. Instinctively she began to walk in the direction of St. Ambroise Street.

She had no real plan of action. She still refused to admit that all she had done to get in touch with Jean had been in vain. Now, overcome by fear and misfortune, she imagined that luck would be with her today and she would meet him at last. But even without this hope she had drifted toward the part of the suburb she associated with his life, with no guide but this mysterious intuition.

At Atwater she turned down toward the canal. The open taverns on her way exhaled their smell of stale beer, and the snack bars, frequented by newspaper vendors, mostly small, tired-looking Jews, gave off an unbearable rancid odour of fried food. As she turned the corner of St. Emilie she spotted the familiar rig of the tobacco man, an old farmer from whom Azarius bought his strong, bitter smokes; then came the marketplace with its bustling crowd around the stalls of the country folk. Flowers, plants – there were hundreds of them in the sunlight in their fragile shallow crates; ferns waving their frothy green in the sooty air; jonquils, pale yellow, bent by the slightest breeze; bright-red tulips bursting with life; and behind this garden scene the stalls with their ordered displays of apples, blue onions veined with violet, fresh lettuce glistening with drops of water. . . .

Florentine turned away, wounded by this feast of colours, this abundance of good smells in which she could take no pleasure. Oh, spring was taking its vengeance for her neglect! It spread all its riches before her eyes, wafted toward her the living perfumes of greenery from the hothouse, of the sugar bush, of docile animals caged for the market. The thick, golden syrup, the maple-sugar cakes, the long-legged hares suspended by their hind paws, their fur thick with blood, the terrified clucking of hens whose red combs projected between the slats of their crates, and the round, anxious eye of the one that was tossed on the scales: everything was here to tell her that life is good to some and unkind to others.

She hastened on to escape this animated scene from which she felt excluded.

She had often come here in the past to help her father do the Saturday-evening shopping. She had still been small, but loved to carry the big shopping bag. Her father would stop to chat with some robust country woman whose broad shoulders wore the same rough men's sweater she had on today, so Florentine imagined. From her they had bought tiny cucumber pickles, of which Azarius was so fond. Occasionally they would go in the fishmonger's shop and inspect the fish. Her father taught her the names of the carp and the burbot and, when she grew restive, let her touch a great eel swimming in a tank. Oh, what a long time ago that was, those Saturday evenings at the market! And how useless to think about them now! Yet it was true that she had been a happy, pampered child. There were rich children who had not had what she possessed while she was small. As they left the house Rose-Anna would say, "Take good care of the little one, now" – they'd called her "the little one" until she was twelve; and off they'd go, she with her hand confidently in that of Azarius. And her father's conversation during the whole walk! And their complicity when he squeezed her hand a little harder and said, "Your mother said not to get any cream, but what do you say we buy some, just to see how she enjoys it with her porridge!"

Could she have stayed happy if she had gone on in the same old way? Never! She'd made her choice, knowing that she could no more refuse it than stop breathing. And even now, if she had it to do over again . . .

Her thoughts had come full circle. Florentine's expression was so tense and unhappy that she would not have known herself in a mirror. All this mulling over things was no help. What's the good! What's the good! She'd have liked to shout the words aloud and kill the sentimentality that had softened her.

Walking more quickly now, her lips tight and her eyes staring, unseeing, searching for a practical plan, she was rebellious against all humility, seeking only a ray of hope to alleviate her terror. What else mattered? She had to be delivered from her fear.

Continuing toward the canal, she heard a great rattling of chains and the repeated blasts of a boat's whistle. Below the ochre hall of the marketplace with its serrated rower, beyond St. Ambroise Street, the swing bridge pivoted and left two gaps in the road. Between two long lines of waiting cars, Florentine saw the smokestack of a freighter sailing by.

She stopped to watch, not out of fascination, for this sight had always seemed inconsequential to her, but because she now perceived everything with a painful acuteness, and found it paralyzing. All the ships she had ever seen pass by here had seemed quite ordinary, but this one, gliding between the barriers, took on a strange uniqueness, as if such a thing had never happened before. It was a tramp steamer with a grey hull, its sides narrow and battered, still smeared with sludge, and a tall mast marked by the spindrift of the estuary. It had completed a journey between two horizons so distant that they were lost in mists, and now, incongruous in this narrow path that led it through the city, had only one desire: past all obstacles, all barriers, to reach the open St. Lawrence again and the swell of the Great Lakes. The ship slid quietly, lazily along, its crew on deck, some ready to toss a mooring line which they held coiled like a lasso, others hanging out washing between the deckhouse and the bow. It seemed to speak to that poverty-stricken neighbourhood of a life apart from, indifferent to, the ups and downs of a landlubber's existence, with a poignant reminder of the far horizons dormant in the depths of every man's being.

Soon it was sailing between the walls of the factories that border the canal, and the hum of its propellor faded. But other smokestacks were puffing this way from the port, and their sooty plumes formed clouds that followed the shining, watery pathway. There was a tanker, lying low in the water like a pontoon; and behind, it, a barge that looked on the point of sinking under its load of cut lumber, its straining propellors roiling the quiet surface. And there were other masts, other tattered flags moving up between the roofs and painted signs. The operator's cabin and, almost always deserted, a tiny, flat-roofed restaurant stood on the canal bank, blackened by the freighters' soot, melancholy and forsaken, like all buildings stuck in thankless surroundings to serve whatever passes, on a road, a bridge or a canal: the offspring of utility and chance.

Then Florentine realized that she was alone in the world with her fear. She had a glimpse of solitude, not just her own but the solitude that tracks every living being, following on his heels, ready to pounce upon him like a cloud, a shadow. For her this solitude had a strong taste of poverty about it; she imagined, knowing no better, that in comfort or luxury it could not materialize.

Her thoughts led nowhere. She shut her eyes and searched within herself for her imperious desire for Jean – the only part of herself that seemed familiar, after the wanderings of her mind – but all she saw was a shadow play of barges moving morosely in the water, a strange, secret screen, unheard-of and incomprehensible. What she also discovered in her own depths was a horrible feeling of resentment, a rancour so strong that she felt her whole being poisoned by it.

No, Jean could never know the fear that was in her as she walked alone through this spring evening made for laughter, for gently holding hands. That was the injustice that she could not swallow. She thought of his man's life, fulfilling in its freedom, devoid of all regrets, and this thought was a thousand times more unbearable than the awareness of her error. It wouldn't be long until he had forgotten her very features. He would love other women. He might occasionally try, without success, to recall the slightest thing about her. This was what she could not abide. Because she had lost him, she would at least have had him suffer as she suffered. Or seen him dead. This notion pleased her, and she lingered over it. Yes, if he were dead she might feel he owed her nothing. But as long as he lived and breathed she would know the humiliation of not having been able to hold him.

In her heart she felt a muted lament, a low cry, a prayer asking that Jean should love her still, despite the leaden hate she felt for him. If she were to be freed of hatred, freed of fear, he had to love her. And she searched her memory for small proofs of tenderness in things that he had said. She clung to these words as a beggar clings to a penny, turning them over and over, hoping perhaps to see it grow or turn to gold through the simple magic of a wish. But the alms had been too meagre, the gold a speck of dust.

And so this was what made the world go 'round: this was why the man, the woman, two enemies, called a truce to their ancient war; why the night air could turn so soft, and the illusion of a path reserved for these two people seemed to open up before them. And this was why your heart gave you no rest! She forgot the moments of frenzy, the suspended moments of her happiness, and saw nothing but the trap that had been set for her weakness; and this trap appeared to her coarse and brutal, and she felt, stronger than fear itself, an unspeakable contempt for her fate as a woman, and a self-hatred that left her amazed.

She had arrived at the house where Jean lived. With its oozing eaves troughs that dribbled like scupper holes, its flaking paint and the pervasive sound of marine propellors, the place seemed to her like a wretched tub of a freighter laid up in drydock. Florentine walked to and fro before it, hesitating. She had been there twice already but had not mustered the courage to go inside. Then she had sent Philippe with a letter. Her brother had sworn he lost it, and next day demanded a quarter to buy his silence. On the weekend he had returned to the charge, this time doubling his blackmail fee.

Florentine repressed a great desire to run, run anywhere, and keep a trace of her pride intact. But where could she go? To whom could she turn if Jean was still the one she missed? Her mother seemed more and more depressed, ever since their trip to St. Denis. Her father? What support or help had he ever been to them? And Eugène. . . . Ever since she had discovered he had not returned the money to her mother, she would have liked to catch up with him and slap his face and scratch him until he bled. During his last leave she had met him on St. Catherine Street, uncertain on his feet and offering his arm to a loud-voiced young lady. That same evening her mother had served the family bread and a little cold meat, saying that she hadn't had time for shopping. Oh, the taste of poverty that went down with that meal! Florentine's mouth was still bitter with that savour, the food of suffering and resentment that would never disappear. Then, out of anger at Eugène, she had lost all patience with her mother, all desire to help her. And this loss of what was best in herself caused her to resent still more her brother's treachery.

Florentine was distressed enough by signs of loosening ties within the family. But behind these signs she recognized the smell of former lodgings, all the poor houses in which they had been together and yet separated already from one another. She saw, as if she were there again, that whole series of interiors where the same pictures of saints and the same family photos hung before walls that slowly closed in upon her. She thought it must have been from the very depths of her life, from her first childhood, that she had been awaiting Jean.

She took out her compact, patted her cheeks with the puff and, in the mirror in her purse, inspected herself with a mixture of incomprehension, wounded pride and profound self-pity. And she regretted not having bought a straw hat; a ridiculous little thing, all flowery, which she must have noticed despite her distress somewhere on her way, maybe today, perhaps long ago, but she remembered it now, barely bigger than a pair of folded wings, with lots of red, and ribbons crossing at the back. She wondered whether, if she had been better dressed or prettier on this day or that when Jean had seen her, he still would have disdained her. . . .

She went up the two steps and rang the bell. Immediately she saw herself as she must look, and was ashamed to be waiting there, her purse on her arm, stiff as a board, jilted and poor.

The door opened a crack. She heard herself asking for information in a barely audible voice. It seemed to her that if she turned around she would see Jean disappearing around the street corner. She could almost hear him whistling. . . . She thought, All my life I'll see him going away.

As through a fog she caught the words:

". . . left without giving any address." And it seemed to her she had already heard these words, at night, at dawn, whenever she awoke and felt herself faced with the obvious.

Later she found herself walking downcast toward the foundry on St. James Street. Bracelets jangled on her thin wrists and on the brim of her straw hat a small bunch of red glass cherries rattled. These sounds echoed in her head and prevented her from following any thought to its conclusion. She arrived in front of the foundry and remembered how, not two months ago, Jean had greeted her here with contemptuous coolness. She blushed with shame and anger. Why on earth had she come here to be reminded of that humiliation? How could she go to places that belonged to Jean? Suddenly she regretted these things she had done more than her vanished dream.

She turned away. And in the face of her inability to find Jean and win him back – an inability which she now began to think of as her own refusal of him – her fears began to dissipate, and continued to do so the farther she left his neighbourhood behind. Oh, if only she could be wrong, her whole life would be a sweet revenge on this absurd panic, on the terrors that had dogged her steps this evening! She must have made a mistake! Now she remembered that her mother had once . . . And again her fears receded. The alarm bell gradually faded away, and Florentine managed to think of her error as a stupid accident, a piece of carelessness which brooding would only turn into an indelible sin.

At Notre Dame Street, which she entered just above the Cartier movie house, she was relieved to see the street signs and the bright shop windows filled with pretty dresses. For the first time in her life the sounds of a crowded street seemed to her friendly and pleasant.

From a small restaurant came the noise of jazz. Her feet were tired, and she took refuge in the animation inside. She ordered a coke and a hot dog, sat down alone and lit a cigarette. With the first puff she sank into a familiar apathy, deep, deep into the noisy, overheated, shrill half-night that had been the normal climate of her being for many years now, outside of which she had to admit she was lost. She imagined that now she would even be contented back at the Five and Ten, where at least the noise and agitation never slowed. Oh, the horror of the silence she had felt around her this evening! The horror of deserted streets! If ever she kept the trace of a memory of this wretched night, sure as she now was of escaping from it, that memory would be of having been alone, irrevocably alone, while in other streets couples strolled together to the sound of jukeboxes braying their syncopated joy from every small café. She would never forgive Jean for the fact that tonight she had slunk about like a leper, banned from the swift stream of sounds and emotions which she loved so much.

The music stopped, and with it her impression of being safe from loneliness. She slipped a coin into the nickelodeon and, to the accompaniment of a deafening boogie-woogie, took out her comb, her compact and her lipstick, and began to apply her makeup with great care. She would take a puff at her cigarette, lay it down, smear a little more red on her lips, pat more powder on her forehead, one foot tapping to the music beneath the table.

A last look in the glass and she was satisfied. She was pale, it was true, but pretty, prettier than ever, with her hair down and her eyes still wide from the alert of fear. She looked down at her slim body as if she had never seen it. She moved her hair under the bracket lamp to make it shine in her tiny mirror, and stretched out her hands to admire her delicate fingers with their carmine nails. In the presence of her own youth, her fine hair, loosely combed, and the whiteness of her arms, she began to love life once more. She decided to buy the little hat; she knew now where she'd seen it. This would be her revenge on Jean. She'd be so elegant that if he ever saw her he'd regret leaving her behind. Then it would be her turn to be hard and pitiless!

The jazz filled her mind, and the cigarette left her in a pleasant daze. She was thinking of all the finery she had denied herself. Seeing herself in this, in that, she made her choices, determined to give her life such an appearance of happiness that happiness itself would come to dwell there.

She thought of her mother, and the pity and tenderness she felt – resulting from her new-found optimism and her respite from fear – seemed to her to be the unmistakable sign of her own goodness: a notion she found so pleasant that she bathed in it luxuriously for a while. Yes, from now on she'd be a real help to her mother. What did it matter if Eugène and

Azarius didn't do their share? She'd never leave her mother to their tender care!

The light-hearted jazz, the easy tapping of her toe beneath the table presaged the facility with which her new sacrifices would be borne. From time to time a siren wailed, vibrant and impassioned, and she would shiver, imagining herself back at the edge of the canal, where she had glimpsed the grey, melancholy thread of her existence. She took several quick gulps of coke, puffed at her cigarette and shook her head angrily. She set a superstitious deadline for the end of her old life: if nothing was changed when she arrived home, she could conclude that her worries were unfounded. As delighted as if she had found a real solution to her problems, she left the restaurant and started home.

Soon she saw the dining room light shining through the parted curtains. Its humble glow provoked a goodness in her heart that was no longer calculating or defiant, nor a kind of currency with which to barter and exchange; what she felt was an infinite, poignant affinity for this life that was her family's. No longer did it seem harassed and restricting, but rather made beautiful from start to finish by Rose-Anna's courage. Her mother's courage shone out like a lighthouse beam before her. Home would take her in, home would cure her.

Her hand on the doorknob, she paused for one long, ineffable moment. Then she pushed open the door. And it was as if an arctic wind chilled her frail efforts to make a fresh beginning.

TWENTY-TWO

In the dining room, furniture that she didn't recognize was piled against the partition. Strangers' faces were there among the ripped-open packing cases, the washtubs of linen and the chairs piled one on the other to the ceiling.

For a second Florentine hoped that she had come into the wrong house by mistake. But no: behind the piles of mattresses and the shaky cupboards there were too many familiar things to be seen – the old clock, the children's hats, the oilcloth on the table. Then she saw her mother sitting on the edge of a chair, tugging absently at her apron. Florentine, trembling, went to her. Rose-Anna smiled distractedly, then went with her into the kitchen, closing the door behind them. In this crowded space they were alone, with nothing to remind them of the chaos outside. Florentine, aware for a new reason of the flight of time, thought, stupefied, That's right, it's May! It's time to move!

"Sit down," said her mother, as if nothing remained to them but the right to sit in their own kitchen . . . and look at each other . . . and talk if the words came. . . .

She herself collapsed onto a chair. Her time was drawing near. She grew out of breath with the slightest effort.

They stared at each other. No explanation was needed. But Rose-Anna felt obliged to say something. Impatiently, almost nastily, she said:

"The new tenants. Couldn't you guess?" Then her voice grew monotonous and plaintive:

"I thought we'd have a few days grace, but these people had paid. The fact is, they're more at home here than we are. What could I do? I had to let them in."

It can't be, thought Florentine. She was accustomed to their yearly flight – sometimes they'd stayed only six months – but not to this invasion of their home by a bunch of strangers. Hearing the smallest children crying and moaning in the next room, she felt a cold rage. Is this what she deserved to see, after coming home so anxious to find everything in its place, like an infallible sign of safety and security? Why hadn't her father and mother done something sooner to be sure they had a place to live?

"You shouldn't have let them in," she said crossly.

"What else could I do?" said Rose-Anna again. And went on to tell how she had arranged things for the moment.

"It won't be easy tonight. But I spoke to our neighbour. She'll lend us a room. And I kept Philippe's for the little ones – mine, that is," she added, as if the confusion were already dangerous. "I put them to bed as early as I could, you can imagine. The racket they were making with the other kids, that woman's – I don't even know her name – it was enough to drive you crazy."

She stopped and stared at Florentine, who sat like a statue in front of her.

"Where've you been so late?" she asked.

But she didn't expect a reply. Were there any answers to be had in this abyss that so engulfed them you could scream for days and hear no response but the echo of your own despair?

Rose-Anna stared obstinately at a worn spot in the linoleum. In a dull, weary voice she began to enumerate their woes as if it were a relief at last to see them all together, the old, the new, the small, the great, those that lay dormant in her memory and those that pulsed in the heart's freshest wounds.

"Your father!" she said. "Your father! He was supposed to find a house. You know your father. He keeps us hanging till the last minute with his false hopes. False hopes! To hear him talk he was going to find a house. A good house. To hear him talk. But I've got to see to everything. How could I? I spent all my time at the hospital with Daniel. He's in hospital," she said, reminding herself as if she had lost the thread of her tangled skein. "Daniel. And then Eugène! Why on earth did we have to go to the farm? Daniel's been sick ever since. We weren't born to have luck, we weren't. And now it's May there's not a house to be had. Will you tell me where we're going to live?"

Then, behind the ranks of these troubles, clear as they were, she saw a whole legion of others appearing at every turn. She was at a loss, and grew silent. And the awareness of all her secret sorrows inclined Rose-Anna to compassion. She had no hope left for herself, but at least she could spare a little for others.

"Did you have supper?" she asked, her voice disconcertingly tender. "I could make you an omelette. . . ."

But Florentine said not a word. Tears of rebellion came to her eyes. Was this what she had come to experience with her mother? Misfortunes so immense and numerous as these? She felt her last shreds of hope disappear.

She saw Rose-Anna in a dusty dress and with dishevelled hair. The dejection of this woman who had kept her courage through all their misfortunes seemed to her a sure sign of the family's downfall, and her own in particular.

Rose-Anna was tugging at the edge of her apron with a tired, futile gesture she had never made in the past – the grandmother's gesture. Her shoulders rocked from side to side in a sad, monotonous motion, as if she were holding a child, or a thought, or an ancient rancour she was trying to put to sleep. Or perhaps she was merely rocking her fatigue, or all her thoughts together. Everything in her posture reminded Florentine of Daniel, whom his mother took with the same movements to calm him when he had fever.

Daniel! He was so small for his age. He'd always been pale, almost transparent. But before he took ill he had surprised them all by his precociousness. There was an old saying in that part of town: the bright ones don't live long. He was so frail, so serious! What torments he must have been through already! God, I hope he lives, thought Florentine. I'll take his cure as a sign of my deliverance.

Her thoughts were steered at once to her own panic. She felt nauseated. And this time she knew it was useless to struggle against her certainty. She would have to tell her mother. But how? And especially just now! As in the distance she heard Rose-Anna's voice:

"And what on earth's your father doing, out till this hour! He's been gone since two this afternoon. What's he up to? What on earth is he doing?"

This old song that she'd heard a hundred times awoke no reaction in Florentine. She was sinking into a suffocating darkness in which no help, no counsel came from any side, wherever she might turn. She was dizzy. Her stomach rebelled.

When she stood straight again, her face pale and humiliated, her mother was looking at her. Looking as if she had never seen her before, Rose-Anna stared wide-eyed, with an expression of mute horror. Without pity, without affection, without kindness. She shouted, her voice rising violently:

"Now what's this? Yesterday morning, and now again tonight! Anybody'd think you were . . ."

She stopped short, and the two women stared at each other like enemies. All that came between them was the confused sound of a foreign intimacy taking its place in their own home, on the other side of a thin partition.

Florentine's eyes gave way first.

Once more she sought her mother's eyes. She blinked back her tears, her lips quivered and her whole body was in anguish. It was the one time in her life that her expression held this call for help, the call of a hunted creature. But Rose-Anna had turned away. Her head hung low and she seemed to have become inert, indifferent, half asleep.

Florentine saw herself at an infinite distance, young, gay and feverishly happy because Jean was there. This far-away joy was unbearable to remember, harder and worse than a spoken reproach. She turned, opened the door violently and ran and ran, in a gust of wind that seemed to wrap itself around her body.

TWENTY-THREE

Running anywhere, blindly, hating the echo of her footsteps in the silence of the empty streets, Florentine fled from her own fear, fled from herself. Suddenly she remembered that Marguerite had often invited her to spend the night at her place. She had never become very close to girls of her own age. She imagined that they envied her and might play her some unpleasant trick, or simply found them boring. Of those that had been nice to her at work she had found none so irritating as Marguerite, whose loud demonstrations of friendliness she had never been able to discourage with her own mockery and impatience. But she knew that Marguerite had a kind heart, and in her present dejection needed to be with someone – even someone a little simple-minded – who would take her in gladly and who, above all, knew nothing of her misfortune.

The walls of the great cotton mill on St. Ambroise Street wrapped her in their shadows filled with the humming and whining of their machines. Everything conspired to make her despondency complete: this nocturnal labour whose sounds seemed to come from underground, lonely passersby who stared too curiously at her, the sky which was clouding over, and the trees in the courtyards waving and breathing together in a low murmur that presaged a downpour.

She emerged into a clearing between the tall textile mills, and recognized the green gables of the house in which Marguerite lived with her aunt, in an alley called St. Zoé. It was one of those old farmhouses, a few of which are still to be found in the area, surrounded by the march of factories and warehouses; the more they are attacked by dust and soot, the fussier they are about lace curtains in their windows, fresh outside paint and a polished threshold.

A light was on in Marguerite's room upstairs. Florentine, not daring to knock and afraid that Marguerite's aunt, a stern and starchy old lady, might answer the door, went over beneath the lighted window. She called softly first, then more loudly. Finally a shadow appeared behind the curtains. Florentine, panting, whispered:

"Marguerite! It's me! Hey, let me in. Don't make a lot of noise!"

When she was in Marguerite's room and sure that the rest of the house was silent, she realized that she would have to explain her visit at this hour of the night. What time was it anyway? She had no idea. Had she been wandering alone the whole evening, or all her life? She was terrified of giving away her secret. Her throat dry, she stammered:

"They're just about to move out of our place. There's no room to sleep."

But she took Marguerite's hand with a nervousness that gave her away, squeezed it hard and begged:

"Keep me, please! Can I stay?"

Marguerite wrapped her dressing gown tight around her

and, wanting to look her best for her friend, ran her hand through her short, tousled hair.

"Why sure," she said. "We can have a chat, we can have a good long chat about all kinds of things, eh?"

But she noticed Florentine's pale face and her wild eyes and asked:

"What's the matter? Are you sick?"

"No, no I'm not," Florentine protested.

She had flopped in an armchair and her trembling hands went from her dishevelled hair to her handbag which she was somehow unable to open. Her reflection in the mirror on the closet door horrified her. Then, repeating those automatic gestures which had helped her in the past, she made a pitiful effort to straighten her hair and, succeeding in standing up, found a lipstick among Marguerite's things and began to cover her dry, chapped lips. Before she had finished she turned away, unable to bear the sight of herself in the mirror. Her shoulders slumped and she gave a little heart-rending laugh, disillusioned, infinitely sad.

"What on earth do I look like, Marguerite?" she asked plaintively. "I've got ugly, haven't I?"

"Why, no!" said Marguerite. "You always look nice, even when you're tired."

"Yeah," said Florentine weakly, "that's it . . . I'm really tired." Then, broken and defeated, she admitted, "I want to go to bed, Marguerite. I want to sleep."

Her cry was a doleful complaint rather than a wish, and it came out as of its own volition.

"My God, how I want to sleep!"

The tiny bed, pushed against the wall, was unmade.

"I'll change the sheets," said Marguerite. "It won't take a minute."

She went out to get fresh linen. Alone, Florentine ran to the mirror and there, with no one to look on, stared long at this new image of herself as enemy – these features that she hardly knew, so wild that she found them frightening; and she could barely hold back her tears. The doorknob turned, and she hurried back to the chair, as if she had been sitting there the whole time. Soon the fresh sheets, turned back invitingly, called her to rest, and she took off her shoes, stockings, sweater and skirt, and with a single bound threw herself on the bed. The coolness of the cotton on her tired limbs was too sweet, and suddenly she lost control and burst out sobbing. She raised her hands to her eyes to hide her expression from Marguerite, exasperated and angry with herself. And she turned to the wall and beat on it with her head in self-punishment, moaning softly.

Marguerite let her weep for a time, then came close to her chilled body and laid an arm around her shoulders, talking to her as to a child:

"Come, tell me what's wrong. Sometimes that helps."

She felt Florentine stiffen, and insisted:

"Tell me what it is!" And as one tries to get a child to speak: "Was it something your mother said? No? Is it your boyfriend? He's not the only one, you know. There's other fish in the ocean, they say. It's not that? Is it because people are talking?"

"Who's talking!" cried Florentine violently, still sobbing. "Who? Who's talking about me?"

"Nobody, nobody, I just wondered . . ." said Marguerite, who had several very precise examples in mind. "You mustn't cry about that, now, come on. They're only gossips, you mustn't pay any attention. I know you couldn't do anything wrong."

Marguerite's confidence, as well as a certain reticence which Florentine sensed, made her furious. She pulled away to the very edge of the bed and declared:

"If you won't tell me who's talking, that's your business, don't tell me." Then she cried defiantly, "And there's nothing wrong with me, nothing at all!"

Shaken by fresh sobs, terrified by the gulf between herself and the other girls in her circle, she dug her nails into Marguerite's shoulders as if to transfer her own unbearable anguish to the other, to take it out on some human being.

"Put the light out," she begged.

In the dark it was even worse to be given over to her own solitude, the frightening, impersonal solitude that was her lot and hers alone, one not to be rejected or even shared.

Marguerite was quiet now, warned of the truth by a very sure instinct. It had not escaped her that Florentine had changed in the last few weeks, and that the other waitresses were slyly watching her every move with a faintly hostile curiosity, often exchanging a look of complicity and understanding.

Good God, is it possible? she thought. And she was surprised to feel no contempt for Florentine, though she had always been severe in her judgements on love outside of wedlock. She had even made fun of it, and perhaps enjoyed the kind of scandal the waitresses spread around at the Five and Ten. And here she was, thinking only of protecting Florentine from the ruin she foresaw ahead of her.

What could she do? She was so young – in fact not much younger than Marguerite, but more frail and fragile and therefore more to be pitied; prettier, too, and thus the more exposed. What would she do, poor Florentine, pretty and all as she was? Would they dismiss her from the store? And what might she not do in her despair?

Grief and pity and a rebellious need to do what her heart told her took hold of Marguerite.

She wasn't yet sure if she would have the courage, but she tried to force herself into the position where courage would come.

"Listen, Florentine," she said. "Maybe you're in a jam. If that's what it is, I'll help. Do you hear, I'll help you through."

But this was not enough, and she knew she had to get in deeper yet to overcome the egotism of nature that prompts us to stand aside from others' problems.

Marguerite suspected something of the sort, and murmured:

"Listen, Florentine, there are ways. Other people have come through it. I'll be with you, Florentine, I promise. And I'll stick up for you, what do you think? Just let them say one word at the store, I'll be ready for them. It'll just be a secret for the two of us."

Thinking of the difficulties they faced, she nevertheless talked of how she could help, and Florentine, too stunned by anger and amazement to say a word, let her go on:

"I've got a little money saved up," she said. "That'll be a help. I'll lend it to you, if you're too proud to take it."

Florentine was still silent. She was thinking, too. But far from being touched by Marguerite's offer, she was petrified that her secret had come out so easily, and especially that Marguerite dared to mention it . . . to talk about what would happen later, that event so terrifying that she herself could not envisage it. What a fool Marguerite was! What a great idiot! A stupid fool! At all costs she must stay quiet, take it easy. And, above all, destroy this idea the big ninny had got into her head.

"You must be crazy!" she said, half angry, half mocking.

"You're really crazy with all your ideas. I tell you nothing's wrong. It's just nerves. It's only nerves."

She repeated the word, raging and defiant as if to convince herself. And when she saw Marguerite half convinced and penitent she felt such relief, such progress toward her own deliverance, that she hastened to pile on more reproaches:

"It's a good thing you were only joking, or I could get mad. I'd leave here in a minute if I knew you thought that about me, what you just said, there. Now take it back, or I'll be mad. You must be crazy, you and your crazy ideas!"

Then she pretended to yawn and stretch, as if she were dead-tired, and said firmly:

"Now let's get some sleep, so we don't look too dumb in the morning. Good night."

She wanted to escape from any further concern on Marguerite's part. When she finally heard her even breathing she felt free to move. Lying on one elbow she stared into the dark.

At first she was surprised at the strange calm she felt. Confronted with the obvious by Marguerite's remarks, whose pity had been more convincing than nature's own warning, she had no use at this point for regret or shame. She simply wondered, her cold hands pressed against her throat, what she was going to do. She stared at the darkest corners of this unfamiliar room as if it were in a far country. But always the same question returned to haunt her: What, oh what am I going to do?

She rubbed her eyes, she pressed her hands to her temples as if she could squeeze out a hope or a solution. She forced herself to think logically. She remembered a factory girl who had told her a most horrible thing one day as they walked down the street together. She also remembered that on that day life had seemed a cruel venture. But there was nothing to be done about it. . . . She toyed with the idea, stiffening at the idea of physical pain, knowing she would never accept it. Whenever she thought about such things, or about what the girl had confided to her (it had stuck in her memory like a poisoned dart), a different vision rose in competition, mingling the church, the holy images and the burning candles, the morning when she had gone to Mass with Emmanuel. Days of pure and innocent joy came to her mind. Then she felt cut off from light, from the sun, from life itself, and close to death. She thought of doing some violence to herself, but abandoned the notion, knowing she could never go through with it.

Again the maddening question throbbed against her temples. What was she to do? Confess? Confess this to her mother? Never. . . . But what then? Tell Marguerite? Her throat tightened. That would never do, either. Marguerite, and all her promises to help: imagine her not talking! She could well afford to play the sister of mercy, that one. Nobody liked her, nobody would go out with her, except Alphonse who didn't have a job, and she likely gave him money! Marguerite was somebody who knew nothing about life. She probably was just curious, that was why she put on the kindness act. Just so she could spread the story afterwards. Women! she thought, contemptuously. Could a woman help another woman? But who, who was going to help *her*?

She thought of a different way out. She was still young and pretty. Other men besides Jean Lévesque had noticed her. So many of them had paid attention to her at the restaurant! She dwelt a while on this possibility, but the memory of her physical experience renewed her despair.

Until dawn she lay trembling convulsively and weeping with her face in the pillow so as not to waken Marguerite, this enemy who *knew*. Finally a pale sunbeam found its way beneath the lowered blind and into the room. Only then did she stop tossing and turning. She lay quiet, dry-eyed. She felt that she had been submitted to such torture during the night that her heart at last had lost all feeling. Her love for Jean was dead. Her dreams were dead, and with them her youth. At the idea that her youth was dead she felt a last twinge of pain, as slight as a spreading circle on the water which leaves only calm behind.

And indeed she was calm now, with a stupefying peace that went down to the deepest layers of her being. No more memories, an end to joy, an end to all regret. What was left was a passive waiting, contrary to reason, contrary to herself, no longer desperate but still less susceptible to hope: a simple kind of waiting inhabited her spirit, as if it had come to stay.

Her decision was made. Whatever happened, whatever the result, she would never tell anyone. She would allow herself to live, accept what others did to her and around her, and she would wait. For what, she didn't know, but she would wait. She was sustained by a pale and feeble thread of pride at not having given herself away, and also by the thought that she had won time in which to reflect.

The neighbourhood was waking up. She heard wheels bumping along the rough street and bottles rattling in a basket as the milkman passed, then a happy whistled tune and the cheerful sound of trotting hooves. In her heart the need to live in spite of everything found its expression in a stubborn defiance. This was not the end. Because she couldn't have what she wanted, she refused whatever was offered; but there must be miracles, she thought, for people like herself, bold and self-sufficient. Her eyes, heavy with sleep, were fixed on the thin ray of sunlight growing stronger in the room.

TWENTY-FOUR

After Florentine had fled from her parents' home, Azarius returned at around ten o'clock.

"I found just the thing," he said, still in the doorway. "Five rooms, a bathroom and a bit of a balcony. And a little yard in the back to dry your clothes, Rose-Anna. I made the deal. If you want, we can move first thing in the morning."

Rose-Anna had remained slumped over the kitchen table after Florentine left. It took a while for Azarius' words to penetrate her torpor. At first she heard only the sound of his voice, but slowly the words sank in. Her hands moved in the air, as if trying to overcome the sullen weight of inertia. Then, suddenly, she was on her feet, reaching out for support. A gleam of relief lit her brown eyes.

"You're fooling! You found one? You found a house?"

For the moment that was enough. Where was it? How was it? She didn't even think of asking these questions. They had found a shelter, a corner for the family, an exclusive refuge for its joys and sorrows. This in itself was a kind of grace, a touch of order in their disarray. She forced herself to get under way. She now realized to what extent she had been revolted by the notion of sharing a roof with strangers. Their whole way of living exposed to the gaze of outsiders! No, a shed, a barn, any black hole would be better than the torture she had been through for the last hours.

She looked up courageously at Azarius. Energy was coming back to her in rapid, consoling waves. A woman of the working class, she seemed to have an inexhaustible source of energy. Holding the edge of the table, she leaned toward her husband.

"Listen," she said, "why don't we move right now, tonight? It's not too late!"

Azarius looked at her with surprise and, finally, submission. Ever since the night when he had dreamed of running away he had been twice as gentle as before, as if he were trying to pay a heavy and implacable debt to Rose-Anna. And his latest bad luck had inclined him to a kind of passivity toward her orders. More lost than he had ever been, humiliated, hemmed-in, learning at last to hide his thirst for freedom, for a fresh start, he was almost pathetic in his readiness to please her.

"I'd put us down for a truck tomorrow morning, but I don't see why I couldn't get it tonight. I'll go and see right now, if you like. Take me fifteen minutes."

"Go ahead," she said energetically. "If we hurry we can get a few beds up there and sleep without the strangers this very night. That's worth a bit of extra bother. You can always come and get the rest tomorrow morning."

And she added, more softly:

"You know, two families getting up together tomorrow morning – we'd all need the stove and the sink at the same time, it just doesn't make sense. And besides . . ."

She raised her arms and let them fall wearily to her sides.

". . . besides, it's nice to be *home*, Azarius!"

He left at once, and she started in bravely, collecting frying pans, pots and saucepans and packing them in cardboard boxes she had kept ready for the move, first a layer of folded linen, then a row of pots and pans, then another layer of linen. Kneeling on the kitchen floor, she filled one large box, glancing from time to time at the clock. Lord, how slow she was! Often out of breath, she would have to stop and give her heart a rest.

She finally had to admit that she couldn't do it all herself. Much against her will she had to wake the children. Stealthily she opened the dining room door and tiptoed across the room. The privacy of the other family was for her inviolable. She respected it with the same intensity as she protected her own. The boards creaked despite her care, and she cast a compassionate glance at the strangers' children sleeping on chairs put end to end. She was not indifferent to the universality of misfortune, but she was suspicious of pity spread too thin. She was accustomed to shutting off too much concern for others, economizing tenderness and keeping watch on her own impulses of generosity. Charity began at home. Just now her reticence fell away, and her usual reserve, as she spoke to the mother:

"You make yourself at home, now. Just use anything you need. We won't be in the way for long."

She was relieved, as if she had rid herself of her vague burden of resentment.

She went into Philippe's small room and called softly to her children in the dark.

"Get up," she said, "and don't make a sound."

Their eyes blinked and they sat up frightened in their beds. She helped them to dress.

"We're going home," she said.

Her voice in the half-dark was firm and reassuring.

She dressed them all except Gisèle, whom she left to sleep, and took the others out on tiptoe, bringing along their quilts and pillows.

In the kitchen she calmly gave each one his task, not losing a minute about her own work. Kneeling on the floor again she said:

"Yvonne, you're not a butterfingers. Take my best dishes and wrap each one in newspaper. Each one separate, now," she warned.

"And you, my little man," she said to Albert, "don't make a racket and don't bang yourself, and go get Mamma's washtub behind the door."

Lucille, too, wanted a job. Rose-Anna said:

"All right, you can help Yvonne, but mind you don't break things, eh, child?"

They were surprised at this tone of their mother's, so calm and placid, almost grave. Their fears had turned to something like joy. Philippe came home, and his mother didn't even ask him where he had been or frown as she usually did. She quietly told him to go down to the cellar and bring up more boxes. Not a single reproach!

At first the children worked silently, but then, emboldened by their mother's serenity, they began to show their enthusiasm for this midnight move. Their voices rose, and little arguments broke out as they all tried to perform the same task at once. Rose-Anna still didn't get angry. It seemed as if she'd never get angry again! But she was tired, and she did need a little quiet.

"Hey," she said. "Don't make such a racket! This isn't our place anymore."

And with the shade of a tired smile she added:

"Just try to contain yourselves! It won't be long. We'll soon be home."

Home!

That was an old word, one of the first the children had ever learned. You used it without thinking, a hundred times a day. It had meant so many different things! They'd used it once for a dank basement apartment on St. James Street, and again for the three-room place where they had stifled under the roof of a dingy building on St. Antoine. Home was an elastic word and even meaningless at times, for it evoked not a single place but maybe twenty shelters scattered through the neighbourhood. It was rich in regrets and nostalgia, and it always meant uncertainty. It was related to the annual migration. It was coloured by the seasons. It sounded in your heart like an unforeseen departure, a flight, for when you heard it you could imagine that you also heard the shrill cry of migratory birds.

As she said the word, their small faces looked at her, lit up with happiness, but with a shyness too that made them all stop talking at once!

But Rose-Anna, having given them something to dream about, knew that she had to protect them against illusions.

"Now, don't start thinking we're moving to some millionaire's apartment," she said. "There'll be lots of dirty corners to clean out. Remember how dirty it was when we arrived here? You can't expect they'll leave it clean for you." And that reminded her: "Did anybody think about a broom? That's important. We'll be glad to have a broom on hand when we get there. With a little water and a broom you can get rid of the worst dirt you ever saw. I always say, a broom, the first go-off!"

She was not usually very loquacious with her youngest

children. The language established between them was one of unspoken tenderness and friendly scolding, rather than conversation. But this evening, upset by Florentine's departure, she tried to atone by drawing the little ones closer to her. Tonight she felt so lonely that she would have tried to make friends with the least of living creatures.

She talked to them continually, as if they were grownups. Instead of placing herself at their level, she called them up to hers with a kind of tender gravity. She told them astonishing and serious things, looking them straight in the eye. Or she disconcerted them with a word said in passing, thrown away, or a sigh that belonged to the new confidence she placed in them.

"Sure, we've got our troubles," she said. "It's not very nice, moving like this in the middle of the night. But I don't know, just look at other people, we're no worse off than they are. With the war and all, there's some a lot more miserable than we are. Poor folks, and what troubles!"

Then she was silent, wondering if she should tell Azarius tonight about Florentine running away, or if she should leave it until morning. Suddenly she saw that she had done well not to mention the scene, that this was a bad dream that must always remain a secret.

Several boxes were filled now. All together they started on another, kneeling around it in the middle of the kitchen. Rose-Anna felt an urge to stretch her arms around them all, to include them in a single embrace and reassure them.

"Whatever it's like it can't be worse than our last house," she said. "Now that was tight quarters for you. At least we've got more room in the new one. Five rooms, your father said. Maybe there's one for you, Yvonne. We mustn't build castles in Spain, that's a waste of time till we see the place, but five rooms sounds better than here. There's a balcony, your father says. We can put some flowers out there. And a yard, that'll be handy, we'll grow a few vegetables if it's big enough. And like I said, never mind about the dirt. You can always get rid of it somehow."

All this time their busy hands were emptying the cupboards and stripping the walls. The homey atmosphere dissolved. The only things preserving it were the old clock on its ledge trimmed with crepe paper, and a few caps hanging on the wall.

Their best times had always been just before a move.

When Azarius came back, the kitchen was already filled with big boxes tied with cord and piles of utensils. They had the knack of moving swiftly, and could decamp in an hour like gypsies. Ingenious and skilful, they knew how to pack a multitude of objects in easy loads.

Together they began to carry their things to the light truck, with a marvellous kind of tacit agreement on how it was to be done. Philippe and his father carried the heaviest things, one walking backwards, and Rose-Anna looked after the fragile articles, putting them carefully in the depths of the space beneath the tarpaulin. The little children ran behind her, one with the precious kitchen clock in his frail arms, another with a smudged, limp doll she had just spotted under a pile of washing. Albert, grown provident and wise, brought up the rear, tripping under a load of firewood that came right to his chin.

Oh, the strange things that make up a household, and how pitiful they look when exposed in this way one by one, without a house or home!

In the light before the door a group of onlookers and children stood gaping.

"Hey! The Lacasse family's moving! Looks like they're in a hurry."

Rose-Anna heard the remark and blessed the night that covered their departure, obscuring their poor belongings.

Too often had they moved in the light of day, when their yellowed mattresses, rickety chairs with legs in the air, scratched old tables, rusty metal bedsteads, blotched mirrors – all the visible signs of their indigence – took their place in the great procession of families filling the streets each first of May, on the move, their tatters flying in the wind.

At last their most necessary effects were piled in a well-established and traditional order: food in a large basket which Rose-Anna took herself; night clothes in an old suitcase; then the table, the chairs and even the kitchen stove. Rose-Anna had been very firm: "You've got to unload that tonight, right away, Azarius. Late or not. Who knows, tonight or early tomorrow morning we might need hot water."

When the kitchen was almost empty it looked very big and strangely mute to Rose-Anna when she went in alone for a final look. Her pretext was that she wanted to make sure nothing had been forgotten. This was her best guess at the confused feeling that brought her back and held her in this naked room.

Here Eugène had spent his last night before joining up, and this roof would never see him with his family again. Who knew if they would ever see him again? And here Daniel had played his innocent games with his serious face before the illness struck him down. And here, on a cold and grey October dawn, she had discovered she was about to be a mother, at age forty, and for the twelfth time. Here Florentine had looked at her with supplicating eyes.

Florentine! Her first child! Her heart went out to the girl, though she was still filled with anger, doubt and disappointed love. The whole thing didn't make sense. For sure, Florentine would come back, she'd explain. And maybe there was nothing to explain. Rose-Anna clung desperately to that hope. Florentine, as gentle and pious as Yvonne when she was younger, couldn't have done such a thing. Now Rose-Anna was full of regret for her own behaviour. She ripped a leaf from the calendar still hanging on the wall and scribbled with an awkward hand: "We've moved. You can sleep in Philippe's room tonight, and tomorrow I'll send Yvonne or Lucille to the store to show you where we live." She hesitated a second, then wrote: "your mother."

Relieved, she took her coat and hat. Softly she opened the door to the dining room and, without putting a light on, took from the buffet a few pious objects from which she was never separated.

The woman whose name she didn't know shifted in the dark. Rose-Anna, moved, wished her a good night.

"Nobody'll be back tonight except maybe my daughter," she said. "We're leaving now. You're in your home now."

Behind her Azarius entered. He went to Philippe's room and took Gisèle in his arms, wrapping her in a woollen blanket. The three of them, very close together, left the house.

She took the sleeping child on her lap, and Azarius started the truck. The rumbling of the motor echoed to the very depths of her tired brain. She turned to spy through the rear cab window to make sure the children were all in the truck. She saw them standing or perched on the piled-up furniture, silhouetted against the raw light of the arc lamp. Everything she had been able to save from disaster was there, and she felt most of her riches were intact. A twinge of guilt touched her believer's heart: she had doubted divine providence, she had for a time refused to hope. But this regret itself, the moment she felt it, had brought her close again to the One who had been the source of her courage. She laid her hand on Azarius' arm and said softly:

"All right, we can go!"

He drove off quickly, the street dark in front of him. He had never been in the habit of recognizing his own responsibility in his family's poverty, but this midnight flit caught him with his defences down. An emotion he had seldom felt tightened his throat.

He pushed the truck a little too fast, and the tires squealed at the first sharp corner.

Much later that night, when the children were asleep on the mattresses laid on the floor around her, Rose-Anna was awake and wondering: is this a house where people can be happy? She had always thought that some houses had a predisposition to happiness, and others, by a quirk of fate, were destined to shelter nothing but misfortune.

She still hadn't had a good look at it. They had forgotten their light bulbs, and had pitched camp by the flame of Azarius' lighter and many matches.

She hadn't seen the house, but she had had the feel of it, smelled it, touched it and, above all, listened to it.

Shortly after midnight she had felt a long tremor at the approach of a train. She understood at once, and with the courageous goodwill that sustained her, resigned herself to the fact: there was always a drawback. There had to be. Sometimes it was the lack of light, or a factory nearby, or not enough rooms. Here, it was the railroad.

No wonder we got it cheap, she thought. This close to the tracks, you can hardly live in it. I'll never get used to that noise.

But she didn't give up. Not yet. She never gave up that quickly.

You've got to take the good points with the bad, she thought. In the morning I'll see how it really looks. Mustn't see the dark side right away.

Azarius moved beside her. She leaned toward him and laid her hand softly on his arm to see if he was awake.

"You can't sleep?" she asked.

"No."

A long silence; then:

"Are you juggling ideas too?"

He mumbled a vague reply and buried his face in the pillow.

Every moment of every day and night he was able to take the measure of his failure now. Even his family's poverty, which for years he had refused to admit, began to grow famil- iar to him, but like the memory of a companion that one has left behind. Rose-Anna . . . She'd been a young girl at his side, then tired, then overwhelmed, and here she was sleeping beside him on a kind of pallet, on the floor. He could hear whimpers from the children in their sleep.

He rolled and tossed again, and Rose-Anna said:

"Don't think so much. It gets you nowhere. You tire yourself out for nothing."

On her elbow beside him, she began to talk as she did to her children when they couldn't sleep:

"We're still together, Azarius. We've still got our health and strength. What worse can happen to us now? We'll get along, and we'll use our two pairs of arms to do it, believe me. Juggling ideas won't help. That's foolishness!"

She had to stop speaking for a moment. Her baby was very active inside her this last while.

She tried to find a more comfortable position; feeling sleep approach in spite of everything, she said in a voice that was growing heavy:

"Sleep, my poor man. Sleep, if you can. Sleep helps you to think straight. Sometimes a good sleep does the most good."

A little later, at about dawn, when he had fallen asleep at last, she got up courageously to explore their new home. Barefoot, she went from room to room. Then she dressed and put on her shoes.

At six in the morning, when a pale ray of sunshine had made its way through the sooty windows, she had been working for a long time already, on her knees on the floor, damp locks sticking to her forehead, and in front of her a big pail of dirty water.

TWENTY-FIVE

Emmanuel left the train at St. Henri station around nine that Saturday evening. The night air was fresh and pleasant, with distant stars that shone through a lattice of clouds.

It was a warm, languorous evening, pierced regularly by the siren's wail, and perfumed by the biscuit factory. Along with this insipid smell, but very faintly, a whiff of spices rose from the lower regions along the canal and rode on the breeze to this slight elevation in St. Henri.

An evening such as you wouldn't see twice a year in the suburb, and never in the neighbouring areas, which remain unvisited by these odours of spice, these whiffs of illusion. Yet it seemed to Emmanuel that he remembered a host of such evenings in his youth as he wandered these parts. It was an evening when the poor population of spinners, mill hands, puddlers and working women seemed to have deserted their houses with one accord and taken to Notre Dame Street in search of some adventure. Emmanuel, too, had often wandered through such evenings, searching for some undefined joy as spellbinding as the vault of the sky above his head.

He walked to the end of the platform, taking in the familiar sights and smells of the suburb. His village in the big town! For no part of Montreal has kept its well-defined limits or its special, narrow, characteristic village life as St. Henri has done.

Children were playing hopscotch near the station and their shouting pierced through the whistle of the locomotive. It was picking up speed between the tiny fenced-in backyards, the thin trees and the loaded clotheslines, which make up our glimpses, swift and depressing, of the intimacy of poverty as seen from trains when they enter great cities.

Emmanuel saw the steeples of the parish church above the clouds of train smoke. His neighbourhood carried on with its everyday life, indifferent to the constant gaps caused by travel and departures. On Notre Dame the woman from the fruit store was wrapping vegetables. Her busy form went to and fro behind the store window. The vendor of French fries passed with his van drawn by a wretched nag with a long, sad neck. The bookseller nearby was selling cards. In front of The Two Records, passersby slowed down to hear the radio, its voice pervading the street. Housewives were hurrying, hugging large bags of provisions. Above the roofs the switchman in his cabin leaned out from time to time through a sooty window to see the crowd pass by from his bird's-eye vantage point. All the windows were open, and the sounds of living, clattering dishes and conversation floated in the air as if the partitions of the world had been abolished and human life was on display in all its warmth and poverty.

Below sail the flat lighters, the freighters, tankers, the Great Lakes barges, the grey canal boats, bringing St. Henri the smells of all the products of the world: the great pines of the North, tea from Ceylon, spices from the Indies and nuts from Brazil.

Nearby, in the rue du Couvent, St. Henri also shelters a life that is closed and provincial behind a certain grill: that of its nuns, who file past two by two when the parish church bells ring the forty hours devotion or Sunday vespers.

In daytime there is the pitiless reality of labour. But at night there is this village life, when chairs are pulled out to the sidewalk or people sit on door-sills and the talk passes from one threshold to the next.

St. Henri: ant-heap village!

Emmanuel, who had travelled now and matured rapidly in a few months, returned to the suburb with the clear eyes of an observer. He saw St. Henri as he had never seen it, with its complex yet open weave. He liked it all the more, as we like our village after returning from some expedition, simply because everything is still in its familiar place, and everyone says hello!

In high spirits, he slung his duffle bag to his shoulder and was on his way.

What an evening! he said to himself, as we sometimes congratulate ourselves on the weather or our own good humour.

Then he stopped, uncertain. On store fronts and street corners he could see the news bulletins bearing the brave, pathetic orders of the day from General Gamelin to the French troops:

*Defend your positions
to the death.*

He was suddenly plunged back into the absurd. Scenes of blood and suffering appeared before his eyes. For a moment he ceased to see the tails of smoke that rose so straight from the chimneys into the clear sky. He ceased to breathe easily, as if the air had thickened. A subtle malaise that hung over the suburb became perceptible to him. He noticed the gravity of the workers, their lunch boxes under their arms, their caps pulled down, going about their business with more anxious looks than usual, as if concerned over a disaster without yet perceiving that it could touch their lives. At the same time Emmanuel noticed how few young men were strolling the main street, and how many of those were in uniform.

Frowning, he went on his way. He came to the Five and Ten store, and thought of Florentine. He stopped a moment to glance in at the restaurant, but the crowd was so thick around the counter that he couldn't see her. He would have loved to go in and speak to her. But in that crowd, he thought, how could I get a word in? Then he considered waiting outside until closing time, which was not far off. But he was dusty from his trip, and thought a wash wouldn't hurt before seeing her. He flushed with pleasure and went on toward his home, whistling *Amapola*, which the nickelodeons were blaring as he passed. His whistling turned to the kind of stubborn reassurance to force one's good humour or persuade oneself that all is well.

Ten minutes later he was hugging his mother and his sister Marie. His duffle bag dumped on the living room floor, he showed them pictures of his regiment. While they passed the snaps around and tried to pick him out of the groups, he slipped away to his room. It looked out on the square, and the trees, not far from his window, were full of the chirping of birds. The fountain sang its liquid song.

Emmanuel leaned out the window and took a deep breath of air perfumed by lilacs; then turned to his ablutions. As he shaved, he thought affectionately of this small room, and wondered at the pleasure he felt at being in it. Only last year he couldn't wait to get away, execrating the insipidity of civilian life. Now this room was thoroughly pleasing. His ties were hanging from a ring in an orderly way, bright ties, gifts from his sister, which he had thought ugly. He wished he could wear one tonight; maybe the blue one with the polka dots or the red one with black stripes. He noticed his pipes in their rack on the dresser, and found it odd that he used to smoke a pipe – when he was very, very young! About eighteen, in fact!

There were so many things, so many memories, that took him by surprise as he touched a pipe or an ashtray that still gave off the musty smell of cold tobacco, or a snapshot of himself stuck in the mirror frame. How ridiculous he looked, there in the country, with his naive and miserable air! What a boring young man he must have been!

He returned to the window, still whistling *Amapola* which he couldn't get out of his mind, then, suddenly serious, went to the mirror of his clothes cupboard and began to examine his face. Florentine! Would she like him? Would she see anything pleasant in these features he was inspecting so critically? Would she see from them that he was sincere, very fond of her, and above all miserable without her?

He saw himself as one sees a stranger. His mouth was thin and serious. A certain shyness made him look younger than he would have liked. But in the lights of his grey-blue eyes passed shades of thoughtfulness, of boldness, of sadness. A lock of blonde hair fell over his forehead. He pushed it back impatiently and tried several ways of combing his hair to make himself look older.

Then he went again to the window and leaned his elbows on the sill. Florentine! He was torn between the desire to run to her and the desire to stay here and dream about her in the soft spring air. When had he started loving her?

Was it the first time he had seen her in the restaurant? Or when he danced with her until they were out of breath? Or in the army camp when, in the evening, she would appear in the clouds of cigarette smoke that hung in the canteen? Little by little she had become for him a familiar ghost, when, broken with fatigue, he would stretch out on his narrow bunk for hours, his eyes closed. Oh, Florentine! Had he been wrong about her all those evenings when he had, in his fancy, danced with her, chatted with her, explored the city with her, eaten and laughed with her! Did she correspond to his dreams, to the strange creature who had haunted his hours of boredom; or was she quite different, and would he have to teach her to love him? The Florentine of his dreams loved him already. She followed him in every step taken by his thoughts. But the live Florentine? . . .

Downstairs in the living room Marie Létourneau's soft laughter could be heard from time to time. Emmanuel listened for this fresh, delicious laugh that was his sister's. She almost never laughed. Perhaps it was his arrival that brought about the change, and she was trying to keep him in the house with her gaiety, becoming quite a different person. His heart went out to her with infinite fondness. Yet he knew that, though he had just come home and despite the affection he felt for his sister and mother, he was already impatient to go out. It was as if he had only one evening of happiness ahead of him, and in that evening he had to spend a treasure of emotion to last a lifetime.

Finished at last with his toilette, he went down the stairs four at a time. With a quick, embarrassed "Good night" he was outside, and felt as if he had escaped from a prison. Oh, a pleasant prison, to be sure, but one that got on his nerves at times. Rid of his heavy bag, he took off at a fast clip. The

GABRIELLE ROY

thought that his mother might find out where he had headed for annoyed him for a moment. Then he thought she would have to know some day, promised himself that he would speak to her at the first opportunity, and brushed off the thought with a toss of his head.

His stride was lithe and rapid. His condition had improved with military life. His head was now held straighter.

As he reached Beaudoin Street he was happy, self-assured. For his first visit to Florentine, marking the beginning of their new relationship, it seemed appropriate to appear at her home, like a serious suitor. He smiled at these words, which had always inspired him with an unholy terror.

He recognized the house, though he had been there only once, on the morning – how he remembered it! – when he had brought Florentine, half asleep, home from Mass. He knew the house, indeed, but saw for the first time that it was a very small, very poor house. The discovery enriched his love: how could she live in such a place, spruce and vibrant as she was!

He found no bell, grew impatient, and began to knock. He stuck out his chin and ran his finger around beneath his tunic collar. His forehead broke out in a light sweat. He wiped it self-consciously and smiled at himself and his nervousness.

A woman, tired and nervous, opened the door.

No, the Lacasse family didn't live here anymore. They moved. No, she didn't know where to. Maybe her husband knew. Yes, she could ask him.

After a long wait she came back with an address scribbled on a piece of brown paper. Emmanuel took it and left, stammering his thanks. He had trouble finding the new house, but passersby directed him to a blind alley opening on the rue du Couvent. No sidewalk led to the building. It was stuck right beside the railway tracks, a hundred yards from the station. From the platform's end where he had stood, thought Emmanuel, he had been a stone's throw from Florentine's house.

He didn't know at first if he should try the front door. The soot from the railway was so thick, it looked as if this door hadn't been used for months. But he tried his luck, and shortly after Rose-Anna came hurrying out.

She recognized him, though she hadn't seen him since the days when she was a cleaning woman for the Létourneaus. Her face lit up.

"Oh! It's you, Monsieur Emmanuel!" she said.

She was dressed in an ample housecoat and there were streaks of dust on her face.

She wanted him to come in and sit down. She insisted, leading the way into the only room she had managed to brighten up and make inviting. Here the portraits of the ancestors and saints recreated an atmosphere that had been resuscitated a dozen times. He couldn't refuse this mark of politeness and esteem, but all the time he was sitting there he suffered from uncertainty on the one point that interested him. Finally Rose-Anna broached the subject.

"Was it to see Florentine?" she asked, catching his eye.

Emmanuel nodded quickly, with a smile.

"She's not back yet," she said, and looked down.

There was silence between them. Rose-Anna, disappointed, was trying to find a way to explain her daughter's strange conduct without hurting the young man's feelings, and especially without putting him off. But how could she say that Florentine now came home only to eat and sleep, and that even then she kept the most frightful silence? How could she tell him that Florentine was no longer the carefree, happy girl he had met one evening? Yet she could read in his face such frankness, such strength of character, that she felt ready to confess many things to him that she would never have told her own husband. And perhaps Emmanuel could give back gaiety to Florentine. Maybe he was the one she missed so much, without really knowing it. Because Florentine had really told her nothing the day she ran away. And when she returned the next day she merely said she had been too tired and nervous to know what she was doing.

Rose-Anna felt a faint glimmer of hope.

"Did you try at the store?" she asked. "She may be working later than usual. It's Saturday, you know. . . ."

He smiled, knowing she couldn't have stayed so late at the restaurant. Rose-Anna tried something else:

"Sometimes she spends the night with her girlfriend, Marguerite L'Estienne. Maybe that's where she's gone tonight. Sometimes they go to a movie together, or they go for a walk, I suppose, when the weather's fine."

She stopped, embarrassed at the idea that Emmanuel must find it strange, her not knowing where her own daughter was. Partly to change the subject, to thank him for his visit and show how it had pleased her, and partly to express the esteem in which she held the Létourneau family, she began to ask news of each of them.

"Your sister Marie, and your mother, I hope they're well? Please tell them I've not forgotten them."

"And they haven't forgotten you," replied Emmanuel warmly, not thinking much about what he said; of all that Rose-Anna had told him he had remembered just one thing: Florentine must be with her friend Marguerite.

He stood up without rushing his departure but with an impatience so obvious that Rose-Anna understood and didn't prolong the parting. She accompanied him to the door and repeated, rather awkwardly, her good wishes for his family. Then, as country folk do, she stayed in the doorway a moment watching him go, and called after him:

"Now you know the way, come and see us. You may have better luck next time."

Suddenly she remembered her farewell to Azarius long ago, when she had been leaning like this on the door frame, calling into the wind which bent all the weeds in the yard:

"You can come back, now you know the way. . . ."

She was so moved that she went inside hurriedly, blinded by she knew not what regret or what small surge of youth.

Emmanuel had almost disappeared, kicking up the gravel of the path with his heavy boots. At the intersection of the railway tracks with the rue du Couvent he stopped to reflect. Then his decision was made. He walked toward St. Zoé alley, for he recalled a Marguerite L'Estienne in that distant part of the suburb. Perhaps she was the friend of Florentine's. As he hurried along he felt a growing anguish. What if he had to spend his whole evening without Florentine at his side? He had so little time. Two weeks' leave were soon over. Every minute had to count double.

Marguerite was not at home. Her aunt didn't know where she had gone.

In his heart Emmanuel had dreaded this moment, knowing well that cold reason would get the better of him and assail him with a host of doubts: after such a brief friendship, could Florentine still care for him? Hadn't she made other friends in his absence?

He wandered down Notre Dame, exposing himself to doubts like an undefended land. But he no sooner gave up hope than he returned and clung to it again. In a way he was certain that he would see her this very evening. He stared at the girls out walking in groups, then limited his inspection to those with boys. He chewed over Rose-Anna's words until he fancied he had found a hesitation hinting that Florentine was out with someone else. He thought of Jean Lévesque and frowned. The way those two nagged each other, could they be friends? But such things happened. People continually at each other's throats, hurting each other, but irresistibly attracted. Yet she was so proud, and Jean so biting and sarcastic – it was impossible. And anyway, Jean had written a note to say he'd left St. Henri for good, and was going to work at Saint-Paul-l'Ermite. He had added in English as a P.S., "*Out for the big time!*"

Emmanuel arrived on the hump of St. Henri. His walk had made him thirsty. He hurried toward The Two Records.

TWENTY-SIX

Several men were standing in the middle of the restaurant, motionless and silent. Others, leaning on the counter, forgot to smoke their pipes. The radio was bringing news of the war. Very often these days regular programs were interrupted by bulletins with the latest happenings. There had just been a break in a program of light music and the announcer's voice came on. After a short newscast the music began again. The listeners relaxed and several began to talk, when a hollow voice rose in a kind of lament:

"Poor France!"

Emmanuel lit a cigarette feverishly. He wanted to forget these concerns, at least during his leave. He frowned, puffed too quickly at his cigarette, seemingly in the grip of some violent emotion.

The man who had just spoken was beside him, his elbows on the counter, his face in his fists. He straightened up slowly as if his shoulders bore more than their own weight. Emmanuel, seeing his face, recognized Azarius Lacasse, who had done some repairs around his parents' house. Emmanuel held out his hand with the easy cordiality that won people's confidence.

"Monsieur Lacasse, I'm Emmanuel Létourneau," he said. "I'm a friend of Florentine's."

Azarius looked up, surprised to hear his daughter's name. His only reply was, "Things look bad, eh? Poor France. Poor France."

He seemed deeply moved. This strange man, who had looked on at the downfall of his family without admitting his own defeat, this lazy man, this unstable dreamer, as people said, seemed close to despair because in a distant country that he knew only by hearsay the fate of armies was being decided in a bloody battle.

When he said "France," the word took on a familiar tone, but it was an incantation too, a combination of an everyday reality with some rare and prodigious marvel.

"A beautiful country, France."

"How would you know?" scoffed the young usher from the Cartier movie house. "Have you been there?"

He never missed a chance to pick a fight with Azarius who had reproached him once for not being in the army.

"How do I know?" said Azarius in a strong, rich voice, without a trace of anger. "How do you know the sun is good? Because according to the asterologists it's billions of miles away and you still feel its warmth every day, and see its light, eh? And the stars, those little pinholes to hell and gone out there! Thousands and thousands of miles away, you can still see their light on a good dark night!"

He was in his stride now, his voice swelling with an unpolished, natural lyric strain:

"France," he said, "is like the sun and the stars. It may be far away, maybe we never saw it. We're French from France but we left. France, we don't really know what France is. No more than we know what the sun and the stars may be. Except it gives off light day and night. Day and night," he repeated.

He looked down at his idle hands with the astonishment he always felt at seeing them so white and soft and useless, then he raised them in a dramatic gesture.

"If France should disappear," he said, "it'd be as bad, you might say, for the world as if the sun fell down."

There was silence. All these men, even the most unfeeling, loved France. Across the centuries they had kept a mysterious and tender attachment for the land of their origin, a vague but constant nostalgia that was seldom expressed but was as close to them as their tenacious faith and their language with its naive beauty. But it surprised them to hear the simple truth expressed by one of themselves; it embarrassed them even, as if someone had obliged them to bare themselves to each other.

Emmanuel had followed Azarius' speech with astonishment at first, then with a surge of sympathy. Finally he felt a certain reservation, knowing that this patriotic outburst didn't satisfy his own thirst for justice. He stood thoughtfully aside, as a few of the older men came over to Azarius and one of them clapped him on the back and cried:

"Well said, Lacasse!"

Behind the counter Sam Latour was scratching the back of his neck, more deeply moved than he would have liked to admit, and without knowing it filled with the same vibrant pride he felt each year during the St. Jean Baptiste Day speeches.

"Yeah, and all that don't help much," he said, trying to bring the conversation back to more comfortable ground. "It's just too bad they didn't get ready for war instead of stickin' their heads in the sand. What did I tell you, Lacasse? I said their Imaginot Line wasn't up to much! Imaginot, Imaginot! Sounds like imagination, and that's about what it amounted to."

"In the first place, it's not Imaginot, just Maginot," said Azarius. "That was the name of the engineer that drew it up, a fellow called Maginot."

"It's still an imagination."

"Could be. But that's not here nor there," said Azarius. "A fort is just a fort. It's not the country. A country, now, that's somethin' else. It don't mean the country's finished just because a fort blows up."

He was getting the oratorical urge again, and the agreeable feeling of swaying his audience. He turned, not as if he were addressing a group of idlers but replying to the murmur of an immense crowd.

"It's not the end of France," he said.

"I told you their Imaginot Line wasn't worth a dang," Latour began again. "I told you, it's like me here behind the counter. You've only got to come around the end . . ."

And he went through his familiar demonstration. But Azarius interrupted him almost violently:

"It's not the end of France. Every time France went down she came up brighter and better than ever. It's not the first time we've seen her hour of danger. We've seen that in history. But in that hour of danger there's always been somebody to lead her to victory. In the old days she had Joan of Arc. Then she had Napoleon. And don't forget Marshal Foch in the last war. Who's it going to be this time? We don't know, but he'll be there. In her hour of danger France has always had her liberator."

He stopped to wet his lips and look around for approval. But the men were reacting against the emotion he had aroused in them, and in a mood for joking.

"By golly, you've got your history down pat, Lacasse," boomed Latour. "You been goin' to night school?"

The men laughed.

"What do you know! Where's he find time to study?"

"He sure learned his lessons!"

"Oh, I read a little. I learn a bit," said Azarius curtly.

His disappointed, nostalgic gaze fell on Emmanuel.

"You're lucky," he said. "You've got the youth and the uniform and the weapons to go and fight."

"Hey, you're talkin' like the old man of the tribe," said Latour. "You're not a dang day older than I am."

"I'm no spring chicken anymore," said Azarius. There was a sudden break in his voice.

But almost at once he drew himself up and faced Emmanuel, as if to measure himself against him. His blue eyes were flaming.

"I salute you!" he said loudly, and went out.

Emmanuel left the restaurant shortly after him.

He had been moved by Azarius' words, and intrigued by the man's complex personality. Apparently he had never been able to provide properly for his family, yet he radiated strength and conviction. Emmanuel suspected that curiosity had played a role in his emotion. As thinking of Florentine's father was a way of being near her, he tried to define the impression Azarius had made on him.

He felt that he had come away with a fine and generous idea, but he also perceived that it could be dangerous and he hesitated to make it his own. Of course, he too loved France. Like all young French-Canadians educated in colleges that had remained true to French culture (without always doing it justice), he had absorbed certain conservative ideas: the survival of the race, fidelity to ancestral traditions, the cult of the national anniversary. All these were fossilized rituals that had nothing, it seemed to him, that might appeal to or nourish the imagination of youth or even exalt their courage. His father, for example, fervent nationalist that he was, had done all he could to dissuade Emmanuel from taking arms and flying to the defence of that France which he pretended meant so much to him.

Yet Emmanuel too had been an adherent of this national cult, which at that time seemed to be undergoing some rejuvenation. Perhaps he, like Azarius, had wanted to go beyond mere fidelity to the past. Even when he was young he had perceived the glory and beauty of the living France of today. He loved France, he loved humanity, he was distressed by the suffering of the conquered peoples, but he knew that suffering had existed before the war, and that there are means other than war to relieve it.

Despite his tender nature he was more open to justice than to pity, and wasn't sure whether the slow martyrdom of China or the frightful poverty of India didn't revolt him more than the invasion of France. It was at this point, tangled in these difficult considerations, that he lost sight of the impulse he had obeyed when he volunteered to fight. But it irritated him to reduce all these questions to how they affected him, and he rebelled. He knew the time would come when he would have to channel his thoughts into something that would be his own truth, his undeniable truth. But not tonight. He wanted first to enjoy a few days of relaxation, and his thoughts of Florentine consoled him.

Walking aimlessly, he found himself several times in the rue du Couvent, a few steps from the Lacasse house, but he didn't dare to knock again for fear of being a bother to Rose-Anna.

At eleven o'clock a fresh hope occurred to him and he went to lie in ambush outside the Cartier theatre. He scrutinized some thirty movie-goers as they came out. Suddenly a young girl seemed, from behind, to be the image of Florentine, and he went up to her holding out both hands. She turned around and saw a man so disappointed that she broke into peals of laughter.

He gave up his search, reproaching himself for mistaking the girl for Florentine. Now that he thought about it, she didn't resemble her at all, she wasn't the least bit pretty, and he'd have liked to admit his mistake to Florentine and laugh about it with her. But how was Florentine, really? Did he know her at all? Was she naturally happy? Was she sad? Hot-tempered or gentle? Pretty hot-tempered, he thought, remembering her anger with Jean and himself in the restaurant. But all those coarse men around her! And that awful job! How tiring it must be! He tried to recall her features, shutting his eyes to see her as she had been at the Five and Ten that day. His other meetings with her had added nothing to that vision.

Since that first day his picture of her had been precise and clear: the straight nose, the ardent eyes, the fine skin of her cheeks, almost transparent, and even the little vein in her neck that swelled at the slightest emotion. He remembered a remark of Jean's: "She's too thin." No, he thought, she's delicate, very delicate. He loved this word, which for him was the very definition of Florentine. It would be the first one he would use in trying to describe her to a friend. He repeated it to himself as he walked. It broke his heart to think of the wretched quarters of the Lacasse family, and of Rose-Anna sitting opposite him, so gentle and resigned. She must have been slim and pretty too once upon a time, he thought.

As for Florentine, "That's no place for her," he said aloud. He thought of the noisy, common bazaar that was Notre Dame Street, and the house covered with soot, shunted up beside the railway. "It's no place for her," he repeated, as if by protesting against her fate he might succeed in altering it.

From every store, wide open on his way, a strong, metallic voice escaped into the street. A word was lost between shops, but from one to the other the same voice continued, disconnectedly. A hundred radios, behind and in front of him, stuttered out their fragments of news, trying to remind him of the world's agony. He heard them but refused to listen, shutting out this invasion of shadows, of terror, accepting only isolated words which, devoid of sense, still horrified him.

He was too impulsive to dwell long on today's disappointment. I'll see her tomorrow. Tomorrow! he thought. And the word filled him with a tantalizing anxiety. He would have liked the night to be over, and then he thought it was perhaps better that he hadn't seen Florentine at once on his arrival. This way, all his joy was still to come, his store of joy was intact, untouched.

Tomorrow, he said to himself, calling on his patience. But he knew that his patience wouldn't last. Going home, at any rate, was out of the question. His mother would want to know, "And how did you spend your evening, dear?" and grate on his disappointment. He might then confess how he had gone out for nothing, and she would scold him gently, saying (and how sure he was of her words!), "But for goodness sakes, Manuel! You could have the pick of the most distinguished girls in St. Henri!"

"Distinguished" was a word she often used. He smiled. Was Florentine distinguished? Of course not. She was a poor girl from a poor suburb, with crude expressions at times, and gestures that were wrong. She was better than distinguished: she was life itself, with her knowledge of poverty and her revolt against it, with her long, floating hair and her little stubborn nose and her odd expressions – hard truths at times.

No, the more he thought about it, the less he believed his mother would approve his choice. A pity, but it didn't change his mind. Yet he wasn't ready to confront the opposition of his family. He couldn't stand anything tonight that would thwart his mood.

What then? Look up an old friend? He couldn't think of one that he really wanted or needed to see. They all seemed to live on a different planet now. He was too upset and angry with these young people who, with a war on, continued their lives as if nothing had happened, preoccupied by their petty personal quarrels.

Tonight he felt a desire to probe the mysterious troubling depths of his anxiety, since he had been unable to forget it. He had the feeling that he would derive more benefit from talking to the first person he met than from some long discussion with people from his own world. He believed that he and the workers he had seen tonight were pursuing their paths with the same burdensome enigma on their minds. Within himself too many things were still unexplained. He had always felt this desire to penetrate the soul of the masses, but never with such intensity. It was as if by coming nearer to the working class, staying in its midst, he was continuing his search for Florentine, a search that would lead him to a better understanding of her and break down the obstacles that lay between them. Yes, he wanted to hear a voice tonight that spoke Florentine's language.

Suddenly he thought of his old school chums on St. Ambroise Street, the ones who gathered at Ma Philibert's place. He saw their faces marked by disappointment and hardship. How could he have forgotten them, the first friends? He had known them and their shivering poverty since he was a child, and had seen them as a living reproach raised up between himself and a certain kind of comfortable life with which he might otherwise have been quite satisfied. Now, as he thought of the divergent paths he and they had followed, he was curious, in a melancholy way, to know what had become of them. He thought: It's easy to predict a future for Jean. When you're not hampered by scruples, you succeed. But what about Alphonse and Pitou and Boisvert?

TWENTY-SEVEN

The restaurant door was wide open. The walls, darkened by smoke, were visible with their cobwebbed corners. The place seemed empty and gloomy. It was not until Emmanuel went inside that he saw Alphonse sitting motionless in his usual spot by the unlit stove. His feet were up on a second chair, and his hands were clasped behind his neck. He seemed to have been staring glumly for hours at some invisible point.

"Alphonse! How are things?" he asked, laying his hand lightly on the other's shoulder.

Behind the drape that concealed the back room he could hear Ma Philibert puttering around. At about eleven o'clock she began making supper for her husband who came home from the factory at midnight. A cabbage boiling in the kitchen filled the restaurant with its pungent smell.

Emmanuel turned a chair so that he could sit astride it facing Alphonse.

"Keeping warm, eh?" he joked, nodding at the cold stove.

Alphonse opened his eyes a little wider, then half closed them again as if the light were intolerable.

"A stove's always company, lit or not lit," he said.

He reached out a hand for a cigarette, waited patiently without budging while Emmanuel gave him a light, then shifted his weight on the chair.

"The winter's over, you know," said Emmanuel, laughing.

"You don't say!" said Alphonse, and fell silent again.

"Where are the other guys?" asked Emmanuel.

"No idea."

Then he began to laugh, a hurt, ironic laugh.

"You mean you haven't seen Boisvert?"

"No, I just got home."

"Well, you missed something."

His tone, loaded with implications, usually got him an attentive hearing. But as Emmanuel didn't encourage him, he lapsed into a semblance of hostile silence, which lasted too long for his taste. He cast with fresh bait.

"*There's* a guy who's doing all right out of this war."

"Yeah?"

"Yeah, with bells on. He's got a job, and new shoes, a new hat, a watch with a six-month guarantee, and Eveline into the bargain. If you hear bells ringin' tomorrow or next day, that's his wedding. Monsieur Boisvert will be coming down the big aisle with Mademoiselle Rochon of the Five and Ten store hung around his neck for the rest of his life. She's one helluva protection against conscription. The guy's protected from head to foot. He's even taken out accident insurance. In case somebody walks on his corns while he's crossin' the street. Some kind of a child prodigy, that kid. And that's how he'll be his whole life, if he lives to be eighty. Don't you remember? A little snotnose, bummin' cigarettes right an' left, and when he had some, 'What's yours is mine and what's mine's my own.' He shoulda been a capitalist. 'They're mine,' he'd say. 'If you want cigarettes, buy some. Do like I do. I earn mine.' A guy can go far, you know, with ideas like that."

"So he has a job, at last!" said Emmanuel.

"Yeah, and you'd think he was the first guy in the world ever had one. My office this, my office that, my desk, my pen, all my things. . . . He's up to his neck in figures, morning till night. And when he wants a rest from that after work, he calculates down to the penny what his weddin' goin' to cost. Boisvert's buyin' his household at fifty cents a month, the way you buy prunes. Fifty cents on the fridge, fifty cents on the iron, fifty cents on the clothesline and fifty cents on the ring. He even knows what it's going to cost him five years from now to get his pinstripe cleaned, and it's not even out of the tailor shop yet. If you want a three-lesson course in how to succeed in life and get married on ten bucks a week, go see Boisvert. He's got it all written down in a little book. A real case, he is. A small-time Rockefeller with three dimes to his name."

Emmanuel laughed heartily. He suspected that Alphonse had tried to borrow some money from Boisvert and had been turned down.

"And what about Pitou?"

"Dunno. That gang's too fast for me."

"Well then, what about yourself?"

"You can see, eh? All alone in the boat. The last of the unemployed. The last of his kind. A real curiosity!"

Clowning, enjoying his own phrase, he repeated:

"All alone in the boat."

"Come on," said Emmanuel. "You're nuts! A guy never had a better chance than nowadays."

"Just listen to him talk!" said Alphonse. "A real little gent!"

He pulled his knees up to his chin, sat up awkwardly, with grimaces of pain, rubbed his hips and wagged his head like an old man. The wail of a siren came from the distance. He stood up.

"Buy me a coke, why don't ya?" he whined. Then he changed his mind.

"No," he said, "let's get outa here. The old lady's gonna turn up any minute and kick me out. There's no puttin' up with her now her handsome little Pitou don't come around to serenade her anymore. And she's started asking questions, like when's a guy gonna pay up. Now I ask you! Come on," he growled as Emmanuel pulled back the drape and said a few words to Ma Philibert. "You want to hear me talk, eh?" he said from the middle of the room. "All right, you're gonna hear me talk."

Once outside he seemed to have forgotten that Emmanuel was there. He dragged along, his leg still asleep, flexing his knee like a drunk. As they passed near St. Zoé Street he seemed to realize where they were, and cried:

"Hey! Not in there! I don't want to see old Guitte just now!"

"Guitte? Guitte who?"

"Marguerite L'Estienne. You know, I drop in at the Five and Ten too sometimes. You musta seen her when you went to say how de doo to your girlfriend, *la belle* Florentine!"

"Lay off Florentine," Emmanuel said curtly.

"Okay, okay, I didn't say nothin'," cried Alphonse. He added boastfully:

"I was supposed to take old Guitte to the movies t'night and pay her the treat. Didn't find the cash. She may still be waitin', for all I know."

"I'll bet she won't wait a second time," said Emmanuel.

"It's funny, though," Alphonse replied, "there's women, they don't like to be too certain of a guy. But she's a good, big old girl, our Guitte. I wouldn't mind so much if she hadn't lent me all that money. Look, she bought me this hat! And the shoes too, I think."

"Aw, shut up!" said Emmanuel.

They walked along in silence. Then Alphonse pointed to a lighted attic room on St. James Street.

"Hey," he said, "my dad's on his little stint in town!"

"Your father? That's right. He's the only family you've got left. Don't think I ever saw him."

"One thing you missed," sighed Alphonse. "My dad's a character, he's a real character."

He asked for another cigarette.

"I'll pay you back all at once," he said, "and the dollar, and the drinks . . ." He stopped for a light, looking curiously at his hands which were trembling. "Say, have you ever been at the dump?"

"The dump!"

"Yeah, the one at Point St. Charles."

"Never."

"No, eh?"

He smiled oddly, and suddenly launched into a morbid, astonishing story which Emmanuel at first thought was a complete fabrication.

"I knew a guy," Alphonse began, "he'd built up a little business at the dump. He picked up all the old pots and pans and he fixed them up and straightened them out and then he sold them to an old Jew. Sure, it wasn't a big business. Some weeks there wasn't much old metal, but sometimes there'd be whole truckloads of lard pails and my buddy, there, he'd have a good day.

"He had a room in town. But there's thieves on the dump, just like any place else. So this guy built a summer cottage right on the dump, so he could keep an eye on his stuff. Those days there was a whole village in that place, a collection of shacks about the size of a dog kennel. You didn't need a building permit and you didn't have to look far for boards. I tell you, you can't believe all the material there was at that dump. There was bed frames and sheets of galvanized iron, and heavy cardboard, not too dirty. You'd dig around there and pick whatever you needed, bits of pipe, four sheets of tin for the roof, and you chose a lot where it didn't stink too bad, right down by the water. You know, there's people ready to pay a thousand dollars to have a cottage and their Sunday visit down by the river. The guys at the dump, they had all that for nothin', except the Sunday visit. And the quiet! You gotta go a long way to find quiet like at the dump. Just like a grave-yard, sweet death well-buried. You didn't hear nothin' at night but the rats goin' at the rotten garbage, and runnin' off with the big chunks of old meat. You left the city behind, the city an' its relief cheques and a bunch of tramps lining up for their bread tickets and all the racket about God knows what, and the streetcars goin' clingety clang and the big cars spoutin' fumes at you as if you had the plague. An' you had no more smoke there, nothin', you were right at home.

"Well, to get back to my handyman friend, there, the guy had ended up havin' a pretty nice life. He didn't owe a cent to nobody, he didn't cost the city a cent. And he was bringin' up a kid in town, doin' pretty good by him. Then whattaya think? The city health officers come for a peek at the dump – it seems some poor devil was found dead all alone in his shack and the rats got at him – and do you know what they did, Létourneau? Those gentlemen from the health office, comin' down to the dump holdin' their noses with both hands?"

Alphonse wiped his forehead.

"Well they set fire to the whole village. They set fire to it, Manuel. They burned the whole shebang, the doghouses, the old mattresses, the bugs . . ."

He was breathing rapidly, as if exhausted by telling his story.

"But when you're used to country air you always come back. The guys built that damn village up again. Not one shack less, not one shack more. Just like before. Same chimneys as big as a flower pot on the roofs. Same pots on the fire inside. And all those thin cats that came back when the people did, from all the places where they didn't get fed right – great big fightin' cats! And maybe you won't believe it, but flowers started growin' in front of the shacks. I suppose it was seeds that came on the wind. An' you can say what you like," he said defiantly, "it's not such a bad life down in that country – an' it is another country! It's not the same country at all! You run your business real quiet, nobody bothers you, and Saturday nights if you don't know what to do with yourself and you miss people and that other country, why you just go into town and make the rounds of society. You pay a visit to the people in the other country!"

Emmanuel was silent; he had no doubts about the truth. He was embarrassed at having been admitted so deeply into Alphonse's life without being able to help him.

"Alphonse," he said, "why don't you join up? A guy forgets his little troubles once he's in the army."

"His *little* troubles!" repeated Alphonse.

They were just arriving at the St. James Street tunnel. Alphonse tossed away his cigarette. He stopped in the light of a green lamp burning in a niche of the wall behind a wire grill, casting a glaucous pool on the sweating concrete. Alphonse's dark locks were dishevelled by the wind, which rushed into this underground burrow. His face appeared to Emmanuel striped with black, as if he were behind bars.

"Listen, Manuel Létourneau," he said, "I'm going to tell you another story. Believe it or not." He gave a stifled laugh and went on. "One fine day, after I heard you make your very fine speech, I went to join up too. Yes, me. The very next day it was, if I remember right. In any case, it was with a bunch of recruits goin' through St. Henri. There was the drum, and the best-lookin' guys up front and the poor bastards in the back. You musta seen that, eh? They put the tough guys in front and then at the back the guys that're draggin' their feet, they don't show so much. Not a bad trick!"

"I didn't know. Why didn't you tell me?" interrupted Emmanuel.

Alphonse shrugged irritably.

"Anyway, there I was on the sidewalk, stickin' up like a fencepost, lookin' smart as hell, I don't think. I stood on one foot, then the other, tryin' to unfreeze part at a time, when all of a sudden I see this gang arrive. The drum was drumming and the fine fellows up front were flappin' their wings and you'd have thought they were gonna dig a gold mine or find a new Klondike at the end of the world or somethin' better yet. 'By gum,' I says to myself, 'it's a long time since you've seen boys as well fed and dressed, 'Phonsie. Why don't you try it yourself?' I says. And that's how I ended up in the gang with the rest of the jobless.

"There was one guy right beside me, and he winks at me, eh? Well, I winked right back. I don't like a guy that makes friends all that fast, but what the heck, when you're takin' a stroll that could end up God knows where, you've gotta be a bit sociable with the guys swarmin' alongside, right? I guess the wink said, 'I fall, you pick me up. You fall, I pick you up.' Kind of a bargain. Funny when I think about it, how fast you can make a bargain with guys that don't give a damn."

"Go on," said Emmanuel.

"I'm just getting to the best part. No sooner have I got this buddy in the army, but they get us liftin' one foot, then the other, and left, right, you catch on fast. Then away we go like the devil as far as the barracks. What a bunch of nuts! And we picked up more the farther we went. Around Atwater alone we picked up three or four, I think. You know, once you're in, you can't wait for some other sucker to join too. I couldn't be happy that day unless I saw a lineup behind me as long as the railway and then some. I'd turn around sometimes to see how big our gang was gettin' but it was never enough to suit me. I couldn't understand those guys that stayed on the sidewalk just watchin' us go by. 'Come on in,' I says to them, 'it's lonesome as hell in our business unless you got the whole earth lined up on your side.' But the little guy beside me, the winker, he wasn't lonely, not a bit. He was a good-lookin' little guy too, all curly haired and healthy, fat cheeks and not a hair on his face. He never stopped singin' the whole time. 'Save your strength,' I says to him, 'you're gonna run out of songs before we find a place to sit down.' But if you ever saw a kid proud to play the man, he was the one. We turned a windy corner and the wind got into our rags fit to whip them off our backs, and there's my little guy shoutin' into my ear, 'Hey, bud, there's a future in the army!'

"On the other side there was an old guy marching, all wrapped up in the wind like a bag of laundry. Well, he was over forty, and a bit out of wind, you can imagine. But he says to me too, as we're fightin' our way up a hill, 'There's a future in the army.' You sure hear some funny things there, marchin' along with a gang that's joinin' up. A future! Seems there wasn't a one that wasn't thinkin' about the future! Well, I thought about it too, marchin' along between those two, the little guy and the old guy who'd had his future already. . . ."

"Well," said Emmanuel.

"Don't get your tail in a knot," said Alphonse. "Here I am tellin' you a story people are goin' to listen to ten years from now. They're goin' to understand it twenty years from now. And all you can say is, 'Well?' Well, I'll tell you all about 'well.' We get to the barracks and they put each one of us through his questions, just like the priest, but they're getting us ready for Extreme Unction, not communion. Just the same it seems you got to know quite a bit for the last rites. You must have gone through that too. I don't know if your officer was as dumb as mine. There can't be many alive like that guy. There he is, an' he pulls out this pen and sits square like he's on a throne, and he blows his nose and scratches his head and straightens out his legs and then he asks me some arithmetic. If I'd had a pencil and paper and been alone to think about my business, it would have been a piece of cake to find the answer, but he lets me have it just like that. I got no time to think about anything and first thing I know he's mad as hell. 'Where have you been all your life? Did you never learn anything?' he says. 'Where have you been?' I ask him right back. 'Not down by the canal, I guess.' 'That's for sure,' says he. 'That's what I thought. No offence,' says I.

"After that they take me in naked to see the doctor. 'Open your mouth. My Lord,' he says to me, 'I never saw so many rotten teeth in my life. Have you never been to a dentist?' After that there was another one who gave me hell because I'd never gone and bought glasses instead of all-day suckers when

I was ten. The funniest of all was the guy that called me all kinds of names because I'd been brought up on beans and fricasseed onions instead of good pasteurized milk. But never mind, I wasn't discouraged. 'There's a future in the army,' I said to myself. 'If the little guy and the old guy and all the papers in town say so, it must be right. They're goin' to crank me up and I'll be all fit for their future.'"

There was a silence, interrupted by the clanging of the warning bell. The street was filled with a roar and the earth trembled under the giant passage of a locomotive.

"Wouldn't they take you?" asked Emmanuel, unable to bear any more of this vindictive tale.

Alphonse broke into uncontrollable laughter which shook him as a strong wind shakes a tree standing exposed and unsupported.

"Always in a hurry!" he said. "In a hurry to get back to the gang. You'll always be in a hurry, you will. But wait a minute. What you're goin' to hear now is the funniest of all. Imagine this: they took the old boy and patched him up like new. They made a different man of him, I tell you, gave him glasses, tore out his tonsils, vaccinated him from head to foot and stuffed him full of vitamins. They even straightened up his nose, it was a bit crooked. And the little guy – no problem there. He had all his teeth, all his hair, two legs and two arms, and all his good humour too. . . ."

He took Emmanuel's arm and squeezed it hard, as if for a final farewell.

Then his expression turned gloomy and indifferent.

"Okay, okay, it's all right. Well, good-bye, good-bye, Létourneau. See you next armistice!"

And away he went, the tail of his overcoat flapping in the wind. His tall, thin shape disappeared in the tunnel.

Emmanuel stared after him. Alphonse seemed to him as dead as all the future dead in battle. Crushed by all he had heard, he went his separate way, mulling over a thought which had turned to an obsession, a refrain in his head not to be dismissed: Peace has been as bad as war. Peace has killed as many people as war. Peace is as bad. Peace is as bad. . . .

TWENTY-EIGHT

Late as it was, Emmanuel gave no thought to going home. He was absorbed in his internal debate. Azarius Lacasse, Alphonse Poirier – he couldn't forget these two beings that had by chance been revealed to him in all their solitude. Why? he wondered. They're both strangers to me. I mean nothing to them. They mean nothing to me. Why did they come upsetting me tonight? Suddenly he realized that their failures had called in question all his fine, youthful ardour, his faith in goodness, his enthusiasm, his drive toward action.

"You're very lucky, young soldier!" Azarius had said to him. And the other one too, poor devil, had said the same thing in his bitter, roundabout way. Lucky! Life must have been horrible for some if they envied him not so much his uniform and his pay but his bayonet, his gun and all the tools of death! And without even having a clear idea who they were to be used against. Alphonse, for example, couldn't possibly hate the enemy as he hated his own country. Was Alphonse the only one of his kind, this unnatural creature? Not at all. Emmanuel could have named twenty, fifty, a hundred like him. Perhaps less bitter but on the same downward slope. What could you offer these men, the ones still hesitating? How could you lead them off to war? With a fife and drum? Emmanuel shuddered, for he thought he had just made a frightful discovery, a fact that defied the imagination: to make war you had to be filled with love, with a vehement passion, exalted, intoxicated, otherwise the whole thing was inhuman and absurd.

What passion then was strong enough to lift men's hearts and draw them in like this? An ideal of justice, beauty, brotherhood? Did he still possess such an ideal himself? That was the sore point. Alphonse had no such ideal, nor did Azarius. And he, Emmanuel, could he still keep intact his ideal, the passion of his youth, or would he succumb to making war without realizing where it was taking him? St. Henri had him in its power, like a prison of doubt and uncertainty and solitude. He decided to go up to the mountain. At times that walk had brought him peace.

He left behind the odours of grain and oil and sweet tobacco. Here, high above the suburb, he could breathe a different air, healthy and pure, redolent of fresh leaves and watered lawns. Westmount greeted him: city of trees and parks and silent houses.

He turned west and soon arrived at the armouries. A young soldier was on sentry duty there, with fixed bayonet. Emmanuel was on the point of murmuring a greeting to this unknown comrade-in-arms when he glimpsed his face.

It was Pitou, marching up and down in front of the armouries, stomping, clicking his heels, about turn, quick march, all alone in the night, rifle at the slope.

Already trained, he didn't stop when he recognized Emmanuel, but his face lit up with pleasure.

"Hey, Manuel!" he said softly, resuming his rhythmic tread.

"Pitou!" said the other, falling into step beside him.

For a time they marched together, as if the soldier on duty had acquired a shadow to keep him company in his monotonous comings and goings. Then Pitou turned abruptly, stomped to a halt. His eyes lit up with mischief.

"Thumbs up," he said in English.

"Thumbs up!" said Emmanuel.

For the first time he uttered these words with a shade of hesitation, as if his thoughts had refused to follow.

"D'you like it?" he asked.

"You bet," said Pitou, again in English.

On his freckled redhead's face, which flushed so easily, there was intense excitement. His grin almost burst open his round cheeks, shining like polished apples.

"We'll get together," Emmanuel promised.

"You bet! In England!"

"Bye, Pitou."

"Bye, Manuel."

Emmanuel continued on his way, slower now, his head cocked slightly to the right. At last he was completely alone with his thoughts. He remembered the conversation at Ma Philibert's and wondered if he had played a part in Pitou's decision. This power of persuasion, which he had often seen at work on his friends, frightened him. Could he perhaps convince others without convincing himself? Was he going around firing others' enthusiasms without keeping a spark for himself?

Pitou, he thought. Pitou in the army! It seemed incredible, impossible. Pitou, the kid of their group, the one they'd still had to protect not so long ago! They'd called him Chubby, or even Baby-Face. He could hear the sound of the gang running down there along an old towing path, and Pitou, out of breath, shouting, "Hey! Wait up! Wait up! I'm coming!"

They'd try to leave him behind sometimes, just to tease him, or because they found him too young for their games.

But Pitou always turned up behind them, a funny shape in his too-short pants which stopped at his fat calves, his shirt too big and his face shaded by an immense hat. To see him from above, at a distance, you'd think it was a self-propelling hat climbing the slopes, rolling down, activated by some magic power. He was always behind, but never discouraged.

Those were the days when, trotting in single file, they'd go down to the old canal to swim. They'd find a spot where the abandoned canal gave passage to reflections of leisurely clouds, and rippled between gently sloping banks where almost no one passed. Clumps of trees here and there were like a wood or forest to them, and a field with a single cow grazing on it was their prairie. That had been the countryside of their childhood! Alphonse, who always chose the hardest path, would talk of going on, never stopping, stealing a boat and heading anywhere. Even then the open sky had filled him with bitter confusion, a feeling of freedom, the obsession with going back, the regret at being unable to push on to the limits of solitude. Pitou, struggling after them, would get caught on a barbed-wire fence or fall in a water hole, always holding them up, and Alphonse would shout, "Why don't you go home, you little pest!"

Later, Pitou had known how to make them wait up. One evening they heard sounds of music from behind a stack of railway ties by the canal. With nothing but his mouth organ, Pitou had held them the whole evening. Alphonse, reconciled, demanded arrogantly: "Come on, give us *Home on the Range*."

Then there'd been the circuses and travelling concerts in the suburb, Pitou out in front with his spellbinding music. And the guitar! Warm, stuffy evenings, not a breath of wind.

And Pitou on the canal wall, his legs dangling, taking them on his fantastic trips – Pitou, whom they had so often threatened to leave behind!

They asked him, "Where the heck did you get the zing-a-ling?" And Pitou, beaming, replied, "There was this old Jew, an' he told me, 'If you can play a piece right off, you can have the zing-a-ling.' So I got the zing-a-ling."

But as time went by, the tunes Pitou extracted from his guitar grew more and more melancholy. Sometimes when they asked him for a happy song, he would say, "Aw, leave me alone!" And he'd be perched up there on Ma Philibert's counter, asking himself and everyone else, "Is there one job in this town? One lousy job?" As his legs dangled you could see the holes in the soles of his shoes, and his worn-down heels.

Pitou, in the army! Emmanuel couldn't get over it. And Alphonse had known, but in some shadowy way was suffering from the knowledge, because he had refused to talk about Pitou. Then Emmanuel remembered: the "good-lookin' little guy, the winker . . . all curly haired and healthy . . . the little guy with all his good humour. . . ." Good God! It had been Pitou there beside Alphonse in the ranks.

He's a kid, thought Emmanuel. Nothing but a kid. Yesterday he was playing his mouth organ and guitar, now he's handling a bayonet. And another thought went through him like hot iron: Pitou didn't need to feel bad about not working. Pitou was earning his living at last, a bird's living, slim pickings were all he asked. Pitou could be happy now, no wonder he stamped his heels so hard. He was happy. He was handling his first working tool!

Emmanuel bowed his head as if he were crushed by the weight of human folly.

The stars were unusually bright. You had to go up on the mountain to see them emerge so stunningly from the depths of infinity. Emmanuel recalled Azarius' words: "France is like the stars, they still give their light at night-time when it's ever so dark."

The expression had seemed very fine to him as it came from Azarius' lips. He had even felt a surge of enthusiasm. But now he wondered if the world was not about to see a night without light or stars. And he wondered if that night had not begun long before the war to engulf the world in its shadows.

Where could you find a light to guide the world?

He was climbing up a street which, with its warm stone houses, Georgian windows, lawns and honeysuckle bushes, was the very evocation of English cosiness. The abyss that lay between his thoughts and this mellow, impregnable calm drove him deeper into his melancholy. Emmanuel had never resented the rich. In the old days, when their noisy gang had ventured up the mountain on a still night to the cry of "Let's go see how the millionaires live up there!" it was not to commit any acts of vandalism but to fill your lungs with fresh air and, secretly taken by such beauty, store up an eyeful of it.

Emmanuel didn't hate the rich. Perhaps he had never been deprived enough to share Alphonse's morbid envy of them.

But as he strolled amongst these princely mansions his uneasiness increased. It wasn't resentment or disgust, or even his old embarrassment as a guy from the working-class neighbourhood in this rich·part of town. It was an indefinable malaise, nothing more. All the troubles and anguish of the lower town seemed to have stuck to him when he left, and the higher he climbed the more tenaciously they clung to his body. And now it was as if he had no right to enter this citadel of calm and order with the stink of poverty clinging to him like the odour of a sickroom.

Finally anger took possession of him. It was his turn to ask the question already raised by so many others: We, down there, the ones who join up, we're giving everything we have to give, maybe our arms or our two legs.

He looked up at the high grills, the curving driveways, the sumptuous façades, and completed his thought: Are these people giving all they have to give?

The stone, the wrought-iron grills, tall and cool, the doors of solid oak, their heavy brass knockers, the iron, the steel, the wood, stone, copper and silver seemed to come to life with a sneer that was taken up by the luxuriant bushes and trimmed hedges, making its way to him across the night:

What's this you're daring to think, poor creature that you are? How dare you try to put yourself on our level? Your life? Why, that's the cheapest thing on the market! Stone and steel and iron, gold and silver – we're the things that last, and cost the most!

"But a life! A man's life!" Manuel protested aloud.

A man's life indeed! Nobody's ever put a price on it. It's such a small thing, so ephemeral, so docile. . . .

Wearied at last by the burden of his thoughts, Emmanuel arrived at the Westmount Lookout. Leaning on the parapet he saw the thousands of lights below.

He felt an intense distress. It seemed to him that he was alone in the universe, on the edge of the abyss, holding in his hands the most fragile, tenuous of threads, that of the eternal human enigma. Which of the two, wealth or the spirit, should sacrifice itself; which of the two possessed the true power of redemption? And who was he to attack this problem and, tonight, to bear its burden? He was a man who until now had lived a comfortable life, without great worries or excessive ambition, an ordinary young man like many others. If events had not thrust him into this dilemma, he might never have encountered a worry more serious than the everyday concerns of a mediocre existence.

The consciousness of his own ignorance was added to his solitude. Only his solitude was measurable: he could judge its depth by the freedom' of the winds playing about the heights where he stood; and its duration, by the distance that separated the mountain from the suburb.

Leaning on the parapet, he searched the distance among the lights to the southwest, sparkling like fireflies against a lake of darkness, and chose one that might be Florentine's.

TWENTY-NINE

The restaurant had seemed very gay to Florentine, with its touch of the garden café beside the river – a place where her regrets might withdraw their pursuit, or her thoughts take a less painful turn.

A few Chinese lanterns were swinging from the branch of a tree in front of the door, its gentle movement shaking and mingling their lively colours. A garland of coloured light bulbs framed the doorway. Having made this concession to the picturesque, the owner had turned his energies to a series of posters on which he advertised every product he sold and a few more besides. The narrow façade and decrepit walls of the restaurant literally disappeared behind these ads: women in bright bathing suits on a tiny beach were supposed, for unknown reasons, to represent the mildness of a certain brand of cigarette. Others, still more scantily dressed, vaunted a well-known thirst quencher. Painted tin sheets, large and small, had been crammed together on the building's front with advertising of all sorts. The effect was wild and gaudy, but Florentine loved it. You just couldn't go in a place like that with gloomy thoughts.

Under a makeshift bower that created a scanty patch of shade stood a single small picnic table of rusty metal on which a brewery trademark was barely visible. Venturing toward it, Florentine murmured:

"Say, it looks real nice here!"

Hoping to please her, Emmanuel had invited her to this restaurant on the outskirts of town. But she had refused to have anything but a coke and a hot dog.

Inside, more Chinese lanterns hung from the ceiling, moving gently in a breeze from the river. The tables were painted bright red and the walls were covered with primitive paintings of Japanese pagodas, triremes cutting through a chalky sea, Hindu temples on a muddy background. There was a nickelodeon in one corner, and Florentine kept Emmanuel busy playing the same vibrant, syncopated piece.

The owner had served them their light meal, and they were now almost alone. From time to time a couple would come in to buy cigarettes and go off again, laughing and teasing on the riverside path.

The day was not turning out as Emmanuel had imagined. Yet the element of the unforeseen with its suspense was not unpleasant. He was continually waiting for a word to be spoken between them, a gesture, which would irrevocably change the course of their lives.

That morning he had gone to High Mass in St. Henri Church, hoping to see Florentine there. His shyness had the upper hand again and he wanted to meet her by chance rather than risk another visit to her home. He would never forget the mixture of joy and hesitation with which she had greeted him. As if she were fighting back her pleasure at seeing him . . . yes, that was it, as if she were struggling against a natural desire to see him and an equally natural instinct to flee.

The rest still seemed strange and complex. Florentine, at the church door, dressed in her Easter best! Not knowing what to say, he had mentioned her new finery, squeezing her arm a little at the same time. She had granted him a brief, tense smile and then frowned as if he had displeased her. But she said:

"You see everything, eh? There's men that never see what a woman has on!" As if he could forget her black dress at his party, or her green uniform in the store, and the pink paper flower she stuck in her hair!

They went down the church steps together. Could he really be there beside her in the sunlight, knowing at last all the details of her new costume! And the joy of saying to himself, We're leaving the church together, we look like real lovers. But he didn't understand her mood. She walked beside him, biting her lips and casting sideways glances at him that were hesitant, perplexed and almost hard. And the words they had exchanged in the crowd inside – embarrassed, very embarrassed, though he remembered every nuance and intonation:

"You haven't changed, Manuel!"

"You neither, Florentine."

"Are you on your way overseas?"

"Yes, very soon. I've got two weeks' leave, and then . . ."

"So it's your last furlough! That's not long. . . ."

She had said "That's not long" in such a strange, meditative voice that he had leaned over greedily to see if her eyes explained what her words had left unsaid. But she had looked away, swinging her handbag nervously.

Why had she said "That's not long"?

He stretched his hand across the table and took her fingers.

A little haughtily, half joking, yet genuinely concerned, she asked him:

"What were you juggling in your head? You were cooking up something, I'll bet you two bits."

"I was thinking about you," he said very simply.

She smiled with satisfaction, withdrew her fingers which he was pressing too hard, and took out her compact. Since they'd been together he had seen her make up her face three or four times. He found it amusing, like a kitten washing its whiskers. He had noticed that she pursed her mouth and stiffened her face when she powdered her nose, and that she never failed to take a little spit on her fingertips for her lashes, curling them gently with her nail.

He was more entertained than astonished by all this, but what intrigued him was to catch her continually poring over her tiny mirror, absorbed in her own reflection, and somehow quizzical or doubtful about what she saw. What on earth did she find there that was so upsetting?

For a time they sat there, glancing warily at each other. Then she said:

"Put a nickel in the machine, Manuel."

He was no longer surprised by her need for noise and movement. Since the previous evening he himself was in an over-excited state that matched hers. He went to the music box and chose a piece he particularly liked. It was from *Bitter Sweet*, a melody that expressed for him the bitterness and delight of seeing her again.

"What's that you put on, Manuel?"

Then she stiffened. *I'll see you again, whenever spring . . .* The sentimental phrase pierced her heart. Her lipstick skidded onto her cheek. She saw herself again at the entry to the movie theatre the night she had begun her descent into the unknown, the night of her downfall.

"Let's dance," said Emmanuel. He took her gently in his arms.

All day he had been hoping to hold her for a few moments to the rhythm of a waltz, and feel the warmth of her body.

As she danced she barely saw what she was doing or where she was going. She was remembering how cold she had been as she waited in front of the theatre. That was an arctic night! And all the dark streets by which Jean could have arrived – silent, deserted and empty! *I'll see you again* . . . The nostalgic refrain filled her with gloom. Everything was ugly in the depths of her thoughts. No hope, no joy. And the cold! A whirling winter wind chilled her heart. No one had come through the storm that night. No one, for that matter, had ever come.

"You're not following," Emmanuel reproached her gently.

And he began to sing softly in her ear: *I'll see you again* . . .

She was waltzing stiffly with him, stumbling, trying to sound the depths of those strange words that reached her from so far away, words which Emmanuel was now repeating in her ear. She saw someone sitting in the movie, comforting herself with the thought that Jean must have been delayed. How could she have been so naive, so silly, such a child! Suddenly she wanted to take her revenge on Emmanuel. She would have liked to find an unkind word, just one hard word, to wound him and see how suffering looked on someone else.

"We danced so well together last time!" said Emmanuel.

He noticed that her cheek was smeared with lipstick, and offered his handkerchief, but she didn't notice his gesture. He wiped her cheek himself, very gently.

Then she broke into a mocking, bitter laugh:

"Look at you! You've got it all over. There. Anybody would think we were in love!"

She knew she had gone too far and that he was hurt. She had not really wanted that. Hurt him a little, yes, but not insult him and turn him away from her. She had to stay friends with Emmanuel. She shook her long hair and gave him a smile that was more provocative than friendly.

For a moment the cherished notion he had had of her dissolved. In its place he saw a girl who was nervous, unstable and loud, with too much makeup. This can't be Florentine, he thought, I'm losing my mind, I must be wrong. But a second later he saw a simpler, sadder truth: she was like himself, anxious and caught among conflicting emotions.

"Let's go," she said, "there's nothing doing here. D'you want to go?"

Wherever they stopped, she was the one who wanted to leave. It's harder than I thought, she said to herself, to pretend I love him . . . and make him love me. But she knew that despite her feelings her mind was made up and would not change.

He helped her on with her new coat. She had told him with a touch of defiance: "Yeah, it's new this spring. It cost a lot. Do you like it?" The coat was of light knop wool pleated from the hips and with a great tortoise-shell buckle, and it could be seen in all the stores of St. Henri. It had broken his heart as she said, "Well, do you like it or don't you?" He had replied, "Yes, of course, it's really nice, Florentine."

He had thought of all the clothes he would like to buy her since she was so fond of dressing up. He imagined going with her into stores and helping her make her choice. He felt very daring as he said, "Florentine, you may think this is a bit odd, but would you let me buy you a really nice dress before I leave, as a going-away present?" He hesitated, almost certain that she would refuse. But to his astonishment she grasped both his hands and said with real joy, "Oh, Manuel, you couldn't do anything I'd like better."

She made him hold her gloves and handbag while she put on her hat, a little toque covered with greenery and stiff flowers.

"What about my hat? Do you like it too?" And she threatened: "You better!"

She took her handkerchief from the bag he was still holding, smiled briefly at him – a slight apology for the delay – and began powdering herself again before the wall mirror. How stupid he must look, he thought, with all these women's accoutrements, the open bag for her to rummage in, and her scarf, her gloves . . . But it was precisely this, he knew, that he would remember later: standing behind Florentine, waiting for her to turn around and tell him she was ready to take her place at his side.

They resumed their walk by the river. They had left St. Henri without any idea how they would spend their day. Florentine had said, "Let's go up on the mountain," but on the way had changed her mind: "Let's go to Lachine." At first he had thought she shared his feeling of wanting to go everywhere on his last furlough. By now he realized, from a few chance remarks, that she had no interest in the landscape and didn't even see any part of it, missing the unusually clear sky, the movement of the ships and sailboats on the river; and farther out, the enchantment of the islands, half inhabited or deserted, which had always fascinated him. He had tried to interest her by telling her their names and something of their history.

Earlier in the afternoon on the boardwalk at Verdun, among the noisy, colourful crowd, all that had interested her was searching for faces she knew. "I don't know a soul here," she had said, as if irritated and astonished. Unable to bear the idea that he might enjoy the sight of the promenade, she had grown mutinous and insistent: "There's nothing to see here. Let's go somewhere else, Manuel!"

Each time she laid her slim, ungloved hand on his arm Emmanuel saw the gesture as a timid expression of her desire to touch him, and it made him happy. It made him forget his efforts to excuse the girl's ignorance and lack of tact, as if he were trying to repress some warning or instinctive caution.

Now she said wearily:

"Where are we goin', Manuel?"

He suggested that they go over to the South Shore and visit the Indian reservation, Caughnawaga.

She seemed surprised by what he told her about it, and he gathered from her simple questions that she knew practically nothing about the surroundings of Montreal.

"If only I had a month I'd show you a lot of places," he said.

"Well, you've only got two weeks and we're not about to go running over there to look at the savages."

He offered her a ride in a skiff, but she hesitated, not wanting to admit her mortal fear of the water. At last he suggested with some regret:

"D'you want to go to the movies?"

That might well have tempted her. But not now. All she wanted was a particular certainty. She wished that it were already dark around them. She would have preferred night to the most beautiful sunlit day. She longed for the dark and for Emmanuel to put his arms around her and tell her he couldn't live without her. Why didn't he say it? That's what he was thinking about all the time. If he'd admit it, her mind could be at ease. She would be one stage further in the plan she had formed the previous night when her mother told her of Emmanuel's visit.

From time to time she turned to peek at the young man from under the fringe of her lashes. She could see him holding her bag at the restaurant. He loves me, she thought, he's crazy about me. And in fact there was so much tenderness in his eyes when he looked at her that she felt a little ashamed. Then she would think, It's his tough luck if he loves me so much. It's just crazy! And because her vanity left her no peace, she tried to convince herself that she, in her own way, was in love with Emmanuel.

She was able to succeed as long as she made no direct comparisons between him and Jean. When that happened she assumed a disdainful pout, scrutinizing him brusquely as he walked beside her, saying to herself with a touch of pride: Jean would never give in on every little thing like he does. And she became bolder in her designs.

She was stumbling with her high heels, so obviously tired that Emmanuel grew concerned. "Look, you can't even walk anymore," he said, and helped her by putting his arm around her waist. He pretended to joke: "You're going to wear out your fine shoes." But there were dark lines beneath her eyes and her face was pinched. She had grown very pale. He asserted his authority and they took a bus back to town.

Just before reaching Verdun, Florentine suppressed a sigh and said:

"Let's get off here."

They could see the rapids on their right. The swaying of the bus made her sick and weak, and her willpower was failing with her strength. She was afraid of falling into a torpor in which everything would become immaterial to her, and she tensed in an effort to seem gay and even attentive to Emmanuel.

"It's so nice here," she said, "the water and everything," but looking only at her clasped hands. "Let's get off and see if anybody's fishing."

When she was small Azarius used to bring her to this part of the shore on Sundays fishing for burbot. She felt a desire for Emmanuel to understand her through knowing about her childhood and to love her for what she had been as a child. She leaned her head gently toward his shoulder.

"My dad and I, we used to come here together. Oh, that was a long time ago. I'd take off my shoes and stockings and play in the water. I must have been five or six then, I guess."

It was the first time she had mentioned her family to him, as if she had been too ashamed or proud to do so. That she confided in him ever so slightly touched Emmanuel. He took her hand and squeezed it gently. Vaguely moved by her memory of the past, she went on, her eyes vacant:

"My dad was good to us kids when we were little. My dad . . . some people talk about him, they say he's not a hard worker and can't keep a job. But my dad was always good. It's just, he didn't have much luck."

She repeated "My dad, my dad" like a refrain, a kind of prayer, an excuse, a plea, through which, as she relieved him of guilt, she also excused herself. Emmanuel, attentive and sympathetic, encouraged her to go on.

In his expression she discerned a pity that was too specific.

"Come on, let's get off," she said, her nerves on edge.

They were near the power station, walking slowly, Emmanuel holding Florentine back to spare her. It seemed to him that she had opened to him such a pitiful and unhappy corner of her heart that a lifetime wouldn't be enough to console and guide her. The simple words "didn't have much luck . . ." seemed to sum up a whole lifetime, and he was moved almost to tears.

He tried to quiet her mood by the touch of his hand on her arm. She was turning out to have unsuspected depths, and this discovery added to his concerns and tenderness.

Florentine, trying to hurry, was tight-lipped. She felt that she had been a fool to reveal even the slightest corner of her life or to have shown him the least glimpse of the bitter sweetness that remained in her heart. Sweetness brought you nowhere. That's what had ruined them all. It wasn't for her, not ever. In her anger at herself she tried to stay ahead of Emmanuel. The path narrowed to go between great rocks, and here he allowed her to precede him, enjoying the sight of her ahead. He loved her skipping gait and the way she shook her brown hair over her shoulders.

She had left for this hike dressed up as if for church. She even had her gloves, which she took great care not to besmirch. Now she folded them and gave them to Emmanuel for fear of losing them. A moment later she wanted them back, and gazed at them on her hands, her eyes shining with satisfaction.

A touch of sunlight, like a golden mist, shimmered over the water, blinding the view of the far shore. Yet the afternoon was growing cooler and the breeze less clement. Soon the day's warmth would have been absorbed by the moving surface of the river, just as every word they had said, every gesture, would subside into the mysterious depths of memory. Emmanuel found the thought so intolerable that he hurried after Florentine, took her by the shoulders and, when she looked up astonished, was only able to offer her a gratuitous smile.

Now she was waiting, her expression hard and almost overbearing. He seemed to be on the point of saying something. She knew from his frown that he was looking for words to express an emotion he had never felt before. Struggling against his passion, he was trying to glimpse how far he dared to go. His lips were trembling and he wiped sweat from his brow. Gently he said, pretending not to be too serious, but with a note of finality in his voice:

"We should have known each other a long time ago, Florentine!"

She felt a sudden panic. If she lost Emmanuel this moment, everything would be finished between them. Everything. This time she would be completely lost. More than her safety and salvation were at stake. It seemed to her that Emmanuel might succeed in restoring her lust for life, her pride, her joy in being well-dressed and irresistible. It was through him she had rediscovered that she was pretty and passionate. Could she let all that be taken from her? She was twisting and torturing the strap of her purse and looking stubbornly away so that he couldn't read her eyes.

"Hey, you're going to rip your purse!" he joked. "Is it new too?" He pretended not to notice that she was sulking.

"Everything's new," she snapped. "I bought all new things this, spring . . . for . . ."

"To make some guy crazy about you?" he finished the sentence for her, half smiling.

Beneath his words she had sensed real distress, which she recognized from having felt it herself with Jean.

Emmanuel was watching her, his mouth tense, his hands clenched behind his back.

"Are you in love with somebody, Florentine?" he asked.

She hesitated. What was the best way to make him crazy

about her? Make him jealous? Maybe. And maybe not. She wasn't sure. And she couldn't afford a mistake. Oh, no! At the restaurant today two couples had come in for a drink. One of the boys had worn a navy uniform. She had glanced at him a few times; perhaps she had smiled and he had smiled back, finding her pretty. How nervous Emmanuel had been! Without a word he had made her change places so that she could no longer use the mirrors to catch the stranger's eye. . . . It would be silly, she thought, to admit she had been in love with Jean.

She poked at the earth with the tip of her shoe and murmured:

"Oh, you know. There's guys at the store, they kid around . . ."

"Yes, I know," he said.

There was a suppressed tremor in his tone. But he feigned indifference, shifting from one foot to the other. At this moment she had an inkling of a strength of will she had not suspected. She felt a growing distance between them which she had to bridge. She burst out laughing, brushed her cheek against his, put a finger on his lips and cried:

"You're crazy! Crazy! Crazy! Before you left you asked me to be your girlfriend. You know right well it was you I was waiting for!"

All the resistance Emmanuel had summoned against the force of his youth crumbled at the single blow. He breathed deeply, as if a disaster had been averted. He knew now that he had been harbouring a bitter doubt the whole day long. At times Florentine's tricks, her irritability, had driven him half mad. He had thought, it's just out of disappointment that she goes with me.

All these doubts were swept away by her simple, affectionate gesture. That finger on his lips! He took her hand and went down with her toward the river, through bushes whose branches cracked as they passed, brushing against her coat, whipping gently at her straight, slim legs, and he felt as if he had found his way to a world in which there was no war, no horror and doubt, or any human anguish; where all was silent but the rustling of leaves and the hushing sound of a silky dress.

Later, when twilight came, they were sitting at the river's edge by a bay from which they could hear, feebly and far away, the sounds of the city. The steep slope protected their hiding place. They were alone with the ancient sound of the river in their ears, and the sight of wading birds among the grasses of the shallow water. A red-winged blackbird fluttered toward a nearby tree, his epaulettes gleaming. The remaining feeble light seemed to be concentrated on this tiny patch of colour as the bird hovered among the reeds, then soared to the elm branch.

In the distance a blanket of deep-violet clouds sank to the river's level.

They had found a great, flat rock on which to rest. Around its base the ripple of a backwash recalled the distant rapids. Emmanuel had spread out his big khaki handkerchief to protect Florentine's new coat. She was perched on the edge, her legs dangling, and he had his arm around her, still intimidated and astonished at the liberties she allowed. For her the night was welcome. Its terrors were gone because it no longer found her alone – it was a good night, it blurred faces, hid features and mingled memories, bringing her a confused impression of forgetfulness.

With a gesture that was caressing and bold, she leaned her head heavily against Emmanuel's shoulder. Night, descending fast, diluted all her memories, and she felt protected by a distance from her past, from her great mistake, so that now she was almost innocent, and thirsting for new attentions. If this stranger beside her was determined to love her, love her madly, perhaps she would still be able to respond. It seemed that from now on love would be no more than soft and timid caresses.

Snuggling close to him, she could smell his hair, his uniform, and she felt an abandon after all, for she loved the forms and gestures of love, and the path to her soul was, finally, through kisses.

She could feel Emmanuel's heart beating faster. She was observing him closely, a part of her inclined toward surrender and softness, another wide awake and implacable. She watched him from under half-closed eyelids.

But he, caught again in the mental torments of the previous night, unable to reconcile his visions of horror and confusion with the idea of happiness, however fleeting, had unconsciously drawn away from her. He was lost and had no idea where to turn. He could find nothing better than to call on Florentine's goodwill to save the two of them.

"Would you wait for me?" he asked suddenly, his voice husky and low. "It's not right, but would you wait? Would you wait till the world is cured again? A year? Two years? Maybe longer! Could you give me all that time, Florentine?"

She pulled back from him, wary of his words. What did he mean? "Till the world is cured . . ." What kind of talk was that? She was fearful of what she didn't understand, but felt sure that at that moment she held their destinies in her hand. She shielded herself with prudence. Oh, she knew well that there was a sentiment which spoke louder than any distress, any language of the mind and heart! Finally, she gathered her strength, her irresistible strength which knew how to force the mind to silence.

Turning her head slightly on Emmanuel's shoulder, she looked at him with anguished eyes.

"Oh, Manuel! You're going away, I'll never see you again! I don't want to wait so long. I'd be too scared you'd have other girlfriends. Just think! Such a long time!"

She was so intoxicated by the sound of her own voice and the momentum of her words that she was close to believing her life would be unbearable if Emmanuel left her alone. Tears glistened on her cheeks. She was weeping for her past folly, for having been unhappy, not for going astray. She put her frail arms around Emmanuel. She was frightened, but she felt that she was reaching her goal by sheer force of will. Her voice betrayed her fear and a kind of anxious triumph. Already she saw herself reborn, loved, prettier than ever, saved. . . .

She waited until the shadows deepened around them, above them; and then in the darkness that was like a heavy wine for her, she gave him her lips, she gave him her mouth in a cool, decisive movement. But a wave of passion seized her. She no longer knew if it was the memory of Jean's caresses or the reality of Emmanuel's kiss that excited her. She subsided into a marvellous forgetfulness, her face turned greedily to Emmanuel's mouth.

He had not dared to hope for this joy. From his first day of leave, in the train, accompanied by Florentine's image in his mind, he had warned himself against being carried away. To marry Florentine just as he was about to leave seemed unjust. He had only allowed himself to dream of two weeks' happy, careless camaraderie. But other considerations had been a part of this reserve: the opposition of his family, above all of his father. But also the pain he would cause his mother, the more cruel because of his departure. And, finally, Florentine's relationship with his family. But he had reached a pitch of fevered exultation in which a hurried wedding with Florentine seemed the most natural thing in the world.

Wasn't everyone marrying in haste, before leaving for the war? Didn't they have their right to happiness before separating, perhaps forever? Could they be sure their joy would await their return, with all its risks and hazards? And was this not a rare grace which must be grasped as it was offered?

He was so shaken by his decision, so wonder-struck, that he forgot it was Florentine who had led him on so far. He thought he himself had made the decision long ago, and that it was as vain to struggle against it as it was useless to combat the madness and disorder that had taken over the world.

Overcome by emotion, unable to string his words together with the slightest logic, he passed all his difficulties by and thus surmounted them.

"Time . . ." he said. "We haven't much. About two weeks."

Time, inexorable time – this was the only obstacle that might defy him.

Surprised by the impatience she had unleashed and carried faster toward the unknown than she had foreseen – this unknown she began to fear the closer it approached – she gave Emmanuel no help. She remained motionless, trying to see in the dark, her eyes wide open.

"The time . . ." he stammered. "Do you think we have enough time, Florentine?"

He took several deep drags of his cigarette.

"About two weeks." He turned toward her suddenly. "We've got time," he shouted, joyous and feverish. "I'll go and see your parish priest tomorrow morning, first thing. We can arrange everything for Wednesday, maybe Tuesday . . . And we'd take a beautiful hotel room. They'd sign us in: Monsieur and Madame Létourneau. . . ."

He laughed loudly, and stopped as he heard his own laugh. He had not heard it for a very long time.

Now Florentine got in the spirit of the thing, dazzled by the prospect, despite her misgivings: those days at the hotel, and Emmanuel spoiling her, buying presents. . . .

Neither of them seemed to think of anything but those few days which would be filled with youth. For him, they would be days of jealously protected intimacy, an escape into a land of sweet daydreams, of exquisite laziness; for her, the flashing lights of the cinema, the department stores, and Florentine there, radiant. And they were so happy with their respective dreams that they kissed impulsively, without restraint.

Then the final dark of night came down on their interlacing forms.

Emmanuel was talking away:

"You'd have an allowance, Florentine. With what I'd give you out of my pay as well, you wouldn't have to work. You could even have your own house."

He was thinking, Her house, furnished however she'd like it, where she could wait for me. . . .

"It won't be so long," he said again. "I mean waiting for the war to end. We're still young. How old are you, Florentine?"

"Nineteen."

She turned toward him as if she were going to confess: At my age you can make a new start. You can forgive me for everything.

"I'm only twenty-two. We'll still be young, Florentine, when I get back. We'll have our whole lives before us and . . ."

He stopped, realizing the contradictions that had gone through his mind in the last few minutes. His desires, timid to begin with, foreseeing only a week or two of happiness, then emboldened by the possibility of their realization, were now running off with the future, trying to extract from time the promise of a lifetime's happiness. His instinct warned him that he was compromising the future. He glimpsed all the dangers for himself and Florentine in his long absence. He saw the solitude of their young years. And he murmured:

"But you know, Florentine, to do what we're going to do, you've got to be very sure you love each other. For life."

It was a kind of prayer he was addressing to her. It was a daring call to the future, whose quality neither of them could imagine in advance. It was even a challenge to that shadowy part of life that extended beyond their youth.

From the river there came now no more than a milky illumination that threw no light around it. Darkness and silence surrounded them.

Emmanuel was searching Florentine's face and going over the few words and gestures that made up his knowledge of her. It was so dark that he could not see her eyes, and in his fear of being alone he took her in his arms. She knew he couldn't see her eyes, and was glad of it, for she felt she would not herself have wanted to see what was in them then. She said very quickly:

"Yes, that's true, you have to love each other for life."

For once she had spoken from the bottom of her heart. No more tempests. No more ecstasy, no more despair in her life. Just a long, flat road on which she was no longer surprised to be, since it meant salvation.

THIRTY

Rose-Anna came very quietly into the room where Florentine was sleeping. On the foot of the bed she laid the green velvet dress Florentine was to wear at her wedding. She put the dainty shoes on the floor and unfolded a pretty, pale-satin slip which she carefully hung over the back of a chair. Then she looked at Florentine who was still sound asleep, her arm over her face. Rose-Anna gently touched her naked shoulder with her fingertips.

Ever since the night when she suspected Florentine's plight, she had felt ill at ease with her. As if she herself bore a part of the shame. She had hardly dared look at the girl, still less speak to her.

True, this embarrassment had disappeared a few days ago. She had been reassured as she saw the colour come back to Florentine's cheeks, saw her apparently happy with Emmanuel. Ingenuously, she had allowed herself to be happy for Florentine, who was making such a fine match. She had even had a few moments of pride, untroubled by the lack of enthusiasm Florentine displayed. But this morning as she was giving a lick of the iron to Philippe's suit she had found, in a pocket crammed with papers, a letter to Jean Lévesque in Florentine's hand.

Her cruellest doubts returned.

It was growing late. Leaning over the bed, Rose-Anna hated to wake her, but finally gave her a little shake.

"Hey, don't you know it's your wedding day? Get up now!"

On her own wedding day, hadn't she wakened at dawn and dressed singing at her sunlit window?

At her words Florentine sat up and looked around, blinking, bewildered. Softened by sleep, her will had lost its power to spur her on, and was replaced by the usual torment of her mind on waking. She bowed her head and dreamed a moment, her eyes staring. Why did she have to wake up this morning? Or ever! But especially this morning. Her stare took on a glint of panic. Then she thought: Oh! This is my wedding day! The day I marry Emmanuel! And the word "wedding," which she had always linked to a perfect happiness, now seemed austere, distressing, full of snares and painful revelations. She saw her mother, heavy and moving with difficulty. A vision of herself as victim of the same deformity was vivid in her mind. She stretched, and felt a shiver in her delicate bones. The thought of the trials she would have to endure filled her with indignation. How she hated this trap into which she had fallen! And wasn't she moving toward it again, this time of her own free will? An expression of refusal and even hate flashed in her eyes. Then she understood the mute reproach in her mother's look, jumped out of bed and began to dress.

Rose-Anna and Azarius had wanted to do things right for their eldest's wedding. Especially Azarius, who had begun to run here and there to scrape up a few days' work. "A time like this, it's no time to count the cost," he said. And for once

Rose-Anna had encouraged him. "You're right, Azarius, we have to make it nice for her." They had spared no expense to buy her a beautiful dress that was well beyond their means. "Don't want the Létourneaus to think she's not good enough for them," said Rose-Anna, with a touch of vanity. "They're not going to say we gave her to Emmanuel in rags!"

She had been up all night putting the last touches to Florentine's silk underthings. Now, sad at heart, she waited for a word or a look from Florentine that might reward and reassure her.

Florentine had to brush her hair before the dress went on. She stood in the half-furnished room still cluttered with crates and big cardboard boxes from the move. She appeared so frail that Rose-Anna was emptied of all resentment.

What on earth was behind this cold and cruel silence of Florentine's? Why couldn't she share her troubles? Oh well, perhaps when she had come back to the house, after Emmanuel left, they'd have a good chat, just between women. But would that be too late? Perhaps it was now that Florentine needed help.

She began to hold out the velvet dress to her, then hesitated, her fingers clumsily running over the cloth, rumpling it unintentionally.

"Listen, Florentine, if you think you're making a mistake, if you don't really want to get married or you like somebody else, it's not too late. You've got to say so. . . ."

Florentine's reply was to grab the dress from her mother.

"Leave me alone," she said. "I can dress myself."

No, she wouldn't go back on her decision. Her life was settled now, once and for all. It wouldn't be what she had imagined, but it would be a thousand times better than what could have happened. And she hurried, she rushed to get dressed up and create a new person, a new Florentine who was about to confront a strange, unknown life and try to forget what she had been before.

She tilted her head back and inspected herself, her eyes half closed. Oh, it was good to see her waist still slim, her body young and supple, after the horrible picture she had had of herself while waking up this morning! She turned, looking over her shoulder, and was so relieved at her reflection that, if her mother had been less severe with her, she would have liked to make some gesture of affection.

For a moment she had been terrified of seeing herself deformed. She must have had a bad dream. . . . Now she was calm. She was going to be pretty, very pretty for her wedding. Emmanuel would take with him a touching image of her when he left. Emmanuel. . . . He'd be far away when she'd lose her slim figure. He'd never suspect a thing.

Rose-Anna saw her daughter's face in the mirror above the table. Her mouth was hard, her eyes determined, almost insolent. This Florentine with the rigid mask, the dark frown, was a stranger to her. The girl she had known could be difficult and irritable, but at heart she was anxious to be pardoned. Rose-Anna felt so sure of defeat that she gave up all hope of asking a direct question. She murmured softly, as if to satisfy the last demands of her conscience:

"Marriage is a serious thing, Florentine."

"Don't preach," said Florentine violently. She was beginning to see the maze of lies and deceptions that lay before her.

"Me, preaching?" said Rose-Anna.

She thought of her old mother, inflexible and cold, and she wondered if she resembled her. She searched for words that wouldn't sound like sermonizing, but it was hard because her whole spiritual life had been nourished by pious brochures.

And she couldn't let herself go in her natural warmth and tenderness because of Florentine's hostility. She began to feel it was her own fault. Hadn't she rebuffed the girl's first attempt to confide in her?

"I don't want to preach, Florentine. I just want you to know marriage isn't just a bed of roses. There's a lot of suffering too."

Florentine was putting on her makeup, tight-lipped. She had banished her mother's warnings and her own waking nightmare, and was substituting fantasies more to her taste: the church aisle where she would walk slowly on her father's arm, the flower-decked altar, the wedding breakfast at Emmanuel's parents' house, all the compliments she'd get, and then their departure in a rain of confetti, the photographer. . . . That would be fun! And then . . . She didn't want to think too far ahead. The parties . . . all the gaiety . . . And Emmanuel: he was a good boy, after all. Yesterday, as they made plans together, she'd been struck by his gentleness. She wasn't moved, but she was reassured.

Suddenly she felt so thoroughly revenged for Jean's jilting her, rehabilitated in her own eyes and those of her family, worthy of their esteem – for otherwise she would have lost that too – she found herself so clever, with her strong will and all, that she smiled a slow, meditative smile which confirmed her unshakeable determination but also her tragic desire to start afresh. She came close to running to her mother's arms, but Rose-Anna turned away, hesitated and went to the kitchen.

Azarius was waiting in his Sunday suit, a rose in his buttonhole. His face, freshly shaved, smelled of talcum powder. In his white shirt with its tight collar he was stiff and hampered, and seemed embarrassed at the thought of leading his daughter to the altar. Didn't he see her still in pigtails? Where had the years gone?

Florentine getting married! And her father still so young!

"You just about ready there, little girl?"

From the window he surveyed what horizon was visible through the sooty panes. A train was passing, and he had to shout:

"It's a beautiful day out, you know? Nothing but sunshine!"

Their last house had been close enough to the puffing trains behind the embankment which closed off Beaudoin Street. But now they were smack up against the tangle of tracks that fan out from St. Henri station. There was no respite possible. The Transcontinental, the trains from Ottawa and Toronto and the commuter trains all passed by their door. Then there were the freights, ponderous, endless convoys of food-stuffs, or long strings of coal cars. Sometimes they would stop, shunt backwards, then advance, and all around the house there would be nothing but the intermittent trilling of signal bells, the shock of buffers, locomotive whistles and waves of smoke. At other times the engine would race by, whistling loudly, and the house was shaken by a prolonged tremor. The windows rattled, things on the walls or in drawers trembled violently.

To make yourself heard over the racket you had to raise your voice to argument level, and people who constantly shouted at each other in this way came to see their fellows with astonishment and barely hidden animosity. Then, when the howling train had passed and the house settled down with sinister creaking sounds, it seemed as if the sun had fallen, and they must wait for another dull day to dawn through the windows opaque with blackened dust.

Rose-Anna was off dreaming of sunshine and breezes, as one pauses in the midst of afflictions to call up distant, incomprehensible ghosts from the depths of memory, seeing them more as intruders than as friends. She saw her own wedding day, clear and blue, with the sound of bells travelling through the village and out over the fields. There were earth smells, and the whole pathway of her youth which she had travelled so often in memory, joys with the healthy, profound savour of country life.

When she returned to look around her at the disorder of the house, she almost hated the happy scenes she had just left behind. What a mockery, those few days of grace at the beginnings of youth, the beginnings of life! And wasn't today's marriage feast another mockery, in the midst of this filthy house which could never become a part of their life?

The wind attacked the panes with clouds of cinders and soot. It seemed that the horizon could find no better place to dump its clinging soot than on these rattling windows. Azarius was there, with his backdrop of whirling dust; yet she knew that he too was absent, escaping for a moment, as she had tried to do. His hand was tapping absent-mindedly on the windowsill.

She watched him out of the corner of her eye. Oh, she knew he had seen nothing of Florentine's nervousness the last few weeks, and suspected nothing of the drama that was perhaps being played out in their lives. He had seen nothing, felt nothing, yet she had never been less inclined to blame or pity him. During the last few days he seemed to have rid himself of some immense burden. His gait was livelier, less discouraged. His face would redden at times, but he had learned how to be evasive when he knew that he was watched.

Rose-Anna thought he was holding back some secret hope. That he, at his age and after all their misfortunes, could still entertain his hopes so boldly, she found more irritating than his keeping a secret from her. Once or twice she had caught him talking to himself. "There's nothing else to do. I've got to make my mind up." When she had asked what that was all about, he had stood up and brazenly begun making jokes. "Never mind, Rose-Anna, your troubles'll soon be over. The money's on its way, and easy street for us."

She was afraid he'd be disappointed again. And most of all, she had learned to fear the incorrigible youthfulness of this man.

A newspaper was lying on the table. Azarius was buying one every two or three days now. She stared at the printed page without much interest. The headlines said: *Refugees on the March*. Just like us, she thought. Always on the march. A little lower down she saw: *New Contingent of Canadian Troops Lands in England*. Mechanically she looked for the date. The paper was yesterday's, May 22.

"I wonder if Eugène's turn is coming?" she said.

To herself she added, Eugène, Florentine, who's next? Will we never be together again? Can that happen already? Her tired gaze took in the room. No, they'd never be happy here! She'd felt it the moment they came in the place. What new threat was hovering over her now? Her heart was filled with foreboding. It must be Eugène. With one trouble out of the way, she was already on the lookout for the next trial, awaiting it almost impatiently, as if by anticipating it she could deprive it of some of its malignity.

"Poor child!" she sighed.

Azarius gave a little start. He thought for a second that she had spoken to him. In other days, to cure him of his illusions and console him for his failures, she had sometimes murmured those words to him, holding him in her arms like a child. A nostalgic desire for tenderness overwhelmed him like a flood tide, and he knew that he would give his life to make her happy. He looked at his wife's face, worn out with fatigue, her forehead with its wrinkles, her hands bleached from the washing. And Florentine's wedding began to arouse old memories in him with a kind of heaviness which must have been there the whole time, only making itself felt now. Finally accepting the fact that Florentine was grown-up and about to leave the nest, he was dumbfounded at what he saw behind him: everything he had done in all those endless days – but above all what he had omitted. That was the worst thing. And Rose-Anna! . . . He was certain now that he had loved no one else in his whole life. Yet at no time had he been able to prove it to her. Well, the time had come. He would make sure she would never again suffer because of him. He shut his eyes.

He had perhaps never been so ready to explain himself, never experienced such a desire to justify himself; but Rose-Anna had just risen to her feet. Coming forward a step or two, she made her effort and smiled with a kind of strained gaiety at Florentine who had just come in the kitchen.

She would later remember that she had just had time to see her daughter into her wedding finery and that she had not even given her a kiss.

Florentine asked:

"Does my dress hang okay, Mamma?"

Rose-Anna made her turn slowly as she examined the dress and stooped to pick off a couple of basting threads. Then Azarius took charge.

"Come quick, little girl, we'll get a taxi down below."

They now lived close to the taxi stand where Azarius had worked a few months before. Rose-Anna, peeking out the windows, saw them cross the tracks. Then, a minute later, they entered a shining black limousine. Azarius had had the idea of making a detour through the rue du Couvent so she could have a last look.

Rose-Anna rubbed at the dirty window and leaned forward to catch a glimpse of pale green and a little hat perched on long chestnut hair which gleamed for a second in the sun. She waved, thinking, That's silly, the car's out of sight already. And anyway Florentine hadn't looked back. Even as she left the house, there had been no sign of emotion, not even a lingering look. She had left as if nothing affected her now, thought Rose-Anna. "Almost as if she was a stranger," the poor woman murmured, close to tears. When she realized that her hand was raised for a tender good-bye, she had only one instinct: to hide somewhere, hide her face, and stay all alone for a long time.

She turned brusquely away from the window and went to sit at a corner of the table, leaning on it, tired to death. She wouldn't lack for chores to take her mind off her troubles. The little ones would be getting up soon; she would wash and dress them and get them ready for school. And she'd have to coax and wheedle Philippe to help her in some small way. No, she had preoccupations enough. But she preferred to think of the thing that caused her pain: Florentine's departure. She wanted to have a few more minutes alone with that pain, to give herself up to it just once more.

Her dressing gown hung partway open, revealing her shapeless body. She saw her legs, swollen and with dark stains and bumps caused by dilation of her veins.

Rose-Anna collapsed on the table, her head in her arms. It was so long since she had cried! It was a relief even to feel the tears begin. But a moment later there were light footsteps and Yvonne appeared in the doorway. She stayed there, fearful, looking at her mother. Then, in a rush, she ran to throw herself at Rose-Anna's feet.

Her mother began mechanically rolling the child's hair around her fingers. Then, as if she had just realized that Yvonne was there, she pushed her back; embarrassed by the child's clear gaze, she covered herself more decently with her dressing gown.

"What is it, Vonette?" she asked.

It was a long time since she had used this pet name. On emerging from childhood Yvonne had grown silent and almost tiresomely serious, with fits of prayer and penitence that astonished her mother. She had even taken offence at this excess of piety, giving the girl small chores to do around the house when she was trying to get away to church. "You serve God best when you help your parents, you know." Rose-Anna would tell her the parable of Mary and Martha, but her memory would trick her and she would confuse the two. "You know, Jesus said it was Martha who chose the better part." To which Yvonne made no reply.

Now she began weeping softly at her mother's knee. Rose-Anna wondered if she had not neglected and misunderstood the child. She lifted Yvonne's chin to look in her eyes, and what she saw moved her deeply. It was an expression of tender pity and protectiveness rather than the mute reproach of other times.

For a moment Yvonne returned her mother's gaze, then put her thin arms around her heavy body.

"Poor Mamma! Poor Mamma!" she murmured.

Rose-Anna noticed for the first time the graceful, developing form of the child beneath her nightgown. Already! she thought, not knowing whether to rejoice or be sad at the discovery.

After a silence, she said:

"You know, you'll soon be as big as Florentine!" And

she asked in a soft, trembling voice: "Are you going to get married too?"

"No," Yvonne replied calmly.

She was squatting at her mother's feet, staring rapturously at the grubby wall as if she saw it illuminated by the sun.

"I'm going to be a nun," she said, her voice singing, soft and winged with sincerity.

"You're going to be a nun," Rose-Anna repeated.

"Unless God takes my life," Yvonne went on. "I offered my life if Daniel gets well."

Rose-Anna's eyes blurred. She had almost forgotten Daniel in the intensity of her worries over Florentine. How could she! Each one of the family had been so preoccupied by his own troubles that no one had thought of the sick boy. Except Yvonne!

She knew that her voice would not be firm. She tried to get up, then looked straight at Yvonne as though she didn't see her, saying quickly:

"I'm pretty tired for going to the hospital today. And the streetcar makes me sick to my stomach, you know. Do you think you could find your way all alone?"

The girl was on her feet with one bound, her eyes shining.

"Oh, yes! I can ask the way. Let me go! And I have an orange left for Daniel. I'll bring him the chocolates Emmanuel gave us. Maybe Jenny will let him have some. His good Jenny! His beautiful Jenny!"

Rose-Anna had told her about his affection for the young nurse, and Yvonne had taken Jenny to her heart, including her in her childish prayers. Now that she had her mother's permission to go to the hospital, so long desired, she hurried to get dressed before Rose-Anna could change her mind.

She was singing snatches of hymns in the next room, something about the lovely month of May. Soon she appeared in her convent uniform, the long skirt flapping around her legs but the bust now too tight.

At the door, before flying on her way, she said very seriously:

"I haven't decided yet what kind of nun I'll be. Maybe for the poor. Or maybe a nursing sister. Either one would be good in God's eyes, wouldn't it, Mamma?"

"Yes," said Rose-Anna, "but don't run when you cross the streets, and look up and down first. And take a few cents out of my purse in case you get too tired."

"I don't need any money," said Yvonne happily.

Then, stiff in her ugly costume despite her graceful body, she ran off. Her arms were filled with packages. Rose-Anna guessed there was more than dainties in the big brown paper bag she was hugging. There'd be holy pictures too, and pious pamphlets, all the things the child hoarded.

At the window, Rose-Anna saw another of her children leave. This trip up the mountain was a serious affair for a child who had never been farther than the church. And because of the conversation they had just had, this departure seemed marked by a special sign.

When Yvonne had turned the corner her mother could barely remember her face. It seemed to her that the child had already withdrawn from this world, and that an impassable distance had been placed between the two of them. Of all the separations that had afflicted her recently, this one seemed the hardest, the most mysterious and irrevocable.

Yvonne was taken from her. But Yvonne had never belonged to her.

Daniel had been crying. His heavy eyelids barely opened on his reddened eyes. For more than a week now Jenny had been on duty in another ward and he saw her only when she passed by and came to tuck him in and leave a whiff of perfume from her blonde hair.

He had demanded her with cries and fits of anger which left him weakened, chilled and sweating. Then he wanted his mother, who also failed to appear.

His small, diaphanous face, the skin tightened over the bones, had taken on a curiously old expression. He was horribly thin. The bed covers lay flat over his weakened body, which seldom moved. In spite of the blood transfusions and ingestions of raw meat they had given him, his illness had made swift progress. Without pain, very gently, he was entering on the final phase of his disease.

Yvonne, with the God-given comprehension of a child, knew as she bent over him that he was about to die. All the strength and willpower he possessed was concentrated in the boy's piercing glance.

He pulled toward him the big package she had brought. His hand was impatient and the bag tore, and he saw all kinds of things tumble onto the bed. There were coloured pictures which fascinated him, and then he discovered a baby chick made of cardboard. It could stand up by itself. Yvonne explained that she had drawn it and cut it out at school before Easter, specially for him.

At the word "school" he pricked up his ears and looked pensive. Then he was back to his exploration of the bag and its surprises. He found a row of little men cut out of white paper, holding each others' arms. This brought the shadow of a smile to his face. Then he left all the things he had gathered to catch an orange which started rolling down the folds in his covers.

He held it up to the light in his cupped hands and looked at it with a puzzled frown. In the hospital they'd often given him a glass of juice that tasted like orange. But an orange wasn't juice, it was a fruit you got at Christmastime. You found it in your sock on Christmas morning, and you ate it, quarter by quarter, making it last. An orange was like a new coat, or a shining flute: you wanted it so much you kept asking for it, and when at last you held it in your hand you had no use for it.

Funny that this Christmas fruit was now his! It wasn't winter, and his mother wasn't coming in with parcels which she'd hide before even taking off her coat. It wasn't winter and it wasn't Christmas, and there he was with a fine orange in his hand, round and soft and full.

But he had no appetite. He let it fall and turned so he could peek at Yvonne. He had liked her before, in that world that was now so different, so far. In the evening she would help him with his lessons. While he was in school he had loved that serious face leaning over the book beside his own, their two voices spelling together, repeating the singing names of the letters. Now he wondered what it meant that she was here at his bedside.

After a while he ventured a timid smile. And Daniel, who had never been demonstrative, reached out a hand and touched her cheek.

His hand wandered over her cheek like a baby's, with its mysterious gestures of possession and curiosity.

Close to tears, she asked him:

"Do you still know your prayers, Danny?"

He nodded faintly, then blushed and murmured:

"Nothing but *Our Father*. . . ."

"That's enough," she said. "*Our Father* is the prayer Jesus taught us himself. Say it with me, Danny."

He was watching her with anxious curiosity, but he began the prayer, stumbling a little, and recited it without her help until he came to *Thy will be done, Thy kingdom come, on earth as it is in Heaven*. Then he seemed confused.

"In Heaven, will there be Jenny?"

"Yes, your good, pretty Jenny will be in Heaven some day," Yvonne replied gravely.

"She's Jenny!" he said with a vehement, defiant tenderness. Then he sighed. "But she doesn't cross herself."

Yvonne hesitated, wet her lips and said with an effort:

"She'll go to Heaven anyway."

"And Mamma?"

"Mamma, you can be sure she will," said Yvonne with more conviction.

He seemed to reflect for a long time, then murmured:

"You too?"

She was all he had left, and he suddenly loved her with all his heart.

"Yes," said Yvonne, leaning down to kiss him.

In that moment, she felt a flood of rapturous, almost frenzied affection. To reassure Daniel, she was ready to compromise her conscience with all its timorous and childish scruples.

"There'll be everything you love in Heaven," she promised in her sweet, childish voice. "That's what Heaven is: everything you love. There'll be the good Holy Virgin, and she'll rock you to sleep in her arms. You'll be like a Christ-child in her arms."

"But I'll have my new coat too!" he interrupted, trying to show his determination.

"If you want it, you'll have your new coat, but you'll have lots nicer things than that. You'll never be hungry or cold in Heaven, Daniel. And nothing will ever hurt. You'll be singing with the angels."

He closed his eyes, wearied with the visions she was calling up before him.

So as not to burst into sobs in front of him, Yvonne quickly stood up, put the orange into his hands and fled, a puny figure in her skimpy dress which flapped about her slender legs as she ran.

Daniel saw her going and tried to call her, but his cry failed to reach her.

A few days later, the day nurse coming on duty found him dead. His life had gone out gently, without cries or suffering.

THIRTY-ONE

Rose-Anna dressed the children as soon as they had finished their midday meal. Astonished by her haste to get them outside, they dawdled and made her angry. They picked away at their food, and couldn't find their things for going out. Rose-Anna hustled them along to the door, sending Gisèle with them, and told Yvonne to take good care of them all.

The child remembered other hurried departures when she was small. Made anxious by these memories and by her mother's pain-distorted face, she hated to leave her.

"Let me stay inside," she begged.

"No, no, I don't need you today. Go and play before school. And stay and play afterwards."

She watched them go, all holding hands, Gisèle in the middle. She heard their voices fade away and wished she could call them back, kiss them again and hold them tight for a moment.

During her pregnancy she had several times felt a presentiment of her own death, and had occasionally even welcomed this idea with longing for rest. But at the sight of her children pausing before the level crossing, then scurrying all at once, probably because of Gisèle who was going with them for the first time – a great responsibility – she imagined all the dangers threatening them today, tomorrow, in the distant future, and put away as a sin her longing for rest and death.

She went back in the house, and the sound of the door shutting behind her rang in her mind. She was alone now, as a woman always is at such times, she thought, encouraging herself. But she had to admit that never had she felt so alone as now. No one could be more alone, no one in all the world.

The house appeared to her in all its frightful ugliness and indifference. Nothing around her was consoling. Everywhere there was disorder, signs of moving, disarray. She had come to this house, as to many in the past, only to clear a place for herself and have her child, before she even had time to put the house in order. Yet never before had she felt so deserted by the very appearance of stability. She was imprisoned between these four walls.

She took a few uncertain steps, stumbling through the kitchen, and knocked on the partition to warn her neighbour, as they had agreed. All morning her pains had followed her, catching up intermittently. At times she had wished for a remittance of the pain; at other times, that it would take possession of her in order to have it over. She had put up with the first attacks without revealing it to her family, keeping busy as usual, with her pride in holding on as long as possible and an almost physical refusal of pity; and – at whatever cost to herself – with the conviction that she was thus helping nature along.

At last the time had come to recognize this pain which she denied the moment it passed, but of which all her life she had been terrified, with a child's terror, well-hidden, well-stifled.

She went in her room, still almost empty and spacious.

At the back – the bed. Rose-Anna lay down. Staring at the grey ceiling, she called Azarius, called him with a low groan. Even alone she was ashamed to confess her body's suffering. Where was Azarius? Why wasn't he with her now? Then she remembered, with a painful effort, as if the most recent events were blurred like the oldest memories. This morning, when news of Daniel's death had come to them, Azarius had rushed to the hospital. Later, as he had not returned, she had agreed with the neighbour's wife on a signal for fetching the midwife. Daniel . . . Azarius . . . Her thoughts revolved around the two of them. Who had died? Daniel, the child? But it seemed to her that her pains came from him, that it was he who was tearing at her body. Poor child! She imagined a small coffin, white and narrow, carried under Azarius' arm. But she mustn't dwell on such things; people said they were bad for a pregnant woman. Yet what could she think about but that shallow coffin, scarcely bigger than a cradle! A burial, a baptism, all the great events of life took on for her the same tragic, fathomless, bitter character.

And were the baby things ready? Yes, the same ones she had used for Florentine. Florentine! Where was she now? Good Lord, she was married! And one day she too would be delivered up to suffering and the humiliation of the body. She'd been glad when Florentine was born. She had always wanted girls. Yet each time at the last moment she had wanted to give birth to a boy who would have less to suffer. Always when the dark and solitude set in, through the body's distress she had dreaded giving birth to a girl.

Her mind cleared and she was back in the present. The clock counted its minutes so slowly that with each stroke of the pendulum Rose-Anna felt herself sink into an infinite abyss, then rise, then sink again. She had heard women say that only the first lying-in was hard. She knew otherwise. She knew that each time the body dreaded a little more this fresh submission to suffering, and that the mind remained more apprehensive there beside the chasm, seeing more distantly each time, farther every time, its lovely years of pure and careless youth, so far, ever farther, deep within the past, farther, farther every time. . . .

She raised herself, wiping her wet forehead. Now she was sure that no one had heard her rap on the partition. The neighbour might have been out for a few minutes when she knocked. She had to get up, get help. At first she thought she had already done so, then she understood she had the task before her. She succeeded in sitting on the edge of the bed. Using the chairs and the wall for support, she managed to cross the immense space between her room and the kitchen. Just a few steps more . . . She touched the wall with her outstretched hands, and began to knock with all her strength.

Was it a human voice that answered through the wall? Were those steps she heard at the front door? A train passed. Its wailing whistle deafened her. With a great effort she straightened up, made her way back to her room and fell on the bed. Now it was herself she imagined in a coffin, with a rosary in her clasped hands. She felt such a need to go gently to her death and escape her suffering that she folded her hands on her breast to resemble the vision.

Slowly it seemed to her that she was a distant spectator of her own last moments, that she was supervising all its stages and would later have to busy herself, when all was over, with arrangements for her own funeral. How would they dress her? The panic of realizing she possessed not a single dress for a decent burial brought her to the surface. She saw the confusion that would reign in her household – the children with no one to dress them and feed them, Azarius, himself like a child, unable to find his collar buttons or his Sunday suit. A thousand worries erupted in her mind. She should have mended Philippe's pants, and she should ask him where he was spending his days, leaving so early in the morning.

She murmured, "Jesus, Maria, later, when the children are grown up! . . ." And she decided: "I'm going to the hospital." She searched for her shoes under the bed. She reached the dresser where her hat was. She didn't know what she'd done with her coat. Where could it be? She looked around the room, and looked again. Her poor things. . . . She was ashamed of them, ashamed to go like this among strangers. Yet a stronger instinct, intent only on defying the frightful power of her pain, ordered her to leave as she was, half dressed. At last she found her coat and went, tottering, not clear as to how she would reach the hospital, half hoping she would never reach it. At the door she ran into the neighbour woman with the midwife.

A few moments later, back in her bed, she thought sadly and with terrible embarrassment, There, I must be in the hospital. She had always had a horror of them. She imagined glaring lights and a horrid setting filled with strangers fussing around her. She had never been able to resign herself to that, not even when the doctor advised it for Philippe's hard birth. They'd caught her this time.

But slowly she knew from the smells and sounds that she was in her own house. She sighed, contented. She risked a glance, tried to come back to the present and make sense of what was happening around her. Two women were busy in the room. "Strangers, after all," she muttered.

That had always been the worst part. Being seen and helped by others. Needing help so desperately. She tried to pull up a fold of the sheet or the quilt.

A stranger? Not really. She recognized the face that was bent over her. It was the same face she had glimpsed during Daniel's birth, and Gisèle's as well.

Strong hands were helping her, to her humiliation. For moments at a time she escaped into the past, to scattered memories. She was drifting like a rudderless boat through past years, seeing the landscape as it retreated swiftly, sometimes a great curve in the river, sometimes a single point on the bank, clear, precise, standing out. She fled on this rudderless boat, reviewing at a vertiginous speed the current of her life which she had ascended so laboriously; things she had barely noticed on the initial voyage assumed a fresh importance now. Everything was moving too fast, and the scene was too disordered for her to find her way in it. The more her visions mingled and were superimposed, the less she understood. She was there, excited, radiant, sweet, engaged to Azarius. As she saw this young girl dressed in bright muslin on a certain summer's day by the banks of the limpid Richelieu, she could have smiled vaguely at her, as at a stranger pleasant to meet but unimportant – an accidental acquaintance. But there she was again, grown old, accepting Eugène's sacrifice, struggling to keep a scrap of money which he took from her, money she needed for food and clothing. . . . Then she stood by the Richelieu again, her summer dress still rustling in the breeze, her hair tousled, the smell of the flowers and the hay caressing her senses.

And here she was walking, walking, through the streets of St. Henri, searching for a house where she could give birth. Then there was a wedding dress to finish in a rush. For Florentine, who was going to marry Emmanuel? No, it was before, while they were on relief. She was sewing to help with the housekeeping money. You mustn't get sick for long, you'd lose your customers. Miss Elise wanted her dress at once. . . .

Oh, God, she had to finish the dress . . . she must get up. . . .
The sudden effort unleashed a sharp wave of pain. Now she
was leaning over a hospital bed. Who was dying? Who was
suffering so? Daniel? Could she do nothing to ease his pain?
Or her own? Their suffering seemed to have joined forces,
melted together in her own flesh. Then a weak cry reached
her ears. She leaned back into the pillows. And almost at
once, through layers of darkness, came a voice:

"Did you see that, Madame Lavallée? Not a whimper!
Not a one! You don't see many that brave, I can tell you."

Not a whimper, thought Rose-Anna. Who had said that?
Then she remembered: it was the midwife who had helped her
own mother. And she felt closer to her mother than she ever
had. A pride and courage swelled in her heart as if new strength
had been transmitted to her from old Madame Laplante.

Her mind wavered between sleep and a thousand small
preoccupations. She stretched out a hand to point to a drawer
in the dresser where the baby's things were to be found. She
had always had them ready – little dresses that weren't silky or
ornate but clean and warm.

Anxious, suddenly devoured by fear, she asked to see the
baby. There was always this fear of having a malformed child.

"It's a fine boy," said the midwife. "He's delicate, but very
lively. I'd say six pounds," she said, trying his weight in her
strong arms.

Rose-Anna had a desperate, dizzying desire to hold the
baby. At last, washed and swaddled in an eiderdown, he was
brought to her. His tiny fists emerged from the blanket. On
his satin cheeks trembled the shadows of his blonde lashes,
fine as down. She had always found the fragility of a newborn
baby very touching. She finally allowed herself to take some
rest, one arm supporting the sleeping child. She felt emptied

of all suffering and distress. After every child she felt this way, languid but courageous, as if she had once more been able to draw on the mysterious, unfailing fountainhead of her youth. It seemed to her that this was not her twelfth child but the first, the only one. Yet this concentrated tenderness did not exclude the others. She heard them come in a little later, led by Yvonne who had taken them for a walk after school. Excited by fresh air and freedom, they demanded their supper. Rose-Anna surprised herself by giving directions to the midwife who, according to the St. Henri custom, filled the office of maid as well as nurse.

"There's a cold roast and some bread," she murmured. "You can give some to the children. And you can see that their things are ready for school in the morning. There's always some little tears to mend."

She was trying to think of all the other things she ought to be remembering. Already her thoughts were back in the daily tangle of small chores. She struggled bravely against sleep, and asked repeatedly:

"Isn't my husband back?"

He had gone out that morning ravaged by chagrin and a feeling she thought she understood: a horror at the life they led and at his own inability to change it. Where could he have gone after he left the hospital? What tortures was he suffering? And what might they drive him to do? Azarius, poor fellow! She had always held him responsible for their poverty, but now it seemed to her he had done his part. A man, she thought, can't put up with as much as a woman. I should have had more patience. He had his sorrows too.

And Rose-Anna, who for so long had taken no thought to please her husband by what she wore, asked for the lace bed jacket Azarius had given her just after they were married. She also asked for a white coverlet which she kept pressed and starched and folded against the worst contingencies of illness and death. For a moment as she saw the two women holding its corners, she caught a whiff of danger, a cold threat coming from the stiff folds which refused to open. Her mother had thought it was bad luck to use the best linen except in need. That need skulked behind words one didn't say aloud: accidents, departure from this life.

Then Rose-Anna had to smile at her silly fears, and gave in to the urge she had always had as a young mother: to appear all in white for Azarius. Her anguish left her, and she dropped off quietly to sleep.

THIRTY-TWO

When she awoke, night had fallen. They had pulled back the curtains to air the room. The red signal lamps of the railway shone through the window. The warning bell rang shrill and insistent, and Rose-Anna thought she heard a despairing cry dragging her from her sleep. Someone needed her . . . someone was calling. . . . She half raised herself in bed and called her husband's name. Azarius! Where could he be? Why was he calling her? Was this another bad dream? No, she was sure that while she slept Azarius' thoughts had gone out to her, and she was warned of some new trouble on its way to her. Her sudden movement had reminded her of her maltreated body. She called his name again, with all her strength, as if her voice had far to go to find him.

This time she heard steps in the next room. Those were a man's steps, for sure. A shy smile came to her lips and she felt an unexpected sweetness, that of rediscovering, after suffering, her old life with its duties, affection and, yes, even its torments and regrets.

The steps were drawing near. It was Azarius, and yet there was something unfamiliar in the sound. She heard the floor vibrate under heavy hobnailed boots. She knew what it was; he'd bought new work boots.

Again she had to think of the past. A May morning. Her yesterday's wash, moist with the dawn, was flapping on the line in the sunlight outside, and birds were chattering. Azarius was leaving for his day's work. She had lain down in bed again after making his breakfast and was listening to his firm step ringing on the sidewalk. He went off singing, Azarius did, on that May morning. She felt confident, confident about the baby that was about to be born – her first. She feared nothing. No misfortune could come near her. She listened for the last trace of sound from her husband's footsteps. With tender gravity she said aloud, speaking to her timid love, to her present, to her future: "He's going off to earn our living!"

God, how happy she had been in those days, and how little goodwill it took to recognize the fact! Suddenly she wished she could detach some joy from her youth, just one, any one, and offer its memory to Azarius.

The door opened a crack, then completely, and she saw her husband's shape against a background of yellow light. Rose-Anna raised herself up in bed, a nervous smile on her drawn face, and held the sleeping baby toward him. Memories could be tarnished by the troubles that clung to them, but the baby – that was their future, that was their real youth rediscovered, the great challenge to their courage.

"Turn on the light, you have to see him," she said. "He's just like Daniel when he was born, remember, pink and blonde, really blonde. . . ."

"Daniel!" he said.

She heard his choking voice. Then he buried his head on the bedside and began to weep with great, surging sobs.

"Daniel is past suffering," said Rose-Anna simply.

She reproached herself, however, for this way of recalling the dead child. Azarius, for his part, had not made her voyage to the depths of pain to understand that death and birth, in that place, have almost the same tragic meaning. She knew that she would miss Daniel a little more, and more intensely, as her daily life took over again and reminded her of him. She knew that her regrets were there, numbed within her brain; but just now Daniel seemed lucky to have escaped his human fate and the share of misfortune she had bequeathed to him. It was as if a balance were re-established.

She took Azarius' hand.

"We can't see each other, Azarius," she said. "Turn on the light."

At first he did not answer. Clumsily, he was wiping his eyes.

"In a minute, Mother. I want to talk to you first."

Silence weighed on them. Then, in an uncertain voice, still gasping and tearful but determined, he said:

"Get ready for one heck of a surprise, Rose-Anna."

Usually this preamble would have thrown her in a panic. Today she merely pressed his hand a little harder.

"What on earth have you been up to now, Azarius?"

There was another silence, inexplicable. At any other time she would have felt it as a brutal warning.

"You're not saying anything, Azarius. So you've been up to some nonsense!"

He sniffed loudly, wiping away a final tear with his hand. Then he got to his feet.

"Rose-Anna," he said, "for a long time you've put up with everything and you haven't said a word, eh? Oh, I know." He brushed away a protest. "I know since we were married you've always had a hard time. It started with little things and then bigger things. And it built up and built up till at last you couldn't even cry anymore, not even when you hid from me at night. Do you think I couldn't see you eating your heart out!" he cried vehemently. "Do you think I didn't see it all? And the worst thing after that was when you went out cleaning for other people and I was too yellow to take any old job, street cleaner or on the sewers."

In his humiliation, his admission of defeat, he felt a kind of intoxication, as if finally he were about to see the light of pardon. His voice broke. When he spoke again his voice was hollow and trembling:

"But you know, Rose-Anna, it was because I couldn't believe we were that bad off. I just didn't want to see it. Instead I thought about the times when we were young and ready for anything. That's what I always saw. I didn't see our misery. Oh, sometimes I did for a minute, when I was clear-headed, but I couldn't really believe it. I could still hear your laugh when you were young, and I couldn't believe a laughing girl like you never laughed anymore. I shut my ears and I shut my eyes. I was like that for a long time. Oh, Rose-Anna," he groaned, "it took me a good ten years to find out what had become of us."

"Azarius!" she cried, trying to make him stop, unable to bear their sufferings in this light. Had she herself not refused to recognize them? "Azarius, don't say that!"

"If I'm talking about all that today," he said, "it's because your poverty's finished, Rose-Anna. Do you hear me, Rose-Anna. There's going to be a new start. And the first thing you're going to do is look for a house to suit you, just as soon as you get back on your feet again. A good house, a bright house, Rose-Anna, like you always wanted. Not one like this where I've seen you not get a wink of sleep, thinking and thinking how we're going to get by!"

A touch of pride and self-vindication swelled in his voice:

"I know you always thought I couldn't do it, I couldn't look after us. Well, by golly, it's done. Everything's looked after. You're going to live like you always wanted to. At least I'll have done that much, Rose-Anna. It's a bit late, for sure, but you'll have a few years of peace and quiet."

"Peace and quiet!" she murmured, her voice a cracked echo of his, incredulous, exhausted. "Peace and quiet!" Then she became herself. "Don't go saying crazy things, Azarius. Don't tempt Providence!" she begged.

He took a deep breath and went on, almost joyously now:

"Crazy things! Crazy things! That's what you always say. Just wait a bit, you'll see what's crazy. Quiet and peace like we never had, Rose-Anna. Just listen: from July on you're going to get a nice bit of money, cash, a nice government cheque that'll come right here to the house. And after that, the first of every month. What do you say to that, eh?"

He was talking with the same joy and satisfaction he had shown in other days when he gave her his whole pay. "Here, that's for you," he would say, slipping the roll of bills into her hand as he held it. "It's all for you." He had seemed to make her a gift then of his well-filled days, of his trade, of his strong arms, and of the future as well, the future to which they both looked without apprehension.

"No, no, Azarius," said Rose-Anna, not trusting her ears. "Don't talk to me about peace and quiet, poor man. That's more than we can ask for. Better not aim too high."

"Too high!" he repeated. "Will you listen when I tell you, you're going to get a nice cheque every month! Your peace and quiet's coming, Rose-Anna, coming in the mail! It's going to fall right in your hand! Every month. But wait a minute. That's just for you. You'll get some for the kids as well. Altogether you're going to have about ninety-seven dollars a month. Is that peace and quiet or isn't it?"

She smiled incredulously, still weak, and so far from any foreboding that she began to make gentle fun of him.

"Same old Azarius! With your furniture business you were going to make two thousand dollars a year, remember? And you were going to make three thousand out of the wrought iron. And with the sweepstake business you were all set to buy a house in Notre-Dame-de-Grace!"

Then, more gently:

"Now don't you worry about it. We'll get along like we always did. With our two pairs of arms. Believe me, forget it. It's better like that. We're better off counting on our arms and hands than getting taken in by wild schemes. Schemes are only schemes. Ninety-seven dollars in the mail? Hey! We never had that much money in our lives! Not for a long time, anyway. That's a lot of money, don't you know? Where on earth will it come from? And why to us, poor fellow? Why us?"

"We've got it, I tell you!"

And he repeated with fresh emphasis:

"It's all yours. You're looked after. Ninety-seven dollars a month. And that's not all. The best of all is . . ."

He strode up and down the room, his hands behind his back, then sawed the air with one hand.

"The best of all is . . ."

He came nearer the bed, breathing rapidly:

"The best of all is, you're going to be rid of me."

He was aware of a terrifying silence as soon as the words were out of his mouth. He had tried to say it lightly, turn it into an affectionate joke, but there was no smile in the silence.

His throat tightened and he felt a sudden melancholy. He went to the window, put one elbow on the dusty sill and stared stubbornly out across the tracks. And he realized that if he had just made a coarse, cheap joke it was because behind it lay the assurance of his own liberation. For a long time he stood at the window looking at the shining rails. They had always fascinated him. Squinting a little he saw them stretch away to infinity, carrying him off to his rediscovered youth. Free, free, unbelievably free, he was starting a new life! His saliva no longer tasted of soot and coal but of the open spaces and strong winds. He thought of the freighters in the canal, which had always given him a terrible desire to leave. He thought of the old countries of which he had dreamed when he was young, the pictures in his schoolbooks, that "France" lurking in the back of all his dreams like an incurable home-sickness. He even thought of the battlefields steaming with human blood, where a man could test his strength. He had a great need for adventures, perils, hazards, he who had failed so miserably in the small things. And he, who had found himself unable to come to the aid of the unhappiness around him, was seized by a fever of intrepidity at the thought of combatting the great afflictions of the world.

His forehead was sweating. He was panting softly. Had he acted to save himself or to save his poor family? Whichever it was, he had a sensation of accomplishment and resurrection.

A soft voice, uncertain and touched by fear, came to him in the dark:

"Azarius, have you found some job out in the country and you're leaving here?"

No reply.

Then her voice came again, hoarse, almost whistling:

"Azarius, put that light on. Let me see you."

Quietly Azarius turned the switch on the bulb that hung from the ceiling.

Dazzled at first, Rose-Anna saw only the movement of his hands, and his face, pale, determined and so young that it broke her heart.

Then she looked down at his shoulders, his body, his legs, in a suit she didn't recognize. Her eyes opened wide, her mouth trembled, and suddenly she cried aloud just once, and the sound was lost as a screaming locomotive passed.

Motionless, Azarius was standing there in uniform.

THIRTY-THREE

The waves of khaki followed on each other, rolling toward Bonaventure station, bearing along in their folds the bright shades of women's dresses, loud songs, laughter, the reek of alcohol, hiccups, sighs and all the clamour of an over-excited crowd.

Emmanuel and Florentine had arrived early and found seats on the benches in the large waiting room. They were chatting, holding hands on top of the duffle bag which lay across both their knees. Snatches of phrases, silences, sudden recommendations – do this, don't do that – and their words, their anguish, were scattered by the scuffing of heavy boots and the thousands of sighs which rose as if relieved and happy toward the vaulted roof.

Emmanuel watched his regiment arrive with unbelieving eyes. Most faces were radiant with joy. One of his comrades approached, staggering, supported by two other soldiers roaring with laughter. Another, his tongue thickened by drink, came by shouting in English, "We're going to see the world! You bet we're going to see the world!" From all sides came the signs of an unwholesome and artificial exuberance.

Emmanuel looked away and put his arm around Florentine.

He had thought it would be easier to leave her if they were married, that he would be reassured by this gesture of confidence in the future. But he was finding out that fragile yet powerful links had already been established between them through a whole tissue of habits. Florentine – trying on the dresses he had bought her, trying on the hats, a thousand times a day! Florentine – always wanting to go out, out in the streets, dawdling in front of store windows! Florentine – so flirtatious with him, yet so sad, so bitter at times. Then, the brief moments of tenderness when she would take his hand and say, "Oh, how I'm going to miss you when you're gone!" The days had gone by like minutes, like a dream. Gone in a flash, he thought. No, the ones who were leaving shouldn't indulge in close attachments!

The crowd was laughing and singing around them. Why were they singing? What were they laughing about? What was so jolly about this departure?

They stood up, silent. Florentine helped him sling his duffle bag on his shoulder and they came to the great waiting hall with arms about each other's waists, like a hundred other couples. The jostling crowd threatened to separate them and they held each other tighter. Near the main entry leading to the platforms, they found a whole group from St. Henri and made their way toward them.

Sam Latour was there. He was shaking hands all around with paternal and comic gestures. His fat face, placid and red, clashed with the flood of violent invective that emerged from his soft mouth: "That swine of a Hitler!" he said. "Somebody try and bring me back three hairs of his moustache. Even better, fetch me his cowlick and I'll make me a floorbrush out of it."

The voice of Azarius Lacasse rose stronger and more persuasive than any. With the authority of a sergeant he went from group to group and addressed them: "Tell the boys in France to hold on till we get there." He drew a folded newspaper from the epaulette of his uniform. He opened it wide and saw the headline: *Allies fall back on Dunkirk*. He struck with his fist at the paper, which ripped in two.

"Don't let them give up till we get there!" he shouted. "That's all I ask! Tell them we'll soon be there, us Canadians, and maybe the Yanks as well before long." He picked on a soldier, young and bewildered, and slapped him on the back. "You there, you're good for knockin' off twenty or thirty Germans, aren't you?" But he added immediately, laughing, "Don't kill 'em all, though. Leave me a couple. Don't end the war too fast, you guys!"

His face was glowing with the purest enthusiasm.

Behind him was another glowing face: Pitou. And behind Pitou was another face, ferocious and inflamed. Emmanuel thought he must be dreaming. Were these yesterday's unemployed? Were these the men he had seen so lifeless, miserably submissive, discouraged to the marrow? Was this Pitou, the musician, who had cheated away his years of idleness with the sound of his guitar?

He looked at Azarius again and was more upset than ever. Was this the man he had seen so despondent no more than a week ago? Was this Rose-Anna's husband?

Why, this man seemed barely older than himself, Emmanuel thought. He gave off a sense of almost irresistible vigour. Quite simply, he had at last become a man, and his consciousness of it gave him this measureless joy.

So this was how salvation came to the suburb!

Salvation through war!

Emmanuel looked at Florentine in a silent appeal. At first he felt a hollow in his breast, a vacuum, then a storm broke loose in his mind. The anguish he had felt that night on the mountain as he looked down on the suburb came back with added violence. He was no longer asking, Why am I going? but, Why are we all going? We're leaving together, it should be for the same reason.

It was no longer enough for him to know his own motive. He had to know the truth that was guiding them all, the principle which had guided the soldiers of the last Great War, without which their departure now had no meaning but was merely a repetition of the same mistake.

He leaned over toward Florentine and asked her the question that was troubling him:

"Why are we going, your brother and your father and I?"

She looked up, surprised.

"You mean, why did you join up?"

"Yes."

"Well, I can only see one reason," she said soberly. "It's because it served your purpose to go in the army."

He looked at her in silence a long time. Yes, he should have thought of that before. She was closer to the people than he was. She knew them better than he did. She had the answers. And he seemed to hear the answer she had given him whispered by those thousands of sighs of relief. And distantly, through that breath of liberation rising from the crowd, he heard the chink of money.

They've been bought, he thought. They've been bought too.

They, above all, he thought.

He seemed to be witnessing with his own eyes the supreme bankruptcy of humanity. Wealth had spoken the truth that night on the mountain.

But in a moment Emmanuel recovered from his discouragement. He thought, no, that's not the whole truth. The ones who are leaving are the least of the profiteers. There are all the Léon Boisverts and Jean Lévesques who'll owe their personal advancement and maybe their fortunes to the war, without running any risks.

But why, then? Why are the regiments on the march? There must be some deep truth, perhaps one not yet known, not even to those who had gone to the other war. Perhaps beneath the tough layer of human ignorance there was an obscure reason which man couldn't express.

Suddenly Emmanuel heard a voice from the crowd, metallic and imperious, a voice in English shouting:

"We'll fight to the last man for the British Empire!"

The Empire, he thought. For the Empire, so that a territory can keep its old boundaries. So that wealth stays on one side rather than the other.

A whole group had started to sing:

There'll always be an England . . .

Yes, but what about Pitou, what about Azarius? Is it for merry England and the Empire we're going to fight? Right now other soldiers, just as frenzied, are singing a hymn to their own country. They're singing in Germany, in Italy, in France. . . . Just as we could sing *O Canada!* No, no, no, he thought vehemently, I'm not going to put myself on any patriotic, national bandwagon. Am I the only one?

He tried to reject the monstrous, paradoxical idea that came to him, but it was irresistible: none of them was going to war with the same goal as the others. Some were going to the end of the world to preserve their Empire. Some were going to the end of the world to shoot and be shot at, and that was all they knew. Still others went to the end of the world in search of their family's daily bread. But what was it there at the world's end that enlightened men on their common fate?

The barriers opened wide and the crowd poured onto the platform. The rest was a nightmare for Emmanuel. He kissed his mother, his sister, his father. Then he embraced Florentine. He had found her frivolous, vain, nervous and sometimes irritable in their short life together. He knew now that she was weak and light-headed, but he loved her all the more for that. He loved her as one loves a child that needs one's help.

He put his arms around her and saw tears on her drawn face. In the last few days he had often been disheartened by her coldness, and equally nonplussed by sudden fits of tenderness or periods of silence. Her tears now moved him deeply.

She was weeping on his shoulder. He could not know that it was from a vague sense of relief, but also from an obscure distress hidden under vanity. She was most impressionable. The whole stage-set of this departure, the tears around them, the hands waving good-bye, all this she found moving in a way as superficial as her nature, without the slightest awareness of what lay beneath. But Emmanuel, believing that she was truly stirred at last, was gratified.

He jumped up on the steps of the car. For a moment he was in suspense, one hand holding the bar, his face tilted, a young man running to make the offering of his youth. His avid curiosity, his interior torment, had found no answer. He was going now, and no longer knew the reason.

Yet he had his answer. It came in a flash. . . . It came suddenly, not from Florentine, who was waving, nor from his mother, so small he could barely see her in the crowd, and not from Azarius, who was running alongside the slowly moving train. Miraculously, it came from a stranger.

She was an old woman he had never seen before, very thin, seeming gently resigned, and lost in this crowd which paid her no attention.

For a second their eyes met, and Emmanuel understood in that same moment. This humble woman was moving her lips as if to give him one last message. The sound of her voice could not reach him, but from the movement of her lips he could see that she was saying, for him alone: "There'll be an end. Some day there'll be an end."

So that was it.

It was this diffused hope, unappreciated by most of mankind, which was causing humanity to rise up once more: war must be destroyed.

Florentine was now no more than a bright patch on the platform. He managed to see her take out her compact and wipe away the few traces of her tears. He closed his eyes and, as if he were already very far away, cherished that image of Florentine and her powder puff. Then he searched the crowd one last time for her thin, small face and her burning eyes. But she had already turned her back to leave before the train was out of sight.

Tired and irritable, Florentine pushed her way alone through the throng and hurried toward the exit without waiting for her father.

The heat and the hubbub in the station had been terrible. Now she felt vaguely sad. There was no hurt, but the impression of a loss the extent of which she was just beginning to realize.

She reached the terrace and stopped to collect her thoughts. What was going on in her mind?

She had accepted Emmanuel's kindness and gentleness as her due. These qualities had not surprised her. But she had been touched by his generosity.

Before he left Emmanuel had given her almost all his last pay, as well as his savings, now banked in her name.

Florentine opened her purse and touched the slim cheque book and a thick roll of bills. She felt an intense satisfaction. Then she grew ashamed of herself and ran to the sidewalk.

She was jostled by a group of young people getting out of a car. Then a woman held out her hand. She was dressed all in black, a frail old woman.

"Have you just been seeing someone off?" she asked. "Was it your boyfriend or your father?"

"My husband," said Florentine simply, but with a touch of haughtiness of which she became aware as the words were out.

"You can be proud," said the old lady before she disappeared.

Florentine stood there for a moment, thoughtful. Then a timid smile, new and fresh, appeared on her tired face. She remembered how people had looked at her during the last few days when they saw her walking arm in arm with Emmanuel. An undefined sadness plucked at her heart.

She didn't love Emmanuel. At least, she didn't love him as she had thought she could love one day. And yet she experienced gratitude or vindication at being loved by him, along with a sincere desire to give him her affection in return.

She looked up and froze. On the sidewalk opposite was Jean Lévesque. He had stopped to open a newspaper under a street lamp. He was wearing a well-cut new suit, which she took in avidly. She even noticed his tie, the same colour as his summer shoes, and his soft felt hat pushed carelessly back. She was comparing him with Emmanuel in his rumpled khaki uniform and his coarse boots. Suddenly she was in a rage at Jean for turning up to diminish the picture she had of Emmanuel. Then other thoughts, more perfidious, passed through her mind. One moment her heart was filled with bitterness; the next, she was on the point of going up to Jean. To show him the ring. And to let him have a good look at her pretty silk print dress and the dainty shoes Emmanuel had bought her before he left. And the beautiful suede purse. He had chosen everything for her. It was stupid, really, to be so well-dressed for nobody. Just one minute, she thought. Just to show him I can get along without him. To see his eyes flame up, and then laugh at him and leave him, revenged, contented, happy, yes, really happy! Her heart was beating so hard that she was breathless, peeking at Jean and yet fearing that he might see her.

He looked up, folded his paper and walked toward her. Holding her breath, her palms moist, she turned her back to him and slipped into the shadow of a parked car, waiting for him to pass, her temples throbbing. She had to hold back not to cry out or make some gesture. Then she left, hurrying. She crossed the street almost at a run and went toward the suburb. She ran as she had never run in her life.

Later, she walked far and fast, her hair in the wind, not noticing where she went. She was still out of breath, and stopped to rest a second. It was then she was surprised to notice that she was pleased with herself. A satisfaction she had never experienced – self-esteem – astonished her. She felt she was starting a new life.

Emmanuel's return, about which she had never been able to think without fright, now seemed natural. Her path was clear. She was going toward her future without any great joy, but without distress. After the upheaval of the last months, the calm that enfolded her was as comforting as a bench in the sun to one who has walked for many nights. There was scarcely any malice left in her heart. She was able to begin thinking about her child almost without resentment.

It seemed that it was no longer Jean's, but Emmanuel's and hers. She still couldn't think of it with love, perhaps she never would; but slowly she would learn to dissociate it from her own mistake, her grievous error. Emmanuel would take care of them.

Emmanuel. . . . With him she had to admit she was better off than she would have been with Jean. Emmanuel gave himself away by a look, a word, and you knew what to expect. There wouldn't be the exciting emotions, but she could now see the freedom and peace of mind that would make up for them. And she extended these advantages to her mother and the whole family, with the proud sensation of having redeemed herself. For a second she thought of the domineering side of Emmanuel's character, which could be violent on occasion, and wondered if she shouldn't have told him everything. But then she allowed herself a smile at the very idea, and for the hundredth time congratulated herself on the way she had managed the whole business. And now there was no sin, no fault, no past. Only the future counted.

She went down St. James Street, growing dark as she approached St. Henri. All sorts of projects came to mind, new factors in her life, agreeable and consoling. With her mother's allowance and her own they could live well now. Emmanuel had begged her not to go on working, but she thought in her grasping way, I'll go on as long as I can. It'll just be that much more. She became ambitious and felt a secret solidarity with her family. By that she meant her own family and Emmanuel, but not the Létourneaus. Without admitting it to herself, she had been hurt by their coldness, and embarrassed when she was with them.

Reckless with pride and envy, she thought of a house on Lasalle Boulevard, almost as fine as her in-laws', and she knew it was for rent. Why not? she thought. We're certainly not going to go on living in St. Henri! She wouldn't admit to herself that she wanted to break with everything that might remind her of her silly love for Jean Lévesque. She would buy new clothes for her mother and the children. At last we're going to live well, she repeated with satisfaction and a vanity that filled her with contentment. She thought, Mamma can't get over it, but Pappa did the right thing, he did well to join up. It's the most beautiful thing he ever did in his life. And Mamma will just have to get used to the idea. Funny how hard she takes it! She never had so much money in her life!

She was walking quickly, calculating how much they would have when it was added together. She was surprised how well they were going to get along. She was organizing their life logically, cleverly, with a seriousness quite new to her. She saw their troubles fly away – they were gone already. Oh, yes, it was a new life they were beginning.

It bothered her somewhat to think that they, the women, were getting all this money while the men risked their lives; but these scruples were dismissed, and her calculations began again. She thought herself rich, she planned what she would buy, and was delighted at the turn of events. Where would they all have been without the war? She was dazzled by their prospects, very proud and relieved . . . while farther down the train picked up speed through the suburb and Emmanuel leaned out to catch a glimpse of the Lacasse house. A light was burning downstairs. That must be Rose-Anna's room.

The young man watched it go by with silent pity. Then it was far behind him and the train was crossing St. Henri Square.

His nose against the window, Emmanuel saw the level-crossing gates pass by, and the Sacred Heart in bronze, and the switcher's cabin on its piles. He saw a tree in a backyard, its branches tortured among electric wires and clotheslines, its leaves dry and shrivelled before they were fully out.

Low in the sky, dark clouds heralded the storm.

AFTERWORD

BY PHILIP STRATFORD

NINETEEN FORTY-FIVE saw the publication of two remarkable Canadian books set in Quebec: *The Tin Flute* and Hugh MacLennan's *Two Solitudes*. MacLennan's novel described the political and economic tensions of a society in transition; Roy's captured the social and psychological stress of a generation migrating from country to city. His approach was that of the historian; hers more the dramatist's. Through his protagonist, Athanase Tallard, MacLennan traced the decline of an old seigneurial line in the years between the wars; in her portrayal of long-suffering Rose-Anna Lacasse, Roy chronicled the dead-end misery of a working-class family living in the Saint-Henri slums in the last years of the Depression. Both were landmark novels, modern, topical, dealing imaginatively with Quebec reality and Canadian duality.

Although *The Tin Flute*, Roy's most famous novel, has been available in translation for many years, it is perhaps less well known to English readers than *Two Solitudes*. This is unfortunate because it is not only a better novel but marks a turning point in cultural history fifteen years before the Quiet

Revolution. It was Quebec's first urban novel. It banished forever the folkloric, romanticized image of the province which had changed little in the previous three centuries. It set Montreal squarely in the mainstream of subsequent fiction.

In 1941, when Roy started this first novel, she had just returned from two years in Europe where she had gone to study acting. She had decided against that career and had begun to write. Settling in Montreal, she worked as a freelance journalist, discovering her parents' native province for the first time. She herself had grown up in St. Boniface, Manitoba, and had taught in that province for eight years before going abroad. Now in her early thirties, she turned a keen and sympathetic eye on the new world around her. In her articles for *Le Bulletin des Agriculteurs* and other journals, she described not only rural Quebec but also scenes from the life of the urban poor. She herself lived on the border of Saint-Henri and walked its grimy streets, soaking up detail and atmosphere. In her autobiography, *Enchantment and Sorrow*, this is how she wrote of the spell Saint-Henri cast on her.

> I returned deliberately to this district listening, observing, sensing that it would be the setting and to a degree perhaps the substance of a novel. Already it gripped me in some curious way that I still don't understand. Its cries, smells, and reminders of travel weren't its only fascination. Its poverty moved me. Its poetry touched my heart, strains of guitars and other wistful scraps of music escaping beneath closed doors, the sound of the wind straying through warehouse passageways. I felt less alone here than in the crowds and bright lights of the city.

Excited by her new experience and inspired by her reading of the great nineteenth-century French and Russian novelists, she soon began her own book.

At first, *The Tin Flute* was to have been a story of the younger generation, of waitress Florentine Lacasse and machinist Jean Lévesque, of their attempts to escape the grinding poverty of Saint-Henri, and of their bitter, abortive romance. Then, Roy tells us, a secondary character, Florentine's mother Rose-Anna, took the forestage. "She almost forced her way into my story," wrote Roy, "and completely upset my plan for it." In fact, Rose-Anna became the centre of the novel. Trudging through the slushy streets looking for yet another cheaper cold-water flat for her large family, she became a symbol of the monotonous, dispiriting round of life in Saint-Henri. As a character, however, she developed much more than symbolic power. Her tenderness, her courage, her devotion in trying to keep her family together against heavy odds made her one of the great *mater dolorosa* figures in Quebec fiction.

With Rose-Anna as centre, the story became one of the play of many different forces on the Lacasse family, a microcosm of Saint-Henri, which in turn represents the working-class poor in Quebec society. Seeing in her mother an image of the life she is determined to avoid at all costs, Florentine is drawn by the glitter of St. Catherine Street and by the strength and ambition of Jean Lévesque. When Jean disappears, leaving her pregnant, she turns to gentle Emmanuel Létourneau for security as father for her child. Her own father, weak and vainglorious Azarius Lacasse, all sentiment and no sense, goes from one empty scheme to another trying to cheer his family since he is incapable of supporting them. Bearing her yearly child, scraping and patching, Rose-Anna is condemned to see her children one after another disappear into the army, the church, the hospital. The most touching separation is from dying little Daniel who in his last days transfers his affection from his mother to the English-speaking nurse, Jenny; the most ironic is the case of both her eldest son, Eugène, and her husband, who finally find a way to help the family but only at the price of leaving it as volunteers for overseas service.

It is Roy's special gift to enter the lives of her characters with compelling understanding and compassion, even the lives of such minor figures as surly Alphonse, plaintive young Pitou with his guitar, and garrulous, good-natured Sam Latour, members of the restaurant choruses at Ma Philibert's and the Two Records Café that provide a background refrain to the voice of poverty. Also, following now Jean, now Florentine, now Rose-Anna on their solitary winter walks through the neighbourhood, Roy evokes with unforgettable vividness the sights and the smells, the rumblings and the grit, the tawdriness and the brute industrial strength and ugliness of Saint-Henri.

But Roy's keen observation does not stop at the surface of things. She has a dramatic eye. The details she records throw the depths of her characters' lives into sharp relief. Rose-Anna's humiliation at the squeak of her old shoes on the shiny hospital floor; the clear vision she has of finding a sun-filled room for the new child she is carrying, and her sudden realisation that this is just a memory of twenty years earlier when the baby was Florentine; the first night in the new home lit by candles because the previous tenants have taken the light-bulbs; the smear of lipstick on Florentine's face that brings out Emmanuel's tenderness more than all her coquetry does; Florentine dressing for her wedding in the midst of crates and boxes left over from the latest move . . . these and so many other small facts and gestures that Roy has noted or invented give *The Tin Flute* its authenticity and emotional resonance.

Roy also renders brilliantly contradictions in character. Florentine's dreaming and edginess, her vanity and despair, her determination and self-doubt are presented in convincing flux. Rose-Anna's worrying, hopeful, courageous, bewildered character is complex and surprising, never stereotyped. Even the male characters, who are not so strongly drawn, are given their own share of inner turmoil so that weak Azarius, arrogant Jean, and gentle Emmanuel exist in the reader's mind as individuals at grips with life in all its uncertainty. Because they are so vibrant, they rise up out of their crippling environment revealed in their full humanity. With penetrating sympathy, Roy takes us to the heart of their several solitudes.

The Tin Flute is the title provided by the first translator of the novel. Roy's French title, *Bonheur d'occasion*, is better rendered as "Second-hand Happiness." But there is not much happiness of any kind in the novel – the disastrous trip to the country in the borrowed truck, the nervous, reluctant love-making, Jean's desertion, the rushed marriage under false pretenses, the birth of Rose-Anna's twelfth child undercut by Daniel's death and Azarius's departure . . . Perhaps, taken in context, *The Tin Flute* is the best title after all. The specific context is another of those true, touching moments that Roy excels in finding. From behind her lunch counter at the Five and Ten, Florentine watches her mother at the far end of the store turning over things in the toy department. She watches with sudden objectivity and a mixture of embarrassment and tenderness as Rose-Anna picks up a cheap tin flute Daniel had asked for and tries to decide whether to spend the two dollars Florentine has just given her on this promise of momentary happiness or on food or clothing. As Florentine watches her mother's hesitation and furtive manner, her own happiness at having been generous sours, she is flooded by the certainty that she will never really be able to reach or help her mother, and she can feel her heart hardening. All Gabrielle Roy's art is gathered in this brief, poignant scene.

Since its publication in 1945, *The Tin Flute* has received national and international acclaim. In 1947 it received the prestigious French Prix Fémina. The same year, in its first translation, the book won American recognition when it was chosen as a Literary Guild selection and sold more than 750,000 copies. At home the novel, ironically in its English version, won a Governor General's Award for Fiction, and Roy was elected the first woman member of the Royal Society of Canada. This initial success launched a long and distinguished literary career, marked by such popular and artistically success-ful works as *Where Nests the Water Hen*, *The Cashier*, *The Road Past Altamont*, and *Children of My Heart*, and yet Gabrielle Roy never surpassed the dramatic skill and truth to observa-tion and feeling that she discovered in this first novel.

BY GABRIELLE ROY

AUTOBIOGRAPHY

La Détresse et l'enchantement [Enchantment and Sorrow] (1984)

ESSAYS AND MEMORIES

Cet été qui chantait [Enchanted Summer] (1972)

Fragiles Lumières de la terre [The Fragile Lights of Earth] (1978)

De quoi t'ennuies-tu, Eveline? [What Are You Lonely For,
Eveline?] (1982)

FICTION

Bonheur d'occasion [The Tin Flute] (1945)

La Petite Poule d'Eau [Where Nests the Water Hen] (1950)

Alexandre Chenevert [The Cashier] (1954)

Rue Deschambault [Street of Riches] (1955)

La Montagne secrète [The Hidden Mountain] (1961)

La Route d'Altamont [The Road Past Altamont] (1966)

La Rivière sans repos [Windflower] (1970)

Un jardin au bout du monde [Garden in the Wind] (1975)

Ces enfants de ma vie [Children of My Heart] (1977)

FICTION FOR YOUNG ADULTS

Ma vache Bossie [My Cow Bossie] (1976)

Courte-Queue [Cliptail] (1979)

L'Espagnole et la Pékinoise [The Tortoiseshell and the Pekinese]
(1986)

LETTERS

Ma chère petite soeur: Lettres à Bernadette 1943-1970 [My Dearest
Sister: Letters to Bernadette, 1943-1970] [ed. François Ricard]
(1988)